What had she just allowed to happen?

She gasped against his lips and he parted from her, still so close their foreheads rested on one another. Her chest rose and fell with her labored breathing, her body heaving with needs she'd never experienced before.

She pushed against him. He dropped his hand and stepped back.

"What, you didn't like it?"

He knew, damn him, that she liked it! "It wasn't appropriate."

He snorted. "Spare me the scandalized rhetoric. There's no harm in a few kisses."

A few kisses? *A few kisses?* The foundations of her life were rocking like pillars in an earthquake, and he'd dismissed what had just happened as "a few kisses."

"We're not inexperienced, you and I." He paused. "Are we?"

She hadn't thought . . . had entirely forgotten the role she played. When he'd taken her in his arms, she'd acted only as herself and made the unforgivable bungle of leaving behind her mask . . .

Other **AVON ROMANCES**

His Betrothed *by Gayle Callen*
A Matter of Scandal: With This Ring
by Suzanne Enoch
The Renegades: Rafe *by Genell Dellin*
Rogue's Honor *by Brenda Hiatt*
Secret Vows *by Mary Reed McCall*
An Unlikely Lady *by Rachelle Morgan*
War Cloud's Passion *by Karen Kay*

Coming Soon

Before the Dawn *by Beverly Jenkins*
The Maiden and Her Knight *by Margaret Moore*

And Don't Miss These
ROMANTIC TREASURES
from Avon Books

My Wicked Earl *by Linda Needham*
A Notorious Love *by Sabrina Jeffries*
Once Tempted *by Elizabeth Boyle*

REBECCA WADE

AN INNOCENT MISTRESS

FOUR BRIDES FOR FOUR BROTHERS

AVON BOOKS
An Imprint of HarperCollinsPublishers

This is a work of fiction. Names, characters, places, and incidents are products of the author's imagination or are used fictitiously and are not to be construed as real. Any resemblance to actual events, locales, organizations, or persons, living or dead, is entirely coincidental.

AVON BOOKS
An Imprint of HarperCollins*Publishers*
10 East 53rd Street
New York, New York 10022-5299

Copyright © 2001 by Rebecca Wade
ISBN: 0-380-81619-9
www.avonromance.com

First Avon Books paperback printing: September 2001

Avon Trademark Reg. U.S. Pat. Off. and in Other Countries, Marca Registrada, Hecho en U.S.A.
HarperCollins ® is a trademark of HarperCollins Publishers Inc.

Printed in the U.S.A.

10 9 8 7 6 5 4 3 2 1

To Kristen and Carrie, my precious sisters.
This one's yours for a million reasons
but mostly because I can't think of two people
I'd rather share my past and my future with.

Here's to three gray-blonde grannies sitting together
and laughing over things no one else
would find funny.
I cannot wait.

Prologue

Houston, Texas
1878

"**W**ill the defendant please rise."

Jarrod Stone stood, as did his three brothers. Clint and J. T. stood beside him in the first row of the courtroom. Holden stood in front of them at his position at the accused's table. Just like always, Jarrod thought. The four of them against the world, ready to take on all comers.

Heavy on his back, he could feel the attention of those in the courtroom—the crowds who'd come to feast on the details of the trial simply because Holden was his brother. People liked it when bad things happened to the families of rich men. A twitter of anticipation rolled through the space. Jarrod set his jaw against it.

1

"Gentlemen of the jury, what say you in the matter of the State *vs.* Holden Stone?" the judge asked the head juror.

Jarrod's eyes narrowed into a stare that had cowed the most fearsome business magnates in the country as he turned his attention to the head juror. There'd be hell to pay if they found Holden guilty.

For twenty years he'd been the head of this household. As the oldest it was his job, his God-given *right*, to protect the others. If he could have, he'd gladly have shouldered the accusation, the arrest, and the trial on Holden's behalf. For a man like Jarrod, jail time would have been better than being caged in a courtroom, where he could do nothing but watch and wait. His gut churned against the powerlessness of it.

The head juror, a short man with a pockmarked face, pulled taut the paper with Holden's fate, and thus Jarrod's, branded onto it. "We the jury," he cleared his throat, "find the defendant, Holden Stone, guilty of aiding and abetting the crimes of the Lucas gang."

Denial roared within Jarrod. No. *No*! Couldn't any of them see that Holden hadn't done what they accused him of? And yet they dared convict him?

The judge's seat creaked as he turned from the jury box toward Holden. "I sentence you, Holden Stone, to six years in the state penitentiary for your crimes."

The muscles in Jarrod's body braced as if against the lash of a whip on flesh. Six years?

The banging of the gavel ripped across his ears, and then movement and noise trickled through the courtroom. The judge in his flowing black sauntered from his throne, the jurors stirred, the people behind them in row upon row of seats whispered.

Jarrod watched, bile burning the back of his throat, as the bailiff crossed to Holden, gathered his wrists behind his back, and fastened handcuffs to them. His youngest brother hadn't so much as flinched. His profile was hard and expressionless, giving no indication he'd even heard the verdict or the sentence.

Jarrod had seen him do that before—wear indifference like a shield. He wished he didn't still remember the way Holden had looked at their mother's deathbed. A five-year-old in an oversize hat and a too-small shirt struggling hard to pretend that his world wasn't ending. When their mother's chest had stilled, her last labored breath wheezing from her lungs, Holden had lifted his gaze to Jarrod, and Jarrod had read trust in his brother's eyes. That trust had been sacred between them ever since. Inviolate.

The bailiff moved to lead Holden away. Before he could, Jarrod reached out and grabbed his brother's arm. Holden stopped, and their eyes met, as they had all those years before. Oldest brother to youngest.

"I'm going to find him," Jarrod vowed. "I'll get you out."

The bailiff jerked Holden forward, and his brother's arm was wrenched from Jarrod's grasp before Holden could reply. It took mere seconds for them to escort Holden through the back door of the courtroom and out of sight.

J. T. blew out his breath.

"God," Clint said.

Jarrod continued staring at the door, even when it had rested dead in its casing for long moments. He let the crushing reality of what had just happened sink into himself, used its cut to sharpen his resolve. An agent called

Twilight's Ghost was responsible for Holden's arrest. And as the agent responsible, he was also the agent with the power to right the wrong he'd done by accusing an innocent man. Though no one knew the agent's true identity or claimed, even, to have seen the man in the flesh, the people did whisper the name of the man's mistress. Sophia Vanessa LaRue.

At the thought of her, an old remembrance raised its head. A dark-haired girl in a dress of snowy white—he cut off the memory.

Feeling a decade older than when he'd entered the courtroom, Jarrod led his brothers down the center aisle. People made room for them, as people always did. The courtroom doors had been thrown open, and a watery February wind coursed against them, causing Jarrod's greatcoat to billow.

Sophia LaRue was the only lead he had toward finding Twilight's Ghost. So he'd go to her, because no matter how long it took or how much it cost, he *would* locate Twilight's Ghost. And when he did, he'd have both justice for Holden and his own personal revenge against the man.

There was about to be hell to pay.

Chapter 1

~~~~~⌒⌒⌒~~~~~

Blackhaw Manor
Galveston, Texas
One week later

The agent known by gossips everywhere as Twilight's Ghost swabbed her miniature brush into a
pot of lip stain, then dabbed on a nearly invisible quan-
tity of the rosy hue. Sophia Vanessa LaRue rubbed her
lips together, scooted back on her dressing-table stool,
and peered critically at her reflection in the mirror.
Though darkness had fallen, the fringed lamp nearby
provided light enough for examinations.

For this evening's dinner party she'd squeezed herself
into an old black gown. Mrs. Dewberry had done her
best to revive it by stitching dark beading around the
V-shaped neckline and replacing the gauzy fabric of the

sleeves. Still, Sophia could see worn patches near her waist.

Oh, well. It would have to do. *She* would have to do. Her breath blew out in a stream. She'd rather be dressed tonight in men's clothing, stealing through the streets after the city slept, then waiting and watching for the criminals she caught. That was the part of her job that suited her best. Unfortunately, gathering details on people and events through small talk at dinner parties was also part of her job.

Footsteps sounded in the hall. Sophia watched in the mirror as Maggie swept into the bedroom already wearing her nightgown.

Sophia turned on the stool to face her friend. The too-short length of Maggie's gown, threadbare white cotton dotted with pink roses, exposed her feet. The vulnerability of those lovely, big, pale feet tugged at Sophia's heart. Her Maggie. How was she ever going to keep Blackhaw over both their heads?

"God bless, you look gorgeous," Maggie said, planting her hands on reed-thin hips.

"You think this gown is all right?"

"Yes!"

"You're too kind."

"No, I'm not. I have eyes, that's all. Gorgeous, I tell you." She motioned toward Sophia's face. "I'd just slick on a bit more of that lip stain and here"—she reached toward Sophia's snugly bound hair—"let me just loosen this a bit."

Playfully, Sophia swatted her hand away.

Maggie made another darting attempt, and managed to pull free a wisp near Sophia's ear.

"Maggie," Sophia chided with a smile, glancing in the mirror as she tried to smooth the tendril back into place.

"I swear," Maggie muttered, glaring at her in the mirror, "if I looked even a fourth as beautiful as you do—"

"You're *more* beautiful than I, with that copper hair—"

"I'd wear lower-cut bodices, a helluva lot more lip stain, and all my hair down. You're supposed to be a widow, you know. You can afford to test the boundaries a little."

"I know, I know." She'd heard this refrain countless times before. "I like my hair this way." She patted a miniscule amount of lavender perfume onto her neck and went to the armoire in search of her evening gloves.

"Just came to tell you that Knoxley should be here to fetch you any minute," Maggie said from behind her.

"Thanks."

"And with that, I'm going to bed to imagine all the men I wish I had in my life and don't. Should you happen upon someone devastating to look at and available between here and the front door, don't hesitate to summon me."

"Look around." Sophia found her gloves, swiped up her black reticule, then closed the armoire's doors. "This house is big enough that there might be a man hiding in a cupboard somewhere."

"You don't think I've looked?" Maggie stopped on the room's threshold, halfway out the door. "We've been living here for *years*, girl. There's not a not a single well-endowed man hidden in any corner of this house. I would swear to it before witnesses." Ruefully, she shook her head. "One would think the Secret Service would take better care of their agents."

"One would think," Sophia agreed, smiling.

"Have an enjoyable evening," Maggie said as she vanished.

Sophia had just pressed a folded handkerchief into her reticule when a thunderous knock sounded from below. Clearly, Knoxley had arrived.

Despite the early darkness of a winter's night, the lantern fire from Jarrod's carriage illuminated the round face and rosy cheeks of the housekeeper who'd answered his knock.

"My name's Jarrod Stone. I've come to speak with Mrs. Sophia LaRue."

The woman's chin dimpled with consternation. "I'm sorry, but Mrs. LaRue isn't expecting you, sir."

"I realize that; however, I have a pressing matter to discuss with her and need to see her."

"I'm sorry." The woman shook her curly, gray head. She'd clearly had long years of practice turning away unwanted men. "Mrs. LaRue only visits with those callers who have been previously scheduled."

"Tell her that Jarrod Stone is here—"

Another adamant shake of the head. "No."

Jarrod placed his hand on the door and pushed. He hadn't built his empire by waiting to be listed on some damn schedule.

Incredulity wiped clean the housekeeper's expression for a split second. Then she made a sputtering sound and threw her formidable weight against the door.

Never breaking her gaze, he applied steady pressure in the opposite direction, enough to scoot her back without toppling her. When he'd cleared a large enough opening, he strode into the foyer. "Where is Mrs. LaRue?"

"Well, I never!" the woman huffed, swatting her apron into place.

"Are you going to tell me where she is, or would you rather I search for her?" Jarrod asked, rounding on the woman.

The ornery housekeeper squished her lips together. The fire in her eyes supplied his answer.

"Fine." Jarrod cataloged the rooms emptying off the foyer. He'd search for her. Only a few lamps were lit, and he had to squint against the meager light as he peered into one empty parlor after another.

He'd spent the past week tabling his business interests, moving his household here, and buying up every available scrap of information on Sophia LaRue. Evidently, much had changed for the girl he remembered. When her family lost its fortune and her grandmother died of grief because of it, she'd been farmed off to a Catholic orphanage. She'd been raised by the sisters, married to a man named LaRue, and quickly widowed by the same.

But one thing hadn't changed. She was still living here at Blackhaw Manor. Though he'd seen it countless times from the outside as a boy, this was the first time he'd ever set foot inside the house, an elegant dinosaur of a place with an interior that looked shabbier than he'd expected.

The housekeeper scurried toward the back of the building, yelling for "Father."

Deciding the upper stories held his best bet of finding a bedroom and Sophia LaRue, Jarrod climbed the wide,

gracefully curving staircase. He gained the second floor
and thew open the first door he came to. Not only was
the room unoccupied, it was completely without furniture. He opened the next door and the next and the next.
All much the same—vacant rooms with crumbling
molding and tattered wallpaper. When he pushed open
the fifth door, a woman swirled to face him.

He stopped dead. This was unmistakably her. This
was the woman who could and would lead him to Twilight's Ghost.

This was also the girl he recalled from two decades
before.

The artful sweep of her brows perfectly comple-
mented the startling color of her eyes, eyes he'd never
forgotten. They were the color of expensive coffee in a
clear glass container, held to the sunlight. The long, thick
eyelashes surrounding them curled outward, giving her
gaze a sensual cast, as if she knew all a man could ever
want her to know about sex. Those eyes, though, were
the only sensual thing about her.

Except for one stray wisp near her ear, her dark brown
hair was pulled tightly back into a plain, sophisticated
bun at the nape of her neck. Her delicate features reminded him of an ivory cameo. And her posture was
practically vibrating with defensiveness, as if she'd bolt
for the windows at the slightest provocation. A well-
bred, stylish ice princess with the eyes of a siren and a
gown that was showing signs of wear. The age of her
gown and the state of her house made him wonder
whether she loved Twilight's Ghost or whether she might
be desperate enough to trade her body to him for the favors he could do her.

The silence between them pulled taut, crackling the air with intensity.

"Mrs. LaRue?"

Sophia stared at the man, the complete stranger, standing in her doorway. Her pulse thrummed hard and fast. No one *ever* barged into her private rooms. Or at least they never had before. Below stairs she could feign wealth. Upstairs the direness of her financial situation was obvious, so all guests were strictly forbidden.

When he'd thrown open her door, she'd plunged her hand into her skirt pocket, through the slit in the bottom, and around the handle of the knife she always wore in her garter. Her grip on the weapon tightened. "And you are?"

"Jarrod Stone."

Her attention streaked over him. Her brain fought to reconcile the man standing before her with all her restless imaginings of the awful children of Adam Stone. "Stone?" she repeated, voice slightly hoarse.

"That's right. Do you know who I am?"

"Yes." Jarrod Stone, the oldest brother, the oil baron. Late at night, she'd pored over reports of his feats on the battlefield. She'd read of the jobs he'd held in boomtowns across West Virginia. She knew the exact date that he himself had struck oil: July 10, 1868. She'd researched the company he'd founded, knew the names of his key associates, and had memorized the acquisitions he'd made. But none of her studies of him had prepared her for the tangible, physical strength of the man in the flesh.

Mother above, she'd envisioned him fat and beady-eyed with a cane and gold rings. She'd not realized he looked like this—that a man that looked like this walked her world at all. He was dressed completely in black, a specter of a man whose mere shadow dwarfed her. His body, hard and unforgiving with the promise of rigidly suppressed power, stood at least six feet tall. He had raven hair, a serious mouth, and a suit that had probably cost half her yearly income.

She imagined him, suddenly, standing with his legs braced apart on the front steps of his marble mansion, ripping thousand-dollar bills to shreds, and feeding them to twin wolves snapping and growling at his feet. Wolves of white with arresting green eyes identical to their master's.

When he stepped into the room, his dark charisma pushed at her, trapping her where she stood and stealing all the air. That, like everything else about him, completely offended her.

"What do you want?" She held her ground despite her instincts, which were all clamoring at her to flee.

"Your help."

"What makes you think I'd lift so much as a finger to help you?"

"Because I'll give you something in return."

She bitterly resented that he'd venture to show his face here, much less have the gall to expect anything from her. They both knew that his father, Adam Stone, had stolen every cent of her family's money. The loss of the fortune she could bear. That Adam Stone had never been caught, never made to pay for what he'd done to her grandmother was what she couldn't abide. Finding him and seeing justice done against him had been the central goal of her life since she'd been eight years old. It was what had initially driven her to seek employment with the Service. It was what had kept her warm in all the cold times, kept her company during all the lonely times, and kept her fighting to keep Blackhaw through all the times when she'd wanted to give up.

From beyond Jarrod, the voices of her alarmed housekeepers merged with thumping sounds as they rushed up the stairs.

"Your protectors are coming to evict me." A sharp smile lifted his lips.

The thought of her motley band of followers attempting to evict Jarrod Stone was laughable. "I'm not in the habit of entertaining men who barge into my private rooms uninvited."

"So I hear. Your housekeeper was so kind as to inform me of your schedule."

Sophia released her hold on the knife just before Mr. and Mrs. Dewberry bustled into the room. Their hectic movement struck a contrast against Jarrod's profound stillness.

"I'm so sorry." Mrs. Dewberry's face pinkened. "I did not issue him permission to enter. In fact, I told him he could not do so. He pushed his way in." She pointed and huffed. "Pushed, he did."

"It's all right," Sophia placated. "Mr. Stone and I have a matter to discuss privately. I'll be down in a moment."

"Certain?" Mrs. Dewberry asked.

"Certain." She'd hear his piece, take from him whatever she could, and get him out of her sight.

Grudgingly, her eyes shooting daggers at Jarrod, Mrs. Dewberry led her husband out. The latch clicked behind the couple, enveloping them in a quiet marred only by the rustling of a breeze-stirred curtain and the rasping of a loose shutter. The tension in the room heightened. For a man who'd sought her out with such fervency, he seemed oddly content to peer at her in silence.

Then, as if he had every right to do so, he started around the room. He scrutinized the simple furnishings, adjusted a book, examined the sampler Maggie had given her last birthday.

"Mr. Stone."

He picked up the candlestick from her bedside table, weighed it idly.

"Mr. Stone," she said more sharply. "Let's cut to the heart of the matter, shall we?"

"I noticed that several of the rooms on this floor are unfurnished," he commented. He eyed the plain white walls, set aside the candlestick. "Why?"

"I can't imagine what business that is of yours."

"None." His gaze honed on her with enough power to slice stone. "I'm asking anyway."

She crossed her arms over her chest and held her silence.

"It must be expensive, trying to keep up a house of this size and age."

She stiffened. How dare he, with all his hundreds of thousands, point out Blackhaw's shortcomings? Love and fierce protectiveness of the place welled in her breast. She and Maggie both worked their hearts out so that they could keep the house on their salaries. It's all she had left from the old days, thanks to his father, and she was both wildly proud of it and painfully aware of all the improvements it needed that she couldn't provide. "I manage."

"Looks like the west wing was damaged in the war."

"I manage."

"And the east wing, what? Hurricane?"

"You have my attention, Mr. Stone." Her voice sounded as tight as she felt. "Why do you need my help?"

He slung his hands into the pockets of his trousers, an action which pushed back the sides of his coat and revealed a snug charcoal gray vest beneath. He came toward her, too close for comfort, and leaned against the edge of her dresser. The pose was deceptively relaxed. She didn't believe it. There was a tenseness beneath his façade that told her his reason for coming here meant a great deal to him.

"Have you ever heard of a Secret Service agent named Twilight's Ghost?" he asked.

Everything inside Sophia went frightfully still. "Yes, I've heard of him." Most people in these parts had. A denial of knowledge from her might arouse his suspicion.

"Do you know him?"

"No."

"Are you sure?"

"Am I sure?" she asked, indignation in her tone. "Yes, I'm sure." For survival's sake she'd become an accomplished actress over the years. So much so, she sometimes forgot which parts of her were real.

"Here's my problem, Sophie—"

"Do not call me that."

"My brother Holden was falsely accused of aiding and abetting the Lucas gang based on a fourteen-year-old arrest warrant. He was found guilty and sentenced to jail."

Falsely accused, her derriere. Her information on Holden had been unambiguous.

"I've learned that Twilight's Ghost was the agent responsible for having Holden brought in and charged. It seems to me that a Secret Service agent would have more pressing matters to concern himself with than fourteen-year-old arrest warrants. My question for you is why Twilight's Ghost would bother with my brother?"

"I've no idea." Though she knew exactly. Two months ago, her friend Oliver, the man who had once been her grandmother's advisor, had crossed paths with Holden Stone at Austin's train station. Holden had treated him with such hostility that he'd warned Sophia about Holden afterward. Oliver had made her promise that should Holden attempt to harass her directly, that she'd inform him so that he could lend her his protection. Holden's belligerent behavior toward Oliver had struck her as suspicious, so she'd gone back over her information on him, then worked to uncover even more about the youngest Stone. When she'd discovered his outstanding arrest warrant, she'd gladly sent officers of the law out after him. Justice was what she did.

"The only reason I can see for Twilight's Ghost to investigate Holden is if he first decided to investigate my father's crimes."

He was exactly right. So right it frightened her.

"And why would the Ghost reopen the case against my father? There's no reason. Unless, of course, someone . . . his mistress, perhaps . . . asked it of him."

She met his gaze, her face void of expression.

"Your family's fortune was stolen twenty years ago," he said. You're the only one who still cares about my father's supposed crime, the only one who'd have asked Twilight's Ghost to find my father, and the only one I know of who has access to Twilight's Ghost."

He was accusing her right to her face. Worse, he was terrifyingly close to the truth.

"So did you?" he asked.

"What?"

"Ask Twilight's Ghost to reopen the case against my father?"

"No."

He extracted his hands from his pockets and braced them next to his hips against the corner of the dresser. Strong man's hands; big, short-nailed, with veins evident beneath the skin. "No?" he asked, one brow cocked with skepticism.

"No."

"You should know that I don't give a damn about my father. The Ghost can search for him, arrest him, hang him for all I care. But when your lover went after my brother for a crime he didn't commit, he went too far. For that I'm going to hunt him down and see that things are set right."

"I fail to see what this has to do with me."

"You're going to help me find Twilight's Ghost."

The fervor in his eyes seared her. He felt that he and his brother had been deeply wronged, she could read that so clearly. Because of it, he wanted more than his brother's release. He wanted revenge against Twilight's Ghost. Against her.

A shiver of foreboding crawled down the back of her neck. Jarrod Stone was a powerful man and his hatred a powerful force.

Needing distance from him, she strode to the nearest of the room's two tall windows. Others had set out to find Twilight's Ghost and failed. There was no reason to think Jarrod Stone would succeed at revealing her identity. So why were her legs quivering? Why had her mouth gone dry?

She pushed aside the heavy curtain and stared at the property below. Every rise and fall of the earth and every tree in the orchard she knew by heart. "You were right," she said at length, "when you said that I have an interest in finding your father. If someone has reopened the case against him, then I'm glad they have. I sincerely hope they hunt him down in the streets and make him pay for what he did." She slanted her body toward him and met his gaze. "But you've come to the wrong place. I don't know anything about either your brother or the agent you're after. I can't help you."

He didn't so much as blink.

"It seems to me that if you want your brother freed, your best option is to cooperate with the Secret Service. Tell them where your father is." It was the subtlest way she could figure to fish for information.

"I don't know where he is. None of us have ever known."

This time, she let her incredulity show.

He shrugged. "We don't."

She made her way to her dressing table, where her gloves and reticule rested. "This conversation is over," she said coolly. "I have an engagement for this evening."

"I'll pay you to help me find the agent," he said.

Typical that he'd throw money at her. It was the only thing men like him understood. "There's no price you could pay me that I'd accept," she answered, not even bothering to look up as she slid her hand into an elbow-length black glove.

"Isn't there?"

"No."

"Name your price."

Her movements slowed as she pressed her second glove into the V between each of her fingertips. If he wanted her to name a price, she would. A price too high for even his rich blood. She paused to consider a fee that would be suitably outrageous.

"Name your price," he said again.

"Five thousand dollars," she replied. For the first time since he'd stormed into her life, she wanted to smile.

"Five thousand dollars," he murmured. He began to walk, slowly, his head canted forward as if deep in thought. He patted his trouser pockets, then his jacket pockets. He whispered the sum again, reached inside his suit jacket, and extracted an enormous stack of money.

Sophia's urge to smile vanished.

He freed the bills from a platinum money clip, counted some out in rapid succession, and placed them on the foot of her bed. Right there on the white quilt the sisters had stitched for her when she was sixteen.

She surveyed the money and him with triple the astonishment she'd experienced when she'd glanced up to see him towering in her doorway. *Mother Mary.* Jarrod Stone had just laid five thousand dollars on her bed. Enough to both pay Blackhaw's taxes and restore it. What sort of man carried that amount of money around with him? What sort was willing to throw so much away?

His gaze swung to her—triumphant. The glitter in his eyes informed her he was pleased with himself. Pleased in that infuriating, cocksure way only men can be pleased.

"Five thousand," he said. "Plus a tip."

"A tip?"

He tested the mattress by pressing down on it a few times, as if his payment for her help came complete with a complimentary tumble beneath the sheets.

Sophia ground her teeth. Smugness had never been one of her favorite characteristics in others. In a Stone it was despicable. She slid her reticule onto her wrist and approached him, scooping up the pile of money. It would be a cold day in hell before she'd take so much as a penny from Jarrod Stone, especially for the service of assisting him track down herself.

She opened his jacket and, holding her breath at his nearness, returned the money to the inside pocket. "I changed my mind." Her gaze flicked to his. "There's no price, not even ten times this much, that could convince me to align myself with you."

The light behind his green eyes turned deadly cold. "Why?"

She stepped away. "Why? Because your father ruined everything in my life I held dear. And because your money can never buy back my trust in anyone with the last name of Stone." She brushed past him, exited her room, and walked swiftly along the upper hallway. The sound of his footsteps followed her down the staircase and through the foyer to the manor's front door. Sophia swung it wide, ridiculously eager for him to be gone.

Jarrod passed over the threshold obediently enough, but turned after just two steps. Beyond him, on the drive, a carriage waited. Black as Satan's chariot, gleaming with its own lanterns as well as reflected light from the house. "I'm going to find Twilight's Ghost," he said, his tone steely sure.

Because she couldn't stand to look at him anymore, to see the fearsome evidence of his determination, she shut the door right in his face. Then she leaned against it and started to shake.

Jarrod stood unmoving on her front step, staring at the door. When was the last time anyone had shut a door in his face? Hell, he couldn't even recall. Years.

Underneath Sophia's cool exterior, the bristling hostility, and the suspicion that rolled from her in waves, was fire. He could sense it, locked away in places he bet she didn't even know about. Sophia LaRue was fiery. She was smart. She was gutsy. And she'd lied to him.

He turned and walked toward his carriage. He prided himself on his ability to read truth in a person's eyes and body language. She was a better liar than most of the men he faced across the surface of negotiating tables, but she hadn't been good enough to fool him.

When he'd first mentioned Twilight's Ghost, there had been something subtle in her eyes, a small flare was all, that informed him she knew more than she was telling. Of course she did. Cases didn't get reopened on their own.

She was involved with Twilight's Ghost, and sooner or later the man would make an attempt to communicate with her. Jarrod paused and glanced over his shoulder at the trio of smaller outbuildings that squatted behind the great house. He gauged them, deciding which one he'd return to tonight to wait and to watch.

Chapter 2

Sophia crouched in the midnight shadows of the dock. The February cold blew in from the gulf, slicing over her reddened features, curling icy tentacles through the openings in her clothing. She'd thought she'd bundled herself in enough clothing to keep warm. Usually she did. But the drop in temperature tonight had caught her unawares, and now she was stranded here, shivering and wishing for a cup of Mrs. Dewberry's tea.

To divert herself, she scrawled West Indian Rum across the top of the paper she'd brought along, using her knees as a desk. Someone was smuggling the stuff into Galveston, and tonight was the first night in her search to find out who.

Occasionally, thieves were so stupid that they paddled their dinghies full of booty directly up to the far end of the dock. That's why she always started here, to give them the chance to be obvious. If she had no luck, she'd move around the island, leveling her surveillance on inlet after inlet, until she spotted them. It had never been hers to confront the criminals she chased, but rather to research and to watch.

She took a deep breath and rested her temple against the side of the crate she'd folded her body into. The damp wooden box sat on its side, the open top facing the water. She huddled in its back corner, invisible, not only because of her sheltered position, but because of her man's clothing. She wore trousers and a coat made from cheap fabrics, serviceable shoes, and a dingy hat that looked like a thousand others. Anyone seeing her, and some always did as she made her way to and from her late-night destinations, wouldn't think to look twice. In this costume she was the most ordinary and uninteresting man on the street.

In the distance, she could hear the revelry of the Strand. Tinny music, the hum of talk and laughter. For months and years she'd listened to those sounds while sitting alone, accompanied only by ships rocking in inky water.

She cocked her head. She'd heard something. She listened . . . yes. There. Separating themselves from the hum, came footsteps. Heavy ones. Male, creaking along the surface of the dock. Her brow furrowed. Two sets.

She slanted her pocket watch toward the moon and read the time in the pale wash of color. Twenty past midnight. She recorded that on paper.

As the men approached her position, she slid her right hand into her pocket. She could feel her muscles tensing, as her fingers wrapped around the hilt of her knife.

It was the first time she'd had cause to grab for the weapon since meeting Jarrod Stone three nights ago. The image of him, all intensity and arrogance, flashed into her mind.

She shook her head, rattling it—*him*—away.

The footsteps neared. Her nostrils flared with the silent *whoosh* of her breath. They were right behind her now. Then passing.

She eyed the men through a knot in the wood of her crate. They walked hurriedly with their faces cast down. Both wore long coats.

Neither of them was Jarrod Stone, come to exact his vengeance upon her.

A groan grated up her throat and she irritably released her knife. It angered her, how much she thought of the man. Her feet barely touched the floor in the morning before his face entered her mind, and she couldn't fall asleep at night without his memory intruding. The only thing she could credit was that her severe dislike of him kept him at the fore of her mind. That, and the knowledge that he was out there somewhere, stalking her. She, who'd always been the stalker.

Her teeth chattered, despite her best efforts to clench her jaw.

Two men, she wrote on her pad, then recorded every detail about them that she could distinguish. It was too dark to see her own writing, but then she was accustomed to that. She used her fingertips to mark off lines.

Her notes complete, she pulled a spyglass from her jacket pocket. Evidently, the rum smugglers were of the stupidest variety. Even now, through the glass, she could see a rowboat making soundless, almost invisible progress toward the dock. She traced backward, trying to sight the sailing ship whence they'd come. No, she couldn't make it out. Could be any one of several. Which meant she'd bide her time and watch their return trip until she could be sure where they'd gone. Then she'd have to paddle her own tiny vessel out into the harbor, until she was close enough to distinguish the name on the guilty ship's bow. Years ago, she'd learned how easily anonymous ships could be moved between dark and dawn. Rowing out to read their name was the only sure way to identify them.

Then, *then*, she could go home and drink her tea.

An uneventful night, really. Quite boring.

Hell, this waiting is boring.

This was the third night Jarrod had spent here, inside the tiny building holding Blackhaw's tack. So far he'd seen nothing. Realistically, he knew he might have to wait weeks for Twilight's Ghost to show. But God, he hoped not. Inactivity wasn't in his blood.

He stood next to the shack's lone window, leaning against a wall seasoned with the smells of dust, horse, and aging leather. A few more hours and it would be morning, another fruitless night passed, another day arrived. A day he'd pass pacing the floors of the house he'd just bought, ravaged by thoughts of Holden in jail. He'd told Holden he'd find the Ghost and get him out. His youngest brother would be waiting for him to do just that, wondering every day if today would be the day Jarrod kept his promise.

Restless, he stepped across the window to lean against the opposite wall. From here he could observe most of the property's deep rear yard— He straightened. What was that he'd seen? Nothing more than the passing of a darker shade of black against a lighter. Little, but enough to indicate movement. He squinted and angled his head closer to the wall for a wider view.

Again, came the flash of black on black. Relief and anticipation swept through him. Finally, the Ghost had come.

Jarrod watched as a person, a man, moved smoothly through the night toward the tall gate that enclosed Blackhaw's property. When he reached it, the apparition uncovered what looked like a crude rope ladder from beneath a bed of leaves, tossed its end over a spire, and used it to climb up and over. When he reached the inside, he looped the ladder around his shoulder.

Jarrod's unblinking gaze followed his every move. He'd wait for the man to near the back door of the house, which was just yards from the tack shed. Then he'd spring.

But instead of moving toward the back door as Jarrod had expected, Twilight's Ghost veered in the opposite direction and ran along the inside of the fence toward the farthest, most tree-covered corner of the property. Jarrod worked to distinguish the man from the shade cast by branches.

The Ghost paused, then bent and opened a square door that hinged outward from the ground. It appeared to be the entrance to a root cellar. The Ghost looked both ways, then took the first step down into it.

The cellar must provide passage into the house. Swearing under his breath, Jarrod threw open the shack's door and ran toward the cellar, his greatcoat flapping behind him.

Even from a distance, Jarrod saw the Ghost's head come up, the hat brim lifting. In the next instant, the

Ghost leapt from the opening and sprinted in the opposite direction.

Jarrod was already at full speed which enabled him to close on the man as the Ghost weaved through the trees. The rush of Jarrod's breath filled his ears, his chest. He was gaining . . . he could almost reach— When the Ghost was forced to slow in preparation to throw his ladder and climb the fence, Jarrod lunged. His fingers sank into the clothing at the man's shoulder.

With a feral growl, the Ghost rounded. Moonlight skated against the blade of a knife as it sheered through the air toward Jarrod's face. Jarrod careened away from its deadly path. The Ghost hesitated for the barest moment before advancing, slashing the knife upward. Jarrod arched back.

With blazingly fast fury, the Ghost struck out at him again and again, air hissing in chorus with his thrusts. Jarrod ducked and swerved out of the way. His heel struck a tree root and he stumbled backward a few steps, reaching into nothingness for a handhold.

When he gained his balance, the Ghost was gone. He spotted the man dropping to the ground on the far side of the fence. Jarrod gritted his teeth into a snarl and pursued, his feet striking hard against dirt. Two houses down, the Ghost darted to the side, then disappeared around the back corner of someone's home. Jarrod charged after him. Cold air whistled against his face, while heat pounded his blood.

On a straight line Jarrod could have easily caught the man, he was certain. But the Ghost kept veering in and out over murky terrain, navigating it with the advantage of familiarity.

The Ghost led him through the back gardens of two

more houses before a towering iron fence stopped him. Jarrod's instincts surged with satisfaction. The man was cornered.

Without the option of continuing forward, his prey wheeled to the right and ran along the face of the fence. Jarrod angled in that direction, hoping to cut him off. Before he could, the Ghost pushed through an opening in the enclosure. Rusty hinges squealed as the gate's door swung inward.

Jarrod shoved his way through. Beyond, tall plants bowed and sighed from geometric plots. He couldn't see the Ghost—no, there he was, zigzagging quick and silent along the cobbled paths. Jarrod followed as fast as he could, his anger building. He should have had him back at Blackhaw, when he'd grabbed the man's coat. He should have god damn *had* him.

Jarrod tripped and cursed as he ran, tripped and cursed, hating the elaborate tile and the fussy stone borders. The Ghost reached the slatted iron fence on the far side of the garden, turned sideways, and stepped a foot between the rungs.

Jarrod's heart contracted violently. With a final burst of speed, he raced toward the Ghost. The man pushed halfway through. Jarrod was almost there, he could almost—he reached out, his fingers closing around cold air in the instant the Ghost slipped through to the other side. The man took several quick steps backward, then paused.

Jarrod faced him through the bars, his chest hitching. The Ghost had trapped him in a cage of flowers and iron and stone. It might as well have been a cage of fire dropped into hell for all Jarrod liked it. He'd been tricked.

His frustration churned, part-disgust, part-outrage. He never lost. Was never outsmarted.

Jarrod wanted to reach through the bars and take a swipe at the Ghost, like some great, rabid beast. As it was, he couldn't stop himself from wrapping his hands around the bars and rattling them.

The Ghost didn't move a muscle.

Jarrod sucked in breath, trying to get a hold of himself. "I need to speak with you," he rasped, "about my brother, Holden Stone."

From beneath the blackness of his hat, Twilight's Ghost regarded him with uncanny stillness. Foe to foe.

"You falsely accused him," Jarrod said.

The Ghost just stared in silence, his facial features a dark void.

"I'm not going to let my brother sit in jail. So free him."

The agent took one deliberate pace backward.

"If you won't help me now, I'll keep searching for you—as long as I have to."

Soundlessly, Twilight's Ghost turned.

"Stop!" Jarrod yelled. But the man refused to heed his order. "Stop!" Impotently, Jarrod again rattled the bars.

Twilight's Ghost melted into the night like a child returning to the fold. Not even the wail of the wind or the crunch of fallen leaves accompanied him, so alone was he.

Jarrod squeezed closed his eyes. The defeat added another weight to the responsibilities he carried on his shoulders. He could feel this newest one, pushing, grinding him down.

Though the knot of disappointment in his gut told him it was impossible, he nonetheless attempted to wedge a shoulder between the rungs of the gate. His arm fit, but no more than that. The metal stopped him firmly at the swell of his chest.

He retraced his steps through the twisting paths of the garden, until he found the gate on the other side. He skirted around the outside of the estate to the place where the Ghost had vanished. Then he combed the property beyond, searching until his eyes ached for sign of a man the color of wind. He found nothing, and still he continued. Walking and walking, a headache pounding against his forehead and temples.

At last, as dawn was just beginning to pinken the eastern sky, he returned to Blackhaw the way he'd come, over the back fence. The cellar door still flopped open, exactly as the Ghost had left it. He could see now that a metal chain had been wound around the inner handle, so that the Ghost might latch it from the inside.

Jarrod descended the steps. Just as he'd expected, a passageway extended underground toward the house. Daybreak's feeble light cut away and he was forced to hunch at the waist and feel his way. The tunnel ended abruptly. Above, light trickled through the crevices of a wooden portal set flush into the floor of the house.

Jarrod reached up and freed the crude inner latch, then tossed the portal open. He stuck his head and shoulders into what appeared to be the kitchen.

With a screech, the housekeeper skittered away from the counter where she'd been kneading bread. A floury hand flew to her breast.

"Good morning," Jarrod said dryly.

"You!"

"Me."

"Well, I *never*!"

"Tell Mrs. LaRue that she and I have much to discuss."

The housekeeper's graying brows crushed dangerously low over her eyes. She reached for a frying pan. "You're not on the schedule."

"No. She's on *my* schedule now."

A half an hour later Jarrod's carriage rocked to a halt in front of his newly acquired house. He tossed open the carriage door before the servant dashing toward him had a chance to, and stalked up the porch stairs. A second servant held the front door wide.

"Get me Collier," Jarrod said as he entered.

"Yes, sir."

One unaccustomed hallway deposited him into another as he made his way to his office.

The day he'd determined that Sophia LaRue was still living in Galveston, he'd sent agents here to purchase a property for his use. They'd informed him that the owners of this estate were not interested in selling, but like everything in life, the property had indeed been for sale for the right price.

Unwilling to sacrifice any more time, he'd simply bought the furniture with the place. It was adequate enough.

He glanced into a parlor as it sailed past—burgundy hues, sophisticated well-crafted pieces. Nothing about this place, from the smallest detail to the largest, elicited within him a single stirring of satisfaction or pride in ownership.

Upon reaching his office, he lowered into his leather desk chair. He swiveled toward the window to gaze out at the morning while he waited for his secretary.

Idly, he drummed his fingers against the well-worn surface of his desk. Wherever he traveled, his chair and desk went with him. He liked the proportions that had been made for him, liked the familiarity of his own utensils resting in places he knew to find them.

Collier arrived moments later wearing navy trousers with sharply pressed creases down the front and a navy waistcoat over a white shirt. His gold cuff links and tie pin gleamed. Every gray hair on his head and mustache had been combed into place. Quite casual for Collier. Their surroundings were obviously having a relaxing effect on the man.

Collier stood, as usual, at the right front corner of his desk.

The joints of Jarrod's chair squeaked as he rocked it slightly, thinking. "I'm going to kidnap Sophia LaRue."

Unruffled, Collier pulled a skinny sheaf of papers from his pocket.

"She lives at Blackhaw Manor," Jarrod said. "At some point today, she's certain to leave her home. As soon as she does, have some of our men bring her here." That Twilight's Ghost had attempted to sneak into her house proved beyond any doubt that she was linked to the agent. He needed her to get to the man and couldn't afford the time it would cost him to woo her politely into helping her.

The tip of Collier's pen scratched across paper.

"She's not to be hurt."

The older man nodded.

"I think she carries a weapon in her pocket. She was reaching for it the night we met."

The pen rasped for a few more moments, then paused awaiting instructions.

"I'm to be notified immediately when she arrives."

"Yes, sir. Restraints might be in order, sir," Collier said.

"Fine. Have them use a soft fabric."

Collier added the remaining details to his pad.

"She has dark hair, dark eyes, ivory complexion. About five feet eight. Beautiful body, beautiful face. Impossible to mistake."

"Yes, sir."

"That's all."

Collier withdrew.

Propping his elbow on the desk's surface, Jarrod rested his fist against his lips and swiveled to gaze out the window again.

His men couldn't bring Sophia here quickly enough for him. The hours between now and her arrival yawned before him, seemingly endless. He'd count every second of them, he knew. There'd be no sleep. No diversions.

It infuriated him that the Ghost had bested him last night and that anger, combined with the urgency he felt to free Holden, accounted for most of his impatience. But not all. There was something about the woman herself that made him hungry to see her. Something that drew him, something that had its roots entrenched decades earlier.

Unwilling to face the memory, Jarrod walked the short length of hall beyond his office, and opened the back door. Maxine was waiting for him, sitting on her mat, just as he'd expected she would be.

"C'mon, girl."

Her tail wagged in answer as she scurried into the house. Side by side they walked toward the library where they'd pass the day until Sophia's arrival.

* * *

That afternoon, Sophia donned her walking hat. It was an enormously wide-brimmed concoction, covered in cream satin, with a spray of elegant brown-speckled feathers at the side. Even after three years of wear, it still looked grand, so long as you didn't look too close.

She tied the hat's thick ribbon beneath her chin, then pulled her brown coat over her plain green skirt and bodice.

Maggie poked her head out of the parlor. "Do you want me to come with you?"

"No, thank you though. If I can't make it the few blocks to Mrs. McBrayer's for luncheon I'm in trouble."

"It's just that what Jarrod Stone said to Mrs. Dewberry this morning sounded . . . worrisome."

Sophia picked up her parasol. "Well, what's he going to do?" She smiled to reassure Maggie. "Nab me off the street?"

Maggie grinned back. "I wish an oil baron would nab *me* off the street," she said as she ducked back into the parlor.

Sophia let herself out and made her way down the long and winding drive to Blackhaw's front entrance. As she walked, she noticed that the handle of her parasol wobbled like it was about to fall off and that the tips of her shoes bore scuff marks. Mentally, she berated the man she'd supposedly married during her time of training at the Secret Service headquarters in Washington. The Service had felt that a dead husband would give her a great deal more freedom to move through society making alliances and collecting information. They'd been right. Still, what kind of a pitiful, sickly, sniveling husband would die without leaving his wife one blessed cent?

As if she'd marry such a nitwit.

She filled her lungs with the bracing air in an effort to flush out the fear that had nagged her since last night's close call with Jarrod Stone. She needed this, the fortification of sunshine and exercise. It would clear her head, help her think, and serve to reassure her that everything was still well with her world. At the street, she exited the protective gates of Blackhaw and turned toward town.

At the end of the second block, a strange shadow slipped across the edge of her peripheral vision. She glanced in its direction, but saw nothing. Her steps slowed. Warning pricked her instincts just as men sprang from their concealed places around her. She went for her knife, but they grabbed her right arm first, pulling it back as if they'd known what she reached for. A man's hand burrowed into her pocket, then farther, to her garter. His crude fingers found her knife and yanked it free.

Fear cinched her chest as they lifted her into the air. She tried to fight, to struggle, but there were five of them—six. Strangers wearing suits that bulged with concealed weapons.

Trees and sun passed in a blinding blur, then she was inside a carriage, stomach down on the floor. Her cheek pressed into the carpet, forcing the brim of her hat back. *My God, what can they want? Are they Stone's men? They have to be. No, not true, they could be acting on the orders of some other enemy*. Her mind was spinning too fast. She couldn't make sense of anything.

She gasped for breath and thrashed her legs. It was no use. In mere moments, they'd bound her wrists, bound her ankles, and locked her inside.

The horses eased into a gallop.

Chapter 3

~~◦◦∞◦◦~~

Finally, the carriage wheels ground to a stop.

The fear hovering at the edge of Sophia's thoughts intensified. She gritted her teeth, fighting it back. Long ago, she'd learned not to court trouble. She dealt with problems at the moment she must and not before.

Her captors, who had the gall to call her ma'am despite binding her like a trussed chicken, lifted her from the carriage and set her on her feet on a crushed-stone drive. One of them knelt to untie the bonds at her ankles.

Her hat had come off, so she squinted through a wash of sunlight. Desperately, she searched her surroundings for clues that would inform her where she'd been taken.

She didn't recognize the mansion or the acreage that surrounded it as far as the eye could see, but as she peered across the circular driveway she *did* recognize the ebony carriage standing in front of the stables, two workers polishing it to a gleaming sheen. It was the same one Jarrod Stone had parked before her front door.

So he *is* behind this. The image of a dark-haired man with an unwavering gaze cut into her mind, replacing her view of the carriage. He was smiling.

Anger flashed through her, obliterating any relief she might have felt that one of the criminals she'd jailed wasn't responsible. Jarrod Accursed Stone had bodily kidnapped her off the street! He was either certifiably insane or completely drunk on his own power.

"My hat, please," she said tightly.

"It will be brought to you."

She dug in her heels when they tried to lead her forward. Somehow, the dignity of a hat seemed important. "My hat."

Unseen hands from behind settled it askew on her head.

She glared at the house as the guards walked her toward the massive double doors. Like all houses in Galveston, the structure was elevated a good five feet off the ground to protect against flooding. In this case, the arched stone base supported a veritable palace.

White pine clapboards ran between enormous windows flanked with black shutters. Eight round columns stood sentinel at the front of the porch, and traveled upward through the second-story balcony before reaching a slate roof marked with soaring chimneys. Recessed behind the home's square front, two wings jutted outward on either side.

The entire effect was as imposing as the man who owned it.

Mahogany front doors pulled silently back at their approach. The men escorted her into the entry room, where her heels clacked against buffed wood. The interior was cool and rife with the scents of pipe tobacco and roasting beef.

The men walked her past a formal parlor, a dining room with a table large enough to sit forty people, and an immense library. Brooding murals of landscapes decorated the walls. Formally garbed servants swarmed everywhere—carrying fresh towels, dusting the mantels, scurrying around distant corners.

Sophia maintained as much of her pride as she could with her wrists bound behind her back and her hat tilting crazily. They led her down a hall, before opening the final door for her. All the hands gripping her released, and seconds later the soft fabric of the bond slipped away.

"Someone will come to fetch you when Mr. Stone is ready to see you," one of the men said.

Without deigning to look at the speaker, she preceded into the room feeling very much like a prisoner entering her cell. The lock tripped closed behind her in the same instant that she came to an abrupt halt.

Her gaze slowly, disbelievingly, cataloged the details of her surroundings. The more she looked, the more shivers streamed over her. Turning degree by degree in a circle, she probed the space for any sign at all that Jarrod Stone hadn't somehow managed to read every desire of her heart.

This suite was nothing like the masculine rooms she'd glimpsed in passing. The walls here had been painted a calm, cool green—the color of moss under mist—her favorite color.

The bed was covered in white, exactly as her beds of

the past twenty years all had been. Matching sheer white draperies hung at the windows, complementing the icing of lace across the top sill. The artwork—she swallowed. The artwork was all by Asher B. Durand, the American artist she admired most. She went to the nearest piece, a mountainous scene framed in tasteful gold. The signature was authentic. A. B. Durand, dated 1845.

Dazed, she waded deeper into the bedroom. Fresh bouquets of her best-loved flowers, wisteria and daffodils, overflowed the tops of both bedside tables, scenting the air.

The books nestled in the top shelf of the bookcase were by Alice and Phoebe Cary. She pulled one free, skimmed the pad of her finger over the binding, then tilted it open. A first edition, of course. Signed by the authors.

"Oh," she whispered.

On the other side of a connecting door, she found a small room entirely dedicated to clothing. Capes lined with dramatic velvets. Fabrics in the sensual, sophisticated colors of black, red, wine, chocolate, plum. Coordinating heeled slippers sat beneath the clothing, and hats to match rested on the ledge above.

She shut the door on the assembly, afraid to find out whether the clothing had been made to fit her.

When Jarrod Stone had come to Blackhaw a few nights ago, she'd flatly rejected his request for help. At that very time, had this room in this house been waiting in silence? It must have been. He had unmistakably furnished this space just for her, a woman he'd yet to meet. For how long had he been planning to imprison her here?

Sophia ran her hands over her forehead, then clasped

her cheeks as she studied her quarters. Within herself, she worked to throw off the astonishment that was dragging at her so she could revolve this situation clearly in her mind. First, she needed to know exactly what she was up against.

She crossed to one of the windows that faced the property's front drive and fingered back a wedge of curtain. Beyond, she saw guards. Two stood sentinel at the porch steps. One was positioned just twenty or so yards in front of her bedroom. Frustration mounting, she walked to a window facing the other direction, outward from the end of the wing. Three more guards—she recognized some of them from her abduction—were chatting near the stables, and one was lying on a patch of grass directly facing her. He removed a hand from behind his head and lifted it in greeting.

She dropped the curtain with a growl. Ire and a suffocating trapped feeling goaded her as she searched the interior of the space. She rifled through every drawer and nook, pulled the cushions from the furniture, and scooted under the bed looking for anything small enough to use to pick the lock or sharp enough to use as a weapon. She found neither. It was almost as if Jarrod had already combed the space for the same.

After pushing up her sleeves, she got down on her hands and knees and pulled high the corners of the bedroom's two carpets, checking for a hatch leading to the area below the house. There wasn't one. Nor did there appear to be any convenient hidden doors or wall panels masking stairways to freedom.

Disappointment swirled down her. She felt it, physically, tunneling deeper and deeper. Escape was going to be a tough proposition.

Heavyhearted, she moved back to the window facing the front of the property and scoured the drive for some sign of Maggie. When Sophia didn't return to Blackhaw this afternoon, Maggie would come looking for her. Someone, after all, must have seen Jarrod's men abduct her in broad daylight, and even if they hadn't, Maggie would suspect Jarrod first. It was futile to expect her to arrive so soon, though. Really, anytime before midday tomorrow would be impossible because Maggie would need to take news of Sophia's predicament to Simon, their supervisor, before she'd be authorized to act.

Sophia was unsure about how Simon would choose to handle this situation and even less sure about how Jarrod would respond to Maggie when she finally arrived—

A discreet twist of a key followed by a knock sounded at her door.

Sophia answered to find a distinguished silver-haired gentleman standing in the hall.

"I'm Collier Melvin," he said by way of introduction. "Mr. Stone's secretary."

She nodded guardedly.

"I'll take you to him now."

Good. She'd a few choice words to unleash on Jarrod Stone. Mr. Melvin led her on the reverse of the path she'd taken to her room. At the entrance to what she recognized as the dining room, he bowed his chin and gestured her forward.

The instant she entered the room, she spotted Jarrod. His attention riveted on her as quickly, and an electric current snapped between them.

He lounged in a thronelike chair at the head of the acres-long table. She was only vaguely aware of the door closing behind her, leaving her caged alone with the wolf. Though two places had been set, the one to the right of his assumedly hers, no servants waited in the corners here, and only a few of the lamps had been lit. The room was dim, shadowy, dangerous. A perfect place for wolves to circle.

As she approached, Jarrod stood, his napkin dangling from one hand. His suit was as dark as the ones he'd worn both times she'd seen him, his aura of power even more palpable. She halted a few feet from him, so furious that her body was practically quivering with the force of her emotion.

"Are you absolutely insane?" she asked, getting right to the point.

"Insane?" A smile played across those serious lips. "Some would say so."

"You *cannot* snatch people off the street. I—"

"Hungry? I'd like for you to sit with me."

"Sit with you?" She drew herself up, bristling. "This is not a social call. Do me the honor, at least, of acknowledging this situation for what it is."

"What's that?"

"A kidnapping. And may I say, that despite your mind-numbing show of arrogance the other night, I never dreamed you'd stoop this low."

With a resigned sigh, he dropped his napkin on the table, crossed his arms, and regarded her with one brow cocked. His attention moved with infuriating leisure along the neckline of her bodice. "Didn't you like the clothing I bought you?" He lifted his gaze to her eyes. "I'll buy others. Anything you want."

"It's not the clothing. It's the kidnapping I find less than satisfactory."

"Is it the artwork?" His forehead furrowed.

"It's the *kidnapping*, Mr. Stone. Stop being deliberately obtuse. You've committed a criminal act."

"You'd have preferred the artwork of Frederic Church, wouldn't you? I knew I should have gone with Church. The nun gave me both names."

Her heart stopped. "Y-you contacted the nuns?" Her years at St. Mary's Orphanage were a part of her life she kept fiercely private. He'd gone to the sisters, spoken to them about her! He'd rummaged around in her past and emerged with knowledge about her favorite things—knowledge he'd used to create a room for her. Ordinarily, the masks she wore covered and protected her. She wasn't used to someone, especially someone like him, looking at her real self.

Her breath was shaky. She couldn't seem to make it smooth. Her real self wasn't as strong as the parts she played. "That's how you discovered all those things about me?" she asked raggedly.

"Nice women down at the convent orphanage. Very obliging to a generous new benefactor such as myself."

She turned from him, refusing to let him see that his claw had connected with tender flesh. Her teeth bit down on her bottom lip as she moved toward the far end of the table, slow at first, then faster. She focused on her rage, letting it clothe the naked feeling he'd left her with.

Jarrod strode along the opposite side of the table, his gaze scorching her skin.

At the end, she stopped and faced him. He stopped and faced her. The air between them fairly sizzled. "You should know," she said, "that people will be looking for me. You won't get away with this."

"Let them come." She could see his ruthlessness in

the clean line of his jaw, the hewn muscle of his cheeks, the flinty hardness that dwelled behind the green of his eyes. He'd use her weaknesses, exploit her history, anything, to get what he wanted.

"What do you honestly hope to gain by imprisoning me here?" she asked, her voice hollow.

"I saw Twilight's Ghost at your home last night." He waited for her to try to deny it.

She didn't, couldn't.

"You're the only person who can help me get to him, which makes you the only person who can help me free my brother. The least I can do for you in return is furnish you with a place to stay while you assist me."

"When you asked me to assist you in trapping Twilight's Ghost I told you no."

"No wasn't good enough."

How did one reason with a man like this? Widely held social laws like personal freedom didn't seem to apply to him. "You had no right to kidnap me off the street—"

"But I did."

"—And no right to hold me against my will."

"Yet here you are."

"You have no right!"

"What are you going to do about it, Sophie?"

Her mouth worked, but nothing came out. She fisted her hands and rapped her knuckles against the wooden table to punctuate her words. "I find you unforgivably egotistical, greedy, and power-hungry."

"Really? I find you beautiful, smart, and desirable."

She gaped at him with shocked mortification.

He smiled in return. "Here." He pulled a thin, square satin box from within his jacket and skated it across the surface of the table toward her. "There are advantages to becoming my ally."

She scowled. "You cannot really be this daft."

"Maybe I can be." He lifted one shoulder, his towering confidence seemingly impenetrable. "Hopefully you'll like this more than you did the clothing and art."

Lips pursed with irritation, she flipped open the box. Within rested the most stunning bracelet she'd ever seen—a circle of fat round rubies at least two carats each bound together by sinuous strips of gold. It glistened with shooting light, fairy-spun, utterly fantastical, the kind of thing a mythical princess might wear.

Disdainfully, she snapped closed the lid and pushed the bracelet toward him. The box spun back across the shiny surface of the table, bumping softly against his thigh.

"I won't wear your jewelry," she said slowly and clearly, looking him straight in the eye. "I won't eat your food, I won't touch the clothing in my closet, and I won't sleep in the bed you've provided."

"Sophie," he chided, "we both know all this fuss of yours is a game."

"Not to me it isn't."

"You have a service I want, I have the money to pay for it."

"What you fail to understand is that I don't want your money, which means you have absolutely nothing to offer that I desire. I will not help you."

His hands slipped into his pockets, which pushed his jacket to the sides revealing a sapphire blue vest buttoned over his taut stomach. "You're an interesting woman, Sophie."

"Don't *call* me that!"

He chuckled as he walked back toward the head of the table.

"Let me out of here."

"You're free to leave at any time."

"What?"

He settled into his chair and placed his napkin on his lap as if oblivious of her presence.

She edged toward the door. When he didn't make a move to stop her, she ran into the corridor and toward the front of the house. The servant standing in the foyer took one look at her and hastened to open the front door. Sophia bolted through the opening. She was halfway across the porch when two guards stationed at the steps converged to block her way.

"Let me pass," she said, as authoritatively as she could.

"I'm sorry, ma'am, we can't do that."

"Mr. Stone just informed me that I'm free to leave."

"We have other orders."

With a hiss, she marched back to the dining room. Jarrod had been served a bowl of soup in the thirty seconds she'd been gone.

He glanced up at her, blowing indifferently at his spoonful.

"Your guards forbade me from leaving," Sophia stated.

As if he had all the time in the world, he blew at his soup again, then sipped at it with that sinfully handsome mouth.

"Your guards forbade me from leaving," she repeated, louder, refusing to be ignored.

He swallowed his soup, then quietly set aside his spoon. A cleft delved into the skin between his eyebrows. "I can't imagine where they got that idea." He flicked his gaze toward the steaming bowl of soup sitting upon her place setting. "Hungry now?"

Chapter 4

Incorrigible, infuriating, impossible man! Sophia had stormed from Jarrod's presence hours before—it was past nightfall now—and yet she couldn't quit stewing. She'd never imagined that the likes of him existed. High-handed, presumptuous—

A key turned in the lock her door. It was followed by a knock.

Sophia scowled toward the noise, but made no move to rise from the pearl pink sofa where she'd been sitting for some time now, damning Jarrod to hell and struggling to plot her escape. First, she'd glean from one of the servants the exact location of this estate so that should she manage escape, she'd be able to orient herself quickly to evade recapture. Then, though she'd never been much of a flirt, she would try to beguile one of the guards.

After a few beats, the knock came again.

She leaned her head against the sofa's back. She'd already told Jarrod she'd not eat his food, so there wasn't much to discuss.

"Ma'am?" Again, a polite rapping of knuckles against wood.

She sighed and made her way to the door. Jarrod's secretary could simply open the thing if he wished—he had the key. He appeared to be a gentleman, however, and wouldn't invade her chamber unless she forced him to. She accepted what puny privacy the wooden door afforded and spoke through it. "Yes?"

The clearing of a throat. "Dinner is served, ma'am. Mr. Stone sent me to escort you."

"That won't be necessary."

"Ma'am?"

"As I informed Mr. Stone earlier today, I won't be taking meals during my stay here."

She heard the floorboards creek as he adjusted his weight. "Yes, ma'am."

The lock slotted back into place before the sound of his measured footsteps diminished to silence.

She crossed to the window, checking for the hundredth time the positioning of the guards. A fresh shift had taken over from the last, though these men still defended all the same stations.

From the hallway she heard footsteps bearing down on her doorway. This set was entirely different than those belonging to Jarrod's secretary. These were heavier, authoritative, determined and she knew exactly, instinctively, to whom they belonged.

As she swirled to face the door a thrill leapt inside her. An awful little thrill.

She hurried away from the window, visually combing the bedroom for something she could use as a makeshift weapon. Her parasol, maybe. She spotted it leaning against the wall. With a quick lunge, she scooped it up and brandished it like a sword.

Had she gone entirely, fully mad? She exhaled and threw the parasol onto the overstuffed sofa. She couldn't fight off Jarrod Stone with a parasol.

He jammed the key into the lock without finesse.

She smoothed her hands down the front of her green skirts and wished for her knife.

Jarrod didn't even bother to knock. He simply shoved open the door with such force that it banged against the inner wall. His imposing, black-garbed form filled the doorway.

Sophia regarded him with utter disdain, even as his charisma flushed against her like a midnight wind off a tumultuous sea. He stood still on her threshold, just as he had at Blackhaw, and simply stared at her for a long moment.

Her insides quaked. The man was ridiculously good-looking. Hard, without the slightest fuzz of youth about him. And dangerous.

"Evening," Jarrod said.

She returned the greeting with a tense nod. "I'm not surprised to see you've no respect for my personal privacy."

"This is, after all, my house."

Of all the arrogant things. . . . "The decency of a knock would have been appreciated."

"I'll endeavor to remember that next time."

Next time? Just how often was he intending to barge into her room?

He glanced over his shoulder. "You may bring that in."

Two male servants eased into the room carrying a small table.

"There," Jarrod said, pointing to a spot in front of the sofa.

"That won't be needed," Sophia said to the men.

One of them looked hesitantly at Jarrod. "There," he repeated, nodding to the place.

Sophia was forced to scoot out of the way. The instant the table was situated, maids scurried in bearing chairs, flatware, dishes covered in domes, butter, salt and pepper, and a silver vase sprouting two perfect rosebuds.

The efficient whirlwind of staff vanished as quickly as they'd come. Jarrod locked the door behind them, turned, and held up the key. It looked tiny in his hand. "You want to fight me for it?" he asked, challenge and something that couldn't possibly be humor glinting in his eyes.

"Not without my knife."

He smiled a rich man's smile. "Pity." He lofted it into the air, caught it with a swipe, and dropped it into his jacket pocket. He strode to the opposite side of the table, and she found herself facing him, both of them standing behind their place settings, like husband and wife.

"Jewel?" he asked.

"What?"

He pulled a velvet ring box from his inside jacket pocket. "Jewel before dinner?"

"No."

"You don't even want to see it?"

"No," she said firmly, though the curiosity she'd cultivated through a career based on observation and investigation wailed at her decision.

"Very well." He slipped it back into his pocket. "Sit with me?"

"No."

He rounded the small table in two paces, so fast he startled her out of an opportunity to retreat. "I'll stand here next to you, then."

Her skin rushed with heat, a tingling wave of it that rolled up her breasts, chest, face. She averted her gaze to the edge of one immaculately tailored shoulder, but couldn't escape the warmth emanating from his power- ful body or the smell of his cologne—bracing and crisp with just a hint of spice. This was disastrously intimate, just the two of them locked inside her bedchamber, and him looking all of a sudden like he'd be more than happy to eat her up with a spoon.

"I'm glad you decided that we should dine in here," Jarrod said. He was so near she could feel the warmth of his breath against her scalp. "It's more private than the dining room."

"I decided nothing of the kind."

He ran his fingers down the curve of her shoulder, then across the delicate flesh at her inner elbow.

Lightning flashed up her arm. She jerked away. "Sit- ting will be fine."

"Very well." He returned to his side of the table, but didn't lower to his chair until she'd slid into hers.

He was probably the type of man that was aroused by an unwilling woman, she realized with a sick, jumpy feeling in the pit of her stomach. He'd made a profession out of crushing obstacles. Her resistance to him was probably only serving to whet his well-honed instincts to battle and conquer.

She spread the linen napkin onto her lap. He followed suit.

But what else could she do? Acquiescence was out of the question. She couldn't very well hand Twilight's Ghost over to him, and she plain wouldn't free his brother. So she'd simply do the best she could, despite her growing sense that she was in far over her head. Her forte was working alone and isolated. She'd never before been forced to confront an aggressor head-on. She'd no training for this, for being so inescapably close to him. No precedent for Jarrod Stone.

Jarrod gripped the top of the shiny metal domes covering both her plate and his, then raised them at the same time. Steam writhed upward from the plate before her laden with beef, corn, and small potatoes tossed with herbs and seasoning. The succulent aroma caused her mouth to water. Breakfast seemed decades past.

"I decided not to press my luck by trying to force you to eat three courses." Jarrod's words were accompanied by a *clang* as he set aside the domes.

Sophia couldn't recall when she'd last seen such gorgeous food. The beef glistened and dripped with a thin burgundy sauce. Not even Mrs. Akers, the best hostess in Galveston, served food this fresh.

She raised her gaze to Jarrod. Though he sprawled casually in his chair, his eyes belied the ease of the pose. They regarded her like a hawk might a mouse. "Do you have an appetite?" he asked.

She'd vowed not to eat his food. Abstinence in the face of all the niceties he'd offered her was one of the few powers she had. Especially abstinence in the face of food, because while Jarrod was a difficult man, she doubted he was cold-blooded enough to watch a woman starve. Of course, she could be wrong. If he didn't release her by to-morrow, she'd have to find a warmhearted maid willing to bring her food. When the time came for her escape she'd need her strength. "I'm not hungry in the least."

Her stomach chose that exact, inopportune moment to fill the air between them with a hearty growl.

He didn't say anything, just raised one eloquent brow.

Oh, damn him anyway. The injustice of it, all of it, his father's thievery, his kidnapping of her, her renegade stomach, caused a scream to build low in her body and begin to rise.

Jarrod lifted the bottle of red wine, examined the label, then filled their glasses. When he raised his glass, light shot from the crystal and illuminated shades of garnet in the wine. "I propose a toast."

Sophia just glared.

He paused, saw she wouldn't be joining him, and murmured, "To us." After saluting her with his glass, he took a sip. She watched the muscles in his throat work as he swallowed. Even his neck was attractive—tan and masculine. It was foolish, the details she noticed about him, more each time they met. She saw tonight that his forehead was slightly lined by years of tough decisions. His brows were uncompromisingly straight above deeper-set eyes. And his thick, dark hair was messier now than it had been earlier in the day. It looked as if he'd been walking outside and the breeze had rifled through it.

Jarrod set aside his glass and gathered his knife and fork. Instead of digging into the meal, however, he gave her a pointed stare and waited.

"I'm not eating," she said. "I believe I mentioned that earlier."

"What do you hope to gain by not eating?"

"It's a statement of my extreme displeasure."

"I can read displeasure in every inch of you, so you've already made your point. Eat."

"Of all the things you can control, Mr. Stone, or think you can, whether or not I chose to eat is not among them."

"Isn't it?" He leaned toward her, rested his elbows on the table. "I can open your mouth and feed you," he said, gesturing toward her lips with the point of his steak knife.

Uncertainty clutched her chest. "No," she replied, too quickly.

"Very well, then eat."

"I won't—"

"Eat," he growled.

Their gazes and wills locked. The china practically vibrated with the room's tension as all noise in the house faded to silence. Sophia planted her palms on the table, lowered her brows over her eyes, and corralled her nerve. "No," she said into the charged quiet.

"Then you've left me no choice."

Mother Mary, he's going to jab his steak knife against my throat and force-feed me.

Menacingly, he set aside his utensils, reached into his suit jacket, and slid a feather from within. Its wisps stroked along the edge of his lapel as he pulled it free. "You're in trouble now."

Her vision honed on the feather. What could he possibly be intending to do with that?

"Ticklish?" he asked.

"Tick . . ." She couldn't quite form the whole word.

He reached across the table, extending the tip of the

feather toward her face. She swatted it away. It came back again. And again. She batted at it for a few moments before releasing her breath in a huff and folding her hands in her lap. Instead of suffering the indignity of fighting off a feather like a ninny afraid of a fly, she'd simply sit and be impervious.

Jarrod skated the silky feather all over her face while she remained rigid—wordless with frustration. Her subdued scream reached her throat and swirled there, gaining force. He swept the feather across her eyelids, coasted it along the apple of a cheek, ran it back and forth over her lips repeatedly, before jiggling it under her earlobe.

"Eat or I'll continue to submit you to this torture," he said.

"I'm terrified."

The feather danced down her throat then licked along the lowest edge of her neckline, far too near her breasts for comfort. She clamped a hand over the area.

"You don't have much of a sense of humor, do you, Sophie?" he asked.

She shot him a withering look out of the corners of her eyes. "I must have lost it the day your father robbed my grandmother blind."

He pushed from his seat. "That's it." Suddenly he was looming over her, then kneeling before her. Without preamble, he clamped the feather between his teeth and tossed up the hem of her skirt.

Sophia gasped and tried to kick him, but he wrapped a hand around each ankle before her shoe could meet his chin. He yanked her forward. She yelped and had to latch her hands against the seat of her chair or be tumbled onto the floor before him. Aghast, mouth sagging

with shock, she struggled against his hold. How dare—
she couldn't believe— Her brain sputtered simply to
comprehend his audacity.

Easily, he notched one of her calves under his arm and
clamped it there with a power that surprised and dismayed her. Both hands now free, he grasped her remaining foot, then slipped off her shoe and tossed it carelessly
over his shoulder, where it skidded under the bed.

She watched in alarm as he released the feather from
between his teeth. Leisurely, he smoothed the tip of it
along her ultrasensitive arch which was protected by
nothing more substantial than a silk stocking.

Sophia made a desperate grab for the feather.

He jerked it out of her reach and punished her by giving her foot another pull. She was forced to return her
hand to her chair and lock both arms, muscles straining
just to stay seated.

The feather grazed her arch again.

To her horror, a tingling sensation unwound up her
calf and hissed along the flesh behind her knee. She
flinched. Oh, this was awful.

He was watching her face now, gauging her reactions
as he coasted the wretched feather under her toes, then
along the ball of her foot.

She clenched her teeth, trying to disconnect from the
feelings zipping across the bottom of her foot, making
her whole leg quiver. When that failed, she tried curling
in her toes, scrunching closed her eyes.

"Not so immune now, are you?" Jarrod taunted. "And
I didn't even have to remove your stockings."

She imagined her lower body, exposed to his scrutiny,
as his big hands rolled down her stockings, his fingers

rasping against flesh no man had ever seen, let alone touched. . . .

The feather's softness was so light—torturous. It teased its way down her arch, up, down, around her heel, and up. . . . A grin tugged at her mouth. She bit her lower lip, trying to stop it. The feather picked up speed, and the skin on the bottom of her foot roared with sensitivity. "Stop!" she demanded.

"Promise me you'll eat."

The floodgates opened, and she started to laugh.

"Promise," he said.

Her laughter intensified, rocking her shoulders now. She fought to jerk her foot from his hold, but he had her soundly. Moisture fuzzed her vision as she laughed and laughed. She fought harder, wild to take a full breath, to be free of his tormenting tickles. The merciless feather continued.

"Stop!" she gasped.

"Will you eat?"

She rammed her foot toward him, hoping to sock him in the chest. But he took her foot's proximity as an opportunity to blow on it, heightening the sensation.

She screamed with laughter.

"Eat?" he asked.

"P-please," she gulped for air, "stop-p!"

"Eat?"

"Yes!"

Instantly, the feather ceased its torment.

Sophia pulled in a deep lungful of air, sniffed, and groped for composure. "Oh," she murmured and dabbed at the corners of her eyes with the knuckle of her index finger.

Jarrod's face came into focus below her. His eyes sparkled and his lips curved with victory. He eased his hold on her ankle.

This time when she attempted to kick him, she succeeded, her heel connecting soundly with his shoulder. He grunted, but his annoying, cocksure expression didn't lessen as he rose and returned to his chair. Sophia tucked her bare foot under the hem of her dress, snuggling it protectively atop the ridges of her remaining shoe. She couldn't quite meet Jarrod's eyes, so she retrieved her napkin from the floor where it had fallen during her writhing. Another sniff, then she smoothed a wisp of mahogany hair back into place. How did one go about regaining ones dignity after that? She risked a glance across the table.

"Shall we?" He nodded at their food.

"Your behavior just now was appalling." She straightened her posture. "I'm embarrassed for you."

"I'm not at all embarrassed for you. You've got beautiful calves, beautiful feet, beautiful toes."

"I have a lover to tell me so. I hardly need you."

She could tell that her barb had sunk home. His eyes darkened, sobered. All levity between them drained away. Here was another distancing tactic she could use against him—his belief that Twilight's Ghost was her lover. It wasn't much, but at least it returned them to their proper position as adversaries, which was far preferable to him tickling her feet or worse, complimenting her.

"Does he tell you how lovely your face is?" he asked. "How perfect your lips are?"

Her throat thickened. See, this was precisely what she wanted to avoid. She was no expert on seduction, didn't even know how to respond to comments that held as much heat and velvet as his did. Jarrod, she got this impression very strongly, had said these same words to a hundred women. No telling how many he'd manipulated to his will. He was smooth, practiced, accustomed to getting what he wanted, and devilishly good at making a woman wonder what his passion must taste and feel and smell like.

"I'm sure you've seen lovelier faces in your time," she said.

"Maybe." The faraway look in his eye narrowed until she had the impression she was the only woman in the world he'd ever looked at as deeply as he was looking at her now. "Maybe never."

She cleared her throat and concentrated on her food. The sooner she ate it, the sooner she'd be rid of him. With fervor, she sliced off bites of meat and scooped up forkfuls of corn. In between, she primly touched her napkin to her lips and took minute sips of wine—just enough to wash down her food but not nearly enough to fog her senses.

Jarrod ate across from her, more slowly than she did. She was painfully aware of him, of every bite he took, the creaking of his chair, and the way he held his fork.

As soon as she finished, she slanted her utensils across her plate and set her napkin alongside.

Jarrod followed her lead. "Dessert?" he asked, placing the ring box from earlier atop the folds of her napkin.

With a long-suffering sigh, she indulged her curiosity by opening the small box. The black-velvet interior ensconced a diamond ring. In a chest gone still, her heartbeat thumped unnaturally loud. The huge central diamond was cut in a rectangular shape, as were the large diamonds on either side of it, as were the not-small diamonds on either side of them. It was the sort of ring that belonged in a museum behind glass. Like everything about him, it proclaimed how very, very rich he was.

The memory of a gaunt boy with ragged clothing and proud eyes slipped into her mind. Years upon years ago he'd stood on the other side of the fence at Blackhaw, his desperation reaching tendrils across to her as he'd clawed up the food she'd offered. She'd never forgotten him.

Lack of wealth could be far more devastating than the possession of it could ever be good. It was because of the boy who'd come to beg, and the girl she'd been, and so many others in similar situations, that she loathed men of Jarrod Stone's ilk, and detested the way they squandered their money.

The heaviness of his attention grew oppressive.

She flicked a look at him from beneath her lashes. "Don't you think it's a little soon to be proposing marriage?" she asked dryly.

He smiled a wolf's smile. "Take it. It's yours."

She snapped closed the lid. "No. Thank you." Resolutely, she reached across the table and set the box on his napkin. "I've always preferred pineapple cake for dessert. Ask anyone."

"So you don't like rubies, and you don't like diamonds." He lounged against the back of his chair, one knee pointing forward, one splayed to the side. He looked far too much like a man content to pass the remainder of the evening sitting in her bedroom. "What do you like? Tell me, I'll buy it."

"I like freedom, Mr. Stone. It's the only gift from you I'll ever accept."

He studied her as a mathematician might a problem he'd yet to solve.

"Well." She rose from her seat and scooted in her chair. "As enjoyable as this has been, I'd appreciate it if you'd relieve me of your company."

When he didn't move, she gestured impatiently toward the hallway.

He unfolded his frame from the chair. Halfway to the door, he caught sight of her bed. He halted, glanced at her. "Did you mean what you said today, about not sleeping in the bed I've provided for you?"

"Yes."

"I can stay in it with you, if that will make you less afraid of scary beasts."

"Why would I ever trade beasts outside the bed for a beast under the covers with me?"

"There are reasons," he said slowly.

Every fine hair on her body seemed to rise. She wondered what he might look like stark naked, what it might feel like to have him slide that naked body on top of hers, for him to bury his hands in her hair and turn his enormous concentration to the task of ravishing her.

The sound of the key fitting into its hole saved her from her thoughts. She stared at his wide back as he freed the lock. Blessed Mary, she couldn't believe she'd just entertained that little fantasy about him—a Stone without a shred of decency, without even one redeeming quality. That she'd envision coupling with him for even one second. Deplorable.

He pulled the door wide and called for his servants, then looked to her. "I'll be back with breakfast in the morning."

"Back?"

"Until you're willing to eat in the dining room, I'll be bringing the food and the torture to you."

Not likely. He'd bested her once, but she had no intention of allowing him to trap her inside here alone with him again. "There's no need. The dining room will be adequate from now on."

He lifted an indifferent shoulder.

As the servants surged past him and swept the remains of their dinner from the room, his gaze weighed on her. The image of him naked returned to her mind with scorching heat.

Oh, Maggie, she thought, *come for me. Come for me quick.*

Chapter 5

The next morning Jarrod watched from his place at the head of the table as Sophia entered the dining room. She was wearing the same dark green skirt and bodice she'd been wearing the day before, except the cloth was now scarred with crisscrossing wrinkles. She'd slept in her clothes. And from the bleary look in her coffee-colored eyes, she hadn't slept well. Not surprising, considering her determination to spurn the bed.

He set aside his cup and stood as she approached. Last night he'd gotten her to eat. Soon, he'd have her wearing the clothes he'd purchased and sleeping in the bed he'd furnished. She wasn't an impractical woman. In fact, the opposite. He sensed that Sophia was far too practical for her own good.

Jarrod held Sophia's chair, then returned to his place

and assessed her profile in silence. He was a man who recognized rarity when he saw it, a connoisseur of fine things. And Sophia Vanessa LaRue was incredibly fine.

She'd brushed the mass of her dark, shiny hair back into another tight bun. Just one brave strand whispered against the tiny buttons at the back of her neck. He studied the refined slope of her nose, the little groove between nose and upper lip, the delicate line of her chin. Together, they combined to an almost breath-stealing beauty.

Still, what fascinated him about Sophia wasn't her looks—many women with perfect features left him cold. What fascinated him was the contrast between the person she revealed to him—no humor, no flirting, no vices—and the person he suspected she truly was. Despite her guardedness, there was a lushness about her, a richness that reminded him of the liquid chocolate he'd once been served in Spain. However, those qualities lived below the surface, down where the fire was.

Once she'd been convinced to share that fire he could only imagine what it would be like to make love to Sophia. He'd thought about little else for most of last night, except for the times he'd thought about what kind of lover she was to Twilight's Ghost.

Had the man really settled for her beauty alone, when any fool could see there was more? Had he allowed her the remoteness she so clearly preferred? He suspected so. "Are you in love with him?" Jarrod asked.

She scowled at him. "Who?"

"You know who."

"I don't believe that's any—"

"Of my business?"

"That's correct, it's not."

A maid bustled into the room, setting a breakfast of ham, eggs, and buttermilk biscuits before them both. "What can we offer you to drink?" Jarrod asked Sophia. "Coffee? Juice?"

"Plain tea will be fine."

"No sugar or cream?"

"No."

Just plain, brown tea. It was as if she'd purposely cut every indulgence out of her life . . . which was something he could remedy. He'd keep testing her with gifts until he found the one that would provide him with the key to her loyalty.

Once the maid left the room, she set about opening her biscuits with her fork.

He moved the pot of honey, the plum jelly, and the butter next to her.

"I just wanted to make sure you're not one of those women who likes to fancy herself in love," he said. He hoped she was too wise and too battered by life for that kind of foolishness.

Her hands stilled. "I thought this conversation was over."

"No." Jarrod had expected Twilight's Ghost to come for her right away, to attempt to steal her back during the night. He hadn't, which might mean that the Ghost was too stupid to value Sophia or too cowardly to risk himself by fighting for her. If the man left her here without a backward glance, Jarrod wanted to know, for reasons he couldn't fully explain, whether Sophia's heart would be broken.

She eyed him for a long moment. "I'm assuming that you, of course, do not believe in love."

He snorted derisively. "No."

"No?" She canted her head at a thoughtful angle. "What about your brother? I suppose you're going to all this trouble to free him because you have a passing fondness for him."

"That's different. That's family."

Something behind her expression tightened—a very old pain. As quickly as it had opened, the slight window into her heart closed, but not before he understood that she wished she were a part of a family. Of course she did. She'd been orphaned carly and widowed early. For the majority of her life she'd had only herself.

An uncharacteristic sense of guilt jabbed him. As far as families went, he'd been far more blessed than she. Not because he was more deserving, or had done anything to earn his brothers but because blind fate had been generous with him and stingy with her.

She busied herself smearing a pat of butter on her biscuit, where it instantly started to melt. "Is the love between a man and a woman so far inferior to that between siblings, to your way of thinking?"

"Absolutely. There's no history there, no blood, or loyalty. To put your happiness in the hands of another without those things is idiocy."

She drizzled honey on her biscuit before sampling it.

He watched her lips move as she chewed. "Not that there aren't a myriad of . . . things . . . a man and woman can't enjoy together."

It amazed him, this talent she had for not meeting his eyes whenever he spoke carnally. Usually people fidgeted when he stared at them and eventually had to glance his way. But she managed to refrain from doing so with an air of extreme disinterest. She likely meant for her feigned boredom to squelch his attention. Instead it dared him to prove to them both how little he bored her.

Maybe that's why he couldn't stop himself from saying sexual things to her. He couldn't resist seeing how she'd react.

Never had he met a woman who needed to be seduced more than she did. Sophia Vanessa LaRue was practically screaming for someone to loosen her up, to strip her naked, to make her laugh and strain with pleasure. Her husband and Twilight's Ghost had both clearly bungled the job.

His gaze drifted to her breasts. She had voluptuous breasts for a woman with such a lithe body. He could only imagine them unbound, the weight of them in his cupped palms. He'd never favored women of skin and bones. He liked his women to be women—with full breasts—and this one was.

"So do you?" he asked, his voice slightly rough.

"Do I what?"

"Love him?"

"Do I love Twilight's Ghost," she murmured, studying her biscuit. "Yes, I believe I do."

His lips twisted. Her admission rankled, made him wonder why he'd forced it from her when he hated her answer. His restless instincts split between shaking sense into her or taking the back of her head in his hand and kissing it into her.

The maid from earlier returned with Sophia's tea. A second maid followed, carrying the coat Jarrod had instructed her to bring.

Sophia eyed the coat, then looked to him. "What's this?"

"Your new winter coat."

"It's the most wondrous thing I've ever seen, ma'am." The maid carrying it slanted it toward the light so Sophia could get a better look. "Black velvet with this heavenly black fur around the neck, trimming the sides all the way . . . all the way to the floor, around the hem, and around the cuffs. See?" She extended a sleeve for inspection. A sliver of window had been left open to the winter and the breeze sliding through it swayed the opulent ebony fur.

"Oh, and it's beautifully fitted, ma'am. Snug around the waist and the back. Not that I . . ." she darted a look in Jarrod's direction, "tried it on."

Sophia's lack of response caused the maid to squirm. "Truly, it's the finest garment I've ever had the pleasure of touching."

"Then it's yours," Sophia said.

"Oh, no, ma'am." Her eyes rounded with dismay.

"I insist."

"But I couldn't possibly—"

"Certainly, you could."

"No! I—"

"Take it," Jarrod said to the girl.

She paled, nodded, and hurried from the room followed by her companion.

"Care to tell me why I just bought a fur-lined coat for a kitchen maid?" Jarrod asked.

"I don't relish wearing an animal around my neck." She speared a bite of egg. "I like them living."

"I didn't see any animals at Blackhaw."

"We used to have them." She gave him a telling look. "Once."

It surprised him, how much bitterness she still held

toward his father. Usually people's emotions cooled over time and they grew philosophical about past wrongs. Not she. She was still actively blaming his father—him—for the unforgivable. For stealing not just her money and with it the former grandeur of her home, but far worse. For taking her only relative from her.

Primly, Sophia licked a drip of honey off the side of her lip with a glossy little tongue. He had a fierce urge to toss her onto the nearest sofa, pull up her skirts, and bury himself inside her.

"You're not eating," she commented. It was a criticism.

"Why would I when I can sit here and watch you instead?"

In the quiet that followed the conversational tones of his kitchen staff mingled with the clop of hooves as one of the grooms cantered a horse down the drive.

She stared at him pointedly. "Cease saying things like that to me. You waste your breath."

"I never waste anything."

"You waste everything of importance, my time foremost among them."

A polite knock echoed from the doors leading into the hall. He looked up to see Collier standing on the threshold. "Yes?"

"You've a visitor, sir."

At Jarrod's questioning expression, his secretary motioned almost imperceptibly toward Sophia.

"Will you excuse me?" Jarrod asked.

She nodded, her interest focused on Collier.

He strode the length of the table into the hall, then led Collier partway down the corridor. "Who?"

"A woman named Maggie May. She arrived alone asking to visit with Mrs. LaRue."

"I know who she is." Sophia's friend and companion. He'd anticipated that Miss May would come in search of her.

He peered over his shoulder toward the dining room and caught sight of a portion of Sophia's face—an eye, cheek, ear. She reared out of view swiftly. Interesting. Here, finally, was something the ice princess appeared to care about.

"Fine," Jarrod said. "Ensure she carries no weapons. Instruct the guards to take her into the kitchen so the women there can check through her skirts and undergarments."

"Yes, sir."

"Then escort her to Mrs. LaRue's chambers and report to me."

"Yes, sir."

Jarrod separated from Collier and returned to the dining room. He found Sophia back at her place, her demeanor alert.

"Was the visitor here to see me?" she asked before he'd reached his seat.

"Yes."

"And?"

"And you are, of course, welcome to spend time with her."

She immediately scooted back her chair.

"With one stipulation."

Her retreat halted. Glowering, she waited for him to divulge the bad news.

A man acquainted with the value of a well-placed

pause, he took his time settling into his chair. In no hurry, he sipped his coffee, and buttered two biscuits.

By the look of her, Sophia was near ready to explode with impatience. So much so, he had to bite back a grin. Damn, but he liked to rile her, to see her eyes blaze and her chin go rigid and her lips tighten up as if she'd just sucked the juice from a lemon. He started slicing his ham.

"What's the stipulation?" she asked.

"Don't you want to finish your breakfast?"

"Just tell me," she snapped.

"The stipulation is that you not wear that outfit again." He gestured toward it with his fork tines. "You wore it yesterday, and I'm tired of it. I want to see you in the clothes I purchased for you."

"I don't want to wear your clothes—"

"I realize that. So you have a choice to make." He ate a bite of ham, taking his time with it, tasting the salty juice that ran down his tongue as he studied her. "You can either see Miss May or you can continue wearing that gown."

Her eyes narrowed, then narrowed again. They'd come to another stalemate. She took so long to answer that he worried he'd have to look at her in that green bodice until the reckoning.

"I want to see Miss May," she finally decided.

"Then you shall," Jarrod answered. "Collier will return to escort you in a few minutes."

Her gaze traveled over his face, from his brows to his lips before returning to his eyes. "I won't forgive you for this, you know. For holding me hostage."

He ate a bite of eggs, salted them, then tried another

bite. She was wrong, of course. She'd not only forgive him, she'd thank him in time.

"I'm sure bribery and abduction have been profitable for you in the past, but with me you've miscalculated. I've worked hard to earn the freedom I have. When you took that away from me you took something beyond price. No diamond ring or fur coat is going to make me forget that."

He relished her show of temper. She could be a hellion in bed, he just *knew* it.

Clearly, she was more attached to her independence than most, something that had likely resulted from the years when she'd been forced to rely upon the sisters of St. Mary's for food and shelter. Still, he knew the female heart. Underneath the bluster, every one of them, including hers, ultimately wanted to be protected and cared for. She didn't know that yet. She didn't know a lot of things yet.

Collier returned and Sophia went to him immediately. To her frustration, the silver-haired gentleman waited to escort her, his face raised to Jarrod, ears pricking like those of a well-trained hound. How humiliating, to be made to wait for permission simply to return to her cell.

"You may take her to Miss May," Jarrod said.

Collier inclined his head and she walked ahead of him. When he opened her bedroom door for her, Maggie turned from where she'd been standing near the pink sofa. Sophia hurried forward and they met in the middle with a hug.

"Are you all right?" Maggie whispered.

"Yes." Sophia squeezed, Maggie squeezed back, then they parted. Sophia checked over her shoulder to ensure that Collier was gone and the door closed behind him.

"Actually, I'm a bit frayed. Jarrod Stone is certifiably insane."

"Certifiably," Maggie agreed. "Handsome, though. I glimpsed him in passing when his secretary escorted me here."

"Handsome!" She couldn't believe Maggie would point out any redeeming quality in her arch enemy. "You can't really think so."

"Absolutely, I do. So do you."

"No," Sophia answered, scandalized.

"Oh, *please,* Sophia. He makes your mouth water, and you know it. All that dark brooding power. Had he not made his fortune in oil, the man could live luxuriously well posing as an English lord for fashion plates."

"I doubt it." What was she saying? Of course the man was handsome, any fool could see that. Ordinarily, she had no trouble admitting the truth to Maggie, but about *him* . . . she just couldn't bring herself to. "Come." She grabbed Maggie's hand and drew her toward her dressing room. She didn't trust Jarrod or his minions not to attempt to eavesdrop on their conversation. The dressing room was farthest from the door, windowless, and muffled by all those expensive clothes.

Maggie followed, the loping gait of her tall thin body reminding Sophia, as it always did, of a Great Dane puppy with more height and enthusiasm than grace. Once inside, Sophia struck a match and lit the lamp positioned on the dresser adjacent to the mirror. Maggie closed them in.

"This room," Maggie whispered, looking around with awed curiosity. "Are all these clothes for you?" She ran a hand along a silken sleeve, then glanced up at Sophia quizzically.

"I'm afraid so."

"That's . . ." She looked again at the clothes, then back at Sophia. "That's spooky."

"I know. I told you—certifiable."

"It's also somewhat flattering, Sophia, you have to admit." Maggie started going through the racks, assessing each outfit before moving its hanger to the side. "I swear, men *never* do this kind of thing for me. More's the pity."

"So tell me how you found me."

"I knocked on our neighbors' doors. Though Mrs. Pinson from down the street didn't witness your abduction, she did remember the carriage that had been lying in wait across from her house all day."

"And you recognized her description of the carriage."

She nodded. "It matched exactly the description you'd given me of the carriage Jarrod brought with him to Blackhaw. I already suspected him, so Mrs. Pinson simply provided verification. It then became a matter of discovering where Jarrod had taken you. The gossips at the Tremont Hotel proved as reliable as always, informing me that he'd purchased this property just days ago."

"Where is this property, exactly? The servants have refused to tell me."

"It's the Bowmans' old place. Two miles due east of town."

Sophia visualized her location, seeing it like a map in her mind.

Maggie's exploration halted on a dark plum-colored hat decorated with flounces of plum ribbon. "Mind if I try it on?"

"Of course not."

Maggie shed her simple straw hat, releasing long, glossy strands of copper hair to dangle around her face.

While most considered Maggie's skinny, gawky body to be highly unfashionable, no one could dispute the fact that the woman had stunning hair. Maggie donned the plum hat and made a face at her reflection. "Have you ever seen a color that looks worse with my hair?"

Sophia laughed, embarrassingly grateful to have her here. "No."

Maggie reached for another hat.

Content for the moment to wait, Sophia leaned against the wall at the far end of the room and watched her friend. For the first time since her kidnapping, comfort twined through her. They'd worked together for five years, and during that time Maggie had always done this for her, always helped her take herself less seriously. With Maggie she never felt as solemn, dull, and old as she knew she truly was.

"Put something on, Sophia."

She was about to decline as a matter of course, when she thought better of it. From this point on, she'd committed herself to wearing these clothes. Might as well put something on now, while Maggie was here to tell her she looked nice even if she didn't.

Maggie tried on a brown-velvet hat while Sophia wedged off her practical shoes and pulled out a completely impractical pair of red ones with ribbon rosettes stitched onto the toes. Her stockinged feet slid into a fit that couldn't have been more perfect had she been Cinderella and these slippers made of glass. She wanted to hate the shoes. She truly did. And yet it was hard to hate something so frivolous and lovely.

She divested her own clothing and donned the red bodice and skirt that matched the shoes. Then she peered at herself in the standing oval mirror, unsure how she felt about the stranger peering back. The high, silk-trimmed collar of the bodice curved around the back of her neck before dipping into in a low oval just above the cleft between her breasts. The skirt perfectly skimmed her hips before sweeping a graceful line to the floor.

These garments had been made for her. The fabric precisely fit the width of her shoulders, the swell of her breasts, the circumference of her waist, the length of her legs. This ensemble was both more comfortable and more flattering than any she could ever recall owning. And yet, she felt tainted just by putting it on. As if she were betraying her principles.

"You do know, don't you," Maggie asked, "just how astonishing you look in that."

She turned to her friend. "Thank you, but—"

"Sophia, it's not a crime to enjoy a few items of nice clothing, you know. It's practically a feminine imperative." She jauntily retied the brown-velvet bow beneath her chin. "I say luxuriate in what you can while you can."

Maybe. But if Jarrod thought he was going to win her allegiance with a closet full of clothes, he was drastically mistaken. Sophia perched against the edge of the dresser, her relaxed mood gone, and her worries returned. "Did you speak with Simon about my situation?"

At the mention of their supervisor within the agency, Maggie's face sobered. Her hands drifted away from the hat. "I did."

"And?" Sophia's heart shrank in her chest. "I take it he isn't planning to raid this house and rescue me."

"No."

"Not even an attempt to free me using just a piddling agent or two?"

Maggie shook her head slowly.

In some region of herself, the logical region, Sophia had guessed that to be the case. It still pained her unexpectedly to hear it. After all she'd done for the agency, all the times she risked herself, they weren't coming for her. An aged sense of abandonment pushed at her from the inside. Nowadays she could squelch the feeling for months at a time, but it never fully died. It just waited, waited for a situation like this to remind her that no matter how far she'd come, it still had the power to drag her back. She was still ultimately alone.

"Had it been me, I'd have brought a whole army with me, guns blazing," Maggie said. "You know I would have. But he's more cautious, less enamored than I, I'm guessing, of the idea of surrounding himself with an army of good-looking men." She smiled that acres-wide smile of hers that displayed all her teeth.

Sophia couldn't quite dredge up any levity. She was being left here to fend for herself against Jarrod, that's what Maggie was saying.

Chapter 6

Maggie's smile melted away. "Simon's foremost concern is to safeguard your identity as Twilight's Ghost, Sophia. Imagine if agents descended on this place and stole you away. Jarrod Stone, already a man on the hunt for Twilight's Ghost, is smart enough to realize that the Secret Service would never go to such lengths for an agent's mistress. Then there's the problem of where to take you. If you're returned to Blackhaw, what's to stop Jarrod from abducting you again? If you're not returned to Blackhaw, then he'll be supplied with proof that you're not simply Sophia LaRue, beautiful widow. It's too risky."

"I understand."

Maggie's eyes held concern and regret. She doubtless loathed her task as messenger. "Sophia, the work you do is critical in this part of the country. He's not willing to risk that."

She nodded.

"And seeing as how Jarrod's goal is to win your assistance to his cause, Simon was willing to bet you'd be well cared for during your stay." She motioned toward the rows of clothes. "Looks as if he was correct."

"My orders, then, are to stay here and to wait."

"Yes. Though if I return to find you chained in a drafty dungeon, I'll be compelled to take matters into my own hands." Maggie winked.

Sophia crossed her arms and tried to reconcile herself to the idea of staying here—with him—for any length of time. Despite the mature, rational reactions she'd just fed her friend, the idea screeched against every impulse she had. "Did Simon have any other agency news?"

Maggie slipped off the hat and carefully returned it to its place. "You know that local counterfeiter our office has been keeping an eye out for?"

"Yes."

"Well, Simon informed me that Slocum's Mercantile has finally grown weary of being passed fake bills in return for their goods." She picked up her own straw hat, made a face at it, and dusted it off. "According to Simon the agency was able to confirm that the vast majority of the loss they're taking is due to counterfeit bills from the press of the same person, or group of people we've been after. Slocum's is offering a reward to the agent who uncovers them."

"A reward?" Sophia's interest sparked. "How much?"

"Five hundred dollars."

Blessed Mary, with that much money she could pay the taxes she owed on Blackhaw— Her gaze traveled over the walls enclosing her. Hope fizzled. She couldn't even manage to escape from these rooms. How was she supposed to solve a counterfeiting case? "Did you bring me my knife?"

"No. I was worried Jarrod would have me searched before allowing me to see you, and was right to worry. He did have me searched. I managed to bring you some of your toiletries, but that's all." She twisted up her hair and secured it beneath her straw hat.

Sophia pushed away from the dresser and paced the tiny space, toying with her fingernails as she thought. "We need to figure out a way to get me some sort of a weapon. If not my knife, then a gun, a letter opener, something."

"You don't think he might try to physically assault you. . . ."

Vividly, she remembered Jarrod's strong, expert hands holding her foot. A feather dancing torture across her toes. "He's too rich, too powerful, and far too accustomed to acquiescence. I can't predict how he'll respond when I continue to deny him his wishes."

"How do you suggest I smuggle in a weapon?"

Sophia stopped, and ran her gaze over Maggie's clothing. Her attention halted on the plain hem of her friend's gingham skirt. "What if. . . . What if Mrs. Dewberry sewed my knife into the hem of your coat? The fabric of your coat would be weighty enough to conceal it adequately, don't you think?"

"I think you're brilliant, that's what I think." Maggie shook her head, bemusement and respect in her eyes.

Sophia's mind whirled, rotating the situation from all angles, as she'd learned to do when investigating her cases. "And Oliver. Send Oliver here to visit me." Being out of contact with her grandmother's advisor had made her superstitious that he might have unearthed a vital clue in their search for Adam Stone, yet been unable to reach her. Besides, there was no reason why she couldn't continue her quest while confined here. That included bringing Oliver here, and uncovering whatever it was Jarrod knew about his father's disappearance.

"Okay. I'll bring a knife, and I'll contact Oliver."

"Thanks, Maggie." She'd feel ever so much better the next time she faced Jarrod, knowing she carried a knife in her garter.

"The newest items you've ordered are on their way, sir," Collier said. "They'll be here later tonight."

Jarrod rocked slightly in his office chair. Collier, ever proper, liked to use the word "items" for what they both knew were bribery gifts for their beautiful houseguest. Over the years, he'd purchased numerous such presents for women. He'd just never had so little luck in response to them. "Good. What about the search for Twilight's Ghost?" Not one to pile all his eggs in a single basket, Jarrod had hired a cadre of high-priced detectives to hunt down the agent while he dedicated himself to the same goal by way of Sophia.

"Nothing, I'm afraid, sir. They report that they're traveling paths other detectives have previously trodden with the same results. There's plenty of rumor and speculation, but the people know nothing of Twilight's Ghost, have seen nothing of substance. Our men haven't yet found anyone worthy even of payment in return for information."

Jarrod swiveled his leather chair toward the dark window and stared moodily out.

"They report that the man is aptly named."

"He's not a ghost. He's flesh and blood, and there's at least one person out there other than my Mrs. LaRue who must know something. Have them continue."

"Yes, sir."

Maxine ambled into the room, her nails clicking on the wooden floor. She plopped down, laid her head on his foot, and rolled her eyes up at him dolefully.

He reached into a drawer and tossed her a specially made dog biscuit, which she caught mid air. "What about Sophia's husband?" he asked, watching Maxine chomp.

"Nothing there either."

Jarrod's gaze sharpened as it moved to the older man.

"As yet we've come upon no information of him. Not a church record of their marriage, no land ownership deeds, no mercantile or bank accounts."

"Keep searching. I want to know how long they were married, what he died of, what Sophia's life was like during the time after the orphanage and before her return to Blackhaw."

So far that space of her life was a mystery to him. Not that he had any particular desire to hear about Sophia's husband. He didn't. In fact, he instinctively disliked the man almost as much as he hated Twilight's Ghost. Information was strength, however, and the more he knew about Sophia, the more power he had over her.

"Yes, sir, I'll have our men continue their search for Mr. LaRue."

"Tell them to be quick about it." He pictured Holden sitting on his jail-cell cot, his face lifting slowly until his eyes met Jarrod's. "I'm going to find Twilight's Ghost. I want to do it soon."

"Yes, sir."

Jarrod dismissed Collier with a nod, then strode to the back of the house and let himself out, Maxine at his side. He set off toward no particular destination. At least it was quiet here, and open. He loosened his collar. Occasionally, in the rooms of his life—rooms where he negotiated, presided over meetings, planned the expansion of his holdings—he felt like he couldn't breathe. Sophia, he'd been discovering, had the power to make him feel the same way. But for different reasons. She stole his breath from his chest.

Around him the gently rolling, tree-covered hills were painted with different shades of the sun. Golden in places, darker in places where clouds cast their shadows. He lengthened his stride, letting his mind clear, at last permitting his thoughts go to the place where they'd been wanting to travel for days, ever since discovering that the Ghost's mistress was Sophia Warren, all grown-up.

He had been fifteen, that first day he'd seen her.

He was starving, literally. His stomach eating the rest of him up. Still, he'd never have come to Blackhaw Manor, never have stooped to this, if not for his mother. Thoughts of her caused a dull ache to expand in his chest. Since his father had been away from the house so much, working on an investment he said would make them rich, things had gotten bad. He pushed his mother's thin, white face from his mind, forcing his concentration to the house before him.

For what seemed like an eternity he'd been standing here at the gates of Blackhaw. Plenty long enough to stare at the part of the mansion visible to him—a steep roof with lots of gables, expensive-looking windows, and yellow-brick chimneys. He both hated and craved every inch.

His bitter gaze lowered to the trees filled with fruit, just across the bars from him, out of reach. A black-iron gate separated him from the orchard and from everything and everyone inside as surely as oil from water.

The coarse cloth of his shirt itched his skin and let in too much morning air. He shivered and crossed his arms over his chest—then saw her.

A dark-eyed, dark-haired girl in a lacy white dress, white stockings, white button-up shoes. She stood beneath the branches of a peach tree staring at him.

He stood stock-still, wishing in that moment for death. He'd rather anyone else have seen him—her grandmother, a stableboy, one of the uppity advisors his father complained about. From them, he might have been able to do what he'd come to do. To beg.

But not from her. A mere girl of about eight. A rich princess without a spot of mud on her clothes and shoes. For no good reason, she had everything in the world, and he had nothing. She wore silly bows on her braided hair, a shiny pink sash around her waist. She was the most foolish creature on earth, and he hated her for it, for having so much and flaunting it when his mother was dying and his brothers were weak from hunger.

Worst of all, in her expression he recognized pity.

He didn't need to see himself in the reflection of her eyes to know he looked poor, sick, and dirty. He was. The realization of that, regardless of how many times he'd been forced to face it, never failed to disgust him. Mostly because he *felt* different on the inside. He wasn't this person, wasn't meant for this.

What was left of his pride melted into a nauseating mass, and he thought he'd throw up the watery oatmeal he'd had for breakfast, their last.

Without a word, the girl plucked a peach from the tree. Using her skirt as a basket, she picked more fruit and more. A wide selection, until the fabric bowl couldn't hold any more. She walked to the gate, standing just on the other side, and regarded him with a strange soberness—too old and calm for such a little person.

He'd brought a gunnysack with him. Quiet stretched between them in the instant before he grabbed for the fruit, tossing it into the bag. When he'd taken it all, the girl stepped away, her dainty hands releasing the sides of her skirt. She continued peering at him, brown smudges and dust now streaking the front of her dress.

He ran. Carrying the fruit across his back, he had dashed from her like a thief, feeling as guilty, and as branded as if he were one.

For three weeks, he'd returned to the gates of Blackhaw every day. And every day, she'd met him there, passing sacks of food to him without a single word. Each time he took her scraps. And each time the mixture of shame, gratitude, and relief roiling inside made him feel less human. He remembered vowing to himself that he'd be as good as she someday no matter how long it took.

In the distance, a horse whinnied. Jarrod's attention returned to the present with a start. Bitterness lingered in his mouth, no longer directed at the target of the girl, but merely the circumstances of the time.

He wondered how Sophia would react if she knew it was he she'd fed back then, the son of the man she'd one day blame for losing everything.

Maxine loped beside him. He noticed that she'd found a stick somewhere and was patiently clasping it in her mouth. "Here," he murmured, as he took it from her and threw it. He watched, hardly registering the sight, as she went tearing after it.

For years now, he'd remembered that girl in white without malice. With nothing, in fact, but a vague sense of debt. He owed her for easing his mother's final days with all those sacks of food, and for sensing that while he might be able to accept her charity, he wouldn't have been able to bear her words.

He'd never had the desire to see her again, however, and would have been content to thank her for her kindness in some distant, anonymous way. Then all this had happened with Holden and Twilight's Ghost, and they'd been thrown together. There was nothing distant about his association with her now. And nothing, he was certain, he'd yet done for her that she'd view as an expression of thanks.

He wished he didn't see the little dark-eyed girl when he looked at her, wished he didn't still feel this nagging sense of obligation. Without those things, pressuring her to his will the way he needed to for his brother's sake would have been a hell of a lot easier.

Maxine bounded to him, panting. He threw her stick again and she charged after it.

So what could he do for Sophia that would fulfill this troublesome sense of debt? He could discover then give to her whatever it was she valued—there had to be something. If there's one thing he'd learned in his climb from poverty, it was that every person had a price. Perhaps he should alter his tactics, look for her price in other places. It was only a matter of time until he hit on it. . . .

Unfortunately, time, right now, was a commodity far more valuable than money. Every hour it took him to wring the truth from her was an hour Holden was spending in prison. A fact that set his teeth on edge, that never left his mind.

What else could he do for her? Grimly, he smiled. He could do her the favor of ending her relationship with Twilight's Ghost. He himself was no moral paragon. He'd had mistresses and never thought twice about the illicitness of his relationships. Why should he? They'd been greedy women, he was a man with powerful desires. They'd met each other's needs.

Still, what was acceptable for him wasn't acceptable for her. Their discussion over breakfast had confirmed it—he plain didn't like even the *thought* of Sophia having a sexual relationship with Twilight's Ghost. The girl he remembered, as well as the woman he was coming to know, was too good for it. Too good for Twilight's Ghost.

And since he was currently in a position to break their liaison, he would.

Maxine returned, and he sent her after her stick a third time.

There was one more thing he could do for Sophia, he knew. And this one he didn't like. He looked back at the house, squinted toward her chamber.

He could save her from himself.

When she'd licked that drop of honey off her lip, he'd been surprised by how much he'd wanted her. Painfully so. Still, a tryst with him, just like a tryst with the Ghost, wasn't worthy of her. She deserved better, after what life had dealt her.

So while he'd allow himself to compliment her, maybe to touch her just a bit, he'd not allow himself to go farther than that. He'd keep his hands off her, regardless of the restraint it would cost him, regardless of how much he'd relish a chance at seducing the ice princess and discovering just how passionately she could writhe.

He stalked in the direction opposite the house, Maxine trotting beside him. Having a conscience could be damn annoying. Which was why, he acknowledged, he indulged his own so seldom.

For three whole days Sophia survived by following an established pattern. She slept in the bed he'd furnished, wore the clothes he'd purchased, and kept to her room reading, pacing, or otherwise avoiding him at all times except when they ate. At the moment they were sitting at the dining-room table in silence, having just completed a strained midday meal of chicken.

Over the past days, Jarrod had attempted to give her perfume, a sapphire necklace, embroidered lingerie, and emeralds the size of walnuts to hang from her ears.

Regardless of the troublesome current that snapped between them, a fire that grew a little hotter, a little brighter with every meeting, she'd easily declined all his gifts. She leaned back in her chair, interested to see what he'd try to give her next, but unworried about her ability to resist it.

"Will you accompany me outside?" Jarrod asked.

She lifted her brows. She hadn't felt the outside air on her face since coming here. "Why?" she asked suspiciously.

"Because I'd like to rope you to a tree and ravish you."

Her pulse stuttered. "That's not funny."

"You never think anything's funny," he said with a half smile. He assisted her in scooting back her chair.

"The truth is that while I'd like very much to ravish you, I'll wait for you to ask me first."

"That'll be a long wait."

"How long?"

"Longer than the remaining days of your life." She stood, firming her jaw as she faced him.

"Not if I decided to put my mind to it." He assessed her with frank sexuality and something that looked a bit like regret.

Her belly fluttered, the way it had taken to doing lately when he looked at her that way. That I-can-eat-you-alive way.

"Today, however," he said, "I want you to come outside because I have a surprise for you."

"Another gift?"

"Yes, another gift. Am I so predictable?"

"Indeed."

"Then I'll try harder not to bore you. Shall we?" He stepped aside so she could pass.

She walked along the hallway toward the front of the house, Jarrod following like a charismatic black demon. When a servant drew the door open for her, she crossed the threshold then the porch, her eyes squinting as they worked to adjust to the clear February day—

She came immediately to a dead halt, her chest contracting at the sight before her.

At the bottom of the steps pranced a horse, though to call the animal a horse seemed far too inadequate. This creature looked like something Cinderella would have ridden over cobblestones of gold into a castle made of gilt. The horse was pure white with a tail that flowed to the ground and a cascading mane. Its neck formed a high, graceful arch ending in a delicately intelligent face. The animal's body rippled with muscle, the legs tapered to dainty hooves.

She'd adored horses once. . . . Every fantasy she'd ever had of them came rushing back. She remembered for the first time in months—or was it years—her white pony. The pony had been stout and short, with a tendency to bite and a proclivity for rolling in mud. She'd loved him staunchly despite his shortcomings, spent hours riding him, brushing him, leading him in circles, drawing pictures of him. Until he'd been sold like everything else to pay the debts after Grandmother's funeral.

Tears stung her eyes, shocking her. Oh, heaven, she'd nearly forgotten all about that pony until just now. How could it mean anything to her after all this time? How could simply laying eyes on this horse today cause her to feel so forcefully the dreams and wonder of a child who'd grown up?

She stared, mesmerized, at the glorious white horse, knowing only that she'd discovered a part of herself, a love of hers, that had been lost for a long time. Suddenly, brutally, this particular gift of Jarrod's didn't seem so easy to decline.

Chapter 7

She worked to compose herself before chancing a look at him. He hung back slightly, his gaze steady on her, seeming to drink in every nuance of her expression. Which made her very afraid that he'd seen too much.

He smiled at her. Not the usual sharp smile, but one of genuine warmth.

Oh. Entire swarms of butterflies took flight in her stomach. Hastily, she looked away. She schooled her voice to expose no emotion. "What's this?" she asked, motioning her chin toward the horse.

He came to stand beside her. "As a boy, I remember hearing that Sophia of Blackhaw had a white horse."

She didn't so much as blink.

"And since you told me the other day that you have a

fondness for animals despite not owning any currently, I thought you might like this one."

He said it all very casually and noncommittally. By acting as if it didn't matter to him whether or not she accepted the horse, he was clearly trying to make it easier for her to do just that. To accept.

The groom holding the horse's bridle crooned something to her, and the animal threw her head. Flutters of mane lofted into the air, the color of ice in the sun, breathtakingly beautiful. Longing resonated somewhere low inside Sophia.

She laced her hands together and took a step back. Then another. This was ludicrous. She couldn't take anything from Adam Stone's son. No gift could ever make up for the wrong done her family. And nothing could make her forget that this man who offered this horse was the same man who'd stolen her freedom, who'd grind her to dust if he discovered she was Twilight's Ghost. "I cannot accept." Her voice emerged small and stiff.

"Of course you can."

"No," she countered, suddenly afraid. "No, no I can't."

Jarrod muttered a curse and stopped her withdrawal by grabbing her shoulders from behind. She broke his hold by swerving to fight him off, and came face-to-face with the warm bulk of his chest. Maggie had brought her her knife. She wore it against her thigh, and she could pull it free—no. If she used it against him, he could take it from her. Panicked, she made another bid to retreat, but he caught her before she could and lifted her off the ground.

She went taut with mortification. Her hip was

squished against his flat stomach, and the outside of her—her *breast* was wedged against his chest.

"You want that horse," Jarrod said, his rigid features proclaiming to her that he'd not be swayed. Determinedly, he carried her down the steps to the drive. "And I'm going to see that you have her."

She refused to give him the satisfaction of a struggle, so she averted her face and stared over his shoulder. Unfortunately, the view there was no better. Jarrod's minions, including the dignified Collier Melvin, were all watching the spectacle with avid interest. Heat scalded her cheeks.

"Hold her steady," Jarrod instructed the groom.

Alarm clanged inside her. She didn't want to sit on that horse, to ride her. Just think of all the terribly exquisite things doing so might make her feel or want. Most of all, she couldn't allow Jarrod to give her something so wondrous. There was no room for gratitude in their relationship. No possible way she could allow herself to warm to him even the tiniest bit. "No," Sophia breathed, her throat clogging with dread.

"Yes," he answered, as he hoisted her into the air and set her in the side saddle. She gripped the saddle horn sheerly to keep herself from falling off the animal's far side, tumbling on her head, exposing her stockings and drawers, and granting Jarrod and his men yet more to gawk at.

With all her might she fought not to see the horse beneath her, not to notice how it felt to sit high on her back.

A maid dashed from the house with a cloak, a pair of gloves, and one of Sophia's hats. Jarrod took the cloak from the woman and reached up to sweep it over

Sophia's shoulders. She whisked the garment from him and swatted his hands away. Ire shifted inside her, prickly and red. The gall of him to fuss over her in public, as if he had that right.

The maid stood patiently beside the horse, waiting as Sophia fastened the tie of the black cloak, then tugged on the matching gloves. She even handed up hatpins as Sophia reluctantly secured the hat to her hair. The black-trimmed straw number tilted down over her forehead and folded up in back and like every other item of clothing Jarrod had furnished, it fit faultlessly.

From the stables, a groom ran forward leading what was no doubt Jarrod's horse. The animal was all muscle and ferocity. Jarrod mounted up with a command that made Sophia groan inwardly. She kept hoping he'd be inept at some facet of living. In this case, it would have been nice if he'd proven himself a poor horseman thanks to all his years of chauffeured carriage travel. Instead he nudged his horse into a trot looking for all the world like a man born to the saddle.

Though her lovely white horse strained forward, Sophia kept her in check, limiting her pace to a walk. She was plodding past the stables when Jarrod turned his mount and doubled back to her. "Duchess there can move a little faster, you know."

"No. We'll stay at a walk."

"Why?" His horse scooted to the side with mincing steps, clearly eager to unfurl his long legs and carry Jarrod toward the gulf at a blistering sprint.

"I like this speed."

"Not good enough. Try again."

The last thing she wanted was to admit her real reason for wanting to stay at a safe walk.

"You're an accomplished rider, aren't you?" he asked.

"It's not that." Though she mostly traveled in buggies these days, she had plenty of experience with even the most spirited horses.

"What is it then?" he goaded.

Unable to see any way to avoid it, she stared fixedly at her horse's snowy ears and took a deep breath. "I don't wish to injure her, if you must know." To the answering silence she qualified her statement with, "She has very delicate legs."

He didn't laugh, at least, which eased her feeling of foolishness slightly.

"Do you think I'd buy you an easily injured horse?" he asked, his tone utterly serious.

"Not on purpose." She dared to slide her gaze to his. "But horses like this have fragile bones."

"She may look fragile, but she's actually very sturdy. She's an Arabian, a breed with more endurance than any other on this continent. Not only could she gallop across Galveston with you on her back; give her some water, and she could gallop across Texas."

Sophia still wasn't sure. She pursed her lips. Duchess, as he'd called her, was so very fine. What if she stepped in a hole or tangled her tail on a passing branch or was spooked by an animal while Sophia was riding her? She'd never forgive herself. She'd lived without beautiful things long enough to be nervous around them. This horse deserved to be treated with extreme care.

"I rode her myself last night," Jarrod said.

"You're too heavy for her."

"No, I'm not. Nor would I be too heavy for you."

At her dark expression, he chuckled. "C'mon." His horse lunged ahead a few paces. "Prove to me you can keep up." He cantered forward, shooting challenging glances at her over his shoulder. A groan eased up her throat. She couldn't stand it. Couldn't stand not to fly on the back of a fairy horse just this one time, especially today when the air felt so crisp after days indoors. She prayed a quick prayer, eased her hold on the reins, and let Duchess go.

The horse surged forward, moving beneath her with a heavenly smooth gait that lifted and lowered, lifted and lowered her through the air—fast. Gloriously fast as hooves drummed the earth. Duchess's mane snapped toward her face, then fell rhythmically against her gloved hands.

Sophia's breath caught at the sheer exhilaration of it.

They crested a hill and an unblemished panorama of sea spread across the horizon. The two horses lengthened their strides yet again, and wind flushed against Sophia's cheeks and dried her eyes. A tentative smile tugged at her mouth as Duchess raced through the thin fans of water unfurling upon the sand.

For long, heady minutes they soared. In the face of the view, the salt air, the invigorating motion, her mind cleared. Wiped away were her anxieties about Jarrod, about her crumbling house, about the secrecies of her job, about the masks she must present. Gone.

When they neared the place where the sand ended in an outcropping of rock, Jarrod slowed their pace. They walked the horses, giving them time to cool, before Jarrod guided her up the dune fronting the gulf.

Mild disappointment curled inside Sophia. She'd rather have kept up all that wonderful riding right to the moment they returned to the stables. Not only because she didn't want to stop galloping atop Duchess, but because she was afraid to be with Jarrod out here alone. She peered toward the little foamy caplets on the water. Perhaps if she spurred Duchess forward, she could make a dash for freedom. . . . She was being ridiculous. She wasn't a coward. And him being born to the saddle and all, he'd have caught her in an eyeblink anyway.

He came to stand beside her and extended his arms. She nodded, giving him grudging permission to assist her down. It was that or jump.

He gripped her waist and the sensation of his strong hands cupping her middle caused her heart to pick up speed. She could feel the heat from, the press of, each one of his fingertips. He lifted her from the saddle and set her gently on her feet. The second he did, she moved away.

Jarrod watched the play of emotions on Sophia's face, entranced as always by the sides of her. She walked farther from him. He followed. She moved away. He decided to let her have her distance.

She stood silently, content to watch Duchess nibble dune grass. Though she tried to cant her profile away from him, she couldn't quite shield the amazement behind her eyes. Nor could she take back the smile he'd seen on her earlier. When they'd reached the water of the gulf, the ice princess had actually smiled. With true joy. And it had made him feel like a king.

Clearly, he'd been wrong in thinking that expensive trinkets could soften her. She'd shown him today that her key rested in what she was clearly so unaccustomed to— adventure, spontaneity, enjoyment for the sake of it. It was simple really. He should have realized it when he'd tickled her and her stream of laughter had sounded so rusty. All the wonder of childhood—wonder in small things like riding, even—had been squeezed from her too early, and whether she knew it or not, she needed it back. From now on he'd give her something worth more than money—enjoyment.

Looking at her in this moment, her narrow shoulders set defensively against all the cares in the world, caused familiarity to stir inside him. With a rush of recognition he realized that the vulnerability beneath Sophia's tough façade reminded him of his mother. She'd used to stand just like that, with her arms crossed over her chest as if to hold in whatever strength she had left. God knows, she'd needed that reserve of personal strength, right up until the end.

A tenderness that no other woman had roused in him before or since spread through his chest at the memory. His mother had been a believer to the last. She'd read to her sons from the Bible each night before bed, telling them of things that meant more than heat and food and shelter. When all the time their circumstances had screamed how wrong she was. Despite what she'd preached, he'd realized at the earliest age how fundamental money truly was.

In time, he'd made a hell of a lot of it. For himself, and for the brothers she'd entrusted to him, and for her. But she had never seen a penny of it and never would. She, with her chapped hands, and her wrinkled eyes, and her ragged clothing would never sleep in a single room of a single one of his mansions, or eat his chef's food, or wear the silks or jewels he still, to this day, craved to buy her.

Sophia could, though, a small voice inside himself said. Sophia who, like his mother, had stared into the abyss of black, difficult times.

He averted his gaze, suddenly finding it painful to look at her.

His lungs filled with the bite of the February air as his gaze moved restlessly along the line between sky and sea. Whatever his mother would have thought about the tough decisions he'd made to keep his brothers alive, or his ruthless business tactics, she'd have believed it right that he give whatever he could to the girl who'd had Blackhaw stolen from her. He'd seen that girl in the adult Sophia so clearly today, back at the porch when longing had tightened her features.

Turning, he caught her watching him cautiously.

The usual zing of desire arched between them. Lust. He felt it, heavier every time their eyes met. He had enough experience to know it was the kind of instinctive, primal wanting not easily sated. It would keep them rolling in the sheets, limbs intertwined, covered with sweat, panting, him buried deep inside her for hours. Days. "I want to make love to you," he said bluntly.

Her bottom lip trembled a tiny bit before she masked it with a brittle smile. "Funny, I had the feeling you were trying to reform me from my relationship with Twilight's Ghost."

"I am. You're too good to be any man's mistress, including mine." He buried his hands in his pockets. "That doesn't stop me from wanting you, though."

"As if I'd so much as let you touch me."

"Wouldn't you?" He neared. Their gazes locked for a heated moment before, ever so deliberately, he reached out and slowly ran his thumb down her neck.

She flinched, but she didn't jerk away. Her cloak had parted, and beneath her tight burgundy bodice, her breasts rose and fell rapidly. "Don't like my touching you?" he asked in a low voice. "Or like it too much?"

She presented him with her back and walked to the

edge of the dune overlooking the water. The wind pressed her fashionable skirts against her hips and thighs. God, he loved to see her in the clothes he'd bought her. Their cut and quality suited her, like a velvet backdrop suited a diamond. That particular shade of burgundy highlighted the color that was beginning to bloom on her cheeks. And the dipping front of the hat enhanced her smoky eyes, eyes that danced with more life every day.

"Have you ever been made love to well, Sophia?" He spoke the words in a voice that was rough and quiet both as he advanced on her. He came to stand almost flush behind her, intrigued to discover how she'd respond. "Have you ever been so spent afterward you could do nothing but lie naked and unmoving?"

She swallowed.

"Have you?"

"Yes."

"Have you ever wanted someone so much you were consumed with thoughts of him? So much you couldn't eat or drink or sleep because of it?"

Her breasts rose and fell, rose and fell.

"Have you ever given yourself to a man completely, to the point where there was no shame, only lust?"

"What's your point?" she demanded, her vision focused fixedly forward. "Do you in your arrogance think you can render me to those states?"

"I know I can." He measured the tightness of her jaw with his gaze. "You didn't answer my question. Has anyone else ever done that to you?"

"It's none of. . . ." She shook her head, refusing to waste her words telling him it was none of his business. That reprimand hadn't dissuaded him yet, and Sophia doubted it ever would. Mary, if she could only get a hold of herself. Her body was clamoring with quivery sensations not unlike those caused by fear—only better. An ache, a weighty pressure had settled between her legs, and his words kept stirring it, like air against seething coals.

"Has anyone ever done that to you?" he asked, tone firm with an order to answer him.

"Of course," she lied.

"I don't believe you."

"Then stop asking me questions."

"Give me a truthful answer, and I'll stop." He moved beside her.

She slanted her face away, keeping no more than her profile to him.

"Was Twilight's Ghost a good lover?" he asked. "Is that why you're so set on protecting him from me?"

She felt a muscle jump in her cheek. She didn't answer.

"Just what do you think I'll do when I find him? Kill him in cold blood?"

Again, she didn't reply.

"Do you?" he asked impatiently.

She ground her teeth together.

"Do you?" he demanded.

She whipped her gaze toward him. "Can you honestly tell me you have no plans for revenge against him? At the very least, you'll expose his identity so that he cannot work for the Service, so that every outlaw he's ever placed behind bars will know whom to hunt down and shoot through the heart." A lock of hair skated from beneath her hat, she shoved it out of her eyes. "So to answer your question, no, I don't think you'll kill him in cold blood if I hand him over to you. You won't have to kill him personally. He'll be as good as dead anyway."

"Which would mean your chances of using your lover to find my father are as good as gone. Isn't that what you're really concerned about?"

"No, I'm concerned about the man—"

"Like hell."

Never had she met someone who left her trembling in the face of a churning anger she'd not even known she possessed. People had always allowed her her remoteness. Everyone, but him.

A sense of bitter unfairness beat hard against Jarrod's temples. "You're angry about something that happened twenty years ago, and you're refusing to help me free my brother out of spite." He gestured angrily. "Meanwhile, Holden is sitting in jail, waiting on you."

"That's ludicrous," she hissed. "Your brother's imprisonment is not my fault. He committed a crime, he received his just sentence for it."

"He committed no crime."

She blew out her breath derisively.

"He committed *no crime*, Sophia."

She stuck out that lovely chin, unwilling to budge an inch. God, she could be obstinate. He pushed both hands through his hair, letting the blunt tips of his fingers dig into his scalp. Think, he urged himself. The issue that was holding her back from assisting him was in part the Ghost's ability to find his father, thus that was one of the issues that needed to be undone. The obvious answer occurred to him, but he didn't like it and didn't want to pay its price.

He looked into her storm-dark eyes and read there

that she had no intention of relenting, at least not anytime soon. God *damn* it. He waited a moment more, fighting against the decision, searching her posture and his brain for any hint of an easier way.

The woman looked as if she'd like to spit in his face.

Fine. The hell with it, he'd play his card and deal with the cost of it later. "I'll find my father for you."

Above those curly-lashed eyes of hers, her forehead wrinkled. "What did you just say?"

"You want my father. If you help me free my brother, I'll bring him to you. It's as simple as that."

Her expression held volumes of mistrust. "Why haven't you found him yourself in all these years?"

"First tell me why you want to find him at all."

She seemed to swirl the question around in her mouth. "I can't allow him to just . . . just go free. He has to pay for what he did to my grandmother."

"Your grandmother, or you?"

She blinked at him, clearly taken aback. "My grandmother was the only relative I had, so what he did to her he did to me."

He glimpsed more of her soul, the woundedness and the pain, in that moment than was wise for his own self-preservation. "Do you think you'll ever be happy carrying around so much hatred?"

"Do you think you'll ever be happy so long as you treat people like animals to be captured and caged?"

For the first time in memory, he didn't know what to say.

"Now tell me why you've never gone in search of your father," she said.

"Why would I have? He never bothered to search for us after he left."

His words hung for a beat before she nodded. "I see." Her voice was barely louder than the salty wind.

Memories of his father shifted through his mind. He saw himself being hoisted onto broad shoulders, burying his hands into the short, brown coarseness of his father's hair, laughing. He remembered his father sitting at the table with him, lamplight playing over the books between them as he'd assisted him with his studies. He recalled seeing his father, snoozing in his chair, the newborn Holden asleep on his chest.

Adam Stone had been a man of dreams and schemes that never quite came true, but good to him and his brothers up until the moment he'd abandoned them. Jarrod had loved him once, though he could no longer decide whether that had been because his father had once deserved it or because all boys want to love their fathers until their fathers do the unforgivable. And even then want to love them.

For a long time after his father had left, he'd remained loyal to him, harboring hope that he'd return, making . . . and this he couldn't bear . . . making excuses for him to his brothers.

"Think about my offer," he said carefully. "I have vast resources at my disposal and more money than your Ghost will ever see. I can find my father for you."

"Don't you mean you can find your father for Holden?"

"For Holden, then."

Thoughtfully, she made her way back toward the horses, then stopped a few yards from Duchess. She regarded the horse with fearful reverence, as if concerned that Duchess might vanish if she dared touch her.

"Here." Jarrod took hold of her wrist and pulled off her glove.

"Stop!" She tried to yank her hand back.

Ignoring her protest, he herded her forward with gentle but firm pressure, then guided her bare palm flat onto Duchess's neck. He laid his hand over hers, lacing a few of his fingers between. The horse's coat was warm, but the electricity of his skin against hers was warmer.

He heard her tiny, choked gasp and grinned with male satisfaction. "I want you to feel her," he said against her ear, and pushed her hand up the horse's neck. His own sense of touch rushed with life, recording every detail, texture, temperature of her and of the slightly moist, bristly fur beneath. He watched their joined hands travel up and down.

"Enough." She tried again to jerk her hand away.

Instantly, he curved his fingers down, holding her hostage.

"Please." The word held genuine upset.

He let her go.

They faced each other, both of them breathing a little faster than they had the ability to hide.

"Sh-she's an excellent horse," Sophia said stiffly. "But I cannot accept her."

"Cannot or will not?" Her refusal annoyed the hell out of him. Did she have any idea how little Duchess had cost him in the scheme of his wealth? How many horses finer than she he owned? Stables full. Sophia very well would and could accept one small horse from him.

"Will not," she answered, then ended the conversation by reaching up for the saddle horn and awaiting his assistance in mounting.

When he cupped his hands for her, he'd have sworn she purposely gouged the heel of her shoe into them as he lifted her.

By the time they returned to the stables, Sophia had almost recovered from her dismaying physical reaction to Jarrod. When he'd imprisoned her hand against Duchess, she'd felt almost dizzy from his touch, the pulsing warmth and life of his hand, and the ridges of him she'd felt against her back. His hard abdomen, his firm hips, pressing against her. *I want to make love to you—*

Banish it from your memory, she told herself. But the more she instructed herself to do so, the more blatantly she remembered. Did every woman's body react to the touch of an attractive male that way? Or just her virgin body?

No, no it wasn't as simple as that. Other attractive men—kinder, more decent men—had touched her before, and she'd never felt a thing. How abhorrent that Jarrod Stone should have the ability to make her not only quiver, but quake.

Grooms flowed from the stables to greet them, far more than were necessary. That was one of the hallmarks of life inside Jarrod Stone's castle, she'd noticed. Overabundance. Ridiculous man. She wondered if he had any idea that there were starving people in this world.

She walked beside him to the house, trying to present the image of someone whose backside wasn't quite so tender.

The requisite guards parted for them at the base of the steps, and they climbed to the porch, Jarrod insisting on planting his hand against her lower back for assistance.

The doors swung open from the inside, where Collier was waiting for them in the foyer.

"Yes?" Jarrod asked.

"There's a man here to see Mrs. LaRue, sir."

Jarrod's demeanor turned instantly menacing. Sophia could almost see his predatory instincts flaring to life one by one. "Who is he?" he asked her.

"He's not Twilight's Ghost, if that's what you're hoping."

"Would you tell me if he were?" If she hadn't known better, she'd have attributed his darkened mood to jealousy.

She shook her head. She didn't intend to tell him anything about Twilight's Ghost, ever. Certainly not that Twilight's Ghost had no need to call on her at the mansion because the Ghost was already imprisoned here right under his nose.

Chapter 8

"**W**here is he?" Jarrod asked Collier.

"The library, sir."

He started down the hall, the coat of his black suit jacket swelling behind him. She had to walk double time to keep up. In the doorway of the library he halted, master of the mansion, large and intimidating and ready at the slightest provocation to do battle for his brother's sake.

Sophia came to a halt behind him. From just around his shoulder, she watched Oliver Kinsworthy rise from an ink blue chair. The man who had been her grandmother's attorney and trusted friend looked just as he always had. His head, bald except for the fringe of white-gray hair around the bottom, was as shiny as ever. His snowy eyebrows were thick over smart hazel eyes, his white mustache was bushy. He'd doubtless come from his office, as wrinkles marked his shirt at the inner elbows, and the collar looked as if it had already been tugged at. His customary eyepiece dangled from his dark brown vest pocket, a vest that appeared ready to surrender the fight to contain the round expanse of his belly by bursting its buttons.

"This is Mr. Oliver Kinsworthy," Sophia said by way of introduction. "Attorney-at-law."

Despite the wary glint in his eye, Oliver inclined his head politely.

Jarrod looked to Sophia. "May I have a word with you?"

"If you insist."

"I do."

"Please excuse us for a moment," she said to Oliver.

"Certainly."

Jarrod took hold of her elbow and drew her several yards down the cavernous hallway. He stopped her progress by turning inward on her, trapping her against the wall. "I'm not letting you speak with him in private."

"But with Maggie—"

"Maggie is a woman."

Jarrod could glower more frighteningly than anyone she'd ever met. He was dark to begin with, with that raven hair. But when he glowered he seemed to turn darker, his eyes glowing like emeralds backlit with fire. "No chance I'm letting the two of you retreat to your bedroom in private."

"Am I to understand that you don't approve of my being alone in my bedroom with a man?"

"Not at all."

"A shame you acquired this staggering sense of

morality *after* locking yourself inside there with me the other night."

He placed his hand against the wall, inches above her head. "Sophie," he growled, his tone warning.

"Oh, very well. I'll speak to him in the library."

"No. You'll speak to him in the library with me present."

"Why? After seeing him you can't still seriously believe he might be Twilight's Ghost."

He gave her that insolent half shrug. "No, I've seen the Ghost and I know that's not he. Still, he could be the Ghost's emissary or he could be carrying weapons. I don't trust him with you."

She tried to decide whether it was better to send Oliver away or to speak to him with Jarrod present. Her sense of privacy rebelled at the thought of Jarrod listening in. Yet, what if Oliver had news? And . . . perhaps it wouldn't be so terrible for Jarrod to hear more about the kind of man his father was. Oliver's coming might even present her the opportunity she'd been waiting for to decipher just how much Jarrod was and wasn't telling about Adam Stone. Surely he knew more than he let on.

"Who is he to you, anyway?" Jarrod asked.

"Oliver Kinsworthy was my grandmother's advisor. He assists me in the search for your father."

"That's it?"

"That and we're friends."

When he scowled, she strode past him toward the library, wondering what Jarrod would say if he learned that Oliver was the person indirectly responsible for the investigation she'd launched against Holden. Had Oliver not come to her with concerns about her safety after encountering Holden in Austin, she'd never have rolled up her sleeves, done more digging, and discovered Holden's arrest warrant.

It was one thing for the Stone brothers to bear some defensive animosity toward those at Blackhaw who loathed their father. However, it was something else entirely when Oliver had given her reason to suspect one of them might actually come after her. She'd protected herself the way she always had—by collecting information and then by acting on it.

Ironic that her worst fears had still been confirmed. A Stone brother *had* come after her. Just not the one she'd expected. And not for a reason she'd anticipated.

When she entered the library, Oliver rose again, quickly, and took her hand in both of his. "How are you?" he asked. "Since Maggie came to visit, I've been concerned."

Up this close, Oliver's sweet, jowly face had a ruddy cast, and the few broken blood vessels on his nose were visible. She gave Oliver her gamest smile, as if to say that things like kidnappings at the hands of millionaires occasionally happened in life and must be borne with good cheer. "Thank you for your concern," she said sincerely. "I'm quite well."

"I worried . . ." His words drifted off as Jarrod paced into the room, making frigid the atmosphere.

Sophia walked with Oliver to his chair, then settled herself near him at the end of a brown sofa, which promptly dwarfed her. Clearly, the sofa's large proportions had been made for men to lounge upon while smoking, laughing, and drinking whiskey.

Two of the room's walls, those behind her and Oliver, were covered with bookshelves. The third, behind where

Jarrod took a seat, boasted an intimidating fireplace crowned by an oil painting of a ship tossing on a raging sea of blues and grays. Double doors that Collier was quick to shut dominated the fourth wall. Even the air in this room was very male.

Sophia cleared her throat. "Oliver, I don't believe I introduced the owner of this home to you earlier. This is Mr. Jarrod Stone."

Jarrod dipped his chin.

Strained silence invaded the space.

"Have you learned anything new since we last spoke?" she asked Oliver.

"I'm afraid not."

It had been foolish to hope he had, she supposed, though that didn't stop disappointment from trickling through her. They'd been searching for evidence on Adam Stone's whereabouts for years. In all that time, they'd managed to scrape together only meager information. Still, she'd harbored the hope that Adam Stone would hear of his son's sentencing and attempt to reach him.

"Mrs. LaRue tells me you worked for her grandmother," Jarrod said.

"That's correct. She was one of my clients. I served as her attorney and gave her financial guidance."

"And how did you advise her when my father came to her with his idea of building a boot-making factory?"

Oliver shifted uncomfortably, raised his eyepiece, and regarded Jarrod with faint censure. "I advised her against it, sir. There were no other investors except for the late Mrs. Warren, so she'd have borne all the risk. Your father, to be certain, had no capital to contribute."

"No," Jarrod said.

Tension stole over Sophia's body, compressing the muscles at the back of her neck. Oliver had come at her request and didn't deserve Jarrod's browbeating. "Perhaps, Oliver, if you could recount for Mr. Stone the events leading up to his father's disappearance with Blackhaw's fortune. Mr. Stone has expressed interest in assisting our investigation."

He looked at her for a long moment. "Yes, ah," he softly cleared his throat, "I suppose I could do that."

"Thank you."

He leaned back in his chair and returned his attention to Jarrod. "Mrs. Warren's butler was a friend of your father's and the one who introduced him to Mrs. Warren. The first discussion between them took place, I believe, about three weeks before her money was stolen." Absently, he studied his eyepiece, then set about cleaning it with a cloth he extracted from his trouser pocket. "From the beginning, she was extremely interested in your father's proposition of building a factory."

"Why?" Jarrod's posture, one knee pointed forward, one splayed to the side, made him look both casual and foreboding. "Why so eager to invest in something so risky?"

"When her son and his wife—" He glanced at Sophia. "When Sophia's parents were killed in a boating accident, sole control of the estate reverted to Mrs. Warren. Though she was a woman with a great many sterling qualities, financial experience was not among them. Her husband, and after him her son, had always managed the fortune."

Oliver tucked away the cloth, then rolled the circular eyepiece between brawny, age-speckled fingers. "From the start, the responsibility of managing such a large fortune was a difficult burden for her. She immediately wished to increase her holdings, I presume because she hoped she'd feel less burdened . . . more secure, you know . . . with more money in the bank. Doubling her savings quickly was more important to her than safe and steady growth, which led her to make ill-advised investments despite my recommendations to the contrary. By the time Adam Stone came to her, her holdings were perhaps a fifth of what they had been at the time of her son's death."

"Which heightened the appeal of my father's scheme."

"Quite right. As I said, I counseled her against it—"

"Did you have access to her money?"

The eyepiece ceased its movement.

Sophia's attention cut to Jarrod. "It wasn't Oliver who disappeared the day the fortune did."

"It's all right," Oliver murmured. "I'll answer his question. It's a legitimate one." He took a deep, sighing breath. "From time to time Mrs. Warren asked me to courier a transaction to and from the bank for her to sign. So yes, in that respect, I did have some access to her money."

"Go on."

"In the days leading up to your father's disappearance, Mrs. Warren met with him more and more regularly. I believe they crafted the remainder of your father's business plan and drew up a crude layout for the building. I know they projected astronomical earnings, because Mrs. Warren showed those to me. The night the money was stolen, I went to Mrs. Warren one final time, to try and dissuade her. She wouldn't hear of it, informed me the deal had already been struck."

Sophia twined her hands together in her lap, hoping

that if she concentrated on them hard enough, she could fend off the memories.

"The next day, I visited again, late in the afternoon. Mrs. Warren was frantic, said your father was supposed to have met with her earlier in the day. He was four hours late."

Sophia clenched her hands tighter, and still the remembrances of that day came spiraling back. Her grandmother had been dressed in her finery, like always. The fabric of her skirt had twitched, and all her necklaces had clinked together as she'd grown increasingly agitated. Her voice had turned more shrill, her breath less even. Sophia had sat alone at their polished oak dining table watching her in silence, racked with fear, waiting for everything to be fine again. Believing, in those early hours, that it would be.

"Your father never returned," Oliver stated, his voice holding an edge of accusation.

Jarrod's cheeks and jaw hardened with an emotion she couldn't read.

"It was later," Oliver continued, "that I learned she'd given him nearly all the money in her possession. Later still I discovered that she'd accrued debts throughout the city and the state."

The ominous quiet that followed seemed to Sophia to pronounce the smell of the room—that of cigar smoke mixed with the musty scent of old and brittle paper. She could bear anything but this silence in which her beloved grandmother's foolishness hung between the three of them like a sharp, ugly glass bauble the shade of blood.

She schooled her voice to sound matter of fact as she glanced to Jarrod. "It's our understanding that your father never returned home the night my grandmother gave him the money. Is that correct?"

Slowly, Jarrod nodded. "I knew nothing about the money at the time, but that's correct. That's also the night that my mother packed our things and took my brothers and me from Galveston."

"Your mother didn't say anything to you," Sophia asked, "about why you had to leave?"

"Absolutely nothing. She died just weeks afterward, and she took that with her to the grave."

"What did she say to explain your father's absence?"

"Only that he'd gone and couldn't come home for a while." Jarrod held Sophia's gaze.

"You're telling me you know nothing about what happened that night."

"That's right."

"And afterward. Your father never attempted to contact you? Nothing?"

"Nothing."

Sophia's frustration churned. "You've no idea where he might have gone?"

"None."

Was he telling the truth? Could he really know so little about his own father?

"What about you?" Jarrod asked her. "What have you learned about my father's movements after that night?"

"Very little."

Oliver tucked away his eyepiece. "We've had reports of places he might have passed through. Received correspondence from owners of establishments where he might have spent some of the money. Nothing that has led us to him."

"You do know, don't you, that the money's gone?"

Jarrod asked her. "Even if I can find him for you, your money's been spent long since."

She saw Blackhaw in her mind's eye—wallpaper curling away from browned plaster, bricks that wiggled when touched, and glass that bore spidery cracks. "I realize that." God knows, she could use the money, but her desire to bring Adam Stone to justice had never been about that.

"What happened at Blackhaw," Jarrod asked, "afterward?"

"Nothing." Sophia frowned. "That's the end of the story."

"Not the story I'm interested in."

Oliver used his meaty arms to lever himself from his chair. "Mind if I stretch my back?"

Jarrod gestured his acquiescence with the lifting of fingers.

As she'd seen him do a hundred times, Oliver braced his hands against his lower spine and arched backward. A soft "ah" seeped from his mouth. "Not much to tell after Adam Stone's disappearance."

"Tell me what there is," Jarrod answered.

Oliver straightened, rolled his shoulders once, and ambled to the window nestled amongst the bookshelves. His gaze traced the contours of the land outside as he spoke. "Mrs. Warren took to her bed almost immediately. Sophia here tended her, as we had to let nearly all of the staff go."

Sophia shifted restlessly. This was more than Jarrod needed to know, far more than she wanted him to.

"She didn't wish for her friends or anyone else to come calling," Oliver continued, "and see her in what she regarded as her disgrace."

"What was done about the financial situation?" Jarrod asked.

"At first, I thought that if we sold off all the other properties she owned, that we'd be able to keep Blackhaw Manor functioning. When the debts were revealed, however, liquidation became the only alternative."

Sophia's heart was thumping like the beating wings of a caged bird. She'd humiliate herself if she interrupted. But would the humiliation be better or worse than having Jarrod know about the desperation of Blackhaw's last days?

"We sold everything but Blackhaw itself," Oliver said. "The other properties, the horses, the furniture, the jewelry. Mrs. Warren passed away before the end of the selling, and sometimes I think it was a blessing. I'm not sure she could have survived seeing that."

Sophia held herself mercilessly still. At the end, her grandmother had aged a hundred years in just a handful of days. Her sweet, funny, lavish grandma had lain beneath sterile sheets, her body shrunken and her eyes hollow.

Sophia had stared into those eyes, watched as the life had drained from them, knowing as their meager light paled that she was losing the only person she had left. Dying, dying, dying. She'd pleaded with God that her efforts would be enough to somehow keep her grandmother alive. They had to be, she'd thought then in desperation. Who else was there to love her? To be her family? The old terror belonging to the child she'd been curled around her like tentacles of black fog, even now.

"And Sophia?" Jarrod asked.

"You already know what happened to me," she said sharply.

He stared at her without expression, the green in his eyes seeming to shift.

She lifted her chin a fraction, trying to defend herself physically against the reality of having her most private tragedy paraded in front of him. Him, with all his toughness and splendor. Him, who to this day had the luxury of family and the love of his brothers.

"I took Sophia to St. Mary's Orphanage," Oliver said. "Being a bachelor, I knew I couldn't care appropriately for a young girl, and there was no one else."

She had no reason to experience a curdle of shame in her belly, but it was there. The stigma of the abandoned.

"Of course, the house always belonged to her," Oliver said. "It waited only for her to claim it."

"Not much of a prize, was it?" Jarrod asked as he pushed to his feet.

"How can you say that?" she demanded, on her feet as quickly. "That house is—is a landmark, a treasure."

"Quite," Oliver said placatingly.

Jarrod opened the door, called for a servant. As usual, one was almost instantaneously near at hand. "Fetch Mr. Kinsworthy's coat."

The servant nodded and hurried off.

"What methods are you currently using to search for my father?" Jarrod asked, as they gathered near the doorway to wait.

Oliver pulled at the bottom of his vest to straighten it. "We post requests for information in newspapers across the country, have written countless letters to city and county officers asking them to search their records."

Jarrod nodded.

"Will you be assisting us, Mr. Stone?"

"It depends."

The servant returned and handed Oliver his coat.

"On Sophia."

The next day Maggie and Sophia were sitting together in their customary places on the dressing-room floor. As usual, Maggie had ditched her straw hat in favor of a richly decorated one. She adjusted the position of the current hat, a black confection festooned with all manner of dotted lace, then checked her profile in the mirror. "Have you actually seen any of Jarrod's brothers?"

Idly, Sophia thumbed through the stack of mail Maggie had brought her. A letter from one of the sisters at the orphanage, three social invitations. . . . "No."

"Do you think there's any chance in God's green earth that they resemble him?"

"It's a possibility. Why?" She looked up.

"Why? Because I want them for myself, of course. What are their names again?"

"Clint, J. T., and Holden. Three men I promise you you want nothing to do with. They're a slimy, disreputable bunch."

"Yes, that's right, Sophia. I'm a thirty-two-year-old spinster without breasts, and I can afford to be picky."

"Maggie," Sophia warned.

"I'm just saying"—she lifted a bony shoulder—"perhaps they could use the influence of a virtuous wife." She batted her eyelashes.

Sophia shook her head and returned to the pile of envelopes. Two letters from would-be male suitors, and one letter—her pulse hitched—from the state tax assessor's office. Uneasily, she pulled it free.

"I realize the youngest one's in jail," Maggie said. "But what do the other two do?"

"One's a marshall and one's a bounty hunter," she answered distractedly.

"Well, that doesn't sound too disreputable."

"Bounty hunter?" Sophia repeated skeptically.

"I happen to like a man with some mischief in his head."

"You like all men." Sophia turned the letter from the tax assessor over.

"You think there's any possibility of my meeting these brothers of his? Any way you could request it of Jarrod, maybe promise to hand over Twilight's Ghost if one of his strapping brothers will take me to the altar and make me an honest woman?"

"I don't think so."

"No?"

"No."

Maggie muttered moodily before reaching for another of Jarrod's hats.

The letter felt bad to Sophia. The weight of it in her palm just plain felt bad. She stared down at it, sudden dread clumping in her throat. Maybe if she just stuffed it into one of the shoes— Don't be silly. Had her confinement here turned her into such a milksop?

Irritated with herself, she tore open the letter. She was a woman who moved unafraid through the streets at night, an agent, an adult strong enough to bear the responsibility for the fall of thieves masquerading as important men. She certainly wasn't afraid of letters.

The single sheet of paper crackled when she opened it.

"Mrs. LaRue: We regret to inform you that due to

your failure to pay taxes . . ." The words blurred before her eyes and she had to force herself to continue reading. ". . . either for the year 1876 or the year 1877 on the estate located at 2330 Broadway, Galveston, Texas, the property has been slated for auction at noon on March 10. Unless your tax debt in the amount of $468 is paid prior to that day, the house will be sold, with the proceeds reverting to the state government."

Chapter 9

Sophia lowered the letter and stared sightlessly at the wall, feeling every contraction of her heart. Her lips rolled inward to stop them from shaking. They'd finally done it. They'd actually set an auction date. Nineteen days away. Less than three weeks. *Oh, God.*

During her time at St. Mary's there had been just enough left over from the sale of her family's other belongings for Oliver to pay Blackhaw's taxes. When that money had run out, she'd compensated with every cent of her Service income. It hadn't been enough. Not for a long time now. She'd known for the past two years that they'd come after her eventually, but up until today she'd been able to stall them with correspondence and Oliver's legal maneuvering and the insufficient payments she'd sent.

Blackhaw. Her breath burned her lungs. Her proud old house. In her mind it was a meshing of old and new images. Vast acres of thriving orchards, soaring pale brick turrets reaching toward endless sky, war-ravaged rooms, jagged glass begging to be replaced. Mostly, though, it was just . . . hers. The only thing in the world she truly owned and the only possession she loved. To be honest, it wasn't like a possession at all, but rather like a living being that, though not indestructible, had proven more constant than her family ever had.

"I must say that I took a fancy to that last hat," Maggie was saying. "A bit of the air of the rich, wounded widow about it."

Dazedly, Sophia smoothed the letter with shaky hands, folded it along the crease marks, and returned it to its envelope. Adam Stone was trying to strip the final thing from her twenty years after he'd taken their fortune and with it her grandmother's reason for living and life.

Tears threatened to well in her eyes. She sniffed them angrily back. Well, he couldn't have Blackhaw. She had two and a half weeks, at least, to try her damnedest to raise the money she owed.

"However, I'm not entirely won over by this one," Maggie said to her own reflection. "The deep green shade is lovely, but I find this starchy bow on top entirely suspicious. Makes me look as though I've just stuck my head out the window of a train, what with the ends pointing upward like they are. I'd frighten off Jarrod's brothers were they to see me in this. Don't you agree?"

Their eyes met, and Maggie's expression turned instantly concerned. "What's wrong?"

Wordlessly, Sophia handed over the letter.

Maggie scanned its contents. "Oh, Sophia," she

breathed as she read the last line, then rested the letter on her lap. She looked so bereft that Sophia's brittle emotions teetered. She was tempted to surrender her head to Maggie's shoulder and sob. But if she did that, she very much feared she'd never be able to fight her way back up again. "It just means I'll have to gather the money for Blackhaw's taxes before the auction," she said with more confidence than she felt. "That's all."

"How do you propose to do that?"

She shook her head, indicating that she'd no idea. On a wave of agitation, she pushed to her feet and began pacing the small space.

Maggie, still wearing the green hat, slowly straightened. She leaned into one of the clothing racks, her shoulder against the bar, and watched Sophia's movement. "You could always just ask *him* for the money."

"No," she replied immediately.

"Or you could start accepting his gifts, and I could try to sell them for you. That ruby bracelet was probably worth quite a bit, all on its own."

"No." That she'd so much as ridden Duchess was bad enough. Everything she accepted from Jarrod rendered her in some way beholden to him. That sense of obligation would only deepen if his money were going, no matter how indirectly, toward the saving of her home. "No, I don't want him involved in this whatsoever. There has to be another way."

"Well," Maggie drew out the word begrudgingly, "there is that reward I mentioned the first time I visited you here."

Sophia's pacing ceased. She faced Maggie, remembering in a rush about Slocum's Mercantile and the five-hundred-dollar reward they were offering for the capture of a counterfeiter. An overpowering, instinctive sense of rightness filled her. "That's it." She'd find the counterfeiter and earn the reward in time to keep Blackhaw.

"I agree that it has potential," Maggie said. "Except that our mysterious counterfeiter is out there." She jabbed a thumb over her shoulder. "And I hate to be the one to point this out, but you're in here." Her lips curled into an apologetic frown.

"I can't stay in here anymore, Maggie. Not after this."

"Nor can you leave. Simon gave strict orders that you stay—"

"I know. And before this I agreed that the risks of attempting escape outweighed the benefits. They no longer do." She toyed with the fingernails of her left hand, thinking. "I'll leave only at night, only when I won't be missed. I can investigate the case without Jarrod, or Simon, for that matter, being any the wiser."

"Oh, Sophia," Maggie murmured worriedly. "How about this? How about if I investigate the case for you?"

"Thank you for offering, and I'll need your help. But the fact is that I can't bear to remain trapped here for the next nineteen days doing nothing, knowing that Blackhaw's auction date is drawing closer."

Maggie chewed her bottom lip.

"I just can't, Maggie."

"I have the utmost confidence in your abilities, Sophia. You know I do. But think for a minute. What if Jarrod catches you? Your career will be over. Maybe your life, too. There's no telling what he'll do."

"He's not going to catch me. I wouldn't attempt to do this if I didn't believe that."

Maggie regarded her with a deadly solemn expression on features that usually brimmed with humor.

She understood Maggie's concerns, treasured her for them. "I can't let them take Blackhaw," she said softly.

Maggie exhaled, her shoulders slumping slightly. "I know."

"I already have my knife, so I'll only need you to bring my disguise and some lockpicking equipment."

Maggie nodded.

"Oh, and if you can bring me a sketch of the surrounding acreage, as well as the best course to take from here into town, I'd appreciate it."

"I'll do it."

"It would also help to know the positioning of the guards late at night. I can only see the ones outside my windows. There well may be more at other stations around the house. I need to know where."

"Okay. I'll scout out their positions."

"You can use my spyglass."

"Right."

Sophia's mind raced ahead. She could hunt for her counterfeiter through the night and catch sleep between her obligatory meals with Jarrod during the day. Yes, once Maggie brought her the information she needed and the remainder of her equipment, she'd have all the necessities of escape.

"Where are you going?" Jarrod asked, his voice dark against the night air.

Sophia stumbled. "Going?" She tried to look nonchalant. "I'm following you."

"I'm over here." He raised a hand and waved. His grin glistened in the light from the half-moon.

She fought the urge to smile back. Instead, she crossed her arms and angled her steps after his. She couldn't help but notice, as she trudged along after him, that the cold blackness of the late hour suited Jarrod to perfection. It starkened the male beauty of his face and cloaked his body with a kind of dangerous power that only made his shoulders seem wider and his height higher. The savagery of nature under cover of darkness matched a certain savagery inside Jarrod.

She didn't know why she should be surprised. Was it any wonder that the night loved the man? For all she knew Adam Stone could well be the devil's brother, which would make Jarrod too close of kin to contemplate.

After dinner, when he'd suggested they take this outing, she'd been eager to accept because she'd immediately recognized it as an opportunity. After Maggie's visit that morning, a chance to view the back of the house and learn the lay of the surrounding land was welcome indeed. She'd been *trying* to get a surreptitious look at the various planes of the roof when he'd asked her where she was going just now.

They waded farther from the light of the house. She was leaning into the incline of a hill, when the sound of crunching leaves broke the stillness. She turned to see someone—no some*thing*—hurtling toward her. A black shadow, closing the distance fast. Her heart leapt into her throat, and she instinctively lifted her hands to protect herself as the thing raced toward her, then bounded past. Out of the corner of her eye she saw it skid to a stop next to Jarrod. It was a dog, a big one. Though now that the animal was dancing attendance around Jarrod, she could see that it wasn't a scary one.

"Sorry if Maxine frightened you," Jarrod said.

"Maxine?"

"Yeah. I didn't think to warn you that she might be joining us."

"Oh," she replied lamely, at a loss for words.

The best she could make out, Maxine was a retriever with a long coat.

"What have you brought me?" Jarrod asked the dog as he ruffled her ears. "A stick? Okay, just don't blame me again if you can't find it once I throw it."

The dog seemed to nod as she unclamped her jaws so that he could pull free the small branch she'd brought him. He threw it overhanded and Maxine charged after it.

Sophia could only stare, unsure what she was seeing. "That's *your* dog?" she finally asked.

He smiled wryly at her as Maxine returned to him, panting with glee. He threw her stick again. "After a long day's work of torturing small children and robbing old ladies I sometimes like to play with dogs."

Heat rolled against the insides of her cheeks, because that's exactly what she'd been thinking. Good-hearted dogs didn't love men like Jarrod . . . did they? And men like Jarrod certainly didn't ruffle the ears of sweet retrievers named Maxine.

She recalled the image of him she'd had the first night they'd met—Jarrod standing on the steps of a marble mansion, feeding money to twin wolves. That vision couldn't have been more different than this reality. His dog seemed to prefer sticks to cold, hard cash. "Have you had her a long time?"

"More than ten years."

"Oh?" When he failed to explain, she found she was too curious to let it go. "How did you come by her?"

He shrugged it off. "No particular way."

Maxine trotted back to Jarrod. He murmured something to her that Sophia didn't quite catch, then threw her branch for her again.

Warmth curled unbidden inside Sophia. Warmth, oh God, for *him*. She worked to steel herself against it. Maybe there were some things about Jarrod, like the fact that he owned a dog, that she was better off not knowing. Such things threatened the distance she needed to maintain between them.

Jarrod renewed his climb up the hill and she followed in silence. For the first time she wondered just how closed she'd become during all her years of secrecy. So much so that she hadn't been able to dare, just now, to soften her perception of Jarrod in the smallest way? That she couldn't allow any civility at all between them? Yes, that's exactly right, a part of her heart answered. It was the part that had loved her grandmother too foolishly and remembered too well the ache of abandonment.

Overhead, the tree branches, like black lace against the gray of the sky, receded. A circular copse opened on the hill's plateau, and she saw that a table had been set for two. The linens gleamed ghostly white. The silver flatware caught the starlight. And the pale china cups and bowls seemed to glow with their own luster, like the inside of a shell. Behind the otherworldly table stood a telescope, pointed heavenward.

She felt Jarrod's attention without having to look to confirm it.

"What?" she asked. "No servants?"

"I'm certain you're astonished." He came to a stop at the table and motioned to the steam twisting upward from the central dish and the spout of the coffee urn. "They must have just left. It's still hot."

She stood next to him. The table was even more magical close-up. "What is it?"

"Pineapple cake."

Yes. She could smell it now, the scents of baked butter and vanilla. "You told me once it was your favorite," he said.

"It is."

He gazed down at her—that hot perusal again, this time from so close. What did he see when he looked at her, she wondered? Probably a prudish woman with too-big eyes, wearing a scarlet gown that was clearly too grand for her.

"You feed me too much," she said, because something needed saying.

"Nothing that I do for you is too much. More like not enough."

Her mouth went completely dry. That deadly charm again, charm that slid around her like satin and made her want—just for a moment or a minute—to believe it. She eased away from him before hazarding to meet his gaze. "I'm not sure I understand why you brought me all the way out here for pineapple cake."

"Have you ever seen the stars through a telescope?"

She shook her head.

"Good. I wanted to be the first to show you." He used the silver serving spoon to scoop a huge portion of pineapple cake onto a china plate, which he handed to her. Heat seeped through the plate and her gloves into her hands. He poured steaming coffee—no, tea, she could tell by the scent—into a cup for her before bypassing his own empty place setting in favor of the telescope. He squinted at it as he worked to adjust the instrument's height and settings.

She slid into a chair and set her plate before her. Obviously, Jarrod was too engrossed in his telescope to sit with her which made her feel . . . how? Miffed not to be the center of his attention for one tiny moment? No, certainly not. She took advantage of his preoccupation by furtively eyeing the back of the house and the surrounding property.

Her first bite of cake fairly melted on her tongue. Gloriously rich and hot and sweet. Every bit as good as Mrs. Dewberry's. Each mouthful would doubtless deposit itself either on her breasts or her bottom. But when food tasted this delectable, it was hard to care. Someone had even thought to bring whipping cream. She added a dollop and luxuriated in the dessert as she continued to make mental notes regarding the landscape.

"The telescope's ready for you," Jarrod announced.

She slid her attention to him, her last bite halfway to her mouth.

"You can finish that first," he said.

"No, really, I'm full." The portion he'd given her had been truly huge.

He moved to her and used his fingers to press the fork to her mouth. "Finish," he murmured.

She was forced to open her lips and accept the cake or be poked by the fork.

"Have I ever told you I like women with curves?"

She chewed and swallowed as quickly as possible. "Then I shall endeavor to slim my figure."

He smiled wickedly. "No, you won't." He plucked her napkin from her lap, threw it on the table, and drew her to the telescope.

Sophia licked her lips, hoping there were no crumbs clinging there.

"Take a look," he said.

Stargazing didn't particularly inspire her, but since he'd gone to so much trouble, she felt obliged. Somewhat self-consciously, she eased her eye to the eyepiece.

A myriad of stars shone through the rod of the telescope, so close and unbelievably brilliant that she reared back a bit in surprise. As quickly as she did so, however, she was drawn back by the sight. Magnificent. Stars scattered across the sky like ribbons of crystals. These gems twinkled, some more luminously than others. Blindingly radiant. Awe coasted through her as she raised her hands reverently to cup the near end of the telescope. She'd not imagined . . . never seen anything like this.

"What do you think?" Jarrod asked from nearby.

"I . . . They're lovely."

His satisfied silence answered her.

"Which stars am I looking at?" she asked.

"You're looking at a portion of the Milky Way."

"Do you know anything else about them?"

"I know it's called the Milky Way because to the naked eye it looks like milk spilled across a dark table or a band of mist in the sky. It's only with a telescope that you can tell it's actually made up of thick clouds of individual stars."

"Does it shift around the sky like the constellations do?" She often used the moon's position to approximate the hour during her nighttime vigils, but she knew precious little else about astronomy.

"Yes. Sometimes it's so close to the horizon that it can't be seen."

"What else?"

"The Milky Way is an area with more bright stars than any other. Of the twenty-one first-magnitude stars, sixteen are in or near the Milky Way. It's only their distance from the earth that makes them appear small."

She nodded, spurring him on, as she drank in the sight.

"What you're looking at is the rim of our universe," he said simply.

To see this expanded the world as she knew it. As if someone had pulled a scarf from the heavens she'd been seeing all these years to reveal an unexpected, astonishing beauty. It was easy to forget, unless you took the time to look, that such beauty existed in the world.

Foolishly, her eyes teared. It made her feel safe, to see this evidence of vastness beyond herself and be reminded that everything in God's kingdom was truly in its place. Stalwart and lasting. Just for a moment, her awful fears for Blackhaw eased. For years she'd been operating on the belief that if she stopped controlling everything in her life, all she held as precious would fall from her hands and shatter. Maybe . . . maybe there was a larger order that would catch Blackhaw in its sweeping hand.

"Which star do you want me to name in honor of you?" Jarrod asked.

At that, she looked to him, blinking a few times to acclimate her vision. He stood close, his hands buried in his pockets, the flaps of his coat pushed back.

"You can't name a star," she said.

"Can't I?"

She wondered how many times in their acquaintance she'd told him he couldn't do something, and he'd looked at her with that same fate-challenging confidence, and said, "Can't I?" Too many times. "Haven't they all already been named?"

"Not yours."

Magic tugged at her, drawing her back to the telescope for another look. This was silly. He couldn't name a star Sophia . . . could he? No, no, surely not. Except that all of a sudden, she deeply, *deeply* wanted a star named after her.

"That one," she whispered, finding a star off on the fringes of the sight. It wasn't the brightest or the biggest, but it pulsed steadily. It was a mysterious little star, a star of perseverance, its heart beating bravely backward and forward through time. It was a star that *survived*.

She heard him move toward her and reluctantly surrendered the telescope to him. "It's the one far up to the right," she explained. When he was quiet, searching, she added, "About three up from the brightest star and then two over. The one that pulses the most."

"I see it."

"Will you ever be able to find it again?" Even as she spoke the words, she couldn't believe she was asking them, less that she cared.

"Yes, my little doubter, I'll be able to find it again." He glanced over at her. "How could I not? Sophia just became my favorite star in the galaxy."

Goose bumps rose on her flesh. A tight part of her, deep inside, unfurled.

"Want to look at a planet?" he asked.

"Yes."

He returned to the telescope, angling it anew. "There." The motion of the instrument stopped. "Saturn." He stepped to the side so she could take his place.

She was struck first by the rings surrounding it. She was struck second by the steadiness of Saturn's light, so different from the stars of the Milky Way. "Tell me what you know."

"Saturn is the sixth planet from the sun," he said, "but second in size. It has eight moons, unless you count all the millions of small moons that form Saturn's rings."

Amazing. Here she was, her feet planted on ground, gazing at an actual planet, seeing it in detail as it winged its way around and around the earth. She tried to memorize it for the future. The next time she found herself waiting away the night alone on the dock or some sandy bluff, she wanted to be able to look up and remember. "So bright."

"Yes, although Venus is the brightest, then Jupiter, then Saturn. Mars varies, though it can blaze as bright as the last two at times."

Sophia hugged the sight of the planet into herself before straightening. He hadn't moved away, was still standing just inches from her.

"How do you know all this astronomy?"

"I look through the telescope often. But everything I've been telling you tonight I just read in a book this afternoon."

Her brows lifted. "Truly?" she asked, unsure whether to believe him.

He shrugged. "I wanted to impress you."

She laughed.

"By God, are you laughing?"

"I laugh when it's merited." Her smile plucked at the edges of her lips.

"It's about time *I* merited it," he murmured, humor creasing his eyes. Then, as naturally as if he'd done it a hundred times before, he kissed her.

Sophia froze. His warm lips were on hers, friendly,

and affectionate. Then gone, before she could comprehend what was happening.

She stood stunned, staring helplessly up at him. Ensnared in disbelief, dismay, and the power of his spell.

Every shred of the previous amusement left his features. His attention roved from her eyes down to her lips and held there with a hunger so concentrated, so forceful, that her woman's center contracted at the sight of it.

Deliberately, as if daring her to stop him, he slanted his mouth against hers. She should have stopped him, could have. Except she didn't because she, God save her, wanted his lips on hers.

Chapter 10

He pushed his hands up the back of her neck, burying his fingers in her hair and trapping her head in his palms. His lips parted, parting hers as they did so, and his tongue slid inside. Her senses, already drunk on the taste of pineapple cake and the sight of the stars, wheeled.

He drew at her, demanding, wholly dominating, just as he was in every aspect of his life. And hot. Wet. Overwhelming her with the force of his appetite.

Staggered, plunged far beyond her element, she went pliant in his arms and simply let herself be kissed. He moaned and walked her backward until her hips came up against the side of the table. The silverware clanked against the china, a distant sound compared to the rushing in her ears. He possessed her mouth completely, and she let him. Too stunned to do anything but follow his lead.

Her thighs fit snugly between his. She could feel the muscles of them leaping, scorching through her skirt. Shyly, she swept her hands up his broad back, hardly believing that she was touching him this way. Hardly believing it could feel so good to be desired as a woman. She'd never known until now how much she'd longed for someone to look at her and see what Jarrod—unbelievably—saw in her. My God, he truly did want her. The growl in his throat, the thrust of his tongue, the clasp of her head in his hands communicated his need to her.

He tilted back her head, roughly breaking the kiss and exposing her throat. His mouth moved along the slant of her jaw, then down the cords of her neck. She pushed the back of her head more deeply into his hold, offering him more. He kissed her neck, tonguing her, trailing fire down flesh met instants later by the tingle of wind. She clutched at his shoulders, as she would to an island in a pitching sea of feeling and emotion.

He straightened, leaning into her, then he was kissing her again. The heated friction of his lips, the hitch of his breath—it dimmed her awareness, burned it to nothingness.

He dislodged one hand from her hair, pressed it along the skin of her neck he'd just awakened, then lower across her upper chest. The touch of an expert, firm and knowing. He wasn't . . . wouldn't touch her there, surely—he *would*.

His hand blatantly captured her breast.

She gasped against his lips, and he parted from her, still so close their foreheads rested on one another. Without the kissing, his hand on her breast was even more carnal. Pressing in, then rubbing a thumb over a nipple that peaked to almost painful sensitivity. And still he worked her, weighing, stroking. Unembarrassed.

She . . . No man had ever in her entire life fondled her with such intimacy. It was a kind of drunkenness, to be so ruled, so given over into such skillful hands. To experience the lushness of being a woman desired. A wild kernel of daring inside her pined for it to go on. Trembled for it to, despite that it wasn't right, what she was letting him do.

Jarrod Stone. *Stone.* Years, decades of virtue and principles came howling back. What had she gotten herself into? Her breast, he was touching her breast. No, too far. Too much. All wrong.

She pushed against him.

His head lifted so he could gaze at her as his fingers caressed her breast, sending bald feeling whipping through her.

She shoved him again. This time he dropped his hand and stepped back.

Mother Mary, what did I just allow to happen? Her chest rose and fell with her labored breathing. She looked around her, searching for something familiar to cling to. There was nothing. She was draped against the table, her skirts mashed between her legs, a foreign meadow encircling her, and her body heaving with needs she'd never experienced before. Nothing about this was familiar.

Jarrod took a few more steps back. Shadow slanted across his face so that all she could see—or maybe she was imagining even them—were his eyes. Deadly serious eyes, honed on her unrelentingly.

She scrambled inwardly for composure as she smoothed her skirts back into place.

Jarrod didn't move a muscle.

She righted the silverware and straightened the table-cloth where it had bunched. Still, he didn't move.

Steady, she told herself. Steady. She worked to master her voice before braving speech. "I suppose we can both agree that was a mistake."

"What, you didn't like it?"

He knew, damn him, that she'd liked it. "It wasn't appropriate."

He snorted. "Spare me the scandalized rhetoric. There's no harm in a few kisses."

A few kisses? *A few kisses?* Hysteria gurgled dangerously close to the surface. The foundations of her life were rocking like pillars in an earthquake, and he'd dismiss what had just happened as "a few kisses."

"We're not inexperienced, you and I." He paused. "Are we?"

Everything within her crescendoed to stillness. She hadn't thought . . . had entirely forgotten the role she played. When he'd taken her in his arms, she'd acted only as herself and made the unforgivable bungle of leaving behind her mask. He believed her to be a widow and a mistress.

Alarm iced through her. Already she might have communicated her inexperience too strongly through her response to his kiss, giving him an enormous clue, risking her job, her identity, everything.

Had she actually hoped just minutes ago that a few pretty stars could save Blackhaw? They wouldn't save her house, and they wouldn't save her. This was the real world. You were smart and protected yourself, or you were ruined. Her thoughts whirred, seeking ways to right the situation.

"Christ, who were these men you took to your bed?" he asked. "What in the hell were they doing?"

"They were men with more gentleness than you, that's all." Would he believe that? How naïve had her kisses been?

One black brow rose with disdain. "Is gentleness what you want in your lovers?"

"Yes."

"Like hell it is."

She made a big show of lifting her chin. "Regardless of what it is I value in my lovers, I can assure you that you don't have it. I don't even like you."

"You like me more than you'll admit to yourself."

"I like you not at all."

He stalked toward her, measuring her.

Her knees began to shake. In a show of false bravado, she firmed her jaw and held her ground.

He stopped close, continued to gauge her.

How much of the truth did he see in her? The truth was, she didn't want to like him at all, and didn't in many ways. And yet she'd just discovered that she loved his kisses with blazing fervor. It wasn't sane. It made no sense. Even now, she craved for him to touch her breast again so that she could feel that intense shock of pleasure a second time.

He frowned. "I've never seen a woman that begs to be kissed as much as you do."

"Excuse me?"

"It's in your eyes, the tilt of your chin, those damned lips."

"I never!"

"That's right. You've never been kissed the right way until tonight."

She sputtered, feeling ludicrously spited.

"Fortunately," he continued, "you're staying in my home. And I've time on my hands."

Oh heaven, oh heaven. This is bad. But even worse, was the anticipation straining upward within her like a sprout toward the sun.

"It's only kisses, after all." He smiled like the wolf he was. All his supremely well cut suits couldn't cover the ruggedness beneath any more than a wolf wearing a knitted sweater could hide his true nature. Jarrod's earthy upbringing, his ruggedness and strength showed through his businessman's veneer. The truth was in a hundred things, not the least in the way he'd kissed her and in his response to her protestations.

"A lovely offer, but thank you, no." She set off toward the house before she could say or do something else she'd regret. "I'll not be indulging in kisses with you again."

"Yes, you will," he replied. "And often."

Shaking her head, she quickened her pace.

"Afraid to stay?" he called after her.

"Going to bed," she called back without looking at him. "I trust sleep will prove more stimulating than this asinine conversation."

Jarrod watched her behind sway as she picked up her pace yet again, all but lifting her skirts and sprinting away from him. He followed at a distance, battling the instinct to charge after her, spin her around, and cart her to the nearest mound of shrubs to make love to her.

He smiled bleakly. She was twitchy and agitated

enough already. He doubted she'd react well to him stripping her naked behind a bush. He wanted to, though. He finally had her all tousled and flushed and wrinkled—and she was even more painfully desirable that way than he'd imagined.

This attraction between them had been simmering for days. It wasn't going away. Having her under his roof, her constant nearness only heightened his hunger for what he couldn't have.

He pressed his hands up his face, then raked them through his hair. Damn his conscience. As it pertained to Sophia, it plain angered him. Kisses didn't satisfy the driving need he had for her. Eventually he'd either have to incinerate his qualms about seducing her or find someone nearby who was warm and willing and a hell of a lot less prickly than Sophia LaRue.

He walked faster, his long legs eating the distance between them as they crossed the manicured stretch of lawn ringing the house. He reached the door an instant before she did, intending to open it for her. She pushed his hand away. He put it back. She grabbed the knob, and they wrestled with the door for a moment before she yanked at it forcefully.

"I've got it," she bit out, then swept into the hallway ahead of him.

Collier, who'd been waiting for him in the hallway outside his office, swiveled toward them. His secretary watched Sophia flash past, glanced at Jarrod, then set out after her, fishing for the key to her room as he went.

Jarrod halted, eyeing Sophia's retreating back. An erupting volcano couldn't have put forth more sparks. She was some kind of woman, Sophia, frustrating, vengeful, and at times like this damn endearing. As he watched her storm around the corner, a powerful tenderness expanded through his chest.

Yesterday when Oliver had told him the story of her grandmother's death he'd experienced an almost crushing disgust. She'd sat there listening to it, her expression pale but stoic, her hands twisting tightly together. He'd known that it hurt her to hear it, but he'd wanted to fill in the few pieces of her past he hadn't been able to discover. More, something integral inside him had needed to understand just how bad it had gotten for her, the girl who'd fed him when he'd had nothing.

If his father was responsible for what had happened to her, he'd hunt him down and he'd God damn strangle the bastard. Even Adam Stone's abandonment didn't rile him as much as what his father might have let become of the innocent young girl who'd worn snowy white, not knowing the way that life was about to mar her with grime.

He made his way into his office for his standing meeting with Collier. His leather chair creaked as he lowered his weight into it, then swiveled toward the window that framed the hill they'd just come from.

At first when he'd started kissing her, he thought she'd reserved her tongue from him out of expertise. The tease, taunting him. It had worked. Her hesitancy had only fueled his need to *feel* her respond beneath him. When she'd begun to, his blood had coursed through his body, molten hot. It wasn't until she'd pushed him away and he'd seen how frenzied she was that he wondered whether her initial hesitancy might have been genuine.

He could barely comprehend what blathering idiots her husband and the Ghost and whatever other lovers she'd taken to her bed must have been. Had they ever brought her to her own release, even? He doubted it, suddenly. And wanted, just as suddenly, to be the first to do that to her. To watch her while he did it. He could bring her to that place without compromising her. He could do that with his fingers.

He shifted, heavy with need. The woman had either the worst luck or the worst taste where men were concerned. Imagine her striving to defend Twilight's Ghost from him when the man didn't even know how to bed her properly. It was insulting.

With little more than a rustle of trouser fabric, Collier returned. He took up his usual position at the edge of the desk.

"Have our men learned anything new?" Jarrod asked, turning the chair toward Collier.

Collier extracted his papers from his inner jacket pocket. "One of the detectives has located a source who claims to have information on the identity of Twilight's Ghost—for a fee. Our man was able to arrange a time to meet with him to discuss what he knows."

"Who's the source?"

"A fisherman who works down on the docks."

Jarrod scowled. It wasn't much, but thus far the fisherman was only the third person his detectives had found who claimed to have any knowledge at all about the Secret Service agent. The theories of the first two had both run dry. "Have the detective pay the man whatever fee is necessary."

"Yes, sir."

"Report to me as soon as you hear."

"Of course, sir."

"What of Sophia's husband?"

Collier's attention skimmed lower on the page he

held. "We've been able to ascertain that when Mrs. LaRue left Galveston and the orphanage she was gone for just under one year. We've also confirmed that she spent the majority of that time in Washington. That's where she met and married Mr. LaRue, so that's where we've concentrated our search for information on the man."

"Still no luck?"

"Unfortunately, no."

Jarrod suppressed a growl of impatience. Usually his money bought information faster than this. Far faster. "Put more men on it."

"Yes, sir." Collier jotted a notation.

"Do you have anything else for me?"

"Yes, it's in regards to the household here. Mrs. Hoskins, the housekeeper, has informed me that one of the girls who works in the kitchen is with child."

"Unmarried?"

His secretary nodded solemnly.

"Do we know who the father is?"

"She's loath to say, sir."

He could still see the faces of all the women he'd known in the same predicament. During the days when he'd been fending for his brothers' survival, such women had scrabbled alongside him for jobs and money. "Find out if she has a place of her own in which to live. If not, buy one for her. She can leave work, she can continue, or she can leave for now and return whenever she wishes. Regardless, make her a gift of two thousand dollars."

"Yes, sir." Collier didn't need to write it down. Jarrod had given the same instructions numerous times over the years.

"That's all, sir." The older man inclined his head, his

customary good night salutation, before walking toward the door.

"Collier."

His secretary turned immediately.

Jarrod rested the back of his head against his chair and searched the ceiling. A decision had been nagging at him since yesterday. He shifted his weight forward, resting his forearms on his desk. "There's another matter I want investigated."

Collier leafed to a fresh page.

"Namely, my father. I want him found." Even if Sophia refused until doomsday to give Twilight's Ghost over to him, he'd find his father for her. At the very least his family owed her answers. At most, much more. He'd ascertain exactly how much more.

"Contact Allan Pinkerton again. I'll need more men looking for Sophia's husband and more men for this. If he has to bring operatives over from his Colorado offices, then so be it."

Collier nodded.

"The man in charge of the investigation into my father's whereabouts can contact me directly, and I'll provide him with the information he needs. However, Mrs. LaRue is not to be questioned under any circumstances, despite her connection to my father's disappearance. She's not to know about this." He was a pragmatist. His offer to help her find his father was a powerful bargaining chip. So long as there was a chance it would sway her toward releasing information to him about Twilight's Ghost, then he'd keep a grip on it.

"I understand, sir."

"That's all."

Collier left in as civilized a manner as he'd come, the office door clicking closed behind him.

Jarrod prowled from his chair to the window. What would his brothers say about his search for their father? The days after their father's disappearance had been so grim for them all that they never discussed them or the man himself.

In the darkness beyond the glass, he saw his mother's death. Heard the sound of her thin breath. Remembered the weight of the realization that she was truly going to die. He'd understood, then, that the sole responsibility of caring for his brothers was his. He'd done the only thing he could have done—shouldered the role with blinding determination and howling fear.

Holden's face loomed from behind the image of his mother on her death bed, growing brighter, nearer. Holden as he had been then, wearing his treasured possession—a ragged hat. He hadn't even cried. His small fingers had curled around their mother's hand as he'd stared at her unblinkingly.

Lastly, came Sophia's face. He saw her expression when she'd first looked at Duchess—wanting and afraid to want. A study in vulnerability and strength. Heartbreakingly beautiful.

He gritted his teeth as he threw open his office door and stalked the halls toward the master bedroom. He couldn't serve them all. Every day he was near Sophia, he understood more strongly that she needed time to be won. Years of mistrust had wounded her, and he couldn't damn well blame her for being guarded. But he couldn't afford to wait.

His first loyalty was to his brothers, and in this case to

Holden. That loyalty was in his bones, would go with him to the grave and beyond. He couldn't let himself forget why he'd brought Sophia here, why he was slowly gaining her trust. This growing softness he harbored toward her tempted him at times to believe that she was here for him. She wasn't. She was here so he could save Holden, a cause that must and did come first.

The simple fact was that regardless of her reluctance, her hurt, her loveliness, she *must* tell him about Twilight's Ghost.

Inside his bedroom, a carved wooden bed commanded the space. He fisted his hand in the sumptuous maroon covering and ripped it off with a single swipe. Was it fair for him to sleep in luxury when his brother was lying in a jail cell? It was his fault his brother was still there. *His job* to get his brother out, and he was failing.

With a sneer, he seized a handful of his sheets and wrenched them free.

Maggie grumbled the next afternoon as she unwound a man's shirt from around her waist, where she had hidden it beneath her chemise. She tossed the garment to Sophia, who caught it eagerly.

The fabric of her disguise felt glorious to her—coarse, warm, and familiar. Maggie pitched the trousers to her next, and lastly the hat, which Maggie had apparently wedged against the small of her back, underneath both the trousers and the shirt.

"That's the last." Maggie flicked her skirts back into place with an efficient snap. "There was absolutely no chance of my bringing the shoes."

"No?" Sophia hadn't thought of that.

"No. I considered stuffing them into my bodice, toes

pointed outward like breasts, but decided against it." She planted her long hands on her hips. "I worried your guards might suspect something."

Sophia smiled and hugged her clothes snugly to her. They represented hope. These few garments were her chance at keeping Blackhaw safe.

She deposited her armload onto the top of the dresser. One by one she opened the drawers, then jiggled them free. Already Maggie had given her the lockpicking tools, sketches of the territory around the house, and a map marked with the nighttime positions of the guards.

"How are you going to start your search for the counterfeiter?" Maggie asked.

Sophia stashed her hat against the top back panel of the dresser, then slid the uppermost drawer into place against it. "Well, think aloud with me. What's a counterfeiter going to need to do business?"

"Paper and ink."

"Right, and an artist to design the plates."

"Unless the counterfeiter himself is an artist."

"That's a possibility." She worked to hide the trousers behind the second drawer. "What else?"

"A press."

"Exactly. And space for a press, not to mention space enough or insulation enough to muffle the sounds of the press." She leaned against the dresser. "I thought I'd begin tonight simply by moving through the warehouse district, watching and listening for the sound of counterfeit money being made."

She had little expectation of catching the counterfeiter tonight using that method. He was smart enough to have eluded the Service for some time now. Still, it was how she always operated. She began with the broadest possible investigation, giving the criminals the opportunity to be foolish and make things simple for her. Gradually, she'd tighten the net, winding her way in ever-smaller concentric circles, following clues she'd garnered on the circle before, until she'd finally gathered the net so snug that one person was left trapped and thrashing in it.

She slid the final drawer into the dresser, then brushed her hands together as she straightened to face Maggie.

Maggie hadn't made a move to sample any of her hats. Apparently her friend was far too serious about what she viewed as Sophia's impending peril to do so. "How can I help?" Maggie asked.

"You can search through the ownership and leasing information on all the warehouses in town, then try to verify whether or not each warehouse is being used for legitimate business."

"I'll start today." Clouds shifted behind Maggie's typically bright hazel eyes. "It's not too late, you know, to change your mind about trying to sneak away from here."

"I'm not going to change my mind."

"I'll look into warehouse records, and you can just wait and see what comes of it—"

"I'm not going to change my mind," Sophia repeated gently. "I can escape from here and let myself back in without either Jarrod or Simon finding out." She dearly wished Simon hadn't given her the order to stay put. She understood his reasons. Her disappearance would induce Jarrod's suspicion about her identity. And Jarrod probably could kidnap her from Blackhaw a second time if he so chose. Still, she'd have loved to have the freedom to break free tonight and keep on running. As it was, she'd return and bide her time as Simon had instructed.

Maggie still looked worried.

She went to her friend and hugged her, drawing comfort from the green, lemony smell of her soap. "Thank you for helping me," she murmured.

"Thank me when we're all safely back at Blackhaw, taxes paid."

"Okay," Sophia said. "I'll thank you then." When Maggie went to open the closet door, Sophia stilled her. "I think we'd best agree to some sort of communication in case the worst happens. I don't expect it to," she hurried to say, "but we'd be foolish not to establish a plan now."

Maggie gave a quick nod.

"If Jarrod catches me, he'll likely cut off contact between us. Should you arrive for a visit and be turned away, just glance at my bedroom window on the way out. If I can be, I'll be there. If I'm simply standing, that means he refused you visitation because of a reason other than discovery of my identity. Who knows, he's irritable enough he might turn you away for any reason on any given day. However, if I press my palm to the windowpane, that means he's found me out."

"What should I do then?"

"Wait to tell Simon. Give me a few days, then come back. If at any time you see me in the window and I tug at my hair, that means I want you to notify Simon."

"What if I come to visit you, and you're not at the window?"

Sophia grimaced, the possibility turning her cold. "Then tell Simon everything at once."

Maggie studied her somberly.

"We're not going to have to worry about it, because he's not going to catch me," Sophia reassured her.

"I know. I just want to make certain that *you* know that Jarrod's not stupid."

"He's a little stupid," Sophia replied lightly as she opened the closet door and led Maggie into the bedroom. "He hasn't suspected me yet." She said the words not because she believed Jarrod to be the least bit stupid, but out of a perverse need to disparage him. He hadn't been at breakfast that morning. His absence had only served to torture her with even more thoughts of him than usual.

"Sophia," Maggie whispered, wrapping her hand around her upper arm, stopping her progress. "He is *not* stupid. He's a man and, like all men, suffers from the perspective that Twilight's Ghost must also be a man because no mere woman could succeed at evading him. You give him a clue, though . . . it might only take just one . . . and he'll figure it out."

Sophia was forcefully reminded for the thousandth time of the kiss they'd shared last night. She'd be roasted on a spit before she'd admit to Maggie she'd kissed him. Or that she'd already divulged one small clue.

"He built an oil empire from nothing but dust," Maggie said urgently. "He's *not* stupid."

"Easy." Sophia patted her hand, and tried to smile. "I was only teasing. I know how smart he is. Your warning's been heeded."

Frown brackets enclosed Maggie's mouth as she released her hold, then straightened the fabric of Sophia's sleeve. "Be careful."

"I'm always careful."

They walked together to the door and Sophia knocked twice. As always when Maggie came calling, one of Jarrod's guards had escorted her to Sophia's room, locked them in, then waited in the hall to escort Maggie out. Today, the one who'd brought Maggie answered the knock and led Maggie toward the front of the house, but neither closed nor locked Sophia's door behind him.

Sophia's brow knit. Unsure about her newfound freedom, she stepped into the hallway to watch Maggie vanish around a far corner. Nothing happened. Quiet swished about her, beckoning. She took another few tentative steps—

"Afternoon."

Jarrod. Her heart did a crazy *thump bang*. Wildly clashing emotions all jostled for supremacy as she swung to face him.

He was hard to see, leaning against the wall at the far end of the corridor. Curtains had been closed over the window there, leaving a black niche for him, in all his black, with his black hair and black heart to wait in.

So why was excitement the emotion that won out over all others? It practically stole her breath. "I didn't see you there," she said, stating the obvious. His presence was clearly why the guard had left her unattended.

"No."

"H-how long have you been waiting?"

"A while."

How long was a while, she wondered frantically. What if he'd heard her and Maggie talking? The closet was well insulated, but it wasn't inviolate—

"I couldn't hear you," he commented, answering her thoughts.

Relief surged through her. She sent up a jumbled prayer of thanks.

"How do you two communicate, hand signals?"

"No . . ."

"Written notes passed back and forth?"

She shook her head. Something was altered about him today. He was always blunt, but she sensed a rawness in him. A dissatisfaction prowling for prey.

Perhaps she'd better return to her room. She sidled toward the open door.

"If you flee in there, I'll follow," he said, stilling her in her tracks. "I have a key, remember?"

She smiled crisply. "Then I suppose I'll take my chances out here in the hall."

"Wise decision." He walked toward her, all towering charisma and devastating good looks.

She resisted the urge to fidget.

"I want my kiss," he said.

Her throat tightened convulsively with a mix of fear and thrill. She eased against the wall, instinctively seeking protection. "What kiss?"

"You're in my home. And I've time on my hands." He closed in on her. "Am I the only one who remembers this discussion?"

"Apparently, because I replied to you that I would not be indulging in . . ."

He planted both palms on the wall above her head, caging her.

She tried to swallow down a bean-sized throat. When that failed, she reflexively licked her lips. ". . . kisses with you again."

"Sophie," he chastised. His grin was lopsided, but it wasn't innocent. No, that smile was wicked, and it made her pine for wicked things. As if his hands were bound with shackles, he didn't use them at all. He didn't need to. The evidence of his arousal as he angled his body against hers was plenty communication enough.

She closed her eyes, fighting the shattering inside herself. She couldn't let herself be so easily mastered—

His lips grazed hers. She forced herself to remain immobile.

Then nothing. He was close. Even without vision, she knew because she could feel his breath against the edge of her lips and cheek. He didn't move, and she didn't dare to. Oh, God, his body was so near and so hard. What would he do next? Free her hair? Invade her mouth? Caress breasts that were aching for him?

With a *whoosh* of air, he pushed away.

Without daring even to breathe, she waited.

Nothing. He touched her not at all. She cracked open her eyelids.

He'd retreated a few feet away and was watching her intently. "What?" he asked, raising a brow. "You want more?"

More? She wanted it all. "Hardly."

"Until the next kiss, then."

Somehow she dredged up a scoffing sound. "If you'll excuse me." She turned into her room and shut the door. Though she waited, holding her breath, he didn't follow her in as he'd threatened. Instead, he simply locked the door and left.

Sophia promptly collapsed against the wall adjacent to the door, pressing a hand to her chest. Beneath her skin, she could feel the throbbing of her blood. He'd granted her a reprieve. For all her righteous intentions, it had been *he* who'd granted her a reprieve at the crucial second. If he'd kept kissing her, she'd have kept letting him.

Weak, she berated herself. *Weak!*

With a moan she dropped her hand and gazed at the familiar confines of her room. Tonight, she'd escape this place. Tonight Jarrod would be sound asleep and she'd be gone, besting him secretly in one of the few ways it appeared she had left.

That night, Sophia stood to the side of her window, peering out through the crack between the wall and drawn curtains. The guards were all in their usual positions. Maggie's surveillance had confirmed what she herself had been able to see, that Jarrod had concentrated all his security at the front of the house and at intervals around the perimeter of her room. Fortunately for her.

Her gaze moved past the men, to the last of the servants drifting home. Their silhouettes were murky against the misty darkness, but she could see well enough to count each one, just as she'd done every night since coming here. Thus she knew that twenty-four people left the property late every evening, after the house had been put to rest. The twenty-third and twenty-fourth were disappearing up the drive even now, which meant there was no chance she'd meet them on the service stairs leading to the upper floor, and no possibility she'd dash into them as she made her way across the grounds.

She waited until the last shadow of the last servant had melted to nothingness. Tranquillity shrouded the exterior of the house, except for the muffled conversation of the guards and the orange flare of their cigars against the night.

Time to go.

She'd hung her lace-up shoes around her neck, so it was on soundless socked feet that she moved to her bedroom door. Her hands felt stiff as she extracted her instruments from her trouser pocket. For a moment, she simply stared at them, before taking a fortifying breath and slipping one into the keyhole.

Nervousness hummed deep in her belly. She'd never lost that sense of unease—it hounded her before every nocturnal foray she'd ever made as Twilight's Ghost. It was doubly strong, though, tonight. So strong, it seemed to push up her throat.

Blackhaw. She brought the house to the fore of her mind, saw it as a collage of sights, memories, smells, feelings. *For Blackhaw.* She pursed her lips against the queasiness and focused on her work.

The lock was of the ordinary household variety. Not complicated. With a deft turn of her wrist, the bolt clicked free. The sound of it struck her ears with the force of a gong.

Crouching behind the door, she both listened intently for and prayed against hearing someone approach. It wouldn't do, she thought slightly hysterically, to be caught wearing men's clothing and holding lockpicking instruments in her hands.

No one came.

She gave her room one last glance as she mentally ticked off the items she had with her. Knife, map of the territory, lockpicking tools, shoes. That was it. That was everything she needed.

She ensured that every tendril of her hair was tucked securely into her man's hat before cracking the door open, checking both ways down the corridor, and easing into the hallway.

Chapter 11

Hurriedly, she turned to her door and worked to lock it behind her. She felt wildly exposed, with her back to the hall and her disguise a red flag to anyone who might glance her way in passing. But she couldn't very well leave her door open and risk a guard noticing that fact during a routine check of the hall.

Faster, she urged herself. *Faster . . . There. Done.*

Heart knocking, she ran in the direction opposite the foyer, stopping at the door she'd seen Jarrod's servants exit and enter. It opened easily, revealing a stairway beyond.

You see, it's fine, Sophia. Everything's fine, according to plan.

The unlit staircase, cold and gritty against her feet, passed hastily below her. When she reached the upper story, she again cracked the door a fraction and scanned the area beyond. She'd never been in this region of the house, but as far as she could discern, the servants tidied these rooms for guests that never came. More importantly for her causes, she could cross here to the unguarded side of the house with far less risk of chancing upon someone. She simply had to follow this hallway, then find the room that led to the balcony she'd seen from below last night.

One wall lamp burned, its low flame illuminating the corridor. The closed doors were cast in shadow, the wallpaper tan in color with brown fleur de lis scrawling across it. *Go.* Rolling her lips inward, she slid into the hall and, keeping close to the wall, scampered forward. The mouth of the grand staircase passed by, spilling light over her for an instant before dimness doused her again.

Just this last hallway. It ended in two doors facing outward. That one, on the left, was the one with the balcony, she was sure. Her vision latched onto it, her beacon. Not much farther now—

A man's sneeze ripped through the quiet. Her steps slashed to a halt. It had come from the room just to her left. The clearing of a throat followed, then footsteps.

Sophia threw herself toward the door on her right, wildly hoping no one would be within as she hauled it open. The darkness of the interior swallowed her. She shut her door, keeping the knob twisted open so as not to make a noise, exactly as his door opened. Shaking inside and out, she leaned down to look through the keyhole.

She caught a glimpse of Collier Melvin, Jarrod's secretary, before he walked out of her range.

With her free hand, she crossed herself. Her forehead sagged forward to rest against the wood. That had been close. Much too close to bear considering. She'd thought . . . well, she'd thought Collier resided somewhere below.

Silently, she clunked her forehead against the door. What if Collier had left his room just now in order to fetch her for some excursion Jarrod had planned? No, that was crazed thinking. Collier had never come to fetch her once she'd retired. There was no reason to think he would tonight.

. . . However, it appeared there *was* reason to worry that others might be rooming on this floor. Her nervousness churned harder. Maybe Maggie had been right. This was insanity.

Blackhaw. She closed her eyes, holding tight to the word. It was the only thing on earth, damn it, that was really hers. It had been her grandmother's house, and her parents' house before her, and the house of her childhood. There was no one left to fight for it but her. And so she would. Because it held her heart, and if she gave up her heart without a fight, then there'd be nothing left to live for.

Long after a safe amount of time had passed, she eased from the room. Ears straining for any other human sounds, she dashed down the remainder of the corridor. At its end she checked to make certain that no interior light seeped below the door on the left. None did, so she let herself in.

The curtains were drawn, rendering the room as pitch-black as the last one had been. Ever so slowly, she felt her way across it. Her fingertips finally met the crusty surface of a painting. Her hands traveled the contour of the frame, over wall, over wall. Curtain.

She opened the velvety drapery to reveal just what she'd been hoping for—a balcony. And past that, a freedom that swirled with dollops of fog. The landscape called to her almost audibly, a song of challenge, and bravery, and home. Emotion ached in her chest. She was going to make it.

The double doors opened for her. She caught her breath against the flush of cold as she padded to the edge of the wooden balustrade and looked over. Not a guard in sight.

The only thing that stood before her was one enormous pecan tree, spreading its branches to the balcony. The grizzled tree looked as if it had been there long enough to see stranger things than a shoeless woman dressed in men's clothing. This wasn't the first time either, she'd bet, that someone had used its arms as a ladder to grander things than bedrooms offered.

She swung one leg, then the other, over the balustrade and balanced on the strip of wood on the other side. The nearest branch, gnarled and about as thick around as her waist, swept past her at knee height. She took a bracing breath, then stepped onto it, grabbing a thinner, higher branch for a handhold.

The tree held her firm, steady as time. At home, she utilized her cellar for entrances and exits, but she was no stranger to tree climbing. There had been many times at St. Mary's when trees had served her well. It all came back to her now, the chattering of the wind through the branches, the slight sway, the exhilarating height. Added to that, the sensation of the bark against the bottoms of her feet.

She'd donned as many undergarments as possible beneath the shirt and trousers. Still, the chill riding on the damp air zinged the exposed skin of her face, hands, ankles.

She reached the trunk and began her descent, one careful foothold at a time. Twigs broke beneath her feet, gouging flesh usually better protected. No matter. Blackhaw. She drew even with the lower-story kitchen windows, all darkly vacant at this hour. One more step down. *Blackhaw.*

On the lowest branch, she gathered her balance, then leapt to the ground. As soon as she reached cover, perhaps a hundred yards off, she'd don her shoes. Until then, she'd simply run. She took off at a sprint. This she knew well, the churning of her legs, the pumping of her lungs, the feel of lonely air against her face. She glanced back once, then twice. Saw no one.

I did it, she thought as she charged onward.

A smile began to spread across her lips.

Four days later the weather was in the same gloomy mood it had been in the night of her first escape, Sophia noted. Foggy, secretive, and so petulant that it had decided to mask the sun despite the midmorning hour. She lifted a hand to her plum-colored hat to keep it on her head as Jarrod's sailing boat skimmed across the swells.

Wintry as it was, at least the brisk combination of speed and cold was keeping her awake.

"Are you all right?" Jarrod asked gruffly.

"I'm fine, thank you." She glanced over her shoulder to where he sat, manning the rudder. Since their kiss beneath the stars, his disposition had held a sharp edge. Though she'd been trying to read him, to deduce its cause, she'd yet to succeed.

"Need hot tea?" He motioned his chin toward the picnic basket his staff had packed for them.

Inexplicably, the question caused tenderness toward him to swell inside her. He remembered everything she'd ever said to him—like what she preferred to drink and how she preferred it—and he always asked after her comfort. Already, he'd bundled blankets around her and handed her a muff for her hands. Dangerously heady treatment for a woman like her. She'd had only herself to care about her needs for the past twenty years, and in that time had never cared half as much as he appeared to. "I think I'll have my tea a little later," she answered.

He returned his attention to the sea. For the excursion he'd donned his black greatcoat, but had left his head uncovered. Ruddy color burnished his cheekbones, and the breeze rustled his dark hair, lifting sections of it.

He glanced at her, and caught her staring. The intense awareness that lived and breathed between them sprang to life like kerosene tossed on flames. He studied her face almost harshly, causing her lips to heat.

How many times had she been alone with him like this? Too many. Every time she'd felt stripped of protection, and every time he'd reminded her of a wolf, circling.

Madness. She tried to swallow. For all she really knew about the man, he could toss her onto the boat's deck, strip her naked right there in the open, and force himself on her.

Her stomach rolled at the mental picture that presented, but not with revulsion. To her dismay, it groaned with restless desire.

"Now you," he said.

"Excuse me?" she said, jolted from her thoughts.

"Your turn to sail this boat."

"Oh." She waved a hand. "Thank you, no." She'd grown accustomed to her rowboat, but she knew nothing about steering a vessel with a sail.

"I insist," Jarrod replied.

"No, truly—"

"Fine." With a shrug, he let go of the rudder and moved down the bench seat, positioning himself across from her. He rested his elbows on the boat's edge, stretched out his legs, and crossed them at the ankles. The look he gave her was serious, pointed.

The boat began to list. She peeked up at the sail, heard it creak as it swung. Her side of the boat dipped. She jerked her head around, watching as the deep, foaming water neared. Just then a gust caught the sail, pitching her perilously close to the surface. Water spattered against her face, a shock of cold.

Frantic, she looked to Jarrod. Even tilted upward toward the sky, he hadn't moved a muscle.

A second gust nearly capsized them. With a yelp, Sophia scrambled to the rear and grabbed the rudder. She pulled it to the middle, fighting the current to do so. With a tremendous shudder, the vessel began to right itself. "What do you think you're doing?" she yelled at Jarrod, the wind flinging her words back at her.

"Letting you sail this boat," he answered, supremely unaffected.

"We could've been tossed into the water and drowned!"

"I can swim. I'd have saved you."

"You're insane!"

"Perhaps, but only for you."

Oh! Ridiculous man! Quivering with agitation, she

gripped the handle tighter. When the boat had been leaning so wildly, there'd been no fear in his eyes at all.
None. Which made her think he really might have been
perfectly content to be flung into the sea. "What were
you planning to do? Keep me afloat with one arm while
righting the boat with the other?"

"Something like that."

She shook her head, refusing to listen. It unnerved
her, his lack of fear. Jarrod Stone was accomplished,
cocky, and so damn unafraid. Was there anything, anything, that made his chest as tight as hers was now? That
had the ability to ruffle those impeccable black feathers?
How badly she wanted to see that happen.

Wavelets slapped, then split against the bow, the sole
sound. "I feel it wise to inform you I've no idea how to
steer this thing," she said.

"Where do you want to go?"

"Straight toward the dock so that I can disembark."

He muttered something that sounded suspiciously
like, "no sense of humor." He met her quelling glance
head-on, then narrowed his eyes in a challenge partly
sensual, partly playful.

A small degree of her anger ebbed. He was infuriat-
ing, but he was also just a tiny bit . . . a *very* tiny bit, irresistible, too. "Just tell me how to maneuver it."

"At the moment the wind is coming at us from the
side. See if you can't use the rudder to turn her so that
the wind is behind us." He set the sail at a different angle.
"Then we'll be sailing before the wind."

She did as he instructed. The sail flapped and filled
with wind, tugging their boat forward. Despite herself,
she grinned. Who'd have thought she could do that? She
was sailing the vessel.

A thick curve of mist slightly to the left caught her attention. She wanted to race to it, suddenly, and plow through to see what was on the other side. "How can I make it go faster?"

"Now the wind is coming from the left side, or beam, so we have to adjust the angle of the sail accordingly."

He did so, and sure enough, the boat picked up speed. Beneath her she could feel the wood slapping against water as the boat drove forward. More wind, then more licked at her cheeks and pulled loose thick strands of her hair. It felt good to let her hair tumble free, to tilt her chin into the air, to rise to a new and exhilarating challenge. It made her feel alive.

The thicket of fog drew nearer until she sent the boat lunging directly through it. Beyond it, there was more. Ribbons of the stuff to follow and to chase.

With Jarrod's help, she raced the boat in two more lines, laughing at times in the face of so much half-frightening speed. Finally, she executed a shaky maneuver that eased them into a slower pace. The whip of air on her face eased, and she was able to relax slightly.

Jarrod sat quietly, leaning against the boat's side, watching her. Her pulse stuttered at his uncompromising male beauty. The weather around him was drizzly and gloomy, but those eyes of his shone. Mossy green, glinting from an inner light.

She smiled at him. Tentatively, slightly self-conscious.

"Holden was always the quietest of the four of us," he said.

Her smile immediately faded.

"And the most reserved," he continued. "He's always

been content to keep his own counsel and his own company."

"Why are you telling me this?"

"Because I want you to see that he's not a bad person."

"I never said he was."

"No, but it's what you believe. I think it's partially what's keeping you from helping me free him."

She sighed heavily, wishing she could stick her head in a storage hamper, cover her ears, anything but sit captive and listen to him talk about his brother.

"There was a time, when he was about thirteen, that he left for two days. Just left." He leaned forward, settling his elbows on his parted knees and interlacing his hands between. "It wasn't unusual for him to go away on his own for short periods, but he'd never been gone overnight before."

Perhaps because banks aren't open for robbing during the night, Sophia wanted to retort. She kept the words locked behind her lips.

"Clint and J. T. and I were getting our things together to go out and search for him, when he came walking back to the house barefoot. Never would tell us where he'd been or what had happened to his shoes. This was at a time when shoes were scarce around our place."

She was reminded of climbing down and up the pecan tree beyond Jarrod's balcony in her socks, the uneven bark digging into the bottoms of her feet. Her skin there was delicate because as poor as she'd been as a child, she'd always, at least, had shoes. Had Jarrod and his brothers been poorer than that? Her research into the brothers had yielded little about the years after they left

Galveston and before they became men. She supposed
she'd always imagined them living in relative splendor,
thanks to the money their father had stolen from her.

"Weeks later, an old man came to our place wearing
Holden's shoes. He was a distant neighbor of ours. Evidently, Holden had heard in town that the man's wife of
sixty years was dying. Months before, the old man had
sent her to live with a daughter when she'd grown too
sick for him both to care for her and work their farm
enough to feed her. When his wife's time was near, he
had no transportation to go to her, and no money to pay
for any. Well, neither did Holden, but he did have shoes
to give. Turns out, the old man had walked a hundred
miles in Holden's shoes in time to hold his wife's hand at
the end. He came back to return the shoes."

Despite herself, emotion gathered in Sophia's throat.
Partly, at the simple generosity of what Holden had
done. And partly at the thought of being loved like
that . . . so much that a husband would walk a hundred
miles in borrowed shoes, merely to hold your hand and
ensure that his face was the last face you looked upon in
this life. . . . That was love. To be loved with such ferocity must be the grandest gift a person could ever receive.

Somewhere above a gull cawed. It swooped overhead,
white on gray, its wings beating.

Sophia had to wonder who would be there at the end
of her life to hold *her* hand. No one, she feared. She'd
made choices, both relational and professional, toward
that end. And yet there were times, like now, when she
felt her aloneness so completely that an almost incon-
solable sadness settled over her.

"When the old man came back to return the shoes,"
Jarrod continued, "Holden tried to insist he keep them,

but the man wouldn't hear of it. Said his wife would never have countenanced such a thing while alive, so he wasn't about to countenance it in the face of her memory. Holden accepted the shoes, but he never wore them again."

"Why?"

"They'd contoured to the man's feet. Every mile he'd walked was marked on them through dirt and scratches and thin places in the sole."

"That's why Holden threw them away?"

He regarded her for a long, steady moment. "No, that's why he kept them. He still has them to this day."

She blinked at him. A shimmering communication moved back and forth between them. It felt very much like understanding.

"I assume such sentimentality escapes you," she said softly, striving for distance, working to remind herself why she couldn't begin to let herself understand Jarrod Stone.

"Perhaps. But then I've never claimed to be half as noble as any one of my brothers."

There it was, that unflinching loyalty he harbored for his family. She could read it in his stubborn jaw, in the battle-ready cant of his shoulders. At times it submerged, and she was almost able to believe that everything he'd done in relation to her was because of *her*. That he might truly see her as deserving of sumptuous gifts, that he might be pursuing her because he wanted her as a woman. Then it surfaced again, his fierce allegiance to his family, and she was reminded. Jarrod had supplied all of this, from the lovely plum gown she was wearing, to the sailboat she was sitting in, to the picnic basket full of food, for Holden's sake. Not because of her. Holden.

Jealousy clutched at her heart. She wished that Jarrod felt even a small measure of that kind of devotion toward her.

Unable to face him, she looked to the sail and slowly steered the boat into a turn. Would that she could turn from who he was and who she was as easily.

Sorrows sucked at her. Sorrow for what had become of the boy who'd once given away his shoes. Sorrow over deceiving Jarrod. Sorrow because for all that was suspect about Jarrod, his loyalty to his family wasn't. And that one most sterling quality about him was the one she could never honor.

She gritted her teeth and turned the sail more deeply into the wind in order to pick up speed. How dare she grieve for Jarrod's troubles? Ludicrous. It made her angry that she'd even *think* it. The man had stolen her off the street, for the love of God! Did he torture himself with regret over that? Not for a second.

"I've tried to be patient," Jarrod said.

She scowled at him.

"But I need for you to help me free my brother now."

She started to shake her head—

"I'll help you find my father."

"I'd like very much for you to help me find your father," she answered honestly. "But I can't turn Twilight's Ghost over to you. Even for that."

With a growl, he pushed to his feet. He was so tall and broad-shouldered standing like that with his feet braced apart, that he blocked out what little sun there was and cast darkness over her. "If it were just me, Sophia, I'd give you all the time you needed to recover from your love of Twilight's Ghost and to overcome your reservations about assisting me. Hell, I'd give you anything you wanted." The wind whisked open the flaps of his coat and caused it to billow and snap. "However, the time you're taking is costing my brother."

"It's costing me, too."

"Then relent. Give me the man's name."

What an impossible situation. She could never give him what he wanted, and he would never let her go until she did. "I can't."

"Like hell you can't." He kicked an overturned bucket in front of her, then straddled it. His greatcoat fell behind him, his inner thighs bracketed her outer thighs. "If the Ghost is so worthy of your loyalty, then why hasn't he come for you?"

She opened her mouth to answer, had nothing to say.

"What kind of a sorry excuse for a man is he that he would let me take you the way I did? That he would leave you to fend for yourself?"

She didn't, couldn't answer.

"Tell me," he demanded.

"I can't speak for him," she said.

"Well I can speak for myself, and I'll tell you right now that I'd never have let you go. I'd have come after you."

Distressed, she glanced down at the rudder and attempted to distract herself by tying it down.

"Look at me." He nudged her chin to face him. "Whatever he does for you, I can do more. Whatever he gives to you, I can give you better. You can tell me who he is."

"You're right," she said shakily, her senses overrun with his unrelenting pursuit, his nearness, and with a dangerous longing. "I can tell you. But I won't."

He gazed at her unblinkingly. "Name whatever you want. It's yours."

"There's nothing you can purchase—"

"There's always something. Name it, I'll give it to you, and you'll tell me his identity."

"No—"

"Name it, Sophia, and let's get on with this. You've drawn it out long enough. It's past time you divulge his identity."

"I won't."

"It's time you did."

"I won't."

"You *will*," he snarled.

"I—"

He grasped her chin and kissed her, his lips pressed hard against hers, his tongue plunging into her mouth. Ravenous hunger leapt within her, and she responded with equal force and frustration, weaving her hands into the hair at the back of his head, pulling him toward her. It was angry and hot and unapologetically blunt—a kiss that made her tremble with a tempest of desire unlike anything she'd ever imagined. She heard herself moan, sensed her body arching against his.

He bent his head and removed the glove from his right hand with his teeth. "Tilt your head back," he said.

She did, and his mouth immediately claimed the sensitive skin under her ear. She could feel the chill of his nose, the heat of his mouth even as she was aware of his hand penetrating the blankets and the coat that shielded her. She shivered as his fingers slid to the edge of her bodice's neckline. She knew what was coming and *wanted* it. So very badly.

His hand delved into her bodice and captured her breast. The blissful texture of skin on skin drew a gasp from her. Oh, so good— He pulled the fullness of her breast up, over the edge of her garment. Her nipple hardened almost painfully, abrading against the inside of her woolen coat.

He worked quickly with his free hand, ripping open the buttons of her coat. He took the point of her breast into his mouth greedily and deeply. She watched him— dark hair against pale skin—shamelessly suckling her in broad daylight. She buried her hands more deeply in his hair even as tears misted her eyes. She craved to make him love her just a little, for this to be about more than physical attraction, for this to be as precious for him as it was for her.

He was turning more than just her body to liquid— rushing, melting, flowing. He was capturing her soul. And still he tugged at her—suction and warmth. He swirled his tongue around the point of her breast. Then pulled away.

He glanced up at her, one breast bared between them. His eyes were cloudy, his breath ragged against her wet nipple. The urgent pulling sensation between her legs, and within her heart, heightened. He bent his head, lavishing the same treatment on her other breast. Kissing her, cradling her, sucking her, licking. She shifted on the bench seat, impatient. Needy for something—

His mouth released her. Her fingers stroked from his hair as he straightened on his seat, dropping the sides of her coat over her nakedness. Even so, she *felt* her nakedness beneath her coat so powerfully.

She glanced at his ungloved hand. *Mother above* . . . it had cupped her breast, held her up for his lips to feast on. And it hadn't been enough. She was still practically itching, fidgeting with the need for more.

She lifted her gaze and found him watching her—his lips slightly swollen. He didn't say why he'd stopped, and she was too proud to ask.

As modestly as she could, she slanted away from him and fixed her clothing. When she turned back, Jarrod was still studying her. *Thinking about what had just happened between us*, she wondered? *Or thinking about his brother?*

A thought occurred to her, bringing with it a sick twinge in her belly. "Did you . . ." Her words faded. Over the years she'd grown comfortable in her role as silent observer of others, of life. To speak truthfully about her own emotions was far, far harder. "Did you kiss me just now because you hope to gain my help for your brother?"

"Did that kiss feel contrived?"

She couldn't tell him she didn't have experience enough to know. "I'm not certain."

His gaze penetrated to the deepest regions of her hopes and fears. "Every time I've touched you, Sophia, I've done so to serve only one man. Me."

She licked her lips, hating herself because she yearned to believe him even though she realized how wrong, how impossible, how completely doomed were her feelings toward him.

The fact was that Jarrod would never forgive her if he found out that she was Twilight's Ghost. If he discovered her, he would *never* forgive and he would *never* understand. That made honesty impossible. And how could she hope for any kind of relationship with a man who she must constantly lie to, a man who didn't know her identity at the most basic level? She couldn't.

Sophia cleared her throat and reached to untie the rudder. "I'm taking us home."

Late the next night Jarrod was sitting alone in his office, his suit jacket long forgotten, his shirt untucked and half-unbuttoned, papers spread across the surface of his desk. He shook his head, furious at himself for his lack of concentration. This was the first time in remembrance that he was either too disinterested or too preoccupied to focus on business decisions that needed making.

With a groan, he swiveled his chair toward the window. Almost immediately, a fantasy of Sophia rushed to his mind in luscious detail. Her, naked, kneeling between his legs and taking him into her pink mouth. That tongue. Breasts, swinging free. Heavy. Her hair running over his thighs. He could still smell her—clean and warm with a hint of lavender. He shifted, imagining her there, between his knees, imagining the sensation of her—

Just then he saw something beyond the panes of his window.

A shadow. Running.

Chapter 12

Jarrod rushed out the back door of his house. He paused, scouring the dark vista of trees and hills for a hint of what he thought he'd seen. At first, nothing caught his eye. He shook his head, and ran his gaze over the landscape again, straining—

There. A streak of tan where all else was deepest gray. So similar to what he'd seen the night he'd waited behind Blackhaw for Twilight's Ghost that the skin at the back of his neck pricked.

He took off at a dead run. Curses swam through his brain, bitingly fervent. Twilight's Ghost. Here. The man had been coming to see her, after all. Like a damned thief in the night, as was his way. Right under the watch of all the idiot guards he'd hired. Right under his own nose. Making a fool of him.

Jealousy and rage at his own ignorance shot through him. It spurred him to push his body harder and faster, until he was barely aware of his exertion. His legs pumped, he jumped over tree roots, and ducked under low-hanging branches, but he didn't physically *feel* it. The hunt for the agent would end now. Tonight.

Jarrod crashed into a small meadow, just as the Ghost was on the verge of exiting it. The man's hat turned, and recognition fired the air between them like lightning. For an infinitesimal space of time, the Ghost froze, then dashed into the cover of the trees.

Hatred rolled up Jarrod's throat. He'd never been a man to be bested twice by any foe. And he wouldn't be this time. He sprinted across the meadow. Here, there was no iron fence for the agent to cage him in. It was simply man against man, and he was going to goddamn wrap his hands around the bastard's throat when he caught him.

Shrubs and trees flashed past, scratching at his arms and chest through the thin layer of his shirt. He dodged and swerved, gaining on the Ghost with brute speed. As he'd learned the last time, his prey was agile. For moments at a time, he managed to escape Jarrod's sight. Regardless of the whisperings of the townspeople, though, the man was human not ghost. If Jarrod looked closely enough the telltale quivering of a branch always marked his passing. Jarrod raced after those pathway markers until he spotted him again. And he always did, and every time nearer until he'd closed on the man so much he could hear his footsteps pounding the uneven ground.

Jarrod followed him out from under a stand of trees, only to find a steep slope cutting away beneath his feet. The Ghost was half-slipping, half-running down its face, angling his steps toward the right, where more trees offered shelter.

Jarrod plunged after him, taking the hill far faster than was wise, using his hands to keep himself upright as rocks skittered beneath his feet. This hillside was his best chance so far of overtaking the man. Foliage and thickets gave the Ghost room in which to disappear and evade. This hillside offered no such protection.

He drew closer, so close he could make out the plaid of the man's shirt. The dirtiness of his hat.

The Ghost reached flatter ground and scrambled toward cover.

The rage inside Jarrod whipped him on. He hurtled into the air, landed with jarring force at the bottom of the slope, and charged after the agent. Just feet away from him now. Closing. They sprinted together, pursuer and pursued. Darkness sliced over them as they barreled under the overhang of branches.

Just as the Ghost attempted to dart to the side, Jarrod threw his body forward. He collided with the man, and together they crashed to the earth, air bursting from the Ghost's lungs when they hit.

Jarrod pushed himself up from the jumble of their entwined limbs, grabbed hold of the Ghost's upper arm, and roughly turned the man toward him. As he did so, the Ghost's hat slipped free.

Moonlight poured past Jarrod's shoulder to illuminate eyes the color of fine coffee, a delicate nose, and carved cheekbones flushed with exertion. Rich brown hair spilled everywhere, clinging to her temple, cascading onto the ground, curling around his hand that still rested on her arm.

She was gasping for breath as he was, the air between

them misting with labored exhales. Had he . . . God, had he hurt her? He—he'd tackled her. He'd not known it was her. He'd thought . . .

Dazed and uncomprehending, he stared into her eyes. Their piercingly beautiful depths held alarm, fear, and . . .

Apology.

She . . . *Oh my God.* Realization rushed through him with a howl. A howl that was denial. A denial of a betrayal so scorching it paralyzed him with pain. All this time she'd been laughing at him, outsmarting him, holding the keys to Holden's jail cell in her deceitful little hands. She was Twilight's Ghost.

Sophia recognized the exact moment that Jarrod comprehended her identity. His face went slack with shock, and everything behind his eyes seemed to die an instant, icy death. She wanted to sob, to beat on his chest and demand to know why he'd insisted on this. Why he couldn't let her have her secrets?

She'd never wanted to endure this again, this kind of blistering vulnerability. And yet here she was, a victim to it because she'd truly thought she could make it to freedom tonight like she had those other times. Now everything would be lost. She saw it all flash before her—Blackhaw, her career, Maggie, her very life. Emotion swelled high, hammering her temples, pressing at the backs of her eyes. He'd take them all from her because his loyalty and his love belonged to his brothers. She'd never been the one he cared about.

Jarrod jerked away as if he couldn't bear to touch her. When he gained his feet, he staggered back a few steps.

She watched him, eyes watering. *Oh God, Oh God.*

He simply stared at her, his features as sinfully dark,

unforgiving, and brutally handsome as Satan's. His shirt hung open at the neck, revealing a swath of chest muscles that leapt and quivered with the billow of his lungs.

With effort, she pushed herself to sitting. Whatever happened—she struggled for breath—she'd not cower on the ground before him. She'd not let him have that. She was as wounded as a soldier shot through a hundred times, but if he was going to destroy her, then he'd have to face her first—head-on—so he could see her for everything she was and wasn't.

She knelt on one knee, saw that blood was seeping through the fabric there, then rose to her feet. Nowhere to run. Nowhere to hide. Her nails bit into flesh as she fisted her hands.

"You," he accused, his voice rasping.

"Yes."

"You're Twilight's Ghost."

He already knew the answer, but the rigidity of his expression ordered her to speak the truth aloud. "Yes."

The word hovered, refusing to be swallowed into silence.

"How the hell did you get out of my house?"

"I . . ." Her brain spun.

"Maggie." He answered his own question. "She brought you what you needed." He motioned contemptuously to her clothing. "All of this."

She groped for answers but was damned every way she turned—

"How many times have you escaped?" he demanded.

She hesitated to say.

"How many times?" he yelled.

"Five."

"How'd you do it?"

"The . . ." Her heart was clambering its way out of her chest. To reveal information went against everything she'd ever known. "The pecan tree that brushes the second-story balcony."

"Why? What's important enough to sneak away for?"

She rolled her tongue into her cheek.

"No, tell me. I want to know what actually matters to you."

She simply couldn't tell him about Blackhaw and her staggering debts. If she had to bear one more humiliation in front of him just now, he'd break her. "I needed to work on a case."

"What case?"

"A . . . a counterfeiting case."

"I don't believe you. This has to do with my brother."

"No—"

"Yesterday you let me tell you that story about Holden." He spoke in a tone void of feeling. "When I asked you to help me free him you looked me right in the eye and denied me. You told me you couldn't."

"And then I admitted I wouldn't."

The look in his eyes stole the air from her lungs. Where before they'd been dead and icy, now they blazed with fury. She'd always sensed a capacity for ruthlessness in him, but she'd never fully seen it until now, the face of his true anger.

"You'll help Holden now," he said.

"No, I won't. Your brother is guilty of his crimes, Jarrod."

"You're mistaken."

"I don't think so." At least she prayed she wasn't mistaken. If Holden was innocent, she'd brought all this down upon him and upon herself for nothing. She . . .

she wasn't as sure about it as she had once been—desperately, she scrambled for her courage, gathering what remained of it in shaking hands—but she was sure enough. "The evidence on the subject was clear. A jury agreed with me."

"You were both mistaken," he repeated, his voice lashing her like a whip.

"You couldn't have watched your brother every minute when you were growing up—"

"I didn't need to. I know him."

"How completely can one person ever truly know another?"

"Far better than I ever knew you, apparently." His stare raked derisively over her.

Inwardly, she fought a guilt she didn't deserve to feel.

He stalked to a nearby tree and reached for its branch. His hand tightened, loosened, tightened, loosened around its crumbling bark. "What were the charges you brought against Holden really about, Sophia?"

"About?"

His expression held relentless insight. "Tell me you realize that Holden is worth a hundred of my father. Tell me you didn't punish Holden because of some supposed wrong my father did you twenty years ago."

She wanted to deny it . . . and yet over the past days her own motives for prosecuting Holden had muddied in her mind. When the Stone brothers had been one-dimensional characters in her research, she'd hated every one of them. That was before Jarrod had smiled at her, before he'd let her ride a fairy horse, before he'd touched her in ways that made her writhe. And that was before she'd known that Holden had once gone barefoot so an old man could walk to the bedside of his dying wife.

"Tell me you didn't punish my brother for the sins of the father," Jarrod said.

Shame stung her.

"Tell me you didn't."

She groped for the right words to make him understand. "A few months ago Oliver and Holden exchanged words at Austin's train station. Your brother was threatening toward him, and Oliver feared that Holden might also attempt to threaten me."

"What reason would he have to threaten you?"

"I don't know, revenge? It's no secret that Oliver and I have been searching for your father all these years, that we believe him to be a criminal. The guilt we've attributed to your father has tainted all of you by association."

He pushed away from the tree, leaving the branch vibrating angrily.

"All I knew was that Holden might try to harass me. For protection I educated myself on your brother's past. During my research, I uncovered the fact that Holden was still wanted for aiding and abetting the Lucas gang."

"That charge was fourteen years old. Why go after him for it now?"

"For justice's sake. That's what I do. I put away criminals for the sake of justice."

He snorted contemptuously. "What, were you hoping my father would come riding to my brother's rescue?"

She badly wanted to answer no, except that wasn't the whole truth. "Perhaps, in part."

"You were using my brother as bait."

"Isn't that what you've been using me for?"

His brows slashed downward over narrowed eyes. "I'll be using you for another purpose from now on. I'm taking you back to the house."

She watched him, waiting. If she could only articulate it better, perhaps she could make him understand her motives. . . . His expression was endlessly cold. He'd not be understanding anything she had to say tonight.

Corralling every bit of pride she possessed, she picked up her hat from the dirt and walked in the direction of the house.

I'll be using you for another purpose from now on. What would he do with her? How far would he go to avenge Holden and his own injured trust? Far, came the miserable answer. Men like Jarrod never compromised. They used whatever means necessary to get what they wanted, no matter who they crushed or what the cost. She'd understood that all along, and yet her heart had still insisted on coming to care for him. She was about to be shown just how little he cared for her in return.

The weight of her knife pressed into her hip, where she'd secured it beneath the waist of her trousers. She could . . . Could what? Circle on Jarrod and fight for her freedom? Injure him? If she whisked her knife from its sheath, she had to be willing to cut him with it. Her stomach lurched at the thought.

She tripped over a root, and Jarrod caught her from behind. The heat of his hand and fingers seared through her shirt. He let go and she continued walking, trying not to look at him or think of him and berating herself with every step. Common sense dictated that she use her only remaining weapon against him. So what was stopping her? If he were in her position, he'd certainly not hesitate to attack her with his knife. Their intimacies, and all the little things he'd done for her and said to her surely meant nothing to him.

But to her . . . To her they somehow did. She couldn't

bear to make him bleed, any more than she could bear to slice at an injured animal caught in a rusty trap. A trap she was partially responsible for setting.

As they neared the rear entrance to the house, he took hold of her elbow. She could only pray he didn't intend to march her up to Collier, announce her identity, and instruct the man to spread word of it throughout the state.

Inside, the house slumbered. Lamplight seeped through the open door of Jarrod's office as they passed it, but only guttering candles lit the remainder of the way to her bedroom.

Jarrod tested her door, found it locked the way she'd left it, and dug the key from his pocket. Once he'd freed the bolt, he walked her inside and kicked the door closed.

She tried to pull free of his grip. In answer, he tightened his hold on her and twisted her toward him. Unceremoniously, he began running his hands over her.

She stiffened and again tried to retreat. "What are you—"

He caught her by a handful of her shirt fabric and brought her close. "I'm searching for whatever it is that enables you to leave me."

Alarm leapt inside her. She feared her helplessness without her knife and lockpicking equipment, and she feared her body's reaction to his seeking hands. "No," she said, shoving his chest away.

He brought her immediately back. "Yes."

She struggled against him when he reached into one trouser pocket, then the other. Through the fabric of her inner pocket, she could feel every movement of his fingers against her hip. He easily located the tools she'd used to pick the lock.

"Fine," she said, yet again trying to fight free of him. "You have what you want, so let me go."

"I'm not done."

"Yes, you are."

"No." His eyes burned like emeralds held to the fire. "I'm not."

They locked gazes and wills for a long moment. Then, holding her fast with one hand, he used his other to search the rest of her. His palm pressed up and down the insides and outsides of both legs.

Mercy, this was exactly what she hadn't wanted. To be so near to him, to be forced to bear his touch and feel this treacherous wanting for him. It wound upward within her, sinuous.

His palm moved to her abdomen and found the bulge of the knife.

Her eyes sank briefly closed.

He pulled her shirt from her trousers.

She clamped her shirt back into place. That knife was her sole defense. "I need the knife."

"Why?"

"For protection."

"There's no one here to protect yourself from but me, and I'd rather not feel the point of your blade against my throat." He yanked the shirttail from beneath her hold, exposing a line of bare skin above her trousers. Her belly quivered as he brushed his knuckles against the skin there in order to unfasten the sheath.

"I could have used it against you earlier and didn't," she said.

"Maybe you should have." He pulled it free. Then stroked his hand up her ribs and along an arm.

"There isn't anything else."

"You'll understand if I'm disinclined to trust you." He released her only when he'd finished his examination.

She jerked away, flushed.

He stalked toward the door.

"Jarrod."

He paused, hand on the knob.

"What are you going to do with me?" It cost her dearly to ask the question. Yet if she didn't, she'd torture herself with wonderings. Armed with the truth, she'd at least be able to strategize her response to it.

"It's not so much what I'm going to do," he said as he faced her. "It's you. You're going to free my brother."

"I have the capacity to bring charges against people, but once sentencing has occurred I can't just—"

"You'll do everything in your power to free my brother."

"And if I refuse?"

"I'll expose your identity." No wavering showed on his face, no weakness, no indecision. Only determination, merciless and brutal.

Her heart contracted. "Despite what you think of me, I've done a great deal of good over the years." She fought to keep her voice even. Her emotion could no longer move him, but she prayed her logic might. "I have the capacity to put away criminals who don't deserve to be free—men who've hurt and stolen and cheated law-abiding people. If you expose me, you'll take that capacity away from me."

"You mistake me if you think I care."

Ice flowed through her veins.

"You refuse to help my brother and not only will I expose you, I'll do everything in my power to take your house from you."

"Blackhaw?" she breathed.

"Blackhaw," he confirmed.

Dazed and stunned, she watched him yank open the door. Watched it slam behind him. Heard the savage twist of the key. *Blackhaw.* Just when she thought things couldn't get any worse, they had. Her feet fumbled backward until her spine came up against the wall. Not only did he not care for her, he hated her so much that he'd rip her home from her.

She'd known he'd never forgive her if he found her out. She'd known and she'd been right.

Oh my God, what have I done?

She buried her head in her hands and began to sob.

Chapter 13

J arrod was seething.

He wrenched open the wooden doors of the library cabinet. Inside, Collier had neatly stacked every gift Jarrod had ordered for Sophia but had not yet given her. Boxes of all shapes, sizes and colors rested within—a virtual treasure trove.

He wrenched off the first lid and uncovered a porcelain figure of a woman, fashioned by an artist in New York. He hoisted it in his palm, felt its weight, then hurled it across the room. It shattered against a bookcase, its pieces raining to the floor in a brittle chorus.

It brought him little satisfaction. He wanted to scream, to ruin things with his bare hands, to watch blood flow from his skin. Something. Some outlet.

One by one, he ripped lids off the boxes and discarded

items onto the floor, looking for something else he could throw. Nothing else was fragile enough. Just like the woman herself. She wasn't damned fragile enough for him to break. Worse, he didn't want her to be. He admired her strength. God, he loathed the predicament he found himself in, hated this situation that would force him either to break her spirit or let his brother sit in jail.

He kicked a topaz necklace out of his way, unable to stand the sight of it. Come morning, he'd order all of this taken away. It only served to remind him of his own gullibility.

He walked to the rolling cart in the corner and pulled a stopper from the bottle of brandy that rested there. Almost as quickly, he replaced the stopper. He didn't want it. Beyond breaking the crystal decanters and glasses, the contents of the cart held no appeal for him. He'd never been a man to crave oblivion. No, he'd always preferred tormenting himself with his mistakes, every faculty intact. Escape was for weaklings. Staring square in the eyes of the facts was far more difficult. It was also what made a man stronger and smarter the next time.

He paced around the room once, then again. Restlessness ate at him. The already-confining walls of the library seemed to close in even farther, sucking away his air. Each time he passed the banked fire, crimson light washed over his boots.

Finally, he lowered onto one of the chairs. His elbows dug into his knees as he buried his hands in his hair and clasped his head. He'd known from the first, God damn him, that Sophia had lied to him about Twilight's Ghost and that he couldn't trust her. Yet he'd let himself do so, never once imagining the truth. Why? Why hadn't he guessed at it?

The business world he moved in was the dominion of men. A woman secret agent? He'd have sooner guessed that dogs could fly. And have sooner guessed it of any other woman than the reserved Sophia LaRue. Which is why, no doubt, she'd gone as long as she had without anyone suspecting her.

What an idiot he was. He screwed closed his eyes.

His stupidity was bad. But what he must now do was worse. He'd told her he'd expose her and that he'd take her house from her. Either option or both would be simplicity itself to execute. They'd require no more from him than a matter of words.

Except . . . The memory of a small girl in a white dress burned the backs of his eyelids. She held out her fruit to him, using her skirt as a basket. The same girl had been deposited at an orphanage just weeks later, with nothing to her name but a suitcase. And years later the same girl had looked through his telescope and smiled with long-lost awe.

Even so, the man he'd been before he'd brought her into his home wouldn't have hesitated to enforce her co-operation in any way necessary. The mere thought of it now, though, made him physically sick. He hated his weakness more than he'd ever hated anything about himself.

He rubbed his hands down his face, then let them drop between his knees. Dully, he gazed at the carpet. He was no stranger to disliking parts of himself. Since the age of fourteen he'd been forced to do things that repulsed him. He'd done them anyway because he'd been willing to exchange a conscience for what had mattered more—first money, then power.

Was he willing to destroy a wounded woman who'd

just begun to put her faith in him? Not for money or power this time—he wouldn't have hurt her for either of those. But for something that mattered far more to him. Was he willing to destroy her for his brother's sake?

At noon the next day, Sophia stared out her window through eyes that felt as if they'd been glazed with sand. An ache beat behind her forehead, a souvenir of the fitful night she'd passed. She'd tossed and turned, her sleep riddled with terrible dreams and more terrible realities.

Just as she'd suspected would happen, Maggie walked down the front steps and back into her line of view, accompanied by a guard. Jarrod had not let Maggie see her. Of course he hadn't after what had transpired last night. She'd anticipated that he wouldn't—no, expected it. So how come watching her friend leave filled her with a crushing sense of loss?

Maggie climbed into her buggy and set the horses into motion. Before she turned them down the drive, she looked directly to where Sophia stood. Very deliberately, Sophia pressed her palm to the windowpane, signaling to her friend that Jarrod had discovered her identity.

Maggie gave a grim nod and steered the buggy toward Blackhaw.

"Oh, Maggie," she murmured, so softly the sound barely reached her own ears. She needed her friend's humor and hope today. The vicious circle of her own thoughts was already driving her mad, and, clearly, that's just what Jarrod had intended. She'd dressed carefully for breakfast this morning, only to have the meal brought to her in her room by stony-faced servants. It seemed her host no longer had any wish to share his meals with her. He'd sentenced her to isolation inside the walls of her silken chamber.

She watched steam misting the cold glass around the outline of her fingers. She could trust Maggie to do what they'd agreed upon, to refrain from reporting the news to Simon, and to return in a few days to try again.

A knock sounded.

She quickly crossed the carpeted space. "Come in."

The lock turned and the door opened to reveal the same two servants who had brought her breakfast. They now carried a tray of what she could only assume was lunch.

Her spirits dipped even lower.

The male servant set the tray of food on the table in front of her pink sofa, while the maid bustled up the remains of Sophia's breakfast tray. Out in the hall, Sophia caught sight of a burly guard. He stood directly opposite her doorway, exactly as he had when they'd brought the food that morning. Evidently Jarrod was taking no chances of another escape.

The maid hurried off, but the man paused near her door, his hands clasped behind his back. "Mr. Stone would like to know whether you've decided yet to assist him, ma'am."

"I . . . I need more time."

He inclined his head and made to back out.

"I would like very much," she met his gaze unwaveringly, "to speak to Mr. Stone in person." Instinctively, she sensed that imploring Jarrod face-to-face was still her best hope of softening him.

"I'm sorry." The man flushed. "Mr. Stone is unable to see you today. His schedule is very busy."

"I see." She swallowed against the burn of his rejection. "If you would be so kind as to communicate my wish of an audience to Mr. Stone, I would appreciate it."

"Certainly, ma'am."

She glimpsed the implacable face of the hallway guard in the instant before the door closed, cutting off her view. She sighed and made her way over to her meal tray. Beneath the dome she found fried chicken, turnips, pickles, and relish. The same beautiful food as always. At least it didn't appear that Jarrod planned to keep her alive on gruel and water.

Listlessly, she replaced the dome. Her appetite had been whittled away.

She pressed her fingertips to the bones surrounding her gritty eyes and started pacing the length of her cell. Should she do as Jarrod demanded and level whatever authority she possessed to the cause of freeing his brother?

She could go to Simon and explain things. Owing to her compromised identity, she'd no idea how he might react. He might simply cut her loose, or he might be willing to contact the governor regarding Holden Stone. It was possible that the Secret Service could exchange favors with the state in order to secure Holden's release. Such deals had been struck before.

Her skirts swished about her ankles when she turned. Could she live with herself if she set a guilty man free for her own selfish reasons? Her heart quailed.

Was her career worth having Holden Stone on her conscience for the rest of her life? Was the potential good she could do in the years to come as a Secret Service agent worth sacrificing her principles now?

She didn't know. Wasn't yet sure.

If she could only see Jarrod. If he'd only allow her another opportunity to explain. . . .

Collier's forehead wrinkled. "Our man in Washington has concluded that Mr. LaRue, Mrs. LaRue's supposed husband, never existed."

"What?" Jarrod searched his secretary's expression with hawklike concentration. The long, lean planes of Collier's face were as impassive as always.

"The detective insists that Sophia Warren did not marry an Arthur LaRue in Washington."

"How did he come to that conclusion?"

"He studied the census information of 1870 and interviewed every LaRue he could in the entire city. Those findings, coupled with his lack of success in locating either birth, marriage, or death records of any kind, led him to believe that Mr. LaRue was invented."

Invented. Of course. Widows enjoyed far more freedom than unmarried women did. With a dead husband, Sophia would be allowed to attend—alone—events and parties she wouldn't be invited to otherwise. She'd have the independence to move throughout the city and beyond unchaperoned and unsuspected.

All last night and all day today he'd thought of nothing, nothing, but Sophia and her true identity. Now the remaining details fell into place.

"As to—"

"If you'll give me just one more moment," Jarrod interrupted. He still wasn't grasping the full import of this. Sophia was, with extreme likelihood, a virgin. The memory of her kisses seared him. The tentativeness of her pink little tongue the first time. The way she'd quivered when he'd captured her in the hallway outside her room. The way she'd melted into him when he'd taken her breast into his mouth.

Oh my God, untouched. She's innocent—not innocent, he reminded himself grimly. *Anything but innocent.* But she *was* physically chaste, and that knowledge only served to feed the driving, unholy need he harbored for her. It made him hard, just thinking about being the only one to claim her. Those delectable legs around his naked hips, arms around his neck as he sank into the heat of her.

He slowly shook his head before returning his attention to Collier. The man stood patiently, waiting. "Go on."

"As to the search for the agent masquerading as Twilight's Ghost—"

"Cancel it."

Collier lowered his ever-present papers a fraction. It was as close as he'd ever come to questioning whether he'd heard Jarrod correctly.

"Order every man we have working on the search to stop immediately," Jarrod confirmed.

"Yes, sir." He jotted down the instructions.

The last thing Jarrod wanted was one of his detectives stumbling onto Sophia's secret.

"What of the men we have investigating the whereabouts of Adam Stone?" Collier asked.

Jarrod pushed from the chair, startling poor Maxine, who'd been snoozing with her head on his foot. He reached into a drawer and tossed her a treat, which she caught in midair.

Thrusting his hands into his pockets, Jarrod walked to the window. He sure as hell didn't owe Sophia any favors. No reason to waste his money on her ridiculous quest for his father. He ought to let her and Oliver scratch for clues the rest of their lives. He *should*, and yet . . . Damn her to hell. More than anything, he wished he could hate her as he wanted to so that he could do what needed doing for Holden. Up until now he hadn't been able to stomach it, so he'd caged her until he could.

"Have them continue the hunt for my father," Jarrod answered. He told himself the decision was justified. Once she'd granted her assistance to freeing Holden it would only be reasonable to offer her some reward.

Liar. He'd always been scrupulously honest with himself, and that's not why he'd done what he'd just done.

He shoved away the stink of his motivation, flat refusing to face it.

Collier continued on, updating him on happenings within his company. His secretary's words fell around him, meaningless.

All he could think of, over and over again, was that Sophia was a virgin.

Three days! Three days she'd been trapped inside these walls. Restlessness had frazzled Sophia's nerves until she could no longer even bear to sit. She knew the grain of every surface in this godforsaken room. Every page of every book had been flipped through, each item of clothing examined in detail, every brushstroke of every painting pondered until her head swam.

She stood in front of the door, staring at the jamb, an all-out hysterical fit of impatience threatening perilously close. Minutes ago, the same employee of Jarrod's had brought in yet another tray of food, arranged precisely as all the other trays had been arranged. Whereas before, she'd only ever made polite inquiries to him about securing a visit with Jarrod, this time she'd informed him that she must have air and exercise lest she lose her mind.

He'd promised to ask Jarrod right away and left in a hurry. It had been approximately three minutes, she'd counted every second, and he'd yet to return.

Hands planted on hips, she drummed her fingers.

If Jarrod wouldn't let her out of this room, she'd have to . . . she'd have to start beating her fists against the door, or break the windows by hurling items of furniture at them. This punishment had gone on long enough.

She picked up the sound of the servant's footsteps returning well before he knocked.

"Come in."

The key turned and he opened the door partway.

"Did you speak with him?" she asked.

"Yes, ma'am. He said that you may take a walk out of doors in the company of"—he licked his lips, obviously harried by the entire situation—"Jonathan." He gestured to the guard towering behind him.

"That will be fine."

"It's a bit chilly. Would you like to get your coat?"

She snatched up the hat, coat, and gloves she'd already piled on the circular table next to the door. "Ready."

He waved her forward, and she set off without a glance at her hulking chaperone. She could hear him though. His heavy, plodding footfalls reminded her that she was a prisoner *thump thump* prisoner. She, who had always been free to roam dark streets. She, who had *always* before been the one to send others to prison.

The corridors passed in a blur.

She reached the main hallway and turned toward the back exit of the house. She was sailing past Jarrod's office when she glanced over. Instantly, her gait slashed to a halt.

Jarrod's gaze collided with hers, trapping her where she stood as surely and powerfully as any force on earth. Stronger.

Her heart bolted straight into her throat. He was standing, leaning over his desk, one hand planted on the papers spread there, Collier at his shoulder. She recognized well the black of his suit, the cut of his short hair, the olive green of his eyes. She'd somehow forgotten, though, just how straight and mean Jarrod's brows could be, how severe his jaw.

All air and noise seemed to suck from the house. He didn't move in the slightest way, just stared at her.

Wordlessly, Collier eased past her into the hall and melted out of sight.

Jarrod's gaze flicked to her bodyguard. "Wait down the hall."

"Yes, sir."

Sophia stepped into his office. If she could order the scattered nonsense of her thoughts, she could try to talk sense into him. This was the chance she'd been waiting for.

He straightened, crossing his arms over his chest. "Close the door."

She pulled it shut behind her, but moved no farther. Her hand remained wrapped around the knob, clenching it. What was wrong with her? She'd been rehearsing this meeting for days. Now that she'd gotten it, she felt stricken by the mere sight of him.

She cleared her throat, drew herself up to her tallest height. "I'd like to take this opportunity to explain to you . . . Well, to explain to you about my work and why keeping my identity secret is so crucial to my safety. I didn't do a very good job of it the other night, and I thought perhaps if I told you—"

"You've explained enough."

"If you'd just allow me to tell you—"

"We've been over all of this. Let yourself out."

Like a match rasping into flame, her anger rushed to life, heating her cheeks. Would it cost him so much to give her two minutes of his time? She let go of the knob and gripped her coat with both hands. *By God, he'll listen to me.* "What you don't seem to comprehend is that I am an officer of the law. A federal official."

His stare would have sent woodland animals racing into their burrows.

"You're committing a crime by holding me here, and I *insist* you let me leave at once."

"You're not in a position to insist on anything."

"Yes, I am. I have the entire Secret Service behind me. They *will* come for me."

"Really? Do they expend so much effort for agents whose covers have been ruined?"

Her pride warred with her own grave doubts on the subject. "What you're doing, tormenting me for your brother's crimes, makes no sense. I did not fabricate the aiding and abetting charge against Holden, I did not write the warrant for his arrest."

"No, but you enforced it."

Her nostrils flared as she dragged in a furious breath. "I am *not* the one in the wrong. Holden did wrong for committing the crime. You are doing wrong by imprisoning me here. But I only acted as the law and my principles dictated—"

He crossed the distance between them, reaching around her for the door. Instead of yanking it open, however, he paused.

The air froze in her lungs.

His attention dropped to her lips and caught there. She thought she saw longing flicker in his expression, then realized in the next moment she'd been wrong. He jerked open the door, his expression endlessly cold.

"The law and your principles sent an innocent man to jail," he said, his tone low. "So you'll pardon me if I've no sympathy for your plight."

"Jarrod—"

"Speak to me again only when you're willing to help."

She turned to leave. He caught her upper arm. "And make it soon. I'm getting damn tired of waiting."

She stared at him, ire blazing so hot inside her she could hardly think. "Not nearly as tired as I am of you," she hissed, and wrenched free her arm. Pulse hammering in her ears and emotions in turmoil, she picked up her skirts and stalked toward the door. Distantly, she heard Jarrod order the guard to follow her.

Outside, frosty wind poured over her. Steel-tipped clouds scudded across a threatening sky, and in the distance thunder boomed. The weather suited her temper as nothing had in all her days of confinement. She lifted her face to it, relishing its austere and dangerous beauty, walking as fast as her legs would carry her. She was too angry to bother donning her coat, hat, or gloves, even when the first brace of rain pelted her face. She simply pressed forward, letting the air sail into all the dark, hot, fearful places inside. Faster and faster she went, until locks of hair whipped around her face. Until rain fell all around her. Faster, unaware of anything save the elements and her own movement.

She'd almost delved beneath the shelter of the trees when the sound of rustling, then running, penetrated her isolated thoughts. Her attention jerked to her surroundings in time to see a group of masked men descend upon her in a blur. One yanked her arms behind her back, spilling her belongings onto the ground. Another confronted her head-on, pressing his black-gloved hand against her lips to smother her screams before they could begin. Terror arced high inside her, immobilizing her muscles, her brain.

They twisted her toward their cohorts, who were fighting with Jonathan, the guard Jarrod had assigned her. Already, they'd stripped his gun from him, and though he battled them, he was outnumbered two to one and they succeeded in wrestling him to the ground. Sophia tried to look away, but the man holding her mouth and chin jerked her face back and refused to let her turn her head.

Through the intensifying rain she watched as one attacker partially straddled Jonathon, then drove punches into his face. The sound of knuckles crashing into cartilage caused her stomach to contort. They'd kill him. "Stop," she croaked against the wet cloth of her captor's gloved hand. "Please, stop."

Heedless of her pleas, they beat him again and again, until they finally knocked him unconscious. That done, they abandoned his prostrate body and closed in on her. They wore the clothes of workingmen as well as bandannas to hide their faces. Different sizes, builds. Shifty eyes, alight with feral intent. Edgy to hurt her, willing and able to.

Her chest wheezed as she fought for breath.

The one who'd clamped his hand over her lips, removed it long enough to pull his arm back and slap her across the face. The crack of sound fired through her brain an instant before the biting pain. Her head snapped to the side. She blinked at the view of the trees, her vision fuzzed with the brutality of his strike and her own panic.

"You listening now?" he asked. His voice was blunt, without feeling or remorse.

She brought her gaze back to him and nodded.

"What?" he asked.

"Yes," she rasped, tasting blood. Rain ran into her eyes, down her chin.

"The one who sent us doesn't want Jarrod Stone snooping into the theft of your grandmother's money or the whereabouts of Adam Stone."

She struggled to swallow. Fought harder to understand. Jarrod had never investigated the theft of her grandmother's money or tried to locate his father. He'd offered that to her, but only in exchange—

"Convince him to cease his search."

Must be some mistake. Frenzied, she looked from one face to the next. She'd been the only one to investigate Adam Stone and Blackhaw's stolen fortune. Who—who could have sent them? What would they do to her?

The man behind her wrenched her arms in their sockets, and she cried out involuntarily.

"Convince him to cease his search," her captor repeated, "or far worse than this will happen to you and to him."

He brought back his hand again. This time she had a second to brace herself.

The force of his slap blinded her. She was released from behind and felt herself spinning and falling, hitting the earth with jarring force. Then an inner blackness descended with dizzying speed, and consciousness cut away.

Chapter 14

Jarrod saw Sophia fall. "No!" he screamed with raw fury as he ran toward the scene he'd first glimpsed out his office window. They'd *struck* her, and he'd been too far away to stop them.

Her attackers stood looking down at her where she'd fallen. When he was yards away, one of the them glanced up and spotted him coming. Jarrod lunged at the man, swinging with his right. The man darted backward, the blow glancing off his jaw. Jarrod sent his left fist barreling forward and this time connected soundly with the man's cheek. His enemy grunted and sprawled into the dirt.

Rabid, Jarrod turned to the others, who came at him as a pack. He fought them wildly, lashing out with bruising force, fueled by a protective rage that hazed his vision red. He threw off one who tried to subdue him from behind, rounding on the man with a snarl only partially human. He drove his punches into him, unsatisfied until the man fell to his knees.

The remaining men backed away. He charged toward them. They retreated. He went after them and they scattered, disappearing into the trees.

Jarrod turned to Sophia, dreading what he would see. She lay in the dirt, her clothing and hair drenched, one side of her face flush against trampled grass. Blood leaked from her lip and melded with the water running in rivulets over her ashen features.

His heart stopped in his chest. He went to one knee beside her. His outstretched hand hovered over her. "Christ." He didn't know where to touch, where he wouldn't hurt her more. He reached toward her shoulders, paused. Withdrew his hand. Both his arms were shaking with a tremor that delved into his chest, straight to his core. Look at her. Look at what he'd let happen to her.

His own guards ran up to him, guns drawn. He'd been unaware of their approach. Barely even remembered yelling for them to be sent as he'd left the house. He glanced around. All of her attackers had fled.

"You there, tend to him." He jutted his chin toward Jonathan, who lay on the ground. "The rest of you go after the others."

They did so at once, spreading out to follow sodden footprints.

Heart breaking, he carefully scooped a hand under Sophia's upper back, another under her knees, and lifted her against his chest. She was surprisingly light, unbearably delicate. And cold. Far too cold. His gaze never leaving her face, he set off for the house.

"Sophia," he said.

Nothing.

"Sophia," he said again, louder.

Her only movement was the slight rising of her chest. His gut twisted with fear.

All his life he'd been the protector of his family. It was what he was, who he was. His clearest identity, and the only one he was proud of. He abhorred that she'd been injured, and even worse, injured on his property under his care. This was all wrong, heinously wrong. The limp weight of her, the angry red mark scarring her beautiful cheek—evidence that he'd failed to guard her as he should have. He wanted to throw his head back and to scream.

If he couldn't make her better . . .

He looked up at the approaching house, desperate for help. Collier ran toward him, hunched against the rain. "Get the housekeeper," Jarrod yelled, fighting to be heard above the rolls of thunder and wind. "I need warm blankets, medicine, bandages. Then go to the stables and send the hands back for one of the guards. He's down."

Collier nodded and loped for the house.

A maid was standing at the back door, holding it open for him when he arrived. Water splashed from Sophia's gown, a steady stream against hardwood as he carried her to her bedroom.

Yet another maid waited there, door open. He passed her without acknowledgment. Sophia's head lolled to the side as he laid her gently on the bed's white coverlet.

He towered over her, afraid to touch her with his

clumsy hands. He watched her chest, willing it to continue lifting with her breath. Between each shallow breath he died a hundred times.

His housekeeper strode into the room accompanied by the smell of baking bread. A wiry woman with a plain horse face and efficient hands, Mrs. Hoskins took in the scene with a glance, then set aside her stack of blankets, medicines, and bandages. "What happened?" she asked, coming to stand beside Sophia across the bed from him.

"She was slapped across the face."

"How many times?"

His mind reeled at the possibility that there might have been more than one. "I only saw the once."

"Any bones broken?"

"I don't think so."

She leaned over Sophia and began running her hands along her limbs. When she pressed work-roughened fingertips to Sophia's bruised cheekbone, Jarrod squeezed closed his eyes for a moment, then looked away.

"Mary," Mrs. Hoskins called.

The girl posted at the door rushed inside. "Ma'am?"

"Fetch my smelling salts."

"Yes, ma'am." She raced away in a hail of footsteps.

"Mrs. LaRue?" his housekeeper said in an authoritative tone. She waited a few beats, then gently shook Sophia's shoulder.

Sophia didn't respond.

"The first order of business is to get her out of these wet things," Mrs. Hoskins said to him.

He didn't budge.

"If you'll excuse us," she said pointedly.

His eyebrows crushed downward. "I'm not leaving her."

"Mr. Stone, I need to undress her—"

"Do it then," he barked. "I'm not leaving." No way in hell he'd abandon Sophia now.

Thin lips pursed tight, Mrs. Hoskins marched into the dressing room and returned moments later with a white nightgown.

Jarrod paced to the fireplace, then knelt to stack more logs onto the grate. Despite his action, he recorded every sound his housekeeper made, counted every second as it passed. How bloody long does it take to change a gown? He didn't trust his housekeeper's ability to care for her, to keep her from slipping away.

"There we are," the woman finally said.

He crossed immediately back to the bed. Sophia was dressed in the gown, bare feet poking beyond its hem and the contours of her body obvious through the single layer of fabric. Her face and hands had been dried, the blood at her lip dabbed away.

Mrs. Hoskins returned from where she'd set aside Sophia's wet clothing and soiled towels. "If you'll lift her for me, I'll sweep aside the bed linens."

Jarrod watched Sophia's face as he gathered her up. Still nothing. A gleaming lock of rich chocolate hair clung damply to the cords of her throat. Jarrod's heart contracted.

In seconds, Mrs. Hoskins had pulled free the saturated quilt, turned down the sheets beneath, and placed a fresh towel across the pillow. Jarrod lowered Sophia, then leaned over to tuck her feet beneath the tightly made sheets. Her flesh was so cold. He took both feet in his big hands and rubbed his palms back and forth, hoping to warm them.

Mrs. Hoskins bound up Sophia's hair in the towel.

When she'd completed that, they both drew the sheets up over her. Mrs. Hoskins opened a dresser drawer, shook out a blanket, and lofted it over her charge. As the blanket settled, so did the quiet. His housekeeper held herself as still as a pillar, assessing Sophia with her gaze.

"What's wrong with her?" Jarrod asked

"The force of the blow simply rendered her unconscious," she answered without looking at him. "We'll have to wait and see whether she's caught a chill from the inclement weather."

"She's not . . . she's not breathing well."

Mrs. Hoskins glanced up and pondered him for a moment. "Once I revive her with the smelling salts, all should be fine."

He wasn't convinced. He knew how fragile life could be. His mother's had gone as easily as smoke disappearing on air. His mother. God where had that thought come from? As suddenly, he realized it had been there ever since he'd seen Sophia fall. There were similarities between the two women. The pattern of strength overlying gentleness, their sadness, their fundamental goodness.

He remembered at once and with perfect clarity how awful it was to care about someone you couldn't help. Everything he was experiencing now, he'd experienced before. The constriction of worry in his chest, the thoughts that spiraled too fast into nightmares, the powerlessness of being the one sentenced to stand alongside and watch. All of it came back to him, each facet of a helplessness lived twice in a lifetime now. Two times too many.

He backed away a couple of steps. He didn't want to do this again. This was why he hadn't married anyone or borne any children. *This* was why.

A light knock sounded at the door, and Mrs. Hoskins bid the person enter. The maid walked hesitantly inside. "I'm sorry, ma'am. I had a bit of trouble locating them." She handed over the smelling salts, a repentant expression on her face.

"I swear no one could find their own backside in this house without my help," Mrs. Hoskins grumbled as she unscrewed the cap. "You may take that pile to the laundry."

The girl hoisted the stack of discarded linens and clothing, then dawdled, seemingly unsure whether she'd be needed for further chores.

"Leave us," Jarrod said.

She skittered out.

Mrs. Hoskins waved the smelling salts beneath Sophia's nose. Sophia failed to react. Jarrod held his breath. Two more passes beneath her nostrils, and at last Sophia moaned and turned her face to the side.

"Mrs. LaRue?" his housekeeper asked.

Frown lines creased Sophia's brow. Her lips pursed.

"Can you hear me?"

Sophia's eyes fluttered open, and she squinted at the wall, blinked, squinted. *Where was she?* she wondered. Her senses were groggy, her memory muddled. This was her bedroom at Jarrod's, but how had she gotten here? She brought her wrist up from under the covers and saw that she was wearing a linen nightdress. She let her lids fall closed for a moment, to rest. Mother above, but one side of her face hurt and her . . . she tested the inside of her bottom lip with her tongue . . . her lip was swollen and sore.

"Mrs. LaRue?" A woman's voice.

Fighting disorientation, Sophia opened her eyes and

looked toward the voice. Instead of a woman, however, the first person she saw was the most masculine man she'd ever met.

Jarrod stood at the foot of the bed, arms braced at his sides, his height and maleness more glaring than ever in the feminine environment. She'd never seen his features so grave or so colorless. And his eyes were lit with a wildness both stark and urgent. Distantly, she recalled thinking once that she'd give much to see Jarrod Stone upset. This was it, she realized. He was upset about something.

She ran her gaze over him and noticed that not only did his dark hair gleam with moisture, but that his shirt was plastered to his chest. He was soaking wet.

In a rush she remembered her fight with Jarrod followed by the slanting rain, the men in bandannas, the way they'd beaten her guard, the warning they'd given her, and the slaps. "Oh," she breathed, wishing she hadn't recalled it. The smothering fear she'd experienced at their hands *whooshed* around her, squeezing her chest.

"Easy," Jarrod said, seemingly able to read her distress on her face.

"The guard? Is he . . ."

"Fine. He's being tended to."

Her shoulders and neck muscles relaxed against the bed. Thank God for that.

"How do you feel?" Jarrod asked, his tone tight.

"Fine."

"Like hell."

Typical that he'd not accept a perfectly good response. "If you must know, I have a terrible headache."

She brought up a hand and gingerly explored her lip, cheek, and jaw. "This whole side of my face is tender, but that's all."

"Any nausea?" the woman asked.

Sophia looked over to find a practical-looking woman wearing an apron over her gray gown. "No."

"I'm the housekeeper here," she said by way of barest explanation. "Any confusion?"

"A little, right when I awoke. That's cleared away now."

"What about your lip?" Jarrod asked.

"My lip?" There had been times, growing up at the orphanage and during her years as Twilight's Ghost when she'd fallen ill, or injured herself. She'd been the one to worry about herself on those occasions, and even then hadn't wasted much energy upon it. It felt strange and warm for someone to care about something as minor as a headache and a tender lip.

"It bled," Jarrod said.

"I believe it simply split open a bit on the inside," Sophia answered. "It'll heal in no time."

Jarrod's housekeeper began moving about the room, shutting the curtains against the stormy afternoon.

"Can you feel your legs?" Jarrod asked.

"Yes."

"Can you move them?" Through the blanket, he took hold of her toes.

Behind his back, Jarrod's housekeeper rolled her eyes and smiled at Sophia. The woman patted her heart with her hand, then pointed from Jarrod to her.

Sophia shook her head slightly, unable to let the woman believe something so false.

"You can't move them?" Jarrod asked tensely.

"I'm sorry, I didn't mean . . ." She wiggled her toes against his hand. "Yes, I can move them."

He blew out a breath and released her.

"I'll be on my way," his housekeeper announced. She stood with hands stiffly inserted in her apron pockets. "It's my advice, Mrs. LaRue, that you stay in bed for the remainder of the day to rest—"

"Oh, that's probably not necessary. I feel—"

"You'll do it," Jarrod said.

A dimple dug into the housekeeper's cheek, hinting at her private amusement. "I'll order the lights kept low here in your chambers and a bath drawn for you this evening. Both should help to relieve your headache. Should you begin to feel nauseous, dizzy, or confused, inform a member of my staff at once, and I shall summon the doctor."

"Thank you."

"You're welcome." She walked in her sensible way to the door and closed it in a sensible way behind her.

Sophia met Jarrod's gaze. He gave her a long, hard look.

She wasn't sure after the hard words they'd exchanged earlier, how to be around him. On the one hand, she wanted to strangle him for today's argument and for the past days of confinement. On the other, he was the one who'd been standing at her bedside when she awoke, worrying over her split lip and asking if she could feel her legs. "Will you at least sit down?" she asked cautiously. "You're making me uncomfortable, towering over me like that."

Obligingly, he pulled up a chair and sat. As usual, he leaned into the seat back slightly, rested his arms along the armrests, and splayed one knee to the side. "Who were those men that attacked you?" he asked.

"I don't know. None of them were familiar."

"What did they want?"

"They said . . ." Since the first day she'd met Jarrod, she'd been concealing the truth from him. Who would have thought honesty would come so haltingly or feel so strange? "They said they wanted you to stop investigating the theft of my grandmother's money as well as your father's whereabouts."

His fingers tightened convulsively around the ends of the armrests. "What?"

"I know. There must be some mistake—"

"They used you to get me to me?" Violence flared in his eyes.

"It appears that way."

He stormed from the chair. Swearing under his breath, he prowled around her room. Finally, he yanked open the curtains covering the far window. Hands jammed in pockets, he stared stonily out, his frustration all the more powerful for its muteness. The thundering sky and water-drizzled window painted his profile in shifting shadows of gray. The only sounds were the pattering of rain and the crackling of the fire.

Sophia winced against the pain as she eased herself into a more upright sitting position. "Do you have any idea why they'd think that you've been investigating my grandmother's fortune and your father's disappearance?"

"Yes."

She laced her hands together in her lap.

"Because I have been."

Her jaw sagged open slightly. He'd been *what*? But she'd thought . . . he'd only search for his father if she helped him with Holden. He'd said he'd never bothered hunting for his father because his father had never bothered hunting for him. Myriad responses swam through her mind. In the end, all she said was, "You didn't tell me."

"No." He faced her. The gloom of the room darkened one half of his face. "I didn't."

"Why not?" But as soon as she asked the question, she knew the answer. He'd hoped to use the leverage of his offer for Holden's sake. "I suppose"—she licked her lips— "the better question is *why*. Why have you been looking for your father?"

"Is it impossible to believe I did it for you?"

Her world tilted. "I don't know. Is it?" Time stretched, each second heavy with meaning.

He shrugged in an effort to belittle what he'd done. Seemingly preoccupied, he crossed to the bookcase and idly picked up a gilt candlestick.

"Jarrod," she said carefully, "I'd appreciate it if you'd tell me why."

He set down the candlestick. "My family owes you answers about what happened." He eyed the Durand painting, then returned to the window to peer out at the storm. "I have the means to provide those for you, so I hired detectives and took action to do so."

It was the most decent thing anyone had ever done for her. That a *Stone* had done it for her, with or without the promise of her reciprocation, caused a lump of gratitude and confusion to clog her throat. Why couldn't Jarrod allow her to loathe him? Just when she thought she might be able to manage it, she uncovered a part of his personality that drew her like a moth to a flame. That he'd launched a search for his father because he'd felt she deserved answers, was a gift beyond words.

"I'm assuming you halted the search when you learned of my identity," she said softly.

He didn't reply.

Oh, she thought, her heart dropping. Even after he'd found out about her and been so angry, he'd carried on his search. Tears burned the backs of her eyes. This arrogant, difficult, stubborn man had acted out of inexpressible kindness toward her.

She thought of all the years she'd spent hunting for Adam Stone, all the pitiful leads she and Oliver had labored to piece together, the countless letters she'd written and telegrams she'd sent only to find disappointment at the end of every one. Did Jarrod have any idea how crucial this was to her? It was like a wound that she walked around with and worked, and slept, and lived with. But all the time, she was bleedingly aware of its presence. Until someone paid for her grandmother's death, she'd never be whole.

With a knuckle, she swept away the trickle of moisture that had spilled over her lashes. "It's no small thing you're doing for me," she said simply. "I thank you."

"It's only money."

"No. It's far more than money to me. It means a great deal." He could shrug off the clothes, the furs, the jewels he'd offered her. But this was much more meaningful to her than those, and she'd not let him demean it.

After a long silent moment, Jarrod picked up the poker and jabbed the fire with it. The blaze snarled and hissed, black-red wood collapsing in on itself.

"This new information puts a fresh perspective on today's attack," Sophia said. "What do you think?"

Again, he prodded the fire. "I think the man who stole your money realized that I was after him and retaliated against you."

She gave a quick nod. "Your father must have come across evidence of your investigation—"

"What proof do you have that my father stole your money?"

She paused, wondering how even his trademark loyalty could withstand twenty years of abandonment and the obvious facts of the case. "My grandmother gave your father the money for their investment, and he was never seen again. That's my proof."

"Other people had access to the money."

"Not that night. She gave it to him. He left with it."

"According to whom?"

"According to my grandmother."

He set the poker aside.

She didn't want to have to hurt him by convincing him of his father's guilt. "Did the men who attacked me today flee?"

"Yes. I sent my guards after them."

"If your guards were able to catch even one of them, perhaps we can get him to divulge where your father is located."

"And how do you propose we 'get' him to divulge the information we want?" The barest hint of humor played about his serious lips.

"Please. You're the one with all the skill for imprisoning people and bending them to your will."

"Not if you're any indication."

She opened her mouth to retort and realized he had a point.

He scowled at her as he came to stand at her bedside. With him so near she could see the way his wet pants clung to his muscular thighs and smell the sea-and-wind scent of his cologne.

"Are there any other things that you've been investigating that I should know about?" she asked. "The knowledge might serve me well the next time I'm surrounded by big-fisted men wearing bandannas."

"My investigations aren't for you to concern yourself with."

So he'd already retreated behind the wall that separated them. Disappointment swirled within her. "I know there hasn't been much truth between us up until now," she said, choosing her words carefully, searching for new ground on which they could form some sort of truce. "Could there be?

"I don't trust twice."

"And I've never trusted at all. I'm willing to try." She took a breath. "What else have you been investigating?

"Your husband, for one. I know you were never married." The shrewd gleam in his eye told her he also knew what went along with that. Her inexperience.

"Oh."

"Now lie down," he said, placing a hand on her shoulder and guiding her back to a lying position. Before he pulled away, he captured her chin between his thumb and forefinger. "You certain you're all right?"

"Yes."

He nodded and walked toward the door. Halfway there, he looked back at her over his shoulder. "Do you think you'll feel well enough to leave your bed tomorrow?"

"Yes. In fact, I can't bear this room anymore. I'd love to leave it."

"Good, because I'm taking you away from here."

"Where?"

"To visit Holden."

Chapter 15

It had been an incredibly long day. But as Sophia caught her first glimpse of the Texas State Penitentiary at Huntsville, she sincerely wished it had been far longer. A gate of brick sandstone reared upward from acres of desolate, windswept Texas plains. Jealously, the gate shielded the inner structures from view. The only building she could see was the one outsiders must pass through to enter the prison. It, too, had been built of sandstone brick and boasted an enormous wooden door that might as well have been the portal into the land of demons for all Sophia cared to enter it.

The bleak chill of the place leaked like smoke through the cracks and invisible seams of the rocking carriage to infect the air within. She drew her chocolate-colored cape around her and huddled into its rich folds.

As if that was going to help an iciness spreading from the inside out.

They'd begun their journey from Galveston early that morning. By gleaming black carriage they'd made their way to Houston. From there they'd taken the train. And now she found herself shut inside another sumptuously appointed carriage, being transported like a carefully tended pearl in a velvet box to a destination she dreaded.

She glanced away from the menacing view. Jarrod sat across from her, his big shoulders swaying slightly with the coach's movement. His attention was riveted on the prison and the endlessly grim set of his lips told her all she needed to know about the direction of his thoughts.

She hunkered even lower into her cape. She hadn't seen Jarrod yesterday after their talk in her bedroom. He'd sent Collier to inform her that his men had been unable to capture any of her attackers. That had been their only communication until this morning, when they'd gathered on the porch for this trip. The smallness of their traveling party had surprised her. She'd expected Jarrod to travel like some foreign maharaja—servants dancing attendance on his every whim and men staggering under the weight of all his suitcases and trunks. Instead he'd brought with them only two attendants, both women, both for her comfort.

Jarrod had spared the maids this awful errand, leaving them a few miles back at the hotel in town. More's the pity. She'd have happily gone without food for days in exchange for a scrap of light conversation just now.

Instead there was only Jarrod, whose demeanor gave her the sense that she was being taken to the prison not as a visitor, but as one to be admitted and never again set free.

Lips pursed, she looked back to the approaching penitentiary. When she'd asked him why he was bringing her here, he'd said he needed to get her away from his Galveston property for her own safety.

While it was certainly true that Adam Stone had located her there and succeeded in harming her, they both knew Jarrod had brought her to Huntsville for a far less protective reason. In fact, in coming here, he wished to strip her emotionally bare. He wanted her to look into his brother's face, see Holden's hatred of her, and feel the full force of what she'd done.

Today was a reckoning.

She hugged her arms across her chest in an effort to warm herself. Always, she'd taken pains to separate her feelings from her work. She did what she did for justice. There was no room in that for personal knowledge about men better seen strictly as criminals. Without a doubt, she'd never wanted to come to know the brother of one of the men she'd arrested. And she'd never, but *never* wished to face any of those men across the bars of their jail cells. In her line of work such things spelled disaster.

Too quickly their carriage pulled to a stop before the building's main entrance. Jarrod exited without hesitation, held the door open for her, and offered his hand without a word. She allowed him to assist her down.

Outside, the wind snatched at her skirts and whistled around her calves. Yesterday's storms had passed, leaving a blustery day in which periods of sheer sun had occasionally penetrated churning clouds of gray. At the moment, all was entirely gray.

With her gloved hand positioned in the crook of Jarrod's elbow, they made their way up the stone steps. *How many men?* she wondered, stealing a glance upward at the building's front. *How many men have I put behind these walls?*

The door was opened from within by a guard. "Mr. Stone?"

"Yes."

The man stepped aside, allowing them to pass. "The warden told us to expect you, sir."

Jarrod nodded as they walked into the simple entry room. A second guard rose to his feet and greeted them with a nod. Both men were middle-aged, both wore denim trousers and work shirts, and both had been chiseled flint hard by years of doing a tough job in the company of tough criminals.

The one who'd let them in now locked them in. Sophia flinched at the sound of the bolt thudding into place. "Right this way," he said, indicating a door that led to what looked like a small visiting room.

Sophia moved toward it, but Jarrod stopped her short. "I'd rather visit my brother in his cell."

The guard frowned.

"I want to see where he lives," Jarrod said.

The guard gestured to her. "Wouldn't be suitable for the lady."

"It would be more suitable for this lady than you know."

"It's not done that way, sir. We've a visiting room—"

"I realize that. I'm willing to pay for the privilege."

Sophia released his arm as he reached beneath his coat for his wallet. "The warden and I have already come to an arrangement, but I'm certain there's more I could do for this establishment." Smoothly, he stacked one bill after another onto the surface of the desk. "Perhaps a refurbishment of your quarters. Better food for the security staff. Newer firearms." He looked up and met the guard's gaze.

By his harsh expression, Sophia could tell the guard didn't care for being blackmailed. She hoped he'd refuse Jarrod outright. Not only because it irritated her to watch Jarrod buy his way into anything he wished, but because facing Holden in the squalor of his cell struck her as a far worse proposition than facing him inside the visiting room.

The guard's attention flicked to the money, held there a long moment, then returned to Jarrod. "Deke, you already fetched Holden Stone from work detail to his cell?" he asked.

"Yes, sir," his coworker answered. "Hour ago."

"Then you can escort these folks to visit him there."

Sophia's mouth drained of moisture.

The one called Deke led them down the hallway, then out into the walled prison yard. Dead grass crunched under the soles of her shoes as they walked toward the central building. It looked like barracks: long, low, and composed of the same brick as the other permanent structures. In the far corners of the yard wooden buildings were grouped in clusters. They held the prison's industry, judging from the smoke winding from the chimneys and the sounds ringing from within.

When they entered the barracks, dimness engulfed them. Sophia's stomach churned at the smells of unwashed bodies, encrusted dirt, and long-held bitterness. Cell upon cell passed by. They all looked the same to her—three brick sides, the front side constructed of steel bars inlaid with a door. Each contained nothing more than two beds, a writing table, and a porcelain bowl. Obviously, the inmates were at work. Holden had been brought here in preparation for Jarrod's visit, or he'd be with them.

Her anxiety mounted until she could feel her shoulders knotting. The sound of their footsteps rang like death knells in her ears, brutally loud.

Deke finally stopped before a cell and jerked his chin toward the occupant. "Here he is."

Feeling sick inside, she turned to see a man push to his feet. Her breath caught in her throat. He was devilishly tall, his hair overlong and unkempt, and his jaw rough with stubble. He wore the thick shoes of a laborer and the black-and-white stripes of a prisoner. His shirt, carelessly unbuttoned halfway down his chest, clung to contours of muscles gleaming with sweat. His sharp gaze moved over her in a single sweeping assessment. His eyes were bright with intelligence and hooded with secrets held.

Where had the boy who'd given away his shoes disappeared to? There was no evidence of him here. Had she banished the last of that boy? Was the loss of any innocence that had managed to survive within him her responsibility to bear?

When he strode toward them, Sophia had to force herself to hold her ground.

On occasion she'd thought of Jarrod as a wolf. The man before her was a fox—scrappier than his brother but with instincts just as deadly. Where Jarrod was smooth, this man was all hard edges. Except for his lips. He had beautifully sculpted lips, which made her wonder just how many girls across how many counties were mourning him.

Holden reached through the bars and briefly shook hands with Jarrod. The men were close in height and resembled one another in the firm angles of brow and nose. However, Holden's hair was shades lighter than Jarrod's, and his eyes hazel instead of green. No two men could have been more different in dress, or in situation.

"I'd like some privacy," Jarrod said to Deke.

The man nodded grudgingly. "I'll wait at the end of the hall."

Once they were alone, uncomfortable quiet fell between them. "Is there anything you need?" Jarrod asked his brother.

"No."

"Have they been giving you enough to eat?"

"Yeah."

Jarrod eyed his brother's living quarters. On his face, usually a face of impervious power, she now read pain. Whatever his faults, Jarrod Stone loved his brothers. Her emotions twisted in sympathy for how terrible this must be for him, to see his brother like this.

"There are two of you who sleep in here?" Jarrod asked.

Holden nodded. "Me and a horse thief from Kansas."

No more than five feet by nine, Holden's cell was far too small to house a man of Holden's size, let alone two. The bed he'd risen from held a flat pillow, neatly made sheets, and a tan blanket. Paper and a few basic writing instruments were stacked on the desk.

When she looked back to Holden she found him gazing directly down at her. Her heartbeat skittered.

"This is Sophia Warren LaRue," Jarrod said. "She's the granddaughter of Mrs. Warren of Blackhaw. She's also the agent known as Twilight's Ghost, the one responsible for your arrest."

Sophia wound her hands into a ball and tried to arm

herself against the condemnation that was sure to be forthcoming. She didn't know if she could take him yelling and cussing at her at this particular low point in her life when everything was already in tatters.

"No." Holden's brow furrowed. "This can't be Twilight's Ghost."

"I wish I was wrong," Jarrod said tersely. "I'm not."

Holden's lips set into a harsh line.

"I brought her here," Jarrod said, "because I want her to hear from you that you're not guilty of aiding and abetting the Lucas gang."

Holden exchanged a long, searching look with his elder brother. "I can't tell her that," he said slowly.

"Why not?"

"Because I did it."

Jarrod's resulting silence was like a clap of thunder. Sophia watched disbelief, then confusion, shift across his features as he grappled to understand.

She wanted to reach out to him, hold his hand or clasp his arm. Something. She would have, if she hadn't been so certain that he'd reject her comfort. So she simply stood next to him quietly, her emotions wrenching at the look on his face. Oh, this was too horrible. To see all Jarrod's beautiful, noble beliefs about Holden shattered before her eyes. Perhaps better than anyone, she knew how fervently Jarrod had believed in his brother, how hard he'd worked to free him, how deep his love and loyalty ran.

"I thought you knew." Holden shook his head, clearly disgusted with himself and the wastedness of his choices. "I thought, on some level, that you knew I'd done it."

"You never told me you had," Jarrod said, his tone dead to emotion.

"No, and I never told you I hadn't. It's not something I'm proud of."

Tendons worked in Jarrod's jaw.

"You wanted to fight the charges with your high-priced lawyers, and I was willing to let you try."

Sophia sensed in Holden both a wildness that pressed close to the surface and a rage that burrowed bone deep.

"But here I am," Holden continued, lifting work-roughened hands to signal his surroundings. "I did it, and I'm paying for it. So you can stop trying to get me off, you can stop trying to collect evidence, you can stop hounding the agent that put me here. It's over. There's nothing you can do and there's nothing I can do and there's nothing she can do."

The creases around Jarrod's eyes deepened, making him look older. He retreated a few steps, leaned his shoulders against the bars of the opposing cage, and rested his head back.

A place inside Sophia ripped open, and tears stung her eyes. How was it that she could hurt this desperately for him? He'd been right in so many ways to fight for his brother. She'd give half her heart to have him care for her even a quarter as much. And yet, in the most fundamental way, he'd been wrong. To learn that in one moment and be told in the next that there was nothing he could do was the worst possible fate for a man like Jarrod.

"I've a question for you," Holden said.

She met his dangerous gaze and saw that he'd directed the question at her. Cautiously, she nodded.

"Why come after me now?" he asked. "I was a ten-year-old kid when I did that crime. The gang asked me to hold their horses and I did it because we needed the nickel they paid me per day." He made a scoffing sound low in his throat.

He'd held their horses? Sophia hadn't known. The warrant had been for aiding and abetting. She'd thought . . . Well, she thought he'd done more than hold their horses for a nickel a day. The tide of self-loathing that washed through her stole her ability to speak.

Jarrod had been right about her that night that he'd caught her in the woods. Whether or not she'd acknowledged it at the time, she'd punished Holden for the sins of his father. She swallowed thickly. The worst of it was that when she'd had Holden arrested, she'd taken grim *satisfaction* from it. From exacting vengeance on a man who'd once held horses for a nickel a day.

She could see now, the evidence was standing on the other side of the bars, that she'd held far too much hatred in her breast. Now look what her hatred had cost Jarrod and his brothers—something she could never repay.

"So why have me arrested now?" Holden asked. "That was fourteen years ago."

This hallway was her courtroom, and Holden her jury of one. "I . . ." Painfully, she cleared her throat. "Oliver Kinsworthy, my grandmother's attorney, told me that you confronted him at the train station in Austin a few months ago. Afterward he was afraid for me, warned me to alert him if you ever tried to contact me. His fears prompted me to research more of your past than I had before. It was then that I uncovered your outstanding warrant."

Holden said nothing.

She fervently wanted to stop there. There was more,

however, and if she wished to have any kind of respect for herself, she must say it aloud to him. Now. She made herself go on. "For all my grand notions of justice, I'm ashamed to say that the warrant wasn't the only reason I hunted you down. I hated your father for what he did to me, and so I hated you." She looked to Jarrod, then back to Holden. "All of you. I had you arrested, partially because I hoped your arrest might chase your father out of hiding. And partially"—she pulled in an aching breath—"out of revenge."

Holden regarded her through weary eyes decades wiser than his age.

"I stand here today very, *very* sorry," Sophia said.

Quiet descended, circling the three of them, twining them together. In the distance, Sophia could hear the *clang* of industry, the buzzing of a fly, and the guard at the end of the hall idly jangling the coins in his pocket.

"Jarrod," Holden said.

It was as if he was watching and hearing what was going on around him in a haze, Jarrod thought. His brain felt sluggish, uncomprehending. Despite all the money he'd worked so hard to accumulate, he couldn't protect Holden from this, which meant that the world as he'd known it for the past twenty years was gone.

"There is one thing you can do for me, if you're willing," Holden said.

Jarrod pushed away from the bars he'd been leaning against and buried his hands in his pockets. "Of course." His youngest brother had never asked a single thing of him. There was nothing Holden could request of him now that he'd refuse.

"I want you to help her discover the truth about our father and the stolen money."

To hell with our god damned father, he wanted to roar. All of this was ultimately his fault. Had Adam Stone been the father he should have been he'd have kept Holden out of trouble. Despite Jarrod's best efforts at raising his brothers, it appeared he'd failed at that.

"I think we've all lived under his shadow long enough," Holden said. He wrapped a hand around the steel bar before him. "I don't have much in here to call my own. I'd like, at least, my good name."

"A name is what you make it," Jarrod answered automatically.

"It's also what you inherit."

For years, all the brothers had gone to great lengths to act as if they didn't give a damn about their father or his abandonment, or the ugly suspicions that followed them all because of what Adam Stone was rumored to have done. But now, with everything bare between him and Holden, Jarrod could see on his brother's face that their father's guilt or innocence meant something to him. Something important.

"If it's what you want, I'll find him, and I'll find out what happened," Jarrod answered.

"It's what I want."

"Then I give you my word."

This is a very bad idea.

Sophia stood in the hotel hallway outside Jarrod's darkened door. She glanced nervously in both directions. The hour was so late that nothing and no one stirred. So late that she, herself, had been lying in her rented bed underneath crisply laundered sheets until just minutes ago. The bed had become a sort of hell during the hours she'd spent staring at the ceiling, tasting her own regret and bristling with awareness of Jarrod in the adjacent room.

He hadn't said a word on their carriage ride back to Huntsville from the prison. He hadn't joined her and the maids for dinner in the hotel restaurant. And though she'd waited hopefully in the drawing room downstairs after their meal, he hadn't appeared to talk with her. She'd allowed him to flog himself privately as long as she could possibly bear, but even she had limits. Silently, she'd slipped from her bed, donned the bodice and skirt she'd worn earlier, and padded into the hallway.

With an agitated movement, she pushed the long fall of her hair over her shoulder. Already, the tie she'd hastily fastened around it was coming loose. She lifted her fist to knock, paused. Flattened her palm to the wood of the door. Glanced at her own room and seriously considered running to it. To do what? Lie immobile the rest of the night, listening to the sound of his feet treading the floorboards and wishing she could say something to him, offer him some meager solace?

Before she could change her mind, she rapped softly on his door.

Silence.

Her eyes sank briefly closed. She knocked again.

"It's open." The words were spoken without inflection. Maybe a good sign. At least he hadn't snapped at her to leave him be.

She let herself in. Though the corridor had been dim, his room was far darker. A single lamp warred against the gloom, shedding a sphere of light over the bedside table and the sapphire blue blanket covering the bed. Jarrod . . . She had to squint to make him out. Jarrod stood at the half-opened window. Gauzy white curtains writhed in the winter wind that coasted though.

Sophia's skin pebbled, though whether from the cold or from the sight of the man she didn't know. Tentatively, she approached him, able to make out more details the closer she drew. He wore just his black trousers and a white shirt. The shirt hung untucked and unbuttoned, rolled up at the sleeves. His hair was tousled, his arms crossed, his feet bare. He was staring at her.

Abruptly she stopped. Now that she'd come, she'd not the slightest idea how to begin to help him, nor why on earth he might wish to let her. She groped for the right words—

"Come to gloat?" he asked.

The accusation stung like lemon dashed into a cut. "What would I have to gloat over?"

"You won." He presented her with his profile as he gazed out the window. "You were right about my brother."

"Do you . . ." She dared a few more steps toward him, coming to stand at the edge of his window. She gripped a handful of the curtain and struggled to read what was behind his eyes. She couldn't. "Do you truly think there was a winner today?"

He held his silence, and she wanted to scream. Surely he didn't see the world that way—everything a competition between adversaries. "I was correct in believing your brother to be guilty," she said haltingly. "But I was entirely wrong in pursuing him the way I did for the reasons I did. I've never in my life felt less like a winner."

He didn't react in any way.

She fisted her hand tighter in the silky cool drapery.

"I'm sure you'll never be able to forgive me for arresting your brother, and maybe you shouldn't. Perhaps I shouldn't forgive you, either, for imprisoning me in your house the way you did—"

His gaze sliced to her and the words died on her lips. There, finally, beneath his dark brows, behind green eyes, she could see emotion burning.

"Was it so terrible?" he asked in a menacing tone.

"Yes."

"Why do you say yes when you mean no?" He dropped his arms to his sides and moved toward her.

She retreated. He was spoiling for trouble tonight, angry and reckless. She'd thought to soothe . . . But no. She'd no business circling with a wolf who knew far better than she how to attack.

"Why do you seal your lips when you want to laugh?" He stalked her. "Why do you hold yourself away from people when you want so badly to let somebody see? What are you afraid of, Sophie?"

She came up against the door and scrambled for a hold on the knob. She'd come here to open him and his heart wide, not to have her own heart flayed open. "I don't know what you're talking about."

"Why do you say that, when you know too well what I'm talking about? Even now, you're readying to flee. You'd rather flee than face an ounce of truth about yourself."

He was far too close to being right. "You think you know me so well?" she asked scathingly.

"I know you better than you know yourself."

"Then I shall be pleased to unburden you of my predictable presence. When we reach Galveston tomorrow, I'll return to Blackhaw."

His chest hitched with the rise and fall of his breath. "You actually think, for one second," he snarled, "that I'm letting you go?"

Her heart thumped loudly in her ears.

She watched him cross to the washstand. For a long moment, he braced his hands against its sides and stared into the water pooled in the porcelain dish. Then he dipped his hands in and cupped water in his palms.

"You've no right to keep me where I don't wish to be."

He let the water fall from his hands into the bowl with a splash, then raked his wet fingers through his hair as he rounded on her. "Right? Right?" he growled. "You think I got where I am today by operating within my rights? I'd still be in the gutter if I had. I don't give a damn about what my rights are or aren't. You should know that by now."

"You've no *reason*, then, to punish me any longer."

"I've every reason."

"Name one!"

"One. I promised Holden I'd find our father, and you're not leaving until we do." He jerked open one side of his shirt.

Sophia's disbelieving gaze sank to his hands.

"Two. You arrested my brother out of vengeance, but I haven't finished having my vengeance on you yet." He ripped free the other side of his shirt and hurled it into the corner. "And three." He came to her, grabbed her hand, and placed it flush against the fly of his pants.

His hardness bulged there, unrelenting.

"Three, I think about you all the time." He was so close that his words rasped against the skin of her lips. He pushed her hand more forcefully against him, moved it up and down over the ridge of him. "I fantasize about you at night. When I'm with you I want to strip you naked, I want to suck you here"—his free hand slid over the point of a breast, then lower toward the juncture between her thighs—"and here."

She shoved him away. "How *dare* you try to intimidate me, to frighten me this way? Are you so desperate to take your anger out on someone? Or are you simply too fearful that I might actually glimpse a fragment of human emotion in you? God!" Needing to lash out at him, she balled her fist and socked him in the shoulder.

He absorbed the blow by taking a half step back.

She pursued, pushing at him again with the heels of her hands. "I'm so sick of you bullying me! Do you hear me?" Another shove. "Sick of it. Sick!"

He extended his hands to subdue her. She slapped them away, then clasped his face and kissed him with all the pent-up rage and heat that her body possessed.

Chapter 16

He responded immediately, meeting her force with force, their kiss hungry and raw and rough. Yearning for something beyond her reach, Sophia strained into him, dug her fingers into his scalp, feasted ravenously from his mouth.

Jarrod's hands were between them, releasing the buttons down the front of her bodice. They weren't coming free fast enough, so breathlessly she helped him, her fingers fumbling and tripping on the buttons at the bottom.

Night air soared against her skin as Jarrod jerked apart the garment. Because she hadn't bothered with her chemise after divesting her nightgown, she was naked underneath. He pulled her flush against the warmth of his chest.

Sensation spilled from her breasts to the core of her,

pulling at her there. She arched against him once, then again, forcing her soft curves against the textured steel of his body.

He twisted her so that her back fit against the planes of his chest. Then he reached around her with one hand to cup her breast, and with the other he spanned her lower abdomen and pressed her backside against him.

Sophia fought for breath. Oh, the feelings. His lips dipped to her neck and shoulder, and she felt the bite of his teeth. Yes. She let her head fall back. The harshness of this gave glorious vent to her frustrations. She could feel his anger, too. Both of them, butting against each other, lost in needs that had no names.

He bunched a handful of her skirt in his hand. Then took up more and more of the fabric until the hem whisked over her knees, over her thighs. When he discovered she wore no drawers beneath, he groaned and thrust against her from behind.

She almost cried out. Her teeth sank into her swollen bottom lip.

He drew her the few steps backward to the side of his bed, then pulled her against him as he sat, positioning her on his lap. His knees came up beneath her naked ones, and then he spread his legs, opening hers as he did so.

Sophia gasped with anticipation.

His fingers caressed her breasts to aching tightness. While his other hand . . . *Oh, mercy.* His other hand smoothed up her quivering inner thigh to the curls between her legs. Ever so lightly he cupped her there. She writhed against his taut thighs, mindless with the feelings he was strumming from her, greedy in her desire for more.

Deftly, he parted her femininity and the breeze

washed over her most private, most heated place. Her back bowed, and she waited without breathing. He simply held her that way, opened.

He kissed the nape of her neck, lifted and massaged her breasts, but he didn't touch the tight bud between her legs that yearned for it. She shifted restlessly, begging him without words.

"Tell me you want it." His voice was sandpaper-rough against her ear.

She gave a helpless sound of distress.

Still, he wouldn't end her torment, wouldn't give her the pleasure she craved.

"Tell me," he said.

"Yes," she moaned.

His blunt middle finger dipped into her. He didn't go deep. Just lightly in and out, his finger slickened with her own desire. Then up his finger stroked, up, until the pad of it skated across—

Her whole body jerked with the intense shock of pleasure.

Rhythmically, he worked her with nothing but that one finger, circling, probing. The friction of it climbed within her—exquisite agony. Too exquisite. Too much. A frission of fear penetrated her thoughts, then built in tandem with her body's physical ecstasy. Even as she bucked against him, straining toward something she desperately wanted, she realized she was losing control.

She should stop it now. But her body was clenching, like the petals of a flower wrapping inward, gathering all their power for something that would explode them apart. Explode her. She pressed her breast into the hard palm of his hand, rode his hips, opened her thighs wider for him. She'd give in to the call of her instincts for once. She wanted this, God help her, she wanted to *weep* over how badly she wanted this.

Wanted what? Her frenzied brain asked. Him? How much of him? Wanted him to make love to her, plant a baby inside her? There was nothing substantial between them on which to build a relationship. Not enough trust. No promises. No future. Only passion, and tonight, anger.

He lifted her, and then her back was against the sapphire cover, her legs off the bed's edge, and him kneeling between them. No, he couldn't possibly. His face lowered. She pressed her knees together, too modest to contemplate. He moved them gently apart. He couldn't possibly—

He could. At the first touch of his lips against her there she nearly bolted off the bed. *Oh my. Oh my.* She tossed back her head and shut her eyes, consumed by sensation. She'd never imagined such a wicked thing existed. Never imagined feelings so glorious. *Oh my.*

He drew at her, teased, drew at her. Her body clenched tighter. Her hands fisted in the bedcovers, her head thrashed to the side. And still he didn't relent, and she prayed he wouldn't. Let it not end. Let it go on and on and on.

Her body's arousal leapt ahead of her ability to keep pace with it. Leapt again. She tried to grab for breath, to master it—couldn't. And then she was throbbing with a pleasure so overwhelming she cried out. It cascaded over her, rippling, rippling, rippling, until she was left lying slack on the bed, blinking in astonishment.

Have you ever been so spent afterward you could do

nothing but lie naked and unmoving? The question he'd once asked her came back to her now. She'd thought it boastful at the time. She'd been wrong.

What had just . . . happened to her? Maggie had told her about the kind of release a woman could achieve. She'd belittled Maggie's description as overly dramatic at the time. She'd been wrong about that, too.

She was aware of Jarrod standing, of him carefully straightening her skirts.

She pressed her hands to her cheeks and could smell the scent of his hair on her fingers. Her heart twisted with a pain that was tenderness. Could she have come to care about him so much that the mere scent of his hair filled her with affection? No. She couldn't have let herself feel that strongly about him. No.

She clasped closed her bodice with hands that bore his scent and met his hooded gaze. *Yes.* Yes, she could and did feel that strongly about him, she realized with a burgeoning sense of disaster.

The bed frame creaked when he planted a knee on the edge of the mattress. She swung her legs onto the bed and scooted over to allow him space. He stretched the length of his body alongside hers, then pulled the far side of the blanket up and over them, creating what felt to Sophia like a warm cocoon. It scared her, how good it was to lie close to him. To feel as if she belonged.

He propped his head in his hand and gazed down at her. With his other hand he reached out and smoothed a lock of hair to the side of her forehead.

"Jarrod, I . . ." How could she begin to account for what had just occurred between them?

"Do you have any idea how long I've been wanting to do that?" He picked up the softly curling end of another tendril of hair and rubbed it gently between his thumb and middle finger.

She smiled shyly. "A long time?"

"Seems like years."

"But you didn't . . . I mean . . ." She couldn't quite bring herself to talk of his own lack of release out loud.

"It was perfect," he murmured. "It was enough."

He could be so incredibly decent. Memories of all the other times he had been flitted through her mind. She turned onto her side toward him and nestled against the planes of his body, fitting her face against his shoulder. She could stay here forever, breathing him in.

He lifted her chin with his thumb and kissed her slow and gently, the force between them that had been a pounding storm minutes ago flowing now like a summer river. Sensual and languid and adoring. His fingers grazed the underside of her chin as he took his time with her.

The string of kisses traveled over the edge of her lips, to her cheek, to the corner of her eyelid, before he parted from her. "Stay with me," he said.

Had he asked her to dance on hot coals in that moment, she would have. "Stay?" she asked.

"Tonight and with me at my estate when we return. Help me find my father. Not because I'm forcing you but because you want to."

Emotion gathered in her throat. She did want to. But until this moment, she hadn't grasped how dearly she'd longed to be asked instead of ordered.

"Well?" he asked.

"Yes."

"You'll come back with me?"

"Yes."

A slow grin moved across his mouth. "Good." He eyed the path of his knuckle as he trailed it down her jaw, her throat, then all the way down the open seam between the two sides of her bodice.

She shivered. "What would you have done if I'd refused to come willingly?"

His gaze returned to her. "I'd have forced you, of course."

She laughed.

"I'm not ready to let you go yet."

Her amusement eased away. He'd said *yet*.

"As soon as we return, we'll start searching for my father. With you and me both working on it solely—"

She placed a finger over his lips. "Actually, I can't work on it solely just now." Touching him was a wonder. Hesitantly, brazenly, she coasted her finger over his cheek then circled his ear.

"Why?"

She tucked her hand against his chest. "Because I've another case I'm also committed to at the moment."

"The counterfeiting case."

She'd forgotten that he'd made her tell him of it the night he'd chased her down in the woods. "Yes. It's somewhat urgent."

"Why?"

"It just . . . is."

Quiet stretched. Guilt niggled at her for evading the truth. Still, she wasn't about to tell it to Jarrod, not only because she was ashamed of the taxes she'd been unable to pay, but because she'd never risk him thinking that she'd told him about Blackhaw because she wanted his charity. She'd rather lose Blackhaw then have him think that even for a second. No, she'd manage her own problems. As always. "I'll give every spare minute I have to finding your father." It was the most honest thing she could say.

"Do you plan to pursue your counterfeiter as Twilight's Ghost?" he asked.

"I do."

"Not without me."

She raised her brows.

"Have your forgotten what happened last time you left the house?" He stroked his thumb over the area of her lip that had split.

"I've been doing this job unescorted for years."

"And now you'll be doing it with an escort."

"Jarrod . . ."

"Look, you can work on your case all you want. It's just that I'll be working on it with you."

"And the search for your father?"

"I'll call in Clint and J. T. With more of us on it, we'll be able to find him faster."

She thought of all the hours she'd spent moving through the night, cold and alone. It would be like the heat of a fire after years of shivering to have him with her. In fact, it worried her how very much the idea tempted her. Once they located Adam Stone, Jarrod would go and once again she'd be left to walk through the deserted, midnight-dark alleys of her life without him.

"I refuse to let you risk yourself," Jarrod said. "If you were mine, I'd never allow you to do such dangerous work."

Allow her? A bone-deep melancholy overtook her. She dared reach for him one last time, let her hand cup his handsome cheek, her thumb rub beneath one of his eyes. Eyes that were wolfishly intense at the moment, ready to fight if need be to enforce his will. "I guess you needn't worry then," she said quietly, "as I'll never be yours."

Exhausted suddenly, she pushed to sitting. Once she'd fastened a few of the buttons of her bodice, she walked to the door.

She didn't dare look back at him for fear of the pining she'd experience. She opened the door, eased into the corridor, and leaned against it on the outside. Bereft.

I'm not ready to let you go yet. But he would be, one day. Regardless of whatever attraction he harbored toward her, she had no illusions. Jarrod Stone wasn't the kind of man who settled down with one woman. And she wasn't the kind of woman who relished being abandoned.

She'd been left once, standing outside an orphanage with nothing but a valise full of clothes and a heart full of unbearable pain. She'd not risk that again, not for any relationship, and especially not one as fated as hers was with Jarrod. He'd said himself just now that he'd never let her do her work if she were his. Even her job, he'd strip from her if given the chance. The one thing that offered her independence, purpose, and, therefore, protection. The one thing other than Blackhaw she would absolutely never part with.

They were doomed, she and Jarrod. It wasn't like she hadn't know it from the beginning. It was just that it hurt now, with a pain so vicious it stole her breath.

Behind the walls of Huntsville prison, Holden lay on his bunk, peering blindly into the darkness above him. All around he heard the snores and muffled grunts of deep sleep, yet he was starkly awake.

The woman Jarrod had brought with him had been one hell of a beauty, with those dark eyes and that porcelain skin. In a million years he'd never have guessed her to be Twilight's Ghost or imagined that she bore invisible scars inflicted by past pain. Her scars ran deep though, so deep that she still pursued his father after all this time. So deep, that she'd turned her sights on him.

God, I'm so sick of it. Twenty years, and the repercussions of what their father had done still haunted him. He hoped his brother killed their father when he found him. His only regret was that he wouldn't be there to pull the trigger himself.

He pushed a hand beneath his lumpy pillow. Restlessly, he canted his face to the side to stare without seeing at the moonlight that planed against the wall, illuminating the rough crisscross of mortar between bricks.

Memory nagged at him. He frowned, annoyed because it was the same feeling he'd been having for a couple of months. As if something was beneath the surface of his brain grasping toward consciousness, but never quite making it. The harder he tried to remember, the more it retreated behind the fog where most of early childhood had gone. Except that this had retreated even farther. Whatever this was lived behind an iron door, locked away as surely as he was locked away in this hellhole.

With a grunt of frustration, he screwed shut his eyes and tried to see it. It was about his mother, that much he knew. . . .

"Holden," she had said that night. "Get your coat."

"We're leaving?" he asked, looking up from the toy soldiers scattered across the table.

He watched her shake loose her thin hair, then wind it into a tight, new bun. She stared into the chipped mirror that hung near the door as she took pins from her mouth and stuck them in her hair. Her eyes met his in the glass. "We're going out for a few minutes."

Holden looked to his older brothers, who were lounging on the rug at the far side of the room. "I can stay here with them."

"No, Jarrod's not back from his activities yet."

Holden knew what that meant. His oldest brother was either working odd jobs or begging in order to bring home food.

"And Clint and J. T. are old enough to take care of themselves but not old enough to look after you proper. So go and fetch your coat, like I said."

Holden slid off the chair. When he reached the coat-rack, he had to strain onto his tiptoes to lift his coat from it. He grimaced as he put it on and secured the buttons. Everybody in town knew Mrs. Martin had given his mother this coat when her Jed had outgrown it. Mother had let it out at the cuffs twice, and it was already too small for him again. More eagerly, he donned the felt hat he'd inherited from J. T. He liked his hat.

Mother gathered up her own coat, one of Jarrod's old ones. "Boys, we'll be back in a few minutes."

Clint and J. T. nodded like they had better things to do.

Outside it was real dark, and the sky was misting. Mother pushed her arms into her coat, then took his hand in her red one and led him along the road. Some women wore gloves. He'd seen them. But his mother never did, and her hands were always red from all the scrubbing she did.

She increased their pace, and he clamped his free

hand onto his hat to keep it from falling off. "Where we going?" he asked.

"To find your father. He was supposed to be home two hours ago." Her mouth went tight. She looked a little scared.

Worry shifted through him. He kept one eye on the road and one on her. He waited for her to look like she usually did, like things would be okay.

She coughed.

His worry deepened.

She coughed again, something she did often lately. It sounded as if she was coughing all the way from her stomach, and something was loose in there. If she got any skinnier or coughed any more, he was afraid she might die.

He tightened his short fingers around hers and looked at his feet. He wasn't the only one who thought so. He'd seen Jarrod's face when she coughed. Jarrod thought she might die, too.

She coughed so hard that her hand jerked in his.

"Where's Pa?" he asked, looking over his shoulder and wishing somebody was here other than just him in case she needed help. The street was empty. Nobody even moved behind windows. The only thing he saw was an old newspaper blowing down the street.

"Your father was going to meet with Mrs. Warren."

"Who's that?"

"The grand lady that lives at Blackhaw Estate."

"The one that's going to make us rich?"

Her eyebrows pinched together. "Maybe."

That's what Pa said, anyway. He said the lady at Blackhaw was going to make them rich soon. "So we going to the big house?"

"Yes."

They turned the corner, and he saw a dark turret in the distance.

"We're going to Blackhaw."

And then . . . And then nothing. The iron door clanged shut, cutting off the rest of the memory. Holden's eyes sprang open, and he saw the wall of his cell, felt the tension that gripped his body.

There was more, god damn it. More that was important. And he couldn't, for the life of him, remember what.

Chapter 17

"A re you sure you want to do this?" Sophia whispered to Jarrod two nights later.

He gazed at her where she stood, poised on the back step of what she'd told him was Galveston's foremost stationers, her lockpicking equipment in her hands.

"Of course I'm sure," he answered.

"Because, as of this moment you're still untainted by . . . less than savory acts such as this. There's still time to preserve your lily-white image."

"You think me untainted?" he asked, somewhat offended.

Her eyes glimmered with humor.

"I'll show you tainted," he grumbled. "In fact, I'm more than willing to pull you down"—he nodded toward the alley dirt—"and taint you right here and now." He was only half joking. He'd be more than happy to sate the hunger for her that prowled within him. Right here would be fine. He could pin her against the door, toss up her skirts, and enter her standing up. God knows he'd waited long enough.

She must have read his thoughts, because her tongue darted over her bottom lip. It made him crazy when she did things like that with her mouth.

"You wouldn't want to taint me in this outfit," she said, her voice slightly throaty.

"Wouldn't I?" He cocked an eyebrow.

Since he was accompanying her tonight on their first foray as Twilight's Ghosts, she'd ditched her man's costume in favor of the rags and soiled cap of a charwoman. Her hair was tucked up and her face smeared with dust and grime. Like he cared. No mud could mar the luster of her coffee-colored eyes, and no tattered clothing could erase his memory of the pale breasts, waist, hips, and buttocks underneath. Damn, but he wanted to take her.

She glanced down at her costume. "As it happens," she said with a smile, "this charwoman has morals." She turned her attention to working her instruments into the lock. "Could you hold this?" she asked, handing him a slim tool.

Obligingly, he took it. On the way here, she'd led him through the gloom faultlessly and fast, and now her slender hands wielded her instruments with expert precision. She was good at her job. If there were records inside this shop detailing an order for the large quantities and kinds of paper and ink needed for counterfeiting, Sophia would find them. Of that he had no doubt.

Still, it didn't sit well with him not to be the one in control of this situation. So far the most he'd done was follow behind her like some hulking, idiot bodyguard. Which, he reminded himself, was exactly what he was tonight.

He didn't like it. And he didn't like this damn fool clothing. Sophia had bid him dress this way because she wanted anyone who happened to spot them to assume them a poverty-stricken couple. He wore denim trousers that had thinned at the inner thighs and had holes in the knees. The trousers, as well as the faded flannel shirt and the dirt-stained Stetson belonged to one of his stable hands. The man had been hard-pressed to come up with such shoddy clothing. Regardless, that he'd managed to at all informed Jarrod he needed to pay the man more.

"Almost there," Sophia murmured. She extended her palm, and he placed the tool he'd been holding in it. "Just one more minute. . . ." Her beautiful lips pursed in concentration.

She'd wanted to make this foray last night, when they'd returned from their trip to Huntsville. But after her attack followed by two days of ceaseless travel, exhaustion had pulled at her shoulders and dulled her eyes. He'd insisted that her counterfeiting investigation could wait one night and sent her to bed. She'd slept today until noon.

Click. "There," she said, wiping her hands on her apron, then stashing her instruments. "It was rusty."

Jarrod followed close behind her as she entered the blackened building. Unease trickled through him as his gaze swept the murky back room. He absolutely *hated* the thought of her doing this kind of thing alone. Who the hell had hired her for this job, anyway, and in doing so allowed her to endanger herself?

She slid past furniture and supplies into the front

room of the shop. He had to squint, just to make her out. "It's damn dark," he said under his breath.

"Your eyes get used to it in time." She crouched behind a long rectangular shape that he guessed to be the sales counter and began sliding open drawers and compartments.

Jarrod stood in the doorway between the front and back rooms, primed for noises, searching the stretch of barren street visible beyond the front windows. "Find anything?" he asked.

"Not yet—" Hinges whined. "Oh . . . wait. Here we are." The scratch of a match sounded. The halo of a flame lit her chin and cheeks as she touched it to the wick of the candle she'd brought. She fished a holder from her skirt pocket, impaled the candle on it, and set both on the floor beside her. Nimbly leaning over the deep drawer she'd opened, she began flipping through its contents.

"Sales receipts?" he asked curtly.

She nodded.

He set his jaw and tried to gauge how much light her candle was putting off. Not much. It was a small flame, mostly concealed by the counter. Yet if someone with an observant eye walked past the storefront, they'd see it. The memory of watching her slapped by her attackers, watching her tumble unconscious to the ground, seared his thoughts.

"Here's something." She pulled a sheet from the stack and angled it toward her candle. "It's a large order. Though not large enough to create the magnitude of counterfeit bills our man has been passing."

"It's a start," he said. "Surely he wouldn't be so fool-

ish as to order all his supplies from one merchant and induce suspicion."

Her gaze flicked to his. "That's exactly what I was
thinking." She returned to her task. He saw determination in the set of her lips, stubbornness in the bend of her
neck. The woman was tireless. She'd never given up on
his father in all these years, and now she was hell-bent
on finding her counterfeiter, too. She was a fighter, come
one come all.

Affection seized his chest. At times like this, she
could look so earnest. There were parts of her that
seemed so true and yet other parts of her had deceived
him with careless ease. She'd proven to him in the
bluntest way imaginable that she couldn't be trusted, and
still he was tempted to put his faith in her. He, who'd
never been a man to be burned twice. He shook his head,
irritated with himself and his inability to shrug her off.
God knows he'd never had that trouble with women in
the past. Now that it was actually important that he distance himself from her for his own sanity, he was realiz-
ing that Sophia LaRue had gotten under his skin.

He watched her copy the pertinent information from
the receipt onto the paper she'd brought along.

He ground his bootheel into the floor and wished
she'd hurry. He itched to take her out of here and back to
his house and safety. This whole thing was ridiculous.
He had a mind to pay Slocum's one good dollar for
every fake one they'd ever received or would ever receive in order to end this case.

He could guess just how favorably she'd respond to
that idea.

"That's all for this drawer," she said. The hinges again

protested as she slid it back into its space. "They must keep their older records elsewhere—"

Above them, floorboards creaked.

Sophia's attention jerked to Jarrod. They both listened as a man's footsteps moved heavily across the second-story floor. Damn it! They'd awoken the owner. Jarrod reached her in an instant, wrapped his hand around her upper arm, and propelled her toward the rear door. She reached back for her candle and snuffed it with her fingertips before pocketing it.

Muffled voices drifted from above. More movement.

Jarrod hurried her forward. In seconds, they were outside on the step. Sophia rushed to insert her equipment into the lock.

"Just leave it," he ordered, pulling her forward.

"No." She dug in her heels and shook off his arm. "Ghosts don't leave open doors."

His mind filling with curses, he glanced upward. The entrance to the second-story living quarters consisted of a wooden staircase that led to a platform suspended directly above them. Even as he watched, the upper door swung open and light spilled through the cracks between the boards.

Sophia bolted the lock, looked to him, and nodded. But before he could rush her down the alley, a man sauntered onto the platform above. His shadow obliterated sections of the lines of light, and his weight sent flurries of dust twirling down on them. "Who's there?" he asked.

Sophia clamped a hand over his lips. He peeled it free. She pressed her index finger to her own lips, her dire expression urging him to remain silent.

From above, the deadly sound of a gun being cocked echoed through the night.

That did it. Jarrod pulled free his own gun. He didn't want to hurt anyone for protecting his rightful property, but he was even less willing to let Sophia be injured.

"No," she mouthed to him, her eyes horrified.

"I'm coming down." The man stalked toward the mouth of the stairs.

Jarrod pushed Sophia toward the building's corner. She sprinted for it. He barreled after her, glancing over his shoulder as he ran. Just as he looked back, he saw the man stop halfway down the stairs and raise his gun, aiming at them over the banister.

"Faster," Jarrod yelled.

Sophia vanished around the corner just as an explosion rent the stillness. Jarrod hunched against the expected pain of a bullet plowing through his back. Instead, the bullet collided with the wall near his shoulder, pinging him with shards of brick.

He rounded the building's corner and ran down the narrow canyon of space between the stationer's and the adjacent structure. Sophia waited for him, silhouetted by the opening to the street. He motioned for her go on without him. The obstinate woman waited until he'd reached her, then ran just ahead of him. Quick as a cat, she led him across the street and down the mouth of another alleyway.

He looked back to see the man skid onto the road, then charge after them.

Sophia turned down another alley, then another. He could still hear the shop owner behind them, swearing and running. A few more turns into the maze of back streets and passageways, and the sounds of their pursuer grew fainter. Then fainter still, before disappearing altogether.

Jarrod stashed his gun and followed Sophia who continued at a swift pace. She guided him unerringly, never once hesitating, until finally, behind a building on the edge of town, she slowed. Her chest billowing, she leaned against the wooden edifice and watched him. He propped his shoulders against the wall next to her and fought to control his own breathing.

"I can't believe you almost shot that man," she said.

Annoyance flared inside him. "In case you failed to notice, he didn't appear to have a qualm about shooting us."

"No, but that doesn't make harming him right. He was innocent."

"What would you have had me do, stand there with my thumb up my ass while he shot you?"

At his language, a displeased frown stitched her brow. "No, I'd have had us escape by running just as we did."

"Our escape was damned close, Sophie. His bullet missed my shoulder by about an inch."

Her belligerent expression softened immediately. "I hadn't realized . . . Which shoulder?"

"This one." He hefted his right.

She went to it and gently brushed off the mist of mortar, then examined the cloth for holes. "Did any of the brick shards cut you?"

"No."

She kept inspecting the cloth anyway, just to be sure. Only when completely satisfied did she stroke her hand across his shoulder, sigh, and take a step back. "I think I'll have to leave you at home the next time."

"What?" he bellowed.

She scowled and pointed toward the slumbering building.

"What?" he asked, more softly, but equally as irate. "I'm not at fault for what happened back there."

"No, of course not. I just can't bear to have you on my conscience."

"Me on *your* conscience?" He couldn't damn believe her. "I'm telling you right now, you leave to work on this assignment without me while you're under my roof, and I'll bend you over my knee, pull up your skirts, and spank you."

Her eyes, with their amazing long curly lashes, rounded. "Th-that's not funny."

"No, it sure as hell isn't. I don't like this, Sophie. Any of it. I don't like you working as Twilight's Ghost."

She gazed at him for a long moment. "I never imagined you would," she said at last, a hint of resignation in her voice. "This may come as a surprise to you, Jarrod, but I haven't in the past and won't in the future make my life's choices based upon your preferences."

He set his jaw and glared. Back in Huntsville, he'd told her that if she were his, he'd never allow her to do such work. He'd meant it then. He meant it tenfold now. He wasn't the sort of man that could swallow his objections and stand mutely aside while she slipped from his bed to go catch criminals during the dead of night.

"Your property begins just there, over the second rise," she said coldly, motioning with her chin. "I guess we'd best get going."

"I guess we'd better."

They'd walked less than a few feet when he stilled her by taking hold of her arm. She turned to him, eyes wary.

"Did I make my feelings clear regarding you investigating this case on your own?" he asked. He wanted no ambiguity.

"Perfectly," she answered. Then she yanked her arm from his grasp and walked into the gathering heart of the night. It struck him as he watched her that the darkness knew her and that she knew the darkness. Too well. Inexplicably, the observation saddened him.

It made him want to give her light.

The next afternoon, Maggie and Sophia waited together on the covered front porch of Jarrod's house. They both wore full-length coats, gloves, and scarves to protect against a day that had dawned sunny and clear, but cold.

"This is ridiculous," Sophia grumbled. "There's absolutely no reason why we must greet Jarrod's brothers the instant they dismount their horses."

"I already told you," Maggie answered distractedly. She was searching the distance with such fervor that Sophia feared she'd suffer eye strain. "If I'm not the first woman they see upon arrival, then one of the maids that infest this place might catch their eye first." She straightened the hat she'd borrowed from Sophia's closet, a dark green one with a paler green bow at the back, then squinted. "I can't afford the competition."

"I've told you and told you, Maggie, you don't want these men."

"Yes, I do."

"They're probably insufferable, pigheaded"—she thought of Jarrod's threat to spank her—"*presumptuous* scoundrels just like their older brother."

"They're mischievous, is all." Maggie slid her a threatening look out of the corners of her eyes before returning her attention to the far end of the drive.

Sophia studied her friend, torn between laughing and

tearing out her hair. She'd sent for Maggie the night she'd returned from Huntsville. Since then, since learning that Jarrod's brothers would be coming to assist in the search for Adam Stone, Maggie had become Clint and J. T.'s staunchest supporter. She refused to hear a word against them, these two men whom she'd never so much as set eyes upon. In preparation for their arrival, she'd even moved into Jarrod's home as a guest. Jarrod had allowed it because Sophia had asked it of him. But now Sophia wondered whether she should have asked.

What if one of Jarrod's brothers hurt Maggie? Disappointed her? Men, as a rule, were too stupid to see past her friend's tallness and thinness to the golden beauty beneath. *Especially* handsome men. And if Jarrod and Holden were any indication, Sophia suspected both of these Stone brothers would be equally devastating to look at. "If Jarrod's brothers don't appreciate you, Maggie, it's their loss, their fault—"

"Oh!" Maggie grabbed her hand and squeezed hard. "Look."

At the far end of the drive, two men on horseback rounded the curve into view. Both rode with the graceful mastery of men who'd logged years in the saddle.

The dryness of the dirt beneath the pounding hooves of their mounts caused dust to churn high around them, making them look as if they were cantering straight out of the imaginary place where men of mystical proportions lived. Two rugged cowboys, their hats shading their faces, their coats mantling powerful shoulders. Twin coils of rope slapping their saddles. Gun belts ringing their waists. Heroes, both of them. Strapping, strong, chiseled, and brave. The answer to every girlish fantasy since the beginning of time.

Sophia felt Maggie go marble-still beside her. Caught up herself in an uncharacteristic bit of romanticism, Sophia tightly clasped her friend's hand.

"Oh my God," Maggie breathed as the men drew nearer. "I think I'm going to faint."

"Don't you dare. I'll be left standing here, holding your limp body in my arms. What kind of an impression will that make on them?"

"Maybe they like pliable women."

"I don't think so. In fact, I recall that Jarrod made a *point* of telling me the other day that all his brothers have an aversion to pliable women."

"Oh," Maggie said thinly, then swallowed.

In a wave of seething dust, Jarrod's brothers stopped ten yards away. Imagine, four magnificent men all the progeny of Adam Stone.

Both of Jarrod's brothers regarded them appreciatively, though the one with the blonder hair curling from beneath his Stetson did so with an unmistakably flirtatious gleam in his eye. He also had a brash grin—as if he saw something he liked and hadn't the slightest insecurity that they might not like what they saw in return.

Both men tipped their hats. "Ladies," the blonder one said.

"Gentlemen," Sophia replied. She stole a quick glance at Maggie, whose lips were pale. For the first time in memory, Maggie appeared to be at a loss for words.

"I'm J. T. Stone," the blonder one said, "and this is my brother Clint."

"Pleased to make your acquaintance." Clint dipped his chin.

"The pleasure is ours," Sophia responded politely.

"I'm Sophia LaRue and this is my dear friend Maggie May."

J. T. actually winked at her before both men slid their legs over their horses' backs and dismounted.

Sophia studied them as they set to work releasing the girth straps from their saddle rings. Clint was clean-shaven, with broader features than any of his brothers. With his hip-length brown-canvas coat, trail pants, and serious expression, he looked like what he was—a marshal who took laws and justice every bit as seriously as she did.

J. T., on the other hand, appeared far too fun-loving to do the grim work of a bounty hunter. His molded cheeks held the sandy stubble of a two-day-old beard. His beige duster swirled around boots that were worn at the heels as likely from dancing as from pounding sidewalks in search of criminals.

Neither man appeared to be as hardened or as forbidding as either Jarrod or Holden. Fleetingly, she wondered if that was only because they'd learned to mask it better.

Sophia shot another look at Maggie. This time her friend gave her a reassuring smile, then widened her eyes in an expression that said she was happier than a cat who'd fallen into a vat of cream.

Once they'd given over their reins to the stable hands, the Stone brothers climbed the steps. "So what brings you lovely ladies to Jarrod's house?" J. T. asked, slapping his hands together to clear them of travel grime. His charmer's grin made his long-lashed eyes sparkle. "Can't be his winning personality."

Sophia smiled. "No. We're here for the same reason you are, to assist in the search for Adam Stone."

"I see. Is one of you the heiress of Blackhaw?"

"I am," Sophia answered.

"Jarrod mentioned in his telegram that you'd be helping us."

She nodded. It seemed strange to hear him say it like that. To her way of thinking they were helping *her*, seeing as this particular search had belonged to her for close to twenty years. Not that she gave a fig. If Jarrod and his band of brothers wanted to stride in and take over the hunt, she was more than willing to let them. She could barely imagine what her life might be like—how light she might feel—without the black specter of Adam Stone's freedom hovering over her.

She moved her attention to Maggie, only to find her and Clint gazing at one another with grave interest.

"You doing all right there, darlin'?" J. T. asked Maggie, touching her elbow. "You were looking a little peaked when we rode up."

"When you rode up I was suffering from a powerful case of awe." A smile roved across Maggie's wide mouth. "Has anyone told either of you lately how outlandishly handsome you are?"

Clint regarded her with blank shock. J. T. chuckled richly. "Not lately enough and not often enough."

"Well you are. I swear, you and your brothers could start a carnival act and make buckets of money."

"What, like a freak show?" Clint asked, brows lifted.

"Rather like a 'Miracles of Nature' show. I'd be honored to offer my services as ticket taker for such an endeavor."

Sophia inconspicuously tugged Maggie toward the front door. She was relieved that Maggie had recovered from her bout of acute adoration in such fine form. She just didn't want her to overwhelm the brothers at their first meeting.

In the foyer, the men helped them divest their winter things, patiently handing items to the servants who waited in attendance.

Maggie pulled free the beaded hatpin she'd borrowed from Sophia. "Do you like my hat?" she asked Clint, her eyes a transparent window of affection and hope.

"Very much," he answered.

Sophia tugged off her second glove and handed it to J. T.

"I like your hat, too," Maggie responded.

"Thank you kindly." Somewhat self-consciously, Clint removed his hat and combed a hand through closely cropped brown hair that bore creases from his Stetson.

Footsteps rang in the hallway. Before she even looked, the flutter of anticipation in her breast informed her they belonged to Jarrod. Their eyes met with a bolt of awareness.

Oh, how awful. Jarrod stalked her thoughts whenever she was apart from him. Then when she saw him after a separation, it was always the same lately. This catastrophic lurch of emotion, just from *looking* at him. As always, he wore a beautifully tailored black suit, paired today with a charcoal gray vest.

Jarrod smiled with genuine warmth as he shook hands with his brothers. He was the kind of man who rarely if ever gave his love or trust. But once you'd earned it, she understood instinctively that he'd love and trust you forever.

"I see you've already met Mrs. LaRue and Miss May," Jarrod said to his brothers.

"We have." J. T. rested his hand on Sophia's lower back. "Mrs. LaRue was so kind as to make the introductions."

"Yes." Jarrod's gaze turned ominous as he very deliberately removed J. T.'s hand. "Mrs. LaRue is very kind that way. Shall we?" He placed his own muscular hand at her back and guided her down the hall.

"You're looking well," she murmured to him. "I trust you're no worse off for our little excursion last night."

"No, but I'm a damn sight better dressed." He eyed her darkly. "Listen, you take a liking to my brother, and I'll—"

"Spank me?" she asked, then blinked innocently.

He growled low in his throat. "When did you develop a sense of humor?"

"Since I've been forced to deal with you. It was that or go mad."

He grunted. "Spankings are fine, but there are other punishments I'd rather employ." His attention swept over her lips and throat down to her breasts.

The pulse in her neck fluttered wildly.

A servant held open the door to the dining room for them. The massive table within had been cleared of everything but two bulging files. A small-boned gentleman wearing a dapper suit and sporting a combed mustache stood at the far end, apparently waiting for them. Jarrod introduced him as Mr. Tucker from the Pinkerton National Detective Agency as they all settled into chairs near the head of the table. When Clint held Maggie's for her she responded with a meaningful, "Thank you *so* much."

The door to the dining room burst open and Sophia watched in surprise as Oliver rushed in. "Sorry I'm late," he said. "Had trouble getting away from the office." He made a beeline directly to Sophia, then cushioned her hand between his. "Good to see you, my girl."

She smiled up at him. "I hadn't realized you would be joining us."

"Yes, yes. Your host was so good as to inform me of today's meeting."

"I'm glad." Once she'd made the necessary introductions, Oliver lowered his bulk into a chair across the table with a grateful sigh.

"Go ahead," Jarrod instructed the detective.

Mr. Tucker looked around the circle, took a breath. "As you may be aware, Mr. Stone hired our agency some days ago to begin an inquiry into the whereabouts of Mr. Adam Stone and into the happenings surrounding his disappearance. Particularly, Mr. Stone expressed interest in determining whether Adam Stone stole the Warren family fortune."

Tension coiled within Sophia.

"We've yet to track down Adam Stone," he continued, "as Mr. Stone summoned me here while we were still in the process of gathering information. Mr. Stone has instructed me to share with you all that we've collected to this point." He steepled a hand atop one of the files before him. "This is the documentation we've been able to garner about the possible movements of Adam Stone over the past twenty years." He steepled his other hand on the other file. "At Mr. Stone's request we've also collected information on every person employed at Blackhaw Manor at the time of the robbery. This file contains those records."

Quiet swished about the gathering. Sophia stared at the files, wondering if she dared hope that the clue she needed—just that one clue—could possibly be waiting there for her to find.

"Let's get started," Jarrod said, rising to his feet and flipping open the cover of the nearest file.

"So what's really going on between you and Sophia LaRue?" J. T. asked Jarrod late that night. The three brothers were sitting together in the library, Jarrod staring into the steam from his coffee, the other two nursing whiskeys.

"Jarrod?" J. T. prompted.

Jarrod looked up, discovered them both watching him expectantly. "What was that?"

"Sophia LaRue," J. T. prompted. "Last we knew you suspected her of being the mistress of Twilight's Ghost."

Behind Jarrod's chair a log toppled in the hearth, crackling heartily and causing the firelight to stir. "I discovered that she's not and never was the Ghost's mistress."

"No?" J. T. asked.

"No." It was the truth. After their mother's death there had been times when the harsh realities of what he'd had to do to provide for them would have terrified his brothers. He'd lied to them then because it was kinder. He'd never done so since. He was coming close, though, by withholding information about Sophia.

He leaned into his chair, tasted his coffee. He'd revealed her identity to Holden because Holden deserved to know. But he hesitated to tell anyone else, even Clint and J. T., because her safety hinged on his silence. It was a responsibility he took seriously.

"Without the Ghost's mistress to lead you to him," Clint said, "how close are you to finding him?"

"It doesn't matter anymore."

Both brothers regarded him levelly.

"I went to see Holden earlier this week in Huntsville." Jarrod inhaled slowly, fully. "He told me he's guilty."

Clint frowned, creases etching into the skin around his lips.

J. T. stared at him for a few seconds, then knocked back the rest of his whiskey in one swallow.

"Did you know?" Jarrod asked J. T. , who was closest in age to Holden and of them all the one who'd always understood their youngest brother best.

"No, but I suspected."

"God," Clint murmured. "He knew better, even back then, than to aid the Lucas gang."

"I thought so, too," Jarrod answered. "Apparently he held their horses for them for a nickel a day." Jarrod still hadn't accustomed himself to it, to having a brother behind bars that he couldn't help. "When I found out Holden had committed the crime I dropped my search for Twilight's Ghost. Can't very well pursue a man for being right."

Clint nodded.

"I took Sophia with me to see Holden. When he learned that she's been searching for our father all these years, he asked me to help her track him down. Said we'd all lived under his shadow long enough."

His brothers solemn gazes rose to meet his.

"Holden's never asked anything of me until now," Jarrod said. "I'm going to see it done."

"As will I," Clint said.

"And I," J.T. said.

Their words were superfluous. Even before he'd sent the telegram, he'd known they'd come. And he'd known they'd work beside him at all costs until the search was over, the job done, and their brother's only request met.

Holden socked the pillow, rolled onto his side on the cot and flung his bent arm over his eyes. Damn the memories. His lips parted with his breath. He could hear the rasp of his inhales and exhales against the relative stillness. He told himself not to think about it. To clear his head. To sleep. And still his thoughts slid to the night his mother had taken him to Blackhaw.

Even from far away, the house had looked scary to him, like it was haunted. His brothers had told him about dead people that didn't go away. Ghosts. Blackhaw was big and old and expensive. Probably lots of ghosts lived there. He slowed his steps, tugging on his mother's hand.

"Stop that," she said, pulling him forward.

"Mama—"

"Come along, Holden."

Grudgingly, he let her tow him alongside her. With his chin buried in the neck of his jacket, he stared at the house, watching it get closer, wishing he hadn't come. His chest started to tighten. When a dog barked, he jumped and wrapped his arms around his mother's legs. "Let's go back to the house."

"We will, just as soon as we find your father." Gently, she tried to pry his hands free.

He clung tighter. This was bad. He swallowed. They shouldn't have come out tonight. "Please."

She gave the top of his head a sensible kiss. "C'mon now, enough of that. Let's go." She unwrapped his arms from her legs and led him toward Blackhaw's tall fence with the sharp arrows on top.

There were no houses close to here and he wished there were.

"I think I . . ." Mother leaned forward, staring real hard. "I see him."

Relief washed through Holden. He looked up and saw him, too. It was dark on the other side of the fence, but he made out Pa's outline. He was carrying a big case, coming toward them down a pathway with pretty grass on either side. "Pa!" he called out.

His father glanced up. When he spotted them, he left the drive and cut across the grass in their direction. Mother and he hurried to the metal bars.

"What are you doing out at this hour?" Pa asked as he neared.

"Coming for you," Mother answered. "I was worried. You were supposed to be home two hours ago."

"I know. I—" he looked over his shoulder—"I had some important things to do, and time got away from me."

Mother nodded, her face tight. "I'm just glad to see you."

Pa looked down at him. "Hello, son."

"Hello, Pa." Holden smiled. His father was here. Nothing bad could happen to them now. No ghosts could kill them.

"Let's get you home," Pa said. He turned up the collar of his coat and started walking toward the gate.

They walked next to him on the other side of the bars.

Pa looked over his shoulder again. He started walking faster. "Perhaps we should hurry."

"All right," Holden said, and had tried his best to keep up.

Holden waited, patiently in the first seconds, then impatiently as the seconds ticked past and no more of the memory revealed itself. He squeezed his eyes shut. Why did he have this god-awful feeling that despite how fast he'd tried to walk, it hadn't been fast enough?

Chapter 18

Sophia yawned, then widened her eyes at the page before her in an effort to fight off sleep. Since the Stone brothers had arrived yesterday she'd spent nearly every waking minute poring over these Pinkerton documents. They hadn't yet yielded her the clue she sought, but she couldn't shake the feeling that if she just went over them one more time, she'd find the piece of evidence that would lead her to Adam Stone.

She yawned again, so wide that her cheek muscles stretched. Settling into the pale pink sofa and readjusting the tilt of her papers, she tried again to focus on print that kept blurring.

A knock echoed at her door.

"Who is it?" she called as she uncurled herself from sitting and moved across the room.

"A man bent on plundering your virtue."

Her senses rushed to humming life at the sound of Jarrod's voice. All vestiges of tiredness vanished. She stopped on her side of the door, rested a hand to her heart, and smiled with girlish delight. This giddiness that was so unlike her felt surprisingly wonderful. "Bent on plundering my virtue, eh? That doesn't sound very promising."

"Let me in and find out."

She opened the door to find him leaning one shoulder against the frame. The topmost button of his crisp white shirt was undone, and he held a bottle of red wine in one hand. His smile moved like a trickle of warm honey across his lips. "In the mood for plundering I see."

"Only if it's me plundering your head with a blunt object."

He chuckled. "I miss the days when I held the keys to this room and could enter anytime I wanted."

"Really?" She pulled the key from the inside of the lock and spun it around her finger. "I don't."

He made a grab for it. She gave a short shriek and jerked it out of his reach, before safely pocketing it. As she grinned her victory up at him she thought how nice it was to tease and be teased. She'd never had that kind of ease with a man before. It was cozy somehow.

"Care for hors d'oeuvres?" Jarrod asked.

"Hors d'oeuvres?"

"It's almost suppertime, and I thought you could probably use an appetizer."

"Well . . ." She gestured toward the stack of papers on the sofa.

"You can't seriously prefer reading those documents to spending time with me."

He was absolutely right. "Fine. I'll spend time with you."

"In here," he said to someone in the hallway, motioning with his head.

A servant carried in a tray bearing salmon croquettes, cheese and crackers, plates, linen napkins, and glasses. He arranged the food on the squat table in front of the sofa before scurrying out. Jarrod kicked closed the door behind them.

"We could have had hors d'oeuvres with the others," Sophia said.

"I'm sick of sharing you with them."

Her blood surged. "Oh."

He assessed her, his eyes hot with a look so blatantly suggestive her own body seethed in answer. To protect herself, she put the table between them then sat on the edge of the pink sofa. Distractedly, she moved croquettes and cheese wedges onto her plate until she realized she'd filled the tiny circle of china to overflowing.

Jarrod pulled a chair as near to her as he could manage. He poured wine for them both and handed her her glass. The ridges cut into the stemmed crystal felt hard and cool to the touch. No doubt both the glass and the wine inside it were just as expensive as their owner.

Yes, she thought wryly as she set aside her glass, just what she needed. To impair faculties already dizzy at his nearness with wine. A wise choice indeed.

He leaned into his chair, one leg outstretched toward her.

She compulsively popped cheese into her mouth.

He smiled devilishly, as if he could read her distress and had the audacity to like it. He kicked up the hem of her skirt a bit, then slid his shoe beneath and rubbed its tip idly against her instep. "To you," he said as he raised his wine.

"Thank you," she whispered, knowing she should move her foot and finding herself incapable of doing so. She understood that at some point in the future she'd pay with pain for every smile, every kiss, every flirtatious word between them. And yet right now, in this, the only moment that counted, that payment seemed too distant to matter.

Jarrod sipped his wine.

"I've just been looking back over some of the information Pinkerton collected on your father," she said to fill the quiet. "I've thought and thought, but none of this provides me with a new avenue for investigation."

He resettled his shoulders even deeper into his chair. "My brothers think we should split up and speak personally with all the people who worked at Blackhaw at the time."

"I think your brothers are wasting their time even reading about those employees. I know who stole my grandmother's money."

"They . . ." His forehead furrowed.

She waited for him to finish his sentence.

He narrowed his eyes at the door, then at her bed, then at her. Slowly, he brought a hand in front of his face and flexed it, studying the play of muscles with some confusion.

"Is something wrong?" she asked.

"I . . ." He clamped his fingertips against the bridge of his nose.

"Jarrod?"

"My vision, it's blurry."

"Blurry?" Anxiety pierced her. She returned her plate to the table with a clatter.

"I'm sorry . . . I'm . . ." He shook his head. "Sleepy all of a sudden." He leaned forward to set his glass on the table. He'd almost reached it when he slumped. The base of the glass struck the edge of the table and cracked. Wine spilled onto the carpet as the crystal tumbled to the floor.

She lunged toward Jarrod, caught his shoulders, and pressed him back into his chair before he could fall.

"Sophia," he said hoarsely, searching for her.

"I'm here." What was the matter? Her heart sped, beating fearfully against her ribs.

He looked for her, yet couldn't seem to find her.

"I'm here," she said again, gripping his shoulders.

"Something's wrong," he slurred.

"Yes." She darted a look over her shoulder, ridiculously searching for someone to help. The empty room stared back. She shook him slightly. "Stay awake."

"Sophia?" Blindly, he reached for her.

She grabbed one of his hands, pressed it against her waist. "I'm here."

In the next instant, his head lolled onto the back of the chair, and the hand she held went limp.

"No," she breathed. "No." Terror leaping inside her, she tried to jostle him back to consciousness. Except for his erratic breath, he didn't respond.

She took her hands away, made sure he wasn't going to slide onto the floor without her support, then turned and ran. What if something happened to him? The panicked refrain repeated in her mind again and again, faster and faster.

As she flew past the library she spotted Clint and Maggie within, a pile of papers spread before them. Her gaze locked on Clint as she skidded to a halt. "It's your brother." Her voice sounded wild, even to her.

"My brother?"

"Jarrod. Something's wrong. He's unconscious."

His face paled as he pushed to his feet. "Where is he?"

"I'll show you." She led Clint and Maggie back to her room as quickly as she'd come. Jarrod remained exactly as she'd left him. The sight of him like that caused dread to ball in her stomach. It seemed heinous for a man of his power and strength to be lying so still.

Clint rushed to his brother and tried to rouse him. When that failed he went behind Jarrod's chair and hooked his forearms beneath his brother's arms. "Help me get him to the bed."

Both Sophia and Maggie hurried to assist. Clint cleared the pillows from the bed with a swipe, and they managed to lay Jarrod across the mattress.

"What happened?" Clint asked her as he released buttons on his brother's shirt.

"Jarrod brought food. He seemed fine when he came in, but shortly after we started eating he told me his vision was blurry. Moments later he said he was sleepy. His speech—his speech was slurred. Then he asked for me again and again and I answered him that I was here but he didn't seem able to see me."

"It sounds like poison." Clint moved across the room to stare down at the food and at the wine that was soaking into the carpet like blood.

Maggie came up beside Sophia and gripped her hand.

"Did you eat any of this?" Clint asked curtly.

"Yes."

"Did Jarrod?"

"No. But he did have some of the wine."

"And you didn't."

"No."

Clint lifted the bottle and sniffed its contents. "Did this come to you uncorked?"

Sophia tried to steady herself enough to think calmly, to remember. "I don't recall Jarrod uncorking it, so it must have."

"We need to get a doctor. Fast."

"I'll fetch him," Sophia answered. "I know where his office is."

"I can go," Maggie offered.

"No." She'd go insane if forced to stand here waiting and wringing her hands. "I . . . I need to do this for him." Without pausing to collect coat, hat, or gloves, Sophia fled the room and the sight of Jarrod's lifeless body. As she ran from the house to the stables, her heeled shoes pounded hard against the earth. The dusk's chilling wind whipped at her, flaying her worry higher.

When she reached the mouth of the stables, the one boy working within jumped to attention.

"I need my horse," she said breathlessly.

The boy caught the current of her desperation and worked at breakneck pace to saddle Duchess. Sophia snatched a bridle off a peg. Her fingers shook as she fastened the straps around Duchess's head.

"There," the boy said, taking hold of the reins so that she could mount up.

She hoisted herself into the sidesaddle.

"Wait." He grabbed a blanket from a nearby hay bale and handed it to her. "Here you are, ma'am."

She nodded her thanks and goaded Duchess forward.

The horse, seeming to sense her urgency, stretched her legs into a gallop. They charged along the drive then down the road that led to town. Sophia gave Duchess her head, allowing her to carry her so fast that the ground streaked by beneath her.

Jarrod needed her. He'd never needed her before, and if it was the last thing she did, she was going to bring the doctor to him in the shortest possible time. She prayed she wouldn't be too late.

"Faster," she whispered to Duchess as she leaned over the animal's back. She pulled the snapping blanket around her shoulders, taking what thin protection it provided. "Faster."

By the time the doctor turned his buggy onto Jarrod's property some forty minutes later, darkness had fallen. Sophia sat beside Doc Scoggins as tense and tight as a piano wire. Had she been able to speed their return to Jarrod by running behind the buggy and pushing, she'd have done so. It would have been better than sitting here with her hands clenched in her lap while her imagination tortured her with one horrifying scenario after another.

The instant they pulled up in front of Jarrod's brightly lit house, she jumped down from the vehicle. It took the doctor slightly longer to disembark, then gather his leather satchel. She furtively licked her lips and wished he'd hurry.

J. T. met them halfway up the stairs.

"How's Jarrod?" she asked him.

"Not good," he said, his expression grave.

Sophia wanted to wail. At least . . . at least "not good" meant he was still alive. She strove to console herself with that. "J. T. Stone, this is Dr. Scoggins." The doctor was a youngish man, soft-spoken with bookish spectacles and competent hands.

"What can you tell me about the patient's current condition?" the doctor asked, as J. T. led them into the house and along the central hallway.

"He's not regained consciousness and his breath is choppy," J. T. answered.

Dr. Scoggins frowned, nodded.

J. T. escorted them to Jarrod's bedroom, where they'd moved him in her absence. Clint and Maggie stepped away from the thronelike bed, presenting her with a view of Jarrod. Her emotions caught.

The doctor approached him and set aside his satchel. Silence descended as he pressed his thumb to Jarrod's wrist to measure his pulse.

Sophia stood numbly at the foot of the bed. This couldn't be real. She stared at Jarrod mutely—black hair tousled against the white of his pillows, uncompromising facial features, powerfully corded neck, muscled limbs. All of it too slack. Again, it struck her as fundamentally wrong for a man like him to be robbed of his strength.

"You told me, Mrs. LaRue, that he took just two or three sips of the wine?" the doctor asked.

"That's correct." She'd related everything she knew during their ride.

"And this occurred less than an hour ago."

"Yes."

"Ordinarily for a patient who's ingested a poisonous substance, I'd immediately prescribe water and ipecac. With someone who's unconscious, however"—his lips set in a thin line—"there's a danger of choking on the water, and ipecac is out of the question. Have you tried to rouse him?"

"Again and again," Clint answered.

"Well, perhaps if we administer water in very small amounts with a dropper." He moved to his bag and un-buckled the latch. "If someone would be so good as to fetch me some water."

Maggie rushed from the room.

The doctor positioned a clean cloth on the nightstand and set a dropper upon it before turning to the brothers. "I'll need to test the wine he drank in order to try to de-termine which poison was used. Only then can I admin-ister the correct anecdote."

"I'll get the wine." J. T. strode out.

"Mrs. LaRue?" the doctor said.

Dazedly, she moved her gaze to him.

"If I may ask for your assistance." He motioned to the dropper. She approached, and he showed her how to po-sition it within Jarrod's mouth so the fluid would dribble down the side of his throat. Maggie returned with a bowl full of water, and Sophia made her first attempt, cradling Jarrod's jaw with one hand, holding the dropper with the other. The unnatural coolness of his skin sent chills down her spine. *Oh, God, let him not die.*

"Good," the doctor said. "That's just fine. Nice and slow." He watched her as he shed his coat and rolled up his shirtsleeves. "Continue just as you are."

When J. T. returned the doctor asked for both broth-ers' help in testing the wine. All three left for the kitchen.

Maggie neared and softly rubbed Sophia's back.

Sophia had no lighthearted words or optimistic senti-ments to voice. She simply kept filling the dropper, slowly trickling water down Jarrod's throat, waiting for him to swallow.

"I'll give you a little privacy," Maggie murmured.

Sophia was only vaguely aware of the door clicking closed.

Without anyone left to see, she let hot moisture slip from her eyes down her cheeks. When next she drew water into the dropper, she tenderly, almost desperately, brushed the fingers of her free hand along his forehead, around an eye, down his cheek. Tears ran under her jaw and into her collar.

This was her fault. Jarrod had never asked for this. The search for Adam Stone had been hers. Never, never his. If someone was out to hurt one of them, and someone clearly was, it should rightfully have been her. She'd committed to the risks of her job, she'd accepted the dangers. She was the one they'd warned not to continue. Her. Not Jarrod. This wasn't his fight. He hadn't wanted it. He was a businessman, for God's sake. All he'd ever truly cared about was freeing his brother.

She couldn't see, suddenly, the telltale rise and fall of his chest. Frantic, she bent an ear to his lips. Air flowed from his lungs. Jerky and shallow, but audible. As she slipped the dropper into his mouth, the prayers she'd learned in the orphanage rose unbidden to her lips and poured forth in a quiet, unbroken stream.

She prayed and prayed and prayed until her world and all the will she possessed narrowed to include nothing but Jarrod, the water, and her urgent petitions to God.

She'd lost track of time during this endless night. Rhythmically, she drew more liquid into the dropper, moved it to Jarrod's mouth. The doctor had come to her and told her that he'd been unable to determine which poison had been used. That was perhaps an hour ago. Perhaps four. He'd been too compassionate to tell her that Jarrod would probably die. He hadn't needed to say the words. She'd read apology and pity in his eyes.

She'd seen that look before, on the face of another doctor twenty years ago. He'd told her then to sit with her grandmother because the end was near, and he didn't think her grandmother would survive the night. Lord, she hadn't wanted to enter that room and sit with her grandmother. She'd been terrified to see her like that. To watch her die. But she'd made herself go in and she'd sat on the edge of her grandmother's bed and she'd held her hand. She'd done it because there was no one else to do it. And because maybe, if she stayed and held her hand tight enough, her grandmother wouldn't go away and abandon her.

Her heart wrung with pain, reminding her how excruciating it was to be left behind, alone.

She gazed at Jarrod, his handsome face lit by the somber light of the bedside lamp. She never should have let herself care for him. She'd been so wary these many years, so independent and self-sufficient. So careful not to give over her dreams into the hands of another. Then Jarrod had stalked into her life, and though she'd tried to hide, he'd not allowed her to. He'd ripped off her shields and forced her to ride on a fairy horse, and shown her stars, and challenged her to sail as fast as the wind. Anything, anything else she could have withstood. But she'd been helpless in the face of his pursuit to unlock the joy she'd buried so deep inside herself she'd forgotten where to find it.

Joy, indeed, she thought bitterly. Look where his efforts to help her had gotten him. He was lying prone and sick unto death. His vast sums of money and his enormous power couldn't help him now.

"Sophia, let me do that," J. T. said, walking up behind her.

They'd all been coming to her for hours, asking to take over this job. Shadows sitting in the room's chairs, drifting in and out of the room's space. The only constant shadow had been Maxine. Jarrod's dog had been guarding him from the edge of his bed for almost as long as Sophia had been tending him. She tried not to look at the retriever because the dog's sad, dark eyes broke her heart.

"No," she said quietly but firmly to J. T..

"Sophia, you can't go on this way. You need your rest."

"I have to stay a little longer."

"You've done enough already."

"No. I'm not finished yet." She couldn't explain to J. T. or even to herself what her heart believed to be true. That maybe . . . maybe if she kept administering tiny amounts of water to Jarrod, if she didn't leave his side, that he wouldn't die.

That belief hadn't saved her grandmother.

But it would save Jarrod, she stubbornly told herself. It had to. And so she'd stay.

Sophia roused groggily as she was lifted. Granite arms. A rich masculine scent. Jarrod. No. They passed into the hall and candlelight played over the planes and hollows of J. T.'s face.

Her senses groped for a hold on reality. She must have fallen asleep at Jarrod's side. A bolt of alarm followed. "I need to go back."

"I'm taking you to bed," J. T. answered without looking down at her.

"No, I promise I won't fall asleep again. I can go longer—"

"Shhh. Enough. You're exhausted, and I'm taking you to bed."

"He needs water. The antidote—"

"Clint's feeding it to him now. I'll feed it to him next."

"He'll be alone."

"We won't leave him alone for a second, I swear it."

He'll die without me there. The certainty swirled about her in a demon rush, like wind beating off vulture's wings.

J. T. laid her on her bed. As softness absorbed her, wakefulness drifted away, though she tried to grasp it back. This was terribly wrong. All wrong. He'd die without her there to keep him alive.

He'd die.

Chapter 19

Sophia cracked open her eyes. Gradually, the winter sunlight glimmering around the edges of her curtains swirled into focus. It was morning. . . .

Memories of the past night came back to her in a single, violent throb. She pushed herself to sitting. Her hair tumbled around her shoulders in disarray. With a downward glance she discovered that she was still wearing yesterday's wrinkled clothing. She slid her feet over the edge of the bed and her shoes peeked out at her from beneath her hem.

Jarrod. Oh my God, how long have I slept?

She swiveled the little gilt clock atop the bedside table toward her. Eleven o'clock. Eleven o'clock! Dismay rushed through her. So long! When she shouldn't have let herself fall asleep in the first place.

She ran into the hallway.

The house beyond greeted her with deathly quiet. It was the unnatural, solemn quiet of a cathedral, and it caused the tiny hairs on her arms to lift. No maids scurried around corners, as they usually did. No friendly chatter or the sounds of clanging pots emanated from the direction of the kitchen.

Her feet carried her fast, then faster toward Jarrod's bedroom, her panic mounting with each step. She saw no one. The house had been rendered barren, stripped of its life.

A sob climbed up her chest. *Jarrod.*

She pushed open his door, terrified to discover what waited within. Clint and J. T. were standing with the doctor near the bed. Maxine was still at her post, and Jarrod was still where she'd left him, eyes closed, unmoving. The tops of his bronzed shoulders were bare above the line of the sheet.

Sophia eased to a stop. Heart pounding in her chest like cannon fire, she looked to his brothers.

J. T. met her gaze . . . and smiled. *Smiled.*

A wild little hope twirled to life in her abdomen.

"He regained consciousness near dawn," J. T. said.

"He—he actually spoke?"

"Some. He was delirious, but the doctor said that was to be expected."

The flare of hope rose and expanded, heating every chilled, frightened place inside her. "And now?" she asked hoarsely.

"Now he's sleeping," Dr. Scoggins answered. His shirt looked as scrunched as her own clothing did, and red rimmed his eyes. Despite that, she could clearly read the pride in him, the deep satisfaction of a job well-done.

"Sleeping," she repeated, overwhelmed with a relief that was purest white, when everything for so many hours had been filthiest black. She should have known Jarrod would do battle against the poison and win. He was the most willful, hardheaded man she'd ever met.

"A good sound sleep," Dr. Scoggins commented. "He's strong, and his body fought it off. He's going to be fine."

She didn't have the right words to say. Through a mist of tears she brought up her hands, pressed them to her lips, her cheeks, then overlapped them above her heart. "Thank you, Doctor, for your work."

"You're welcome. Thank you for all you did."

"Yes," Clint said. "Thank you."

J. T. nodded his appreciation.

"It was nothing," she whispered as her gaze returned to Jarrod. Their gratitude made her feel like a fraud. If they knew that this was all her fault, they'd understand just how insignificant her efforts had been in the face of her responsibility. "What happens now?"

"We'll let him sleep as long as his body demands," the doctor answered. "Then I'll prescribe a round of treatments that will keep him in bed for two days. After that, he should be well on his way to recovery."

She smiled tremulously, then took her time memorizing Jarrod's face. The straight eyebrows that could lift with humor or lower with danger. The deep-set eyes. The muscled cheeks, burnished this morning with the beginnings of a beard. The hair as black as a raven's wing. All of it she collected in her memory, packing it lovingly there.

"You can come closer," J. T. said with a wry smile. He beckoned her forward.

"No," she said softly and took a step back. It was well past time that she retreat, not just from this room but from this house. After what had happened, she could no longer deceive herself about that. "Please excuse me," she murmured before letting herself out.

"Sophia," J. T. called from behind her when she was only a few yards down the hallway.

She turned. Clint was standing in the middle of the corridor, his hands in his pockets. J. T. leaned against the doorframe of Jarrod's room. Both stances were so like their older brother.

"Where are you going?" J. T. asked.

"I'm going home."

"Home?"

"I still live at Blackhaw, the home my grandmother left me."

J. T. nodded slowly, seeming to measure her. "I know Jarrod would be glad for you to stay here if you're willing."

"For as long as you like," Clint added.

"Of course," J. T. said, "there are no servants for the time being."

"I noticed that," she said.

"Until we figure out who did this—"

"Your father poisoned Jarrod. He's also the one that sent men to attack me in order to scare us off the search."

"That may be," J. T. said, "but whoever did this must have also had someone on the inside in order to have access to the wine. Until we know which servant that is, we don't want any of them lingering around."

Sophia nodded.

"Luckily, Clint here can clean some. And I'm not awful with a spatula." J. T.'s eyes twinkled persuasively. "It won't be the style to which you're accustomed . . ."

"It's not that," she assured them. "It's kind of you to invite me to stay, but the truth is that I've been away from home too long already."

"What about the case?" Clint asked. "We haven't found my father yet."

A piece, a vital piece inside herself, stilled. Cleared. So it had come to this. The road she'd been doggedly following for twenty years ended here in this hallway. She swallowed. "I'm finished pursuing your father. I'm just . . . just finished. People have been hurt."

J. T. regarded her with frank surprise. "You mean this thing with Jarrod?"

"Yes." That, and other hurts. What she'd done to Holden. What she'd done to herself by gathering bitterness and hatred into her breast and using it as fuel. At some point even a dream of justice could cost too much. It was time to end it.

"I'll tell you right now," J. T. said, "Jarrod's not going to give up the search."

"Neither are we," Clint said.

"Jarrod promised Holden we'd find our father," J. T. explained simply.

"I know," she said. "I wish you the very best of luck. I've told Jarrod as much as I can remember about the circumstances surrounding your father's disappearance, and my friend Oliver Kinsworthy knows as much about the information we've gathered over the past years as I do. I'm sure he'll be willing to assist you."

"But not you," Clint said.

"No," she said quietly. "Not me."

The sound of clicking nails heralded Maxine's arrival in the doorway. The dog sat next to J. T.'s leg and looked up at Sophia with her sweet, graying face.

"Where did Jarrod get Maxine?" Sophia asked. For days, she'd wondered about that and about the poverty Jarrod had eluded to after their mother's death.

"It was years ago," J. T. answered. "How old is Maxine?" he asked Clint.

"At least ten."

"I'd say twelve. Anyway, she belonged to one of Jarrod's employees up until the time Jarrod saw him kick her, then beat her with a rope. Jarrod fired the man and kept the dog."

Sophia had figured as much. She thought of all the hours Maxine had spent last night, keeping watch over a man most of the country believed to be a ruthless brute. A brute who had rescued his dog and raised his brothers. "There's one other thing," she said to Clint and J. T., taking time to select her words. "Just how . . . difficult were the years after your mother's death?"

The grimness of their faces in response to her question told her almost everything she needed to know.

"However poor a person can be and still survive," Clint answered, "that's how poor we were for a while. Looking back, I still don't know how Jarrod managed to scrape together enough food for us every month."

"But he always did," J. T. said. "Somehow, he always did."

Understanding wove among the three of them. Blackhaw's demise had absolved no one. It had marked them all in the years that followed. "Thank you for telling me," she said. Then after a few moments, "I—" She gestured in the direction of her room. "I'd best be going."

The brothers dipped their chins.

Sophia turned and walked away from them, from Jarrod.

This was a glorious day, she told herself, a day of thanksgiving. Jarrod was going to be well. If she felt a twinge of heartsickness to be leaving him and his home, to be pulling out of the chase, to be saying good-bye to his brothers, she refused to credit it. Jarrod was going to be well. That's all that mattered.

Back inside her room, she divested every one of the garments she wore, garments Jarrod had allowed her to borrow. After rustling through the dresser in the closet, she came up with the stockings, drawers, and chemise she'd worn here that first day. Jammed at the rear of the clothing rack she located her bodice and skirt, her brown coat, and her cream-colored hat.

The cut of her own clothing, the coarse scratch of its fabric, felt strange to her. She eyed herself in the mirror as she hastily bound her hair. These were her clothes, the only clothes of her own she'd worn in days, and yet they didn't quite seem to fit. In fact, on the whole, she didn't look like herself to herself anymore. Her hair simply refused to be brushed back as tightly as it used to into a bun. A rosy hue burnished her cheeks, and her eyes shone. During her stay, something fundamental had changed.

Relentlessly, she fought to force her hair back into the old ways. Then she collected the bag containing her few toiletries and scooped up her parasol. She revolved in a circle, taking in the room Jarrod had created especially for her.

Everything in it belonged to him. The artwork, the books, the linens. She glanced down at herself, double-checking the items she wore and carried. She didn't want to take a single thing from Jarrod—not a scarf, not a slip of paper, not a hatpin.

Gathering close her pride, she walked through the door without looking back. *This is a happy day*, she told herself. *Jarrod is well.*

Mrs. Dewberry scurried into Sophia's bedroom at Blackhaw ahead of both Sophia and Maggie. In a flurry over their unexpected return, the housekeeper bustled around the room, throwing open the curtains, cracking the windows, and keeping up a steady stream of chatter Sophia barely heard.

How peculiar to be back in this place where nothing had changed, when so much had changed in her heart. Distractedly, she pulled loose the hat bow beneath her chin.

". . . nice pot of tea. How does that sound?"

Sophia turned to find Mrs. Dewberry watching her expectantly.

"That sounds heavenly. Thank you."

"And some peach pie, I think." Mrs. Dewberry wiped her hands on her skirts and smiled. "It just so happens that I soaked the peaches last night and made up a lovely pie for Mr. Dewberry and me just this morning. Still warm, it is. I'll be back in two shakes of a lamb's tail." When she closed the door behind her, the ensuing quiet contrasted sharply with the conversation that had enlivened the space moments before.

Sophia took a deep breath and lofted her hat onto the white quilt. "It seems as if I ought to have something to unpack after such a long absence."

"I know, that is odd, how thoroughly he provided for you while you were gone," Maggie said, flopping into the room's single armchair. "How is it to be back?"

"Lovely," Sophia answered automatically. This was

home. Sweet, unmistakable home, and there was a kind of comfort in that that even Jarrod Stone with all his thousands could never purchase or bottle. So why did she still feel, despite every logical lecture she'd given herself today, so inexplicably melancholy?

Because in coming home she'd left Jarrod behind.

A desolate kind of hollowness dragged at her, making her wish she could crawl into bed, pull the covers over her head, and simply . . . huddle.

Instead, she went to the nearest window and rested her hand on the side casing. Beneath the pads of her fingers she could feel the ridges that had formed when cracking paint had been coated over with fresh. The texture spoke to her of the years and the heritage of her house. Lovingly, possessively, she rubbed her thumb over the surface.

She'd been raised in this bedroom, had looked out these very panes of glass as a small child. The same drive still snaked its way through rolling orchards. The same black-iron gate with spires on top still stood sentinel at the property's rim. The same squirrels dashed across the same ground and climbed the same trees. Blackhaw. The word—the *place*—resonated with her and always would.

Always, she thought with a pang. She no longer had the promise of always. Blackhaw's auction was set for just four days from now, and unless she could find her counterfeiter, collect her reward, and pay the taxes in time, then Blackhaw would no longer belong to her. Her *always* would end in exactly four days, and she, Maggie, and the Dewberrys would be cast out onto the street. Mother above, how could the time have slipped away from her so quickly? "Do you realize we only have a few days left to solve the counterfeiting case?" she asked, turning toward Maggie.

"Unfortunately, yes," Maggie answered.

"So." Sophia shook out her arms and hands, then restlessly began to pace. "Let's go over what we know about our counterfeiter."

Maggie nodded and propped her long, narrow feet on the footrest with the needlepoint cushion of roses. "Well," she began, ticking off one finger, "on your escapes from Jarrod's house you combed the warehouse district."

"Yes, where I saw and heard exactly nothing of import."

"At your request I examined ownership and leasing information on the warehouses." Maggie ticked off another finger. "All appear to be legitimate businesses."

"Or seemingly legitimate."

"I think investigating the warehouses further is a waste of our time, Sophia. The counterfeiting presses could be anywhere. They could feasibly be hidden in someone's backyard shack."

"Right." She paced onward, toying with the fingernails of one hand.

"Which brings us to your ill-fated trip with Jarrod to the stationer's." Maggie ticked off a third finger. "According to the receipt you found there, a Mr. Silas Clarke had ordered a conspicuously large amount of paper and ink."

"Correct." Though she'd heard it all before, hearing it aloud again helped her order it in her mind.

"Our Mr. Clarke is an artist who sells his work off a cart on Main Street. He works in various mediums, including paper and ink. Soft-spoken man. Tall. Nice enough. Especially good at watercolors."

"And potentially as talented at designing counterfeiting plates. Go on."

"He moved here three years ago. No family relations. Clean criminal record, so far as the Agency knows."

"What else?"

"Nothing else."

Sophia perched on the edge of her bed. None of this was stirring her instincts, none of it was heating her blood the way an investigation usually did when she was getting close. She groaned and kneaded her temples. "Mr. Clarke is still our best lead. Do we know where he lives?"

"No, but we could follow him home from his cart."

"I'll do that today. Could be he's living above his means. Maybe he has a costly carriage sitting out back. Or an expensive hobby we ought to know about."

"Could be." Maggie didn't appear very hopeful. "What'll you do if you spot something suspicious?"

"Search his house."

"And if that yields nothing?"

"Then I'll need an opportunity to find out more about him another way, possibly speak with someone who knows him."

Maggie sat up straighter in her chair. "The masquerade ball."

Sophia combed her memory. "The ones the McBrayers give every year?"

"Yes." Maggie's eyes lit with anticipation. "It's night after next. You received an invitation just like always, and I accepted for you, hoping you'd be home by then.

There'll be roomfuls of people to talk with. No telling what you might uncover about Mr. Clarke through a little careful conversation. Not to mention, you'd get to don a costume."

Donning a costume held very little appeal for her. Still, the plan had merit—

A knock sounded at the door. "Tea, darlings," Mrs. Dewberry called. She proudly carried in two plates bearing enormous wedges of peach pie. The smell of fresh pastry crust wafted in her wake. Mr. Dewberry followed his wife, bearing a tray set for tea.

Maggie sprang from her chair and hurried to pull into position the little walnut table that ordinarily clung to the armchair's side. Their housekeeper clucked as she arranged everything, then straightened, and knitted her dimpled hands together. "Do you need anything else?"

"This is more than enough already," Sophia answered. "Thank you."

"Of course, dear. So glad to have you home." She reached out and patted her cheek. "Dinner's at six," she reminded them as she herded her husband out.

Sophia pulled her dressing-table stool up to the table and started pouring tea, while Maggie rummaged around in the bottom of the armoire. "Here it is," Maggie finally declared. She held aloft a bottle of claret as she rose to her feet. "Not a moment too soon."

"None for me," Sophia said as Maggie returned to the armchair.

"Oh, *please*, Sophia." Maggie rolled her eyes and poured a healthy swig into Sophia's cup. "Ordinarily I let you get away with that, but today is not a day for drinking plain tea." She sloshed a generous amount into her own cup, then added three cubes of sugar. On her pie,

Maggie drizzled a river of cream. Paused, made her river into a delta, then set about stirring her tea. Stirring and stirring and stirring, her gaze straying to the windows.

"You miss Clint," Sophia guessed.

Maggie's attention snapped to her. "Not as much as you're pretending not to miss Jarrod."

Because Sophia couldn't stand to think about Jarrod, much less talk about him, she poured her own cream delta atop her slice of pie and took a bite.

"Yes, I miss Clint," Maggie said after a time, "more, even, than claret and pie can cure, which is terribly depressing." She forked off some pie, swallowed. "Have you ever seen such a gorgeous man?"

"He's very handsome."

"He's divine. Wonderful to look at and quiet. I always did like that combination in a man. There's just something about those quiet ones. Still waters and all that." She pointed her fork at Sophia. "I bet he's very well endowed."

"Maggie!"

"Well, I bet he is."

"Margaret Elizabeth May," Sophia whispered.

"I bet Jarrod is too, for that matter."

Sophia could only gape.

"Of course, you probably already know that." Maggie winked roguishly and chewed another bite of pie.

"We were talking about you and Clint."

"I wish there was a me and Clint. But honestly, Sophia." Her expression cleared of humor. "Let's be frank. It's not as if a woman like me is ever going to win a man like Clint Stone. I may as well slam a rock against my head hoping to make water."

"That's not true, Maggie—"

"Yes it is, you're just too kind to say so." She re-garded Sophia soberly. "I don't have any illusions about myself. However, you and Jarrod, now that has real pos-sibility."

"It does not!"

"Why? You certainly can't say he's too ugly or that he won't be able to provide for you."

"No." Sophia frowned. "For one, he loathes my career and has told me he'd never let me do it if I were his."

Maggie's eyes widened. "He actually said if you were 'his'?"

"Yes, and secondly, I think he's far more interested in bedding me than in anything more respectable. Then there's his personality. . . ."

"What's wrong with his personality?"

"Wrong? He's rude, bossy—"

"Protective, smart, assertive, and he makes you laugh. He actually has the power to *make you laugh*, Sophia. He gave you a ride on Cinderella's horse and named a star after you."

She stared at her friend, lips parted to say something when there was nothing to say. Maggie was right, of course. It was silly to keep protesting it aloud. For all his faults, Jarrod had given her the ability to glimpse herself as she might have been without the wounds. For a few hours, he'd allowed her to be free. She heaved a sigh. "I found out today that he adopted his dog after he saw her being beaten."

"And there's the way he looks at you every time you enter a room," Maggie said persuasively.

"He provided for his brothers after their mother died. There was a time when they barely had enough money to eat."

"Oh, and one of the maids told me yesterday that when a member of the kitchen staff found herself in a delicate condition—unmarried, you understand—that he bought her a home to live in, gave her money, and said he'd welcome her to keep working for him."

"Really?" Sophia considered impaling herself on a bedpost and ending her misery.

"And even when you were supposed to be his prisoner he kept giving you all those clothes, the gifts. And he's forever asking after your comfort and worrying over your safety."

"So we've established that he's wonderful." Sophia took in a breath that burned. "It's still hopeless, Maggie."

"Hopeless? I'd sell my eyeballs to receive that kind of treatment from Clint."

She regarded her friend through a haze of pain. It *was* hopeless. To talk about it as if it weren't was not only bitterly painful but a pointless waste of time. She and Jarrod had no future. If only that knowledge had hindered her foolish heart from falling for him so completely.

"All right," Maggie murmured, taking pity on her. "We can try to drown our sorrows in claret if you'd rather not talk." She lifted her cup and waited until Sophia lifted hers. They clinked them together. "Bottoms up."

Sophia took a deep sip, then cradled her cup in both hands. The white walls of this room had always seemed so clean and crisp. Now they looked a bit austere. The green rug patterned with a simple floral motif of flowers and vines was scarred with worn patches she'd never noticed before, and her dressing table bore pockmarks and scratches even Mrs. Dewberry's polishing couldn't erase.

Had she become so spoiled during her time at Jarrod's that her own room looked shabby to her now? No. If Jarrod were here, the surroundings would seem as rich as if they'd been drenched in gold. It wasn't its humbleness that stole the light and life from this place. It was his absence.

Oh, dear. She was in very deep trouble. Hastily, she took another drink.

The great room of the McBrayers' home sparkled not only with sconces of candles and neckfuls of jewels, but with the costumes of their ball guests. Sophia resettled her own spidery mask and smiled politely at a matador and his wife, Venus, as they passed.

Since she'd returned to Blackhaw a day and a half ago, Mrs. Dewberry had outdone herself concocting her black widow disguise. Sophia's ebony mask and her long ebony gloves sparkled with lines of black beads that crisscrossed to form a glittering web. Her onyx princess dress was slim and sleek, cut in one line from shoulder to hem. Around her waist she wore a chain that dipped into a vee in front to suspend a fat fake ruby.

She'd had aspirations of confining her hair into a bun that would call to mind the shape of a spider's body. But since the long dark strands continued to misbehave, she'd settled on arranging it in loose curls at the nape of her neck.

"What a lovely costume, my dear."

Sophia looked up to see Joseph Stewart, an old acquaintance, approach with a smile.

"Why thank you. I very much admire the cleverness of yours." Though one of the largest and most important importers of coffee and liquor in town, he was dressed tonight in the garb of a pirate. A graying, distinguished pirate.

They exchanged pleasantries, then companionably watched the spectacle swirling about them.

"Oh, would you look at this," Sophia said, as if just noticing the painting that hung on the wall nearby. She'd steered dozens of people through this same conversation tonight, though she'd yet to receive a single decent clue about Silas Clarke. Couple that with the fact that his modest apartments had also failed to yield her a clue, and she was beginning to feel desperate.

"Why, yes, indeed." He turned to study the piece, lacing his fingers together behind his back.

"The expression of the young girl is beautifully rendered," Sophia said after a moment. "Don't you agree?"

"Quite, quite."

"I've been considering the acquisition of a few new pieces, myself."

"Have you?" He regarded her with kindly interest.

"Yes and I'm particularly interested in the work of local artists. I thought it might be nice to fill my parlor with Galveston's finest talent."

"What a capital idea."

"Is there anyone here locally you'd recommend?"

"Ah . . . There's Will Doogan, of course," Mr. Stewart said. "Horatio Clem is good. So's Matthew Sage."

"What of Silas Clarke?" she asked smoothly. "Have you had an opportunity to familiarize yourself with his work?"

"Silas Clarke," he repeated, seeming to test the name. "No, no I don't believe I have."

Her hopes dropped.

"Wait." He tilted his head to the side. "Is he the one. . . . I'd stay clear of him, my dear. I heard a rumor about him once."

"A rumor?" For the first time in days, her intuition stirred.

"I hate to spread the things."

"As do I." She waited, knowing he'd be unable to resist sharing the tidbit.

He leaned closer. "I was told some time ago that Mr. Clarke was brought to trial to face criminal charges."

Her pulse picked up speed. "What charges?"

"I'm not sure."

"Was he found guilty?"

"I don't believe so."

That would explain why Maggie had told her he had a clean record. In the eyes of the government, he did.

"If I remember correctly," Mr. Stewart said, "he hired himself capable representation."

"I don't recall hearing a thing about this."

"No, you wouldn't have as the trial wasn't held in Galveston."

"You don't say."

"Again if I remember correctly"—he chuckled wryly and tapped his forehead—"it was held in . . . oh . . . I can't recall. One of the small towns near here along the coast."

She gave an interested murmur. "I shall heed your advice and concentrate my efforts on artists other than Silas Clarke."

"Might be wise."

Inwardly, her thoughts churned. She and Maggie

could split up tomorrow and travel to the courthouses of the surrounding towns.

Vaguely, she noticed that the hum of conversation in the great room had waned. Perhaps if they rifled though enough court records, they could discover just what Mr. Clarke had been accused of. Probably too much to hope that it had been counterfeiting.

The small talk dropped in volume another notch. Brow furrowed, Sophia glanced toward the room's open double doors.

Across the yards her gaze collided with the turbulent green eyes of Jarrod Stone. The stare that bore into her with razor-sharp intensity informed her that the time had come to reckon with the devil.

Chapter 20

Oh, my Lord. Every nerve in Sophia's body sprang to life.

He stood framed in the open doorway, as uncompromising and unapologetic as ever. He'd not bothered with a costume. He wore a plain black tailcoat and narrow black trousers with a band of braid covering the outer seam. His white shirt was snowy against his olive skin, his bow tie impeccably tied. He looked like what he was, a surpassingly handsome, ridiculously rich, absurdly powerful oil baron.

His gaze never veering from her, he strode into the room as if he owned it and cut a path directly toward her. The crowd parted to make way for him, their stares avid.

"Is that Jarrod Stone?" Mr. Stewart asked under his breath.

She couldn't talk, couldn't look away from the spell of Jarrod's eyes, so she simply nodded.

This wasn't the same man she'd left a few days before. That man had been desperately sick. This man betrayed no trace of vulnerability. His gait, his posture, and his expression projected only strength, anger, and a determination so fierce it could have caused cold water to churn into a boil.

Amid a buzz of whispers, he came to a halt before her, towering over her. "Mrs. LaRue."

A shiver coursed down her back, arms, hips. "Mr. Stone."

"May I have a word with you in private?"

It would be better if she didn't. Private meetings with him had almost always ended in disaster for her, both in circumstance and emotion. She shot a look at Mr. Stewart, hoping for assistance from his quarter. Unfortunately, he was too busy studying Jarrod with awed respect to come to her aid.

"Certainly," Sophia said, succeeding at keeping her voice even. "If you'll excuse us, Mr. Stewart—"

Jarrod took her by the arm and dragged her away before she could finish her sentence. His grip, firm and commanding, scalded her sensitized flesh. She glanced down at it and thought how much she'd always liked his hands, the blunt fingers, the veins beneath the skin, the masterful way they touched her.

What an absurd thing to think at a moment like this. She was right this minute on her way to meet her doom, and she was rhapsodizing over Jarrod's hands.

He escorted her from the great room into the hallway and through the first door on their right before releasing her. Sophia walked more deeply into the sitting room, which was furnished in luxurious shades of bronze and ivory. The firelight from the hearth reflected off the silver coffee urn and matching cups that had been assembled on a round table for the guests.

Jarrod shut the door, leaving Sophia brutally aware of their isolation. She turned to face him by slow degrees.

"Take off the mask," he ordered. "I want to see your face."

Her fingers shaking the tiniest bit, she reached up and removed the mask.

He kept his distance, choosing to stand just inside the door. In a gesture now familiar to her, he pushed his coat back so that he could bury his hands in his pockets. "You look surprised to see me."

"I am."

"Did you really think, for one minute, Sophia, that I would simply let you leave?"

"I didn't honestly know what you'd do." She didn't say that she'd lain in bed the last two nights praying that he *wouldn't* let her leave, that he'd do just this, that he'd come for her. Praying those things, yearning for him like a lovestruck girl after a man impossibly out of her reach. Despite everything she knew to be true about their relationship. Despite a maturity she'd cultivated at great cost since the day her grandmother and her illusions had died.

"I lost my mind when I awoke to find you gone." He gazed at her harshly, without trying to soften his statement. "I'd have found you sooner if it hadn't been for that damned doctor you hired."

"He's an excellent doctor—"

"He's an idiot. He got it in his fool head I needed to stay in bed for two days to recover."

"Well, you certainly did—"

"Then my brothers got in their heads that they'd been called upon by God to enforce his orders." He appeared genuinely annoyed, a tower of brooding masculine frustration. "I could have taken one of my brothers, but not both."

"Jarrod," she chided. "Don't be ridiculous—"

"Ridiculous?" He neared, brows lowering into a vee. "I'm ridiculous? What about you? You didn't even take Duchess with you."

"Duchess? No, of course not."

"Why?"

A giggling pair of girls entered the room. Jarrod swung on them, stopping them dead in their tracks. They gasped then skittered backward, tripping over their skirts in their haste to exit.

His attention sliced back to her. "Why didn't you take the horse?"

"Because she doesn't belong to me."

"Like hell she doesn't." His voice rose in volume. "We both know I gave her to you, so what's stopping you? Just try to tell me you don't want her." He motioned angrily toward himself. "Just try to tell me that to my face."

She wouldn't lie to him, so she set her teeth tightly together.

"All of it is yours." He flung out a hand. "The clothes, the art, the jewelry, the damned furs. All of it."

"I can't accept any of those things from you."

"Women always accept the things I buy for them."

He'd compare her to others? "Not this woman."

"Why not you?"

"Because I don't . . ." She'd been about to say because she didn't need his gifts, but that wasn't quite true.

In order to save Blackhaw, she desperately needed the money his gifts could have brought her. "Because I'm independent," she answered in a tone that dared him to find fault. "I take pride in that independence."

"So . . . what, Sophie? You're going to go through your whole life never taking anything from people who want to give to you?"

"And you? Are you going to go through your whole life trying to buy people's loyalty with possessions?"

She drew herself up and matched him glare for glare. By God, if he insisted on doing battle with her, it's a battle he'd get.

On a growl, he stalked away. He went to the fireplace and leaned a hand on the mantel while he stared into the licking flames. Sophia studied the lines of his profile, shoulder, back. He was difficult, confrontational, offensive, and, thank the heavens, he was also gloriously, blissfully *alive*.

Only now, with the physical proof of his strength before her in stunning detail, did she feel able to admit just how terrified she had been that he might die. She could live the rest of her life alone, she'd learned to cope with a solitary existence over the years. But she didn't think she could survive another night like the one she'd endured when he'd lain on death's threshold.

"My brothers told me what you did," he said. "How you rode for the doctor. How you fed me medicine." Their gazes locked. "Thank you."

All the concerns that forever clamored inside of her melted in a silken stream, leaving room for tenderness to come. And come it did, shaking and shuddering.

Because she could see he was waiting for her to accept his thanks, she managed a nod.

"I hate like hell that you had to nurse me." He pushed away from the mantel, though he made no move to come closer. "But I can't be sorry that I was the one who was poisoned and not you."

She wanted to clamp her hands on his cheeks and kiss him. She wanted to curl her fingers into the crisp fabric of his shirt, then tear it off of him. "Did you discover who poisoned the wine?"

"No, but I think we have to assume it was the same person that organized the ambush against you."

"I agree."

He crossed his arms. Her fingertips moved restively over the beading on her spider mask.

"My brothers tell me you've given up your pursuit of my father," he said. "I told them I didn't believe it."

Someone opened the parlor door.

"Out!" Jarrod bellowed.

The door shut rapidly.

"So?" he asked her.

She considered her words carefully. "I could live with the damage my vengeance was doing me on the inside. I understood, when I was attacked, that the risk was worthwhile. But when you were hurt . . ." She licked her lips. "That was unacceptable. The next time someone could be killed."

"Some bastard is out there trying to bully us, and you're going to let him win?" Clearly, Jarrod Stone was not a man who allowed anyone either to bully him or to win against him. Not for many, many years.

"That's exactly what I'm going to do. Revenge isn't worth the risk—"

"What about justice?

"Not even justice is worth the risk. I can't be responsible should harm befall you, or Maggie, or your brothers."

Silence stirred between them.

"I'll find my father, you know." He said the words with such fate-challenging confidence that she doubted whether there was any power on earth that could stop him.

"I hope you do."

"I'll find him for Holden, and I'll find him for you."

She got lost in his eyes, the endless green of them.

"It's the only present I can give you that you might accept." He moved toward her. "Stubborn woman." With a mere flick of his gaze, down and up the length of her body, the air between them turned hot. Pulsing. Heavy with intentions.

"Do you know what I want to do to you right now?" he asked when he was just inches away.

Her own words to Maggie came back to her. *He loathes my career.* She sidestepped, trying to put space between them.

He closed the gap immediately. "I want to strip you naked."

He's far more interested in bedding me than in anything more respectable. She turned from him.

He was there. "I want to lay you on that sofa," he nodded to it, "and spread your legs."

His personality. She veered toward the door, frantic.

He cut off her retreat. "I want to run my hands over your bare skin."

With a mewl of distress that sounded more like a moan of desire, she turned from him, then turned again, until they were engaged in a fated dance, and the room was swirling. He was everywhere she looked. Inescapable. Whispering words that were licking, licking over her.

Her shoulder came up against the wall next to the door, halting her retreat. He trapped her there, leaning his body into hers. He tilted his head to feast on her neck. "I want to enter you. I want to feel how tight you are."

She writhed against him and at her body's telltale movement, he lifted his head.

Muscles strung taut, chest heaving, she met his gaze. In the next instant, he claimed her mouth. Distantly, she was aware of his hands spearing into her hair, clasping her head. She kissed him madly, curling her fingers into his shirt as she had wanted to do moments before. The contact was rough, deep, and starved.

Voices grew nearer and the door opened.

Jarrod dislodged a hand from her hair to slam it closed.

They stared at each other, breath ragged. "That's it," he said, and swung her into his arms. "I'm taking you home."

Her senses reeling, she watched the room blur past. He exited by way of the door at the rear of the parlor, which emptied them into a servants' hallway that ran along the far side of the house.

A trio of maids, trays of empty plates and glasses in their hands, halted in astonishment when they saw them.

"She twisted her ankle," Jarrod said by way of gruff explanation.

The three continued to gawk. Jarrod carried her down the hallway, his powerful strides eating the distance. A frigid curtain of air whisked over them when he kicked open a side door and descended the steps beyond.

Purposefully, he strode toward his carriage, which waited at the front of the house. Gleaming black, just like it had been the night it had waited on Blackhaw's drive, the first night she'd met him. *Satan's chariot,* she'd thought then.

Oh, Mother above. She fisted the collar of his dinner jacket more tightly in her hand. If he was Satan, then she wanted to burn.

Jarrod's driver rushed from his perch to open the door for them. Inside, Jarrod deposited her on the velvet seat, then took the one opposite her. "To Blackhaw," he instructed the driver. The man nodded and hurried to close them in.

Assailed by sudden awkwardness, Sophia righted herself on the seat. The fake ruby around her waist shook as she smoothed her ebony skirts into place. She didn't dare meet his eyes, and yet she knew if she didn't, he'd take it as a sign of weakness. The carriage wheels crunched over brick as they rocked into motion.

She dragged her gaze to his. The kisses they'd just shared hung between them as obvious as the darkness that planed across the hard lines of his cheek and jaw. "You're taking me to Blackhaw?" she asked.

"Yes. It's closer." He reached up and rapped his fist against the ceiling of the vehicle. Immediately, the carriage picked up speed.

She resisted the urge to fuss with her skirts again. What were his intentions, exactly, when they reached Blackhaw? If he dropped her off there, she'd never calm her body from this fever pitch he'd churned it to—

"I'm going to take you to your room, and I'm going to make love to you," he said bluntly. "If you don't want me to, you'd best speak now."

Her mouth went completely dry.

"It's past time we settled this thing between us." He scrutinized her. "Don't you agree?"

She, who never risked anything of her heart, looked him dead in the eye and heard herself say, "I do." And she did, violently, want this. She was sick to death of worrying, of protecting, of fearing a thousand demons. Tonight she wanted more for herself. She wanted to live.

The carriage came to an abrupt stop. Jarrod was outside in a flash, holding the door for her. Slightly unsteady on her feet, she lifted her skirts to step down— He hoisted her in his arms again.

Blackhaw's face rose before her, and then they were through the massive front doorway. His shoes rapped the floor as he stalked toward the staircase.

Mrs. Dewberry rushed out from the door leading to the kitchen.

"She twisted her ankle," Jarrod barked.

The housekeeper's hands flew to cover her heart.

"It's all right," Sophia had time to say to the woman, before Mrs. Dewberry was jerked out of sight.

Jarrod mounted the steps, taking her upward. Upward. His fingers found her hairpins and pulled them free. They went pinging down the stairs. Her hair tumbled from its restraints.

He gained the second story and set her on her feet in front of her door. Before she could so much as get her balance, he was kissing her. She banded her arms around his neck, kissing him back, listening to the growl that mounted in his throat. He walked her backward, grasping at the back of her dress. She felt as much as heard fabric rip. Buttons rained against the floor, rolled. He pushed her up against her doorway. Oh—his tongue. He was laying fierce claim to her with it, possessing everything she had and demanding more.

Blindly, she groped for and found the door handle. When she turned it, they rolled inside. He slammed it shut.

She could drown in these kisses, feed off them for days. More impatient yanking on the back of her bodice. More fabric giving way.

Moon and starlight poured into the room through uncurtained windows, coating the furnishings with ethereal light. That's how this felt. Ethereal. This couldn't be happening and yet she pined for it to be true.

Jarrod's knuckles rasped against her lower back as he freed the last of the buttons, then stripped both her gown and her chemise to her waist.

For a breathless moment, he didn't touch her. Air, still faintly warmed from the fire that smoldered in the hearth, looped around her breasts and curved across her nipples.

When at last he grazed the back of his hand across a breast, her body jerked at the splintering contact. It was already too much, this roar of sensation. He kissed her again, his mouth moving in chorus with the hand upon her breast.

Pressure mounted on the inside of her, toward him, summoned by his touch. It was glorious to feel without thinking. To need and so to take. With a soft cry of impatience, she ripped at his jacket, stripping it from him in the way he'd stripped her. Before she could drop the garment to the ground, he was reaching for the fabric at her waist. He pulled everything, including her drawers, down her legs with a single tug. Then he wedged her shoes from her feet and tossed them aside.

The ruby's chain nipped her skin, cold as the heart of

the gem that nestled just above the vee of her legs. She reached around to unfasten—

"Leave it," he said as he straightened. He lifted her immediately against him, and she spread her legs, wrapping them around his hips. Shocks of pleasure quaked upward from between her legs, where her sensitive folds rubbed against the cloth of his trousers and the ridge beneath.

He set her on the edge of her bed. She kept her ankles locked behind him as he tore off his bow tie and shirt. Her hands extended, reaching out greedily to flatten against his chest. He knelt, his mouth hungrily covering an aching nipple as he ripped open the placket of his trousers.

Her body's cravings were driving her forward, but so were longings held in check for years. Piling one on top the other. Some unformed, some piercing, some old, some she'd never known. She longed for a man, for a husband. To be loved. To be made love to, awoken, stirred, touched intimately like this. Exactly like this, she thought, as she caught sight of his dark head bent to her breast. She longed for *him*.

His mouth lifted to hers, and her eyes sank closed as she lost herself to another drugging kiss.

His fingers found her, down low. Opening, delving inside. She began to move and breathe in time to his motion there. Desire hammered through her and she widened her knees, asking for more. He took his hand from her, used it to guide himself to her opening. She felt the tip of his manhood against her.

She was slick for him where he was rubbing against her, throbbing with emptiness. She pulled away just enough to look at him and found him watching her, reading her face.

She loved him in that moment. Adored everything about him. Found in him a piece of her soul that she'd been looking for, ever looking for, and missing.

"Relax for me," he murmured, his voice whiskey-rough.

She eased her tensed muscles, felt herself open against the hardness of him. He nudged inside, and she moaned. He withdrew, and she squirmed. In and out, just an inch each time. The coil inside of her compressed. Her greedy senses screamed for more, deeper.

His expression grew taut with a concentration that looked like pain. In an inch. Out.

Her breath panted shallowly. Heat misted across her chest, raced in unfurling waves up her body to her face, down her limbs.

Finally, she couldn't bear it anymore. Using her ankles, she pulled his hips toward her. He came forward slowly, gauging her eyes, devouring her with his gaze. Again she pulled him toward her, and this time, with a groan, he answered her by thrusting full inside.

A scream tore from her lips, mostly at the fulfillment of it, partly at the hurt. His powerful body stilled.

"Don't stop," she whispered.

His hands snaked underneath to cup her naked buttocks. He held her steady while he stroked in and out of her, slowly but fully. The pain dissipated in the face of the spiraling, seeking feel of him within her—a part of her. The coil compressed tighter, tighter. She threaded her fingers into the hair at the nape of his neck, and they looked into each other's eyes as he entered her even more deeply. Then faster. The ruby thrummed against her belly, beating in time to their rhythm.

She couldn't think for the blazing intimacy of it. The

surrender was glorious. No masks. *No masks.* Just an honesty that made her want to weep. The physical pleasure escalated so quickly she couldn't regulate it—couldn't control—didn't want to. She could only ride it higher.

Jarrod entered her more thoroughly every time, compressing the coil tighter and tighter. She strained into the feeling, mindless, reaching—and then the coil sprang, and pleasure infused her body in a burst that looked like a shower of white sparks. Her woman's center convulsed with ecstasy around Jarrod.

"Oh," she murmured. This time had been even better than the time before because he'd been within her. "Jarrod." She embraced him to her, chest to chest. His bare skin was warm against her own, slicked with moisture as hers was.

Her moon-brushed world tilted as he laid her back, resting her full across the coolness of white cotton. The ruby fell to the side, its chain leaving a gleaming trail across her waist. Languid and drunk with awe, she studied him as he divested his trousers.

Magnificent in his nakedness, he grazed his chest across the tips of her breasts, then held himself above her with his elbows sinking into the bed on either side of her head. She opened for him and he slid inside her in one sure motion. The friction was different for her this time. Almost a pleasure too sharp to take at first, then . . . then *oh.* She lifted her hands to his face and clasped his cheeks. Their mouths joined, and he kissed her while he made love to her.

Passion rolled over her like the undersides of waves. She was deep underwater, warm water, feeling, feeling. Within her, she felt him grow harder, bigger. She ac-

cepted him, asked silently for more, for it all. His breath
beat against her lips.

He thrust again and again. She felt her body beginning to slip over the cusp. She tried to hold back just
until— He inhaled sharply through his teeth. She
clasped him against her and let herself go, both of them
trembling with the force of their joining, with the shattering release of it, with the magnitude of what they'd
created together here tonight.

He held a portion of his weight off her with his elbows and a knee, but he didn't separate from her, and she
didn't want him to. Her sanity drifted back in strips as
misty as a cloud. He was kissing her shoulder, she knew
that. Kissing it softly, lightly. Let her never forget this,
not a minute, not a second of it.

When he moved onto his side facing her, she sighed
her disappointment.

A grin curled his lips.

She smiled, too, wonderingly. Unable to get her fill of
touching him, she ran her fingertips through the hair
above his ear.

"You steal my breath," he whispered.

From nowhere, tears of joy stung her eyes.

"You're the most beautiful thing I've ever seen," he
said.

"That's something, coming from you." She rifled the
hair at his temple again, though she really wanted to knot
her hand in it and never let go. "You've seen so many
beautiful things."

"None of them were worth half as much as you."

She stilled. She wanted to take that as a promise.
Hungered to read the world into his words. Maybe there
was hope for them. Maybe he loved her and would want

to marry her. Maybe in the same way that she'd made the mistake of hating too much she'd made the mistake of hoping too little. They understood each other, Jarrod and she, on a fundamental level she'd not fully grasped until now. Their hearts at their most basic recognized one another through the eyes of two people who'd scraped and fought and survived.

He moved away.

"Don't go," she whispered, fear leaping within her.

"I'm not leaving you." He kissed her, then lifted her and repositioned her gently so that he could pull the linens down the bed. That done, he climbed in beside her and covered them both with the blankets. Her head fit just beneath his chin, her chest to his chest and her thighs and calves intertwined with his.

She could hear his heartbeat. Steady and sure. She edged even nearer to him and closed her eyes.

I'm not leaving you, he'd said. She hoped he'd meant forever because tonight she'd done more than live. She'd found heaven.

Disgusted with his inability to sleep, Holden threw aside his prison-issue blanket and swung his legs to the floor. Sitting on the edge of his cot, he rested his elbows on his knees and clasped his head in his hands. The floor below him was thick with grit. Even in the darkness, he could make out the dustballs and dirt that the wind sent lapping over his bare toes.

He screwed shut his eyes and squeezed the sides of his head, wishing he could squeeze out the circle of memories that kept playing out in his mind's eye. It was like being forced to sit in the audience and watch himself trapped in the same terrible play over and over and over.

Worse, for this play aborted before the end, leaving him staring with ever-growing frustration at a blank stage.

He groaned as the performance resumed yet again.

"Let's get you home," Pa had said that night. He turned up the collar of his coat and started toward the gates.

He and mother walked next to him on the other side of the fence.

Pa looked over his shoulder again. Then he started walking faster. "Perhaps we should hurry."

"Okay," Holden said, trying his best to keep up. He glanced through the fence toward the big house, to the place where his father kept looking.

A figure on horseback galloped from the shadows.

Feeling sick, he tried to warn his mother. But all that came out was, "M . . . M . . ." Urgently, he tugged on her hand and pointed.

She saw what he saw and stopped. "Adam."

Pa turned and saw him too. The ball in his neck bobbed. "You two stay here," he said. "I'll run to the gate and let myself out."

"Adam—"

But he was already gone. His jacket spread out behind him like wings as he sprinted along the wall toward the gate. The thick case he carried banged against his leg.

The man on the horse charged down the drive. So fast the horse's hooves sounded like the beating of a drum. Pa might not have time to get out before the ghost got him. "Mama," Holden whimpered.

She drew him away from the fence, beneath the shelter of a tree that had no leaves. He pressed his back against the front of her skirts, and she stacked her hands on his chest, clasping him to her protectively.

Pa had nearly reached the gate. The man galloped toward him on his big horse. *Hurry, Pa.* But just before Pa reached the latch that held together the gate's door, the man on the horse cut in front of him, then came to a stop, blocking Pa from the exit.

Holden's chest hitched. Would the man hurt Pa? His brothers called him a baby when he cried, so he bit his lip and tried to be quiet as tears blurred his eyes.

When the stranger dropped to the ground, Pa retreated.

"She gave you the money, didn't she?" the man asked. "She just told me that she gave you the money."

"That's right."

"Give it over." The man stretched out his hand to Pa.

Pa shook his head and took another step back. He clutched the case with both hands.

"Give it over," the stranger said. It was almost a yell.

"Give it to him," Holden whispered. Why wouldn't Pa just give the man what he wanted? It was only money. Tears slipped down his cheeks.

Pa stood his ground. "I will not. This is Mrs. Warren's money to do with as she pleases. She's entrusted it to me on behalf of our factory as you well know."

"Goddamned factory," the stranger swore. "It's going to fail, and I refuse to stand aside and watch her squander away any more money."

"I believe we can succeed—"

Before Pa could finish talking, the stranger pulled a gun from inside his jacket. Pa froze.

"My God," Mother breathed. She drew him farther back beneath the branches of the tree and tried to turn his face to the side.

But he could still see through the break in her fingers.

"It's finished, Adam," the man said in a calm, scary voice. "Hand the money over."

"Hand it over," Holden sobbed. Why wouldn't he give the man what he wanted? He hated his father, wanted to pound his fists against him.

Pa hesitated, then lunged toward the man.

Holden ripped his face away from the restraint of his mother's hand.

Pa shoved the stranger's arm then punched him in the face. The man stumbled to the side, but came back fast. He hit Pa in the chin, then pushed Pa. Pa gained his balance and rounded on the man, barreled toward him—

Boom. Light flashed from the end of the gun.

Mother's whole body lurched. "No," she gasped.

Pa's chest caved in before he fell backward onto the ground. The man moved to stand over him, looking down.

Pa couldn't really be shot. No, no, no, no. He'd get up and hurt the man. He'd come home with them tonight and eat the food Mother had set aside for him. He'd promised to take him fishing.

But Pa didn't get up. He rolled onto his side, then his back, his knees drawn up toward his middle.

Shocked too senseless to cry and too horrified to move, Holden felt his mother start to shake uncontrollably. Pa moved like a snake with its head cut off. Slower, then slower.

"Pa!" Holden screamed.

"Hush." Mother tried to cover his mouth with her hand.

He fought her off. "Pa!" He couldn't be shot. He'd promised to take him fishing.

The man with the gun looked in their direction.

"Pa," Holden begged. "Pa."

The stranger came toward them.

Mother grabbed his hand and tried to pull him away but he couldn't move. He could only watch the man with the gun as the man broke into a run. Coming closer.

With a wail Mother shoved him behind her and shielded him with her body. Her hands clawed into his shoulders to keep him in place.

Beyond her coat, he saw the man stop on the other side of the fence. He scowled at them, his gun held low in one hand. "Who are you?" he demanded.

"A-Adam's wife and son." Mother's voice broke. She was shaking real bad.

"Pa," Holden sobbed. Tears flowed down his face.

The man's lips pursed. "I regret you had to see that, ma'am."

"Don't hurt us, please," Mother beseeched him. She retreated, shuttling him behind her.

"You tell anyone what you saw tonight—"

"I won't!"

"Listen to me," the stranger ordered.

Mother stopped, her breath ripping against the still night air.

"You tell anyone what you saw here tonight," the man said, real calm like, "and I'll kill your boy. I'll kill all your boys. Do you understand me?"

"Yessir," Mother whispered.

"You wouldn't want that to happen now would you?"

"No, no, no." She was crying, too.

Holden saw her tears dully, listened to their conversation dumbly. The man had shot Pa.

"Leave tonight," the man said. "Never come back and never breathe a word of this."

Mother clasped Holden's hand and pulled him. He knew she wanted him to flee, but he couldn't make his legs work.

"C'mon baby," she said frantically. "We have to go."

He only gazed at her.

Without hesitation, she had swept him up in her thin arms and began to run.

Holden raised his head and stared at the brick wall of his prison cell. He knew the face of the man with the gun. It had aged over the years, gone bald. But it was the same face he'd seen at Austin's train station just months before. It belonged to Oliver Kinsworthy, Blackhaw's attorney. No wonder he'd felt such sick rage when he'd seen him.

Oliver Kinsworthy had killed his father for Blackhaw's fortune. All this time, the truth had been locked inside his own mind. *God damn it, I should have been able to remember it sooner.*

He rushed to his feet. Jarrod and Sophia were searching for a dead man. His brain spun. Sophia had told him that Kinsworthy had informed her of their meeting at the train station, which meant the two were still in contact, which meant that Kinsworthy likely knew of Jarrod and Sophia's renewed search for Blackhaw's missing money.

His gut tightened. Hell, he was responsible for Jarrod's involvement in that search. He'd asked it of him. Just how long could Kinsworthy conceal his guilt? And who was he willing to hurt to do so?

He saw again the flash of fire as Kinsworthy shot down their father. In two strides, Holden reached the front of his cell. "Guard!" he yelled.

Men stirred in the adjacent cells, grumbled.

"Guard!" He yelled again. "Guard!"

Finally, one of his jailers appeared at the end of the hall.

Holden's muscles bunched as he tried to rend the metal bars in his bare hands. "I need to get a message to my brother."

The guard, his hulking build covered with slabs of fat, approached.

"It's important that I get a message—"

The guard rammed a hand through the bars, connecting with Holden's chest and sending him back a few paces. "Shut the hell up, Stone. You know the rules."

Holden's fingers curled into fists. He wanted nothing more than to fight the bastard, was itching for it. "I need to get a message—"

"Well you can't. What do you think this is, the fricking post office?" The guard's glare seethed with contempt. "Now shut the hell up, or me and the boys will have to take you out of here and whup the crap out of you." He walked back in the direction he'd come.

"No!" Holden yelled. He went back to the bars, pressed himself against them. "No!"

Chapter 21

Jarrod recognized the exact instant that Sophia eased her warm body away from his. The gray-pink light of dawn seeped through the open windows, illuminating her beautiful back as she slipped from bed.

Halfway across the rug, a floorboard squealed beneath her. She stopped and looked over her shoulder at him. He quickly closed the eye he'd cracked open.

When he heard her pour water into the washbasin, he watched her surreptitiously again. Damn, he loved her body. Her bottom was round and high and full, a perfect fit for his hands. Her waist nipped inward from her hips in a line too perfect for even the greatest artist to capture on canvas.

As she leaned over the dish to soap her wash towel, he

drank in the profile of her breasts, their rosy nipples taut with cold.

His body stirred. He needed to make love to her again, craved to bury himself inside her and have his release. Last night hadn't been near enough. On the contrary, looking at her now, he felt hungrier for her than he ever had before. Like an addiction.

Water trickled against water as she lifted the soapy towel and cleansed herself. A kind of delicious agony tightened his groin as she ran the cloth from her toes up to her thighs. God, she was so concentrated, his Sophia. She even washed with an expression of focus on her features. When she coasted the cloth between her legs, he nearly groaned.

She stilled, then glanced toward him.

He feigned sleep.

More swishing sounds. He watched as she cleaned her upper body, neck, and face, then wrung out her towel and shivered. When he'd told her she was the most beautiful thing he'd ever seen, it had been a gross understatement. He wished there was a word that did her more justice than "beautiful" did.

His lips curved at the memory of her the first night he'd seen her, here in this room. Her hair tightly bound, her face icy white, her posture iron-straight. And now look at her. All rosy and soft, all color and warmth.

She used her wrist to push a long lock of mahogany hair behind her shoulder, then set about brushing her teeth with dental cream.

He wanted to marry her. He'd never been a man content with half measures. No, when he wanted something, he wanted it wholly. And what he wanted, more than he'd ever wanted the money or the power or the possessions, was her. A day with her, a few more nights wouldn't do. He was selfish enough to covet every day of the rest of her life. To demand the right to call her his. To own her love. He needed time enough to treasure her properly, to give her everything the little girl in white had been robbed of.

She tiptoed across to the armoire and hastily donned undergarments.

Once they were married, he'd keep her naked for days at a time and ban undergarments entirely.

She pulled on stockings, strapped her knife to the outside of her thigh, put on a worn-looking navy blue skirt and bodice, and laced up her shoes. It took her only moments at her dressing table to brush her hair, then weave it into a loose, elaborately twisted style that suited her far better than the buns of old. She stood from the stool in a rush.

He closed his eyes, listening to her move toward him, skirts rustling. He could smell the lavender scent of her soap as she bent over him.

He held himself immobile, despite every instinct. Decades of responsibility had fashioned him into a man who protected. He hadn't protected his mother well enough, and her death had been a searing lesson to him. After her, he'd held tight to those he loved, convinced somewhere inside himself that it was his guardianship that kept them from harm.

If given the chance or the choice, he'd control Sophia's actions because that was simply what he did. What would keep her safe. But if he wanted a future with her, he knew he'd have to make his peace with her career. Her work as Twilight's Ghost meant everything to the woman. She'd proven it to him a thousand times, and if he forced her to choose between it and him, as his inclinations were driving him to, she'd choose it. More than that, though. He didn't want to have to force her to choose. He wanted to give her the ultimate sign of his respect by trusting her to make her own decisions.

He would begin this morning. With letting go.

Lighter than the touch of a dandelion, her fingers slid through his hair. *Don't move,* he told himself. *Let her wake you and ask for your help if she will.* Holding himself torturously still, he waited for her to, hoped she would. Her breath soughed against his forehead before she kissed him softly.

Then, too soon, her caress vanished, and he heard the faint sounds of her retreat.

He had to stop her, he couldn't let her go—

The door whispered open then shut.

He pushed himself to sitting. The blankets pooled at his waist. His heart thudded with loss, with doom. He *must* let her go and do her work as Twilight's Ghost. He understood it rationally. Yet doing nothing went against every fiber of him.

He gritted his teeth. Moved to go after her. Stopped.

"Damn it," he said beneath his breath. *Let her go, man.* He understood the kind of woman she was, how stubbornly independent. She'd left him to go hunt down her counterfeiter, and he had to have enough faith in her to let her do what she did best.

She'd be fine, he assured himself. She hadn't found the criminal yet, and there was no reason to think she would today. It was light out. There'd be people around. She was quick and smart.

She'd be fine.

*　*　*

"Thank you," Sophia said to the town of Hitchcock's courthouse clerk, and accepted a stack of papers from the gentleman. She made her way to the empty desk against the wall and pulled up a chair.

Her stomach yawned with hunger. She'd skipped breakfast in lieu of traveling from one small town to the next, examining records in hopes of finding information on Silas Clarke, her artist with a penchant for ordering large quantities of paper and ink. The hour was now approaching noon, and she'd yet to find anything on the man.

She sighed as she stripped her dusty gloves from her hands and set them aside. She prayed Maggie was having better luck.

Industriously, she straightened the stack and pulled it in front of her. But instead of paper and print, she saw Jarrod pulling her hips toward him as he entered her. Saw the color that tinted his cheeks, the passion that clouded his eyes.

Heat blossomed in her belly. She fidgeted in the wooden chair, hooked a finger around her neckline, and pulled in a fruitless attempt to give her lungs more air. If she was honest with herself, this was why the day's duties so far had been agony. She'd been hungry and tired countless times before while investigating her cases. But she'd never been so thoroughly haunted by a man. Jarrod had dominated every thought she'd had today. Riding in her buggy, leafing through records—it didn't matter. She saw, knew, tasted, felt nothing but him. She physically ached to return to him, to kiss him again, to hear his voice, to see him look at her with love. . . .

Irritated with herself, she shook her head to clear her

thoughts. She *couldn't* allow her hopes to tumble so far beyond themselves that she'd never be able to catch them back. The truth was that he hadn't necessarily looked at her with love. It could have been lust, and she wouldn't have known the difference. He'd promised her nothing.

Yet again, she straightened her papers and tried to concentrate. This investigation was crucially important. It was Blackhaw's last chance. The auction was set for tomorrow, and if she couldn't claim her reward money before then, she'd lose her home.

One deep breath, and she forced herself to start reading over the court papers. She searched one sheet at a time for the name Silas Clarke. Not him. Not him. Not him.

She was two-thirds of the way through the stack, her imaginings returning to Jarrod, when she saw it. Silas Clarke. Black script on white paper. She leaned forward, her pulse picking up tempo as she scanned the record. He'd been tried more than three years before for the crime of . . . Her vision skimmed past inconsequential information . . . Counterfeiting.

Victory soared inside her. "I've got you," she murmured, nearly overwhelmed with relief, satisfaction, and accomplishment.

She read the sheet over more carefully, taking note of the particulars. Silas Clarke had been found not guilty. Mr. Stewart had said that was due to good representation. She traced her fingernail down the words. His representation had been . . . Oliver Kinsworthy.

She blinked, surprised. Then glad. Oliver would be able to give her information about Silas not listed on this document. She hurried to her feet, enlivened by a second wind of renewed purpose. She'd go straight to Oliver. He'd help her.

* * *

The weather was turning ugly.

From astride his horse, Jarrod peered to the north-west, where a storm brewed. There, the sky was darkest gray, paler gray strips arrowing toward earth. Rain. Here, the air swept past them on curling rushes of moist wind.

He turned up the collar of his greatcoat and frowned at the surrounding territory of winter-swept forest. "You sure about this, J. T?"

"I'm sure we're heading in the right direction. The house should be over this next hill." Expertly, J. T. maneuvered his horse through a minefield of fallen logs. "But I'm not certain we'll learn anything useful when we get there."

"Worth a try, though." Clint commented.

His brothers had spent the last few days working doggedly on the pursuit of their father. They'd begun in the right place to Jarrod's way of thinking, by filling gaps in the information the Pinkertons had compiled. They'd almost finished piecing together the past and present of every person who had served at Blackhaw at the time of the theft. Almost but not quite. Clint and J. T. had discovered a missing section of Oliver Kinsworthy's history. Finding out just what Kinsworthy had been do-ing during those years was what had brought them on this fool's errand.

Jarrod trotted his horse along the bank of a brook, watching the water bump and glide over rocks and think-ing of the water that had flowed over Sophia's body that morning.

He hadn't wanted to do this today. Hadn't wanted to do anything but stay in bed with Sophia making love, eating, sleeping, making love. He sure as hell didn't give a good goddamn about riding for the better part of two hours just to chase down information on Kinsworthy's dull past. But when he'd returned home this morning and found his brothers on the verge of riding out, he'd decided to go with them. Unfortunately, the activity hadn't diverted him as much as he'd hoped. His body was physically here, but his mind was with her. Going over the events of last night, remembering every square inch of her skin, her every gasp, and glance.

He sighed impatiently, shifted in the saddle.

They crested a hill and a house, set about a quarter mile distant, speared into view.

"Jesus," Jarrod said.

"Quite a house, eh?" J. T. murmured.

"What happened to it?"

Clint squinted at the structure. "Time, I'd say."

They directed their horses onto the road that led up to the grand old relic. The structure was enormous, clapboard-sided, with round-topped windows cut into three towering stories. Elaborate balconies marked its sides, while steepled dormers and turrets jutted from the roofline. A mansion by anyone's standards, except it looked like a monument to greed gone bad because the paint had frayed off the clapboards, the decorative wooden carvings had been stripped dull by water and wind, and the turret windows gaped with jagged holes.

The negative intuition that had been with Jarrod since morning unwound itself and spread. "What does this place have to do with Kinsworthy?"

"About five years after Sophia's grandmother's death," Clint said, "the Pinkerton file lost track of his whereabouts for a couple of years. Sophia, actually, was the one who helped us discover where he'd been during that time."

"Sophia?"

Clint nodded. "She supplemented the Pinkerton file on our father with all the letters Kinsworthy ever wrote her concerning their search. A few of his letters to her were dated during the missing time period and marked with this return address."

"He owned this place?"

"No, not according to the locals. This house has always been owned by the family who built it. Name of Dobson."

"We think Kinsworthy worked here," J. T. said.

They pulled their horses to a stop and dismounted before the stairs leading up to the front entrance. "It doesn't even look inhabited," Jarrod said.

"No," Clint agreed, as they climbed the steps, their boots ringing against brittle wood. "It doesn't."

Jarrod knocked. J. T. and Clint swept off their Stetsons while they waited.

At first, he heard absolutely no stirrings of life from within. Then, as if originating in some netherworld instead of from the back of the house, footsteps sounded. Jarrod fully expected a wizened old man with a cane and a passel of cats to open the door.

When the door swung inward, it revealed a woman instead. A fairly young one with a frail body, a simple tan dress, and sparse mousy hair. She regarded them through eyes as round as nickels, apparently flabbergasted to find three men standing on her threshold.

"Miss Dobson?" J. T. asked.

"Yes."

"I'm J. T. Stone, and these are my brothers, Jarrod and Clint."

"Ma'am."

"Ma'am."

She simply stared.

"We've come to talk with you," J. T. said, "about a gentleman that may have been in your family's employ some fifteen years ago. A Mr. Oliver Kinsworthy."

J. T. had gentled both his tone and manner so as not to scare her. He'd always had a way with women, been able to cater to whatever it was they needed. Jarrod, on the other hand, was atrocious with shy women.

"Yes," Miss Dobson answered. "I know Mr. Kinsworthy."

"I realize this is a great imposition," J. T. said, "but may we ask you a few questions regarding him?"

"I . . ." The sinewy muscles in her throat worked. Self-consciously, she fluttered a hand over the back of her head. "I haven't had my hair properly styled in some time."

She's insane, Jarrod thought.

"It looks lovely," J. T. replied smoothly, his grin warm and complimentary.

She stepped jerkily back, and held the door for them. "Come in."

They followed her into a parlor that contained a rug, a sofa, and three chairs. Every other item that had once graced it was gone. No curtains, no paintings, no tables, no plants, no baubles. He was reminded of Blackhaw's second-story rooms, rooms that stood empty except for tattering wallpaper and faded paint.

The woman sat on the edge of the sofa. J. T. chose the sofa's other end, while Jarrod and Clint settled into chairs.

"Can I offer you anything?" the woman asked hesitantly. "There's—" She rose to her feet as if she'd suddenly remembered she had water boiling on the stove.

All three of them stood.

"There's *cheese*," she said, motioning vaguely toward the back of the house.

"That's a very kind offer," J. T. responded, "but, no thank you, ma'am. We couldn't possibly impose on you more than we have."

"No imposition."

"Thank you, but we couldn't possibly."

She nodded, and they all took their seats for the second time. A momentary shift in the clouds caused sunlight to slant across her face. She was even younger than Jarrod had first assumed. He doubted she'd yet to reach twenty-five. So, why had he thought her older at first?

She had old eyes, he realized, studying her. The delicate skin around them was smooth and young. But those eyes. They'd been aged by shame and poverty and broken dreams of grandeur.

His sense of unease deepened.

"In what capacity was Mr. Kinsworthy employed here?" J. T. asked.

"He was my grandfather's advisor and attorney. They, ah, worked together on my family's business interests from the offices here in the house." More vague pointing toward a general region of the residence.

"Your grandfather, you say?"

"That's correct."

"Did you and your family live here with him at the time?"

"Oh. No," she said with a wistful note. "My parents

both contracted polio and passed when I was very young, I'm afraid."

"I'm sorry," J. T. said sincerely.

"It was just Grandfather and me during Mr. Kinsworthy's time."

"How long did he work here?"

"Two years or so. Up until the fortune was stolen and Grandfather died."

Jarrod clenched the armrests of his chair.

She pursed pale lips. "After that, you understand, I hadn't the finances to keep Mr. Kinsworthy on. A pity, that."

"You must have been very young," J. T. said.

"Oh . . . Not quite ten. Mr. Kinsworthy's the one who took me to my great-aunt Clara's to live. We still correspond frequently, Mr. Kinsworthy and I." She smiled softly. "I think the world of him. He's even offered to help me find the man who stole our family's money. It would be nice"—her gaze flitted around the room—"to restore this place a bit."

Jarrod stared at her, aghast. He was looking at the woman Sophia might have become. Twice, Kinsworthy had gained the trust of his elderly patron, twice his patrons were robbed, twice no one was left to question it but a small girl.

My God. Sophia had been wrong about his father's guilt and wrong to trust Oliver Kinsworthy, her lifelong friend. Jarrod rushed to his feet. "I need a word with you in private," he said to his brothers.

"If you'll excuse us for a moment, Miss Dobson," J. T. said.

"Certainly. I just remembered. I've also a bit of boiled

ham." She stood, smiling hesitantly. "If that would interest you."

"I'll be back in one moment," J. T. promised her.

The three exited the foyer and stood together on the porch.

"Sophia trusts Kinsworthy," Jarrod said. "She could be with him now, for all I know. I'm going to Blackhaw. I don't want her anywhere near him." He strode halfway down the stairs. Turned back toward them. "As soon as you can get away, ride to my house. If I can't find her, I'll contact you there."

"We'll be there," Clint said.

"And for God's sake, find out what this woman needs." He jerked his chin toward the house. "Whatever it is, I'll buy it for her."

Jarrod mounted his horse in a single movement. He reined the beast in a tight circle before goading him to gallop down the road. Overhead, the gray-black skies churned. Wind whipped through his hair and streaked beneath the collar of his coat and shirt.

Sophia had gone today to investigate her counterfeiter, not to search for his father. She'd told him herself that she'd sworn off the hunt for Blackhaw's thief, which meant there was no possible reason for her to visit Oliver Kinsworthy before Jarrod could get to her and warn her.

She was safe and he was overreacting.

His dread worsened. He knelt over his horse's back, urging the animal to go faster.

Chapter 22

❦

"**O**liver?" Sophia knocked on the front door of his home for the second time, then stamped her feet in an effort to warm herself. Her blood, skin, and bones were freezing after the long ride from Hitchcock's courthouse to Oliver's offices in town, then here when his secretary had informed her he wasn't in. The wind wound its way up her body, penetrating straight through her clothing.

Hoping he might be around back, she clasped closed the neck of her coat and hurried to the rear of the house. For almost as long as she could remember, Oliver had lived on this quarter-acre lot on this quietly tasteful residential street. "Oliver?"

Dead leaves tumbled across her shoes when she gained the back-door stoop. "Oliver?" She knocked rapidly.

No answer.

She knocked again as she tested the knob. It turned easily beneath her hand, hinges creaking as the door slid open. For a split second, she hesitated. Surely he wouldn't mind if she escaped the weather and waited for him inside.

She let herself in, the outside noise cutting away as she closed the door. The tick of a clock welcomed her, as did the warmer temperature, the smell of coffee, and the lamps that had been left burning. It looked as if he'd just stepped out for a brief errand.

Rubbing her arms with her gloved hands, she delved into his home. The atmosphere was masculine and muted, comfortable. The artwork hanging on both sides of the hallway watched her pass as she made her way to the front room. Automatically, she reached out to nudge closed a hallway closet that had been left ajar—

Air gusted through the opening, ruffling her hair.

She stopped. Frowning, she opened the closet door, but instead of a closet she found a staircase that led downward to some sort of basement. Darkness shadowed the ten or so steps, but faint light pooled on the floor below. "Oliver?"

Quiet answered.

She took a second look at the door's knob and noticed it had the capability to lock. How odd to discover stairs behind a locking door that looked very much like a closet door. She hadn't even realized this house contained a basement. Curiosity mounting, she eased down the first few steps, then down the rest of the way.

When she reached the bottom she halted. The flame within the basement's lamp sent light flickering over a space perhaps one half the size of the upper story. A printing press stood like a metallic king in the center of the floor. Containers of ink sat upon shelves. On a wide artist's desk piles of money had been stacked. Reams of paper waited in wooden crates.

A chill that had nothing to do with the climate birthed deep in Sophia's stomach. She eyed her surroundings for long moments without moving, her brain turning slowly, like the rusted wheels of an old mill. After a time, she moved around the space, her dull gaze cataloging what her agent's mind recognized but her loyalty refused to credit. The chill invaded her chest, her limbs, her head. She stopped at the room's far end and stared blankly at a newly created artist's plate of a ten-dollar note.

Oh, Oliver. Her thoughts raced back in time, remembering her friend over all the years. All the times he'd visited her at the orphanage and the countless times they'd met to discuss their hunt for Adam Stone. His smiles. The way his speckled hands cushioned hers.

Impossible to reconcile that man with one who could be guilty of counterfeiting. She couldn't force this puzzle piece into the same mold she'd cast of him in her heart.

"Sophia."

She spun toward the sound of his voice.

Oliver stood halfway down the stairs, holding a brown sack. In many ways he looked so familiar . . . his bald head, the snowy white brows and mustache, the too-tight tweed vest. Yet the expression in his eyes, one of sadness and censure, she'd never seen before.

Painful silence strained the air between them.

Disillusionment and confusion tangled Sophia's emotions. Ridiculously, she wanted to apologize for snooping. Especially, *especially*, because in a distant way she realized that nothing could ever be the same for them again, after this, when she'd very much wanted their relationship to continue forever.

He took the last few stairs, stopped at the bottom, then made no move to come closer. "What are you doing here?"

"I came to ask you . . . a question. I let myself in because of the cold, then found the door to this basement ajar."

He didn't answer, just stood there, watching her. The awkward quiet expanded, slinking its way into the room's farthest corners.

"Why?" she asked softly. "Why are you doing this, Oliver?"

"Why?" He shook his head ruefully and tossed his brown bag onto a countertop. "Because large quantities of money are hard to come by."

"Why would you need large quantities of money? You've this house, a flourishing law practice—"

"Do you really think I'd manufacture money for myself?" The wrinkles around his eyes seemed to deepen with disappointment. "No, it's the Southern Army that needs it."

"The Southern Army?"

"Good men, friends of mine, relatives," he said grimly, "fought and died for the right of the South to secede." His lips pursed. "It's a right we were due then and a right we're due now."

"We lost the war," she said feebly.

"I've supported and believed wholeheartedly in this cause for thirty years. I'm no quitter." His eyes blazed with devotion. "They fought and *died*, Sophia. What kind of man would I be if I refused to do whatever I could for the cause? If I refused to do my part?"

"I don't know."

"I do."

"You're paying them?" she asked, slightly disoriented. "The Southern Army?" None of this fit with the man she knew.

"We're gaining strength, but strength takes money that's quickly drained."

Sophia released a painful breath. His convoluted notions of honor and nobility only made this worse. "Perhaps I'd best go."

Oliver rolled his lips into a resigned frown. "I'm sorry you had to find out about this, Sophia."

"I'm sorry, too."

"You're sorry for my sake, I'd hazard to guess. Whereas I'm sorry for your sake."

A frission of fear mingled with her shock.

"This cause is too important," he said. "I can't have you running to the law and informing them of my situation."

What, he'd try to physically stop her? Hurt her? *Her*? He'd not a violent bone in his body and she . . . she was like a daughter to him. For God's sake, he'd hugged her on the steps of the orphanage when she was eight years old— With a sickening lurch, she wondered suddenly what else he was capable of. He'd carted her off to that orphanage because Adam . . . because someone had stolen all their money.

I've supported and believed wholeheartedly in this cause for thirty years.

Mother Mary. He'd been feeding cash to his cause

since before her birth, and certainly at the time of Blackhaw's demise. She felt dizzy with betrayal and heartsickness and her own naïveté. In her mind Adam Stone had
always been guilty of robbing Blackhaw's fortune.
Largely because of what . . . Oliver had told her over the
years. Oh, heavens, Jarrod. Holden. She moved toward
the staircase. Oliver moved, too, so that his bulk squarely
blocked the mouth of the stairs.

She stared at him, anger swirling to the surface.
"You're not going to let me leave?

"I can't."

"We've been friends for twenty years."

"Sophia," he chided, "the most important thing about
honor is that a person can't allow it to be diluted by anything. Even affection. Surely, you've learned that by
now."

"Let me pass." She stormed toward him.

From within his coat, he quietly pulled free a Smith &
Wesson. The round eye of the barrel sighted on her chest.

Disbelief struck her like a punch to the chest. "You
wouldn't shoot me."

"My dear, for the rights of the Southern people, I'd do
anything on earth."

Her breath turned shallow in the face of her reeling
world. Her dear, kind Oliver was willing to kill her—to
kill her—to keep her quiet. She struggled to think as she
retreated. She slipped her hands into her skirt pockets in
a gesture she hoped looked capitulatory. The fingers of
her right hand gripped the hilt of her knife as her gaze
measured the distance up the stairs to freedom.

Could she attack him? She was an agent who acted
through observation, not confrontation. Could she stab

an old man for believing too fervently in the wrong hope?

Upstairs, a door opened and shut. Oliver looked toward the sound of footsteps progressing down the hallway.

A tall, wiry man filled the doorway. Silas Clarke. She recognized him from the day she'd followed him home. Two others came to stand beside Silas. Men whose eyes she'd seen once before, above the lines of their masks when they'd attacked her outside Jarrod's home. Her heart raced. Like an animal cornered, she instinctively backed up until the base of her spine hit the edge of the artist's desk. No farther to go.

"I found her here," Oliver said to the men.

"Well, we can't have that." Silas led the others into the basement. He studied her for a long moment, then shook his head in disgust. "Perhaps you'd best sit down, Mrs. La Rue."

"No."

"Just take a seat right there." He indicated the artist's chair as he approached her. His cohorts loomed behind him.

"No," she repeated.

They closed in, almost near enough to grab her now—She whipped free her knife. Quick as an eyeblink, Silas made a swipe for it. Sophia reared away from his reach and parried, thrusting the blade toward him. He darted backward. "Get out of my way," she snarled, arcing her blade through the air, fighting to hold the three of them at bay.

The one on the right made a quick move in her direction. She swung toward him, even as he was feinting back. Muscled hands closed over her forearm from the other direction. Silas wrenched the knife from her grip.

Terrified, furious, she threw her elbows, squirmed, and kicked. They were everywhere, hauling her off her feet, subduing her flailing limbs. She cried out and tried to fight them off. No luck. They were overpowering her, stronger. The three forced her into the chair—two holding her feet against its legs, Silas behind, trapping her arms behind the chair's back. "I need twine," he bit out.

Sophia struggled, sweat heating her face and neck, strands of hair falling in front of her face, tangling with her eyelashes.

Oliver collected a length of twine from a drawer filled with supplies and tossed it to Silas, who began to bind her wrists.

"Where are we going to take her?" Silas asked.

"Far," Oliver answered. "I don't need to tell you that my neighbors aren't accustomed to hearing gunshots—"

A resounding knock boomed through the house.

All four men froze.

Sophia gasped for breath, tried to pull free her wrists. Silas responded by looping twine around them two more times. Again, came the knock. Forceful, vibrating with impatience.

"Bennett," Oliver said.

"Yes, sir."

"See who's there."

The man grasping her right foot took hold of her left as well, freeing his partner to dash up the stairs.

She recognized the icy eyes of the man at her feet. He'd been the one to slap her that day in the rain. Fear clawing her, she remembered his mercilessness and power. Wondered which servant he'd convinced to poison Jarrod's wine.

This time, knocking rocked the door at the other end of the house. The back door.

The sounds of a scuffle ensued upstairs. A grunt, the breaking of glass, a heavy thud. The three men in the basement exchanged a look. Oliver readjusted his hold on his gun. "Bennett?" he called loudly.

No reply.

Behind her, Silas let the twine he'd been holding fall to the ground. She heard the rasp of a gun sliding past leather as he unsheathed his weapon. Frantically, she tried to yank free the restraint securing her wrists, but he'd looped it tightly and it held firm.

The door at the top of the stairs crashed open.

Jarrod stood on the threshold with his legs braced apart, the silver of the gun he clasped stark against his black greatcoat. He looked like an avenging angel, mad as hell.

Love and relief billowed within Sophia, tamped immediately when Silas and Oliver clicked back the hammers of their guns. There were three of them and only one of him.

Jarrod's forbidding gaze swept the scene, pausing on her for an instant, before coming to rest on Oliver. "You let her go now, and I won't have to kill any of you," Jarrod said.

Lord above. Sophia's muscles strained against the cords at her wrists.

"You're outnumbered, Stone." Oliver's eyes narrowed.

"I've been outnumbered before by better men than you. Let her go."

Sophia saw Oliver's trigger finger whiten as he exerted pressure. "Jarrod!" she screamed.

Jarrod vaulted over the banister of the stairs, landed on the basement floor, and came up swinging. His punch sent Oliver careening into a wall of shelves.

Both men who'd been guarding her ran toward the fight. Sophia stuck out her foot, tripping Silas. He broke his fall with his hands. His gun spiraled across the floor. When he started to push himself upward, Sophia gripped one of the rungs at the back of the chair and stood, swinging its legs at him. She caught him across the back with enough force that the wood splintered. He sprawled to the ground, spewing curses.

Sophia dropped the chair and ran to his gun, kicking it beneath the printing press lest he try to reclaim it. She worked frantically to jerk free her wrists. Jarrod was viciously fighting the man who'd slapped her unconscious, their blows landing with crunching power. Oliver had recovered enough to hold steady his gun, waiting for a clean shot. Movement from above caught her eye. Bennett had come to, and he hurtled down the stairs to help his cohorts. He drove his shoulder into Jarrod's back, snapping Jarrod's head back with the force of it.

Sophia wailed, remembering too well the way she'd watched Jarrod's guard beaten nearly to death by these same men. With a final heave, the twine stretched open enough for her to pull free her hands. She ran toward Jarrod—

Silas grabbed a handful of her skirt and heaved backward. Her knees slammed against the floor.

"Sophia!" Jarrod yelled.

Their gazes met for a split second. He'd knocked Bennett onto the stairs, and blood was gushing from the man's nose. "Watch out," she gasped, as his other attacker coiled his arm for another punch.

There were too many of them. She scratched her way to standing and dashed to help him. Jarrod was breathing hard, a grimace of rage contorting his features. He sent his fist hurtling again and again.

Sophia curled her hands into the back of someone's shirt and tried to pull him off Jarrod. She was shoved away. Her back banged against the wall and pain flashed up her spine, but she returned quickly, fingernails bared, fighting to haul them off Jarrod.

And then there were more fists. Silas was yanked by helping hands into the air, then thrown against the printing press. She looked up to see J. T. growl as he went after the man. She stumbled backward. Clint was there, too, socking Bennett as he tried to stand. And Maggie at the top of the stairs. The scuffle enlarged, fists flying, grunts rushing from split lips.

Her dazed attention cut to Oliver. He raised his gun, determination in his eyes. He was going to start shooting, not caring anymore whether he hit his own men.

She flew at him, managing to strike his gun arm upward just as he pulled the trigger. The bullet howled into the ceiling. Hissing with rage, Oliver turned the gun on her.

"Don't you dare." The muzzle of Jarrod's pistol pressed unrelentingly against Oliver's temple.

All around her, Sophia sensed stillness where moments before there had been hectic motion.

"Put it down," Jarrod said, "or I swear to God I'll kill you."

A muscle near Oliver's eye ticked.

Sophia didn't move, didn't breathe, just stared at the yawning black hole of the gun pointed at her chest.

"Put it down," Jarrod demanded, nudging his own gun so sharply against Oliver's head that the older man flinched.

Slowly, Oliver lowered his weapon.

Sophia's shoulders slumped with deflated tension.

"You're under arrest," Clint said as he gathered Oliver's arms behind his back and fastened cuffs around his wrists.

Sophia looked to Jarrod. He gazed back at her. Blood trickled from the side of his lip.

Her heart twisted at the sight.

She could see his chest pumping beneath the layers of his coat and suit. One of the men lay at his feet. Silas, too, had been knocked out by J. T., who stood with his arms crossed above his prey. Bennett was writhing in pain near the bottom of the stairs, cradling a broken nose.

Maggie picked her way through the rubble. "Are you all right?"

Sophia pushed a chunk of hair out of her eyes with the back of her hand, then nodded, too weak in the aftermath of her terror to speak. Thank God Jarrod was unharmed, that his brothers had come in time to keep him safe. He'd not be crushed and bloodied because of her.

"We returned to your house to find a prison guard from Huntsville waiting for us," J. T. said to Jarrod.

"Huntsville?" Jarrod asked.

"Yeah. In hopes of a messenger's fee, he'd traveled all the way from the prison with a warning from Holden."

"Which is?" Jarrod asked tensely.

"That this one killed our father." Grimly, he inclined his head toward Oliver.

Jarrod's scowl turned frightening as he leveled it on Oliver.

"Holden was only just able to remember it," J. T. said. "He was there that night at Blackhaw with Mother. He saw Kinsworthy shoot our father."

Sophia swallowed a rise of bile.

Oliver looked toward the wall, his mouth tightly sealed.

"He shot him for the money?" Jarrod asked.

Clint nodded. "Mrs. Warren had entrusted our father with it that night for their investment in the factory. Kinsworthy caught up with him before he even reached the gates of the property, killed him for it, and kept it."

A burning ball formed in Sophia's chest. She'd been the first to believe Adam Stone guilty and the last to believe it untrue.

A dangerous pressure built in the room. A pressure borne from the years of stigma and doubt and bitterness the Stone brothers had endured. Sophia sensed it, pumping through her veins, pumping through the veins of Jarrod and J. T. and Clint.

"We rode to Blackhaw Manor to find you," J. T. said to Jarrod. "You and Sophia weren't there, but Miss May was. She's the one who led us here. How'd you know where to find Sophia?"

"When she wasn't at Blackhaw," Jarrod answered, "I went to Kinsworthy's offices. His secretary told me Sophia had just been in and that she'd likely come here." His jaw tightened into a severe line. "She had."

Maggie cleared her throat. "Perhaps we'd best get these boys to the sheriff."

"If you don't mind," Jarrod said to his brothers, "I'd like a word with Sophia alone."

Her heart skipped a beat.

"Do you need my help getting these men upstairs first?" he asked.

" 'Course not." J. T. slung the limp Silas over one shoulder like he might a sack of potatoes, then helped Maggie pull Bennett to his feet. Clint lifted the third, and urged Oliver ahead of him up the stairs, using the point of his gun.

Once they'd straggled out, she and Jarrod faced each other without distractions or noise. She remembered last night in flashes of detail—the flat plane of his stomach, the feel of his hot chest, the fervent look on his face as he'd made love to her. "Jarrod, I. . . ." How did one begin to express this? "I'm so sorry I believed your father to be guilty. I was wrong."

"You had reason to believe what you did." His solemn tone frightened her. "I don't give a damn about that."

"What is it then?"

He swiped at his lip, looked at the blood on his fingers, and angrily cleared the rest with his thumb. She could see tightness invading his shoulders, almost touch the darkening of his mood. Over their weeks together she'd grown attuned to him, to the way his frustration could rise, as it was rising now, to a jagged ridge.

He swiveled away from her, presenting her with his broad back.

Please let him not be about to tell me he doesn't want me. Maybe she could bear it later. But after the beauty of what they'd shared last night, after Oliver's betrayal, she needed him right now. Desperately.

He stalked a few steps away, turned. "Here's how it is."

She held her ground, praying she wouldn't shame herself if he broke her heart.

"I want you," he said bluntly.

Her heart stuttered. Then swelled—

"But I can't do this. I thought I could, but I can't. I can't let you go to your job knowing that every time I do you could be walking into a bullet or a knife." He dashed a hand through his wind-tousled hair. "That's not the kind of man I am. It's not in me."

She couldn't move.

"So you have a choice. Me or Twilight's Ghost."

She understood why he was asking this of her, she did. But it was too much. Old fears twisted around her. He was asking her to put all her hopes and trust—her very existence—in his hands. To risk everything on him.

What if he abandoned her? Where would she be then? Worse off than living the rest of her life without him? Her body, the very material of her tendons and bones longed for him. And yet . . . how could she risk everything? How could she sacrifice the only security she had?

"You've until noon tomorrow to decide," he said, his voice curt. "I summoned my ship into the port a week ago. I'll wait at the dock for you until then." Unspeakable sorrow grooved into his expression. She glimpsed the pain that lived inside him that he so rarely showed.

Then, far too soon, he turned and walked up the stairs, the back of his greatcoat slapping against his heels. His body filled the hallway door, then was gone. And she was deathly alone.

She wrapped her arms around herself and closed her

eyes against the hurt ravaging her insides. He'd given her until noon tomorrow to think about it. But what was there to think about, really? She'd never been a heedless person. She'd always made the safest choices in the interest of protecting herself.

Yes, but *for him*, a part of her argued. He was worth the risk. He could give her the stars from the sky and sea wind across her face. He had the power to make her young again.

She wiped suddenly cold hands down her forehead, her cheeks, her nose, her lips, struggling to compose herself.

By the time she let herself out the front door of Oliver's home, only Maggie remained. Her friend stood in the cold, waiting for her, the breeze mournfully tossing the hem of her coat.

"Come," Maggie said, approaching her and wrapping a comforting arm about Sophia's shoulders. Gently, she guided her toward the buggy. "We need to send word of this to Simon." She smiled sadly, gave Sophia's shoulders a squeeze. "We've a reward to collect and a house to save from the auction block."

"Yes," Sophia said, though she couldn't help feeling that the most valuable reward God had ever given her had just walked out of her life for good.

Chapter 23

The next day Sophia sat beside Maggie on one of the wooden benches that ran down the center of the bank. Her fingers were laced together in her lap, the pads of her thumbs tapping twice every second. She hadn't taken her attention from the clock mounted upon the wall behind the teller's console in exactly seventeen minutes and thirty-three seconds. It was eleven-ten. *Eleven-ten.* Getting to be too late.

She parted her lips, closed them, stared at the clock in utter distress. Maggie patted her knee. But instead of soothing her, her friend's sympathy made her want to jump out of her skin. After a sleepless night, she was ill prepared to deal with this right now. If she had to watch another minute tick by without the teller informing her that her reward money had arrived, these good people of

Galveston, doing their good transactions, would damn
well see her go stark raving mad before their eyes.

Blackhaw's auction was scheduled for noon, just as
was Jarrod's promised departure, and her money should
have arrived by now. Long before now. Immediately
when they'd left Oliver's last night they'd couriered a letter to Simon, informing him that they'd caught the counterfeiter and alerting him to the urgency involved in
receiving the money first thing in the morning. It was
asking a great deal of the Agency, she knew, to move so
speedily on this. Ordinarily the processing and receipt of
rewards took days or weeks. But over her years of service, she'd *earned* this one favor.

She watched the minute hand tick downward a notch.
Eleven-eleven. Simon had sent word straight back, saying that Slocum's Mercantile must first have the opportunity to verify that the counterfeit money they'd been
passed had indeed come from Oliver's basement press.
For her, he'd promised to attempt to complete that chore
yesterday evening so that Slocum's could issue the reward first thing this morning and so that he could trans-
fer it to her account, here.

She and Maggie had been waiting at the bank's front
doors when they'd opened for business this morning.
Hours ago. And still, nothing. She'd planned to take the
reward money to the tax office straight away, so that
they'd have time to cancel the auction entirely. Now she
was going to have to rush straight to the auction itself
and create a spectacle. That's if the money arrived in
time at all.

Did Slocum's Mercantile, did Simon, have any idea
how very much Blackhaw meant to her? Did they have
the slightest inkling? Could they possibly let her do the

work, earn the reward, get this close to saving her only possession, and then allow it to be snatched away? A sob built in her throat.

Eleven-fifteen now. And Jarrod— *Don't think about him.* But she couldn't help herself. Because with each jerk of the clock's minute hand, she felt as if he were being ripped farther from her. There was no choice to make where he was concerned. She'd known that from the minute he'd issued his ultimatum, his lip bloodied from fighting on her behalf. So why had she never felt more desolate in all her life?

If she could only get the reward money and save her house. Then she'd feel better, less barren. Then she'd have something.

Maggie leaned in close. "Yesterday at Oliver's did you see the way Clint felled that Bennett person with a single blow? I swear, I almost expired right then and there. The man is an absolute walking, talking, breathing god. Did you see how he handcuffed Oliver and told him he was under arrest? And then, be still my heart, the way he lifted Bennett over his shoulder as if he weighed nothing and marched Oliver outside? My mouth was so dry with . . . well, *awe* . . . that I didn't dare say a word to him, so when we all arrived outside I just stared at him like some sort of magpie while he loaded up the prisoners. Once Jarrod joined them, Clint tipped his hat to me and said good-bye, and I didn't even manage a gurgle. Have you ever heard of anything so humiliating? Not even a *gurgle*, Sophia."

"I . . ." Maggie's conversation was stringing tighter her nerves. "I'm sorry, Maggie, I just can't think about anything at the moment except the time. Something's wrong."

Maggie pulled in a breath and glanced at the clock. When she saw the time, she pushed to her feet. "I'm going to visit Simon."

"We're not to meet with him at his offices—"

"These circumstances are special. I'll take a careful route and use the back entrance."

"Maggie—"

"I can't let you sit here any longer without information. You stay here in case the money comes in, and I'll go."

Sophia couldn't decide. She glanced from Maggie to the teller.

"I'm going," Maggie said firmly. She pulled on her coat as she rushed toward the double doors.

Sophia thought she'd been desperate before, but Maggie's departure heightened her anxiety by bounds. She started tapping her thumbs three times a second. Eleven-twenty came and went. Eleven-twenty-five. Eleven-thirty.

"Mrs. LaRue?"

Sophia's attention sliced to the teller who'd called her name. The short gentleman with the brown doe's eyes motioned for her to hurry forward.

Too harried to be relieved, almost too harried to be polite, she went to his station and waited while he counted out the bills she was owed. She stashed the small fortune in her reticule, thanked him, then turned and fled. She had just enough time to reach the auction they were conducting at the courthouse.

The day greeted her with a swirl of chilly breeze. She paused on the bank steps just long enough to shove her arms into the sleeves of her coat. Then, clasping her reticule close to her chest, she hurried down the sidewalk.

I want you. Jarrod's words snaked out from the buzzing sounds of the city.

She ducked her head and walked faster.

I can't let you go to your job knowing that every time I do you could be walking into a bullet or a knife. That's not the kind of man I am. It's not in me. His voice tugged at her, insistent, persuasive. She shot a look over her shoulder to where the masts of the great ships pointed into the sky beyond the line of buildings. Her heart lurched.

Biting her bottom lip, she brought her concentration back to the sidewalk passing beneath her feet.

So you have a choice. Me or Twilight's Ghost.

The strips of weathered wood began to slow.

Me or Twilight's Ghost.

Her strides cut to a halt, and she was left staring at a square of unmoving wood.

Who was Twilight's Ghost? Not a real person. Just a mask she sometimes wore. It couldn't keep her warm in bed at night. Couldn't make her laugh. Couldn't cherish her.

The reason she'd been so upset back at the bank, she realized, wasn't because the lateness of her reward money had forced her to face the possibility of losing her house. It was because it had forced her to face the certainty that she could no longer have the house and Jarrod both. And having both was the secret hope she'd buried deep within herself. That understanding came like sunbeams parting the clouds and connecting honeyed fingers with the earth.

It was almost noon, and the advancing hour meant she could have either Blackhaw or Jarrod. Twilight's Ghost or Jarrod. Her old life or Jarrod. She raised her face and peered in the direction of the courthouse, where the auctioneer would be preparing his information, where buyers would be gathering. She blinked. Then with a rippling wave of daring that felt like the rushing of a million bubbles against the inside of her skin, she turned.

And she hurried toward the docks.

Until just now, her decision to cut Jarrod out of her life had seemed palatable. But as soon as she'd started her walk toward the courthouse, actually taken action toward a life without Jarrod, everything had changed. Her choice had become brutally wrong.

She wove through a crowd of people.

Mother above, she was tired of being afraid, cautious, untrusting. She'd needed those mantles once, needed her job to feel secure, and her house to feel safe. She didn't need them anymore. Strips that had bound her for years seemed to unwind from her body and whip away on the crests of the wind. Making her lighter, lighter, lighter.

Her steps increased in speed until she was practically running.

She wanted to love Jarrod and be loved by him, perhaps have children together and share a family. *Family.* The thought resonated down to the very deepest core of herself. Suddenly, she wanted a family with a ferocity that told her she'd wanted it her whole life and wanted it more than anything else on earth.

Getting closer now. The dock was almost in sight. She completed the length of one block, then another, then the last remaining block before reaching the harbor. Thanks to her years of observation from the dock's platform, she knew every supporting pier and plank that composed it. Running amidst and between the stevedores as they unloaded cargo, she scanned faces for a pair of green eyes, for black hair, and straight brows.

She didn't see him. Worry burgeoned, stealing just a fraction of her joy. Her skirts churned around her legs. Anxiously, she lifted a hand to shield her eyes. Where was he? He'd be here. He'd said he would. He'd not leave her.

She found herself at the end of the dock, the wood cutting away to reveal frothing water beneath. Panic rising, she turned in a circle, searching for him.

In the distance, she glimpsed the rear of a sleek ship as it eased out the mouth of the harbor, its sails filling with the gale that would carry it away. Because of its design and newness, it looked very much like the kind of vessel Jarrod would own. Her concern thickened, solidified.

She grabbed the arm of a stevedore as he rose from unloading a sack of salt atop a nearby pile of goods. "Do you have the time, sir?"

"Certainly, miss." He smiled, revealing gaps in his ground-down teeth. He pulled a timepiece from his trouser pocket. "It's twelve-ten."

"So late?" she asked, dismayed.

"No need to trouble yourself there, miss," he said encouragingly. "The day's still young."

"Are you," she licked her lips, "Are you familiar with that ship there?" She gestured to the one that was even now cutting its way into open water.

"Ah, yes'm. It's been in port for two days now. Fine ship, that. Excellent lie in the water."

"Do you happen to know who owns it?"

"You ever heard of an oil baron named Jarrod Stone?"

Every muscle in her body clenched. *Mother Mary, no.* She loved him. No, he couldn't possibly have left her here. She gazed at the ship, his beautiful ship, as it sailed away from her. Sailed beyond her ability to catch it back.

She'd watched dreams die before. But never one that mattered so much and never because of her own stupidity. She'd realized she loved him too late. She couldn't breathe beneath the crush of disappointment.

"Are you all right, miss?"

She nodded mutely.

The man stayed at her side for another few seconds, before finally returning to his tasks.

She remained where she was, staring at Jarrod's ship. Within her mind she saw him, his black hair shining, his piercing green eyes glinting and his lips curved into a smile that promised her she was the only woman in the world.

The tragedy was that she knew for certain now. Now that she'd lost him, she knew that Jarrod Stone had been the right choice to make for her life and for her heart.

Her footsteps sounded as hollow as her insides felt as she approached the courthouse steps. Like an old rag doll, there was nothing left to hold her together except a few fraying threads of stubbornness. She clutched at those and walked doggedly forward.

A trio of gentlemen turned toward her as she neared.

She clasped her reticule full of reward money in both hands. "Did you gentlemen by chance attend the auction of Blackhaw Manor?"

"We did." All three studied her with interest.

"Was it already completed?" she asked, both knowing what they would answer and dreading the hearing of it.

"I'm afraid so, ma'am."

Pain cut at her, surprisingly sharp. She looked away from them for a moment, fighting to retain the last of her composure. She had the money needed to pay Blackhaw's taxes. She didn't have the money it would take to buy the house back from its new owner. "Do you happen to know," she asked, her attention returning to the men, "who purchased the estate?"

"I did," one of them answered. He was a tidy gentleman, with a beautifully cut blue suit and a black bowler.

Her courage wavered and she wanted nothing more than to walk away and shut herself inside her bedroom—where? Her bedroom where? She didn't have a bedroom anymore. "Sir, is there any possibility that you might consider selling Blackhaw to me?"

He shook his head.

"It's been in my family since the time that it was built, and I'd very much like to retain it. If there's even the slightest chance that you might consider an offer, I'm sure that I could come up with a figure that would be palatable. . . ." Her words drifted off. He was still shaking his head. Despite the kindness she read in his expression, she also read inflexibility.

"I'm sorry, ma'am," he said. "While I sympathize with your situation, there's absolutely no chance of a sale."

"But I'm willing to pay whatever is necessary." And somehow she would.

"I'm sorry." His eyes filled with apology. "It can't be done."

She simply gazed at him. How was she going to tell this to Maggie and the Dewberrys? How could she ever make this right to them?

She bit her upper lip and inclined her head. Spine erect with brittle, futile pride, she turned on her heel and walked toward Blackhaw. She needed somewhere to go to cry. And she needed to say good-bye.

Sophia turned her key in Blackhaw's lock, then eased inside. For an interminable time, she leaned against the inside of the door and allowed her gaze to travel over the foyer. The sounds of the house coasted around her. The Dewberrys appeared to be out, and Maggie had yet to return, so without people to enliven the space there was just the music that was uniquely Blackhaw's. A dignified, very quiet music. Punctuated by the creak of the shutter on the second floor and the wheeze of the door behind her as it withstood the wind.

Tears moistened her eyes and slipped free. *Oh, God. This is awful.* The pain of losing Jarrod, of losing this house, twisted like a knife in her belly. She walked into the foyer, glanced at the parlor—and froze.

Blood rushed from her head in a dizzying stream, because there, every glorious inch of his magnificent body slouched in a wing chair, was Jarrod. He was staring into the fire apparently lost in thought, his elbow planted on the armrest, his hand supporting his head. The firelight burnished his profile, the muscular hollow of his cheeks, the grave set of his lips.

He was here. Now she was truly crying, but the tears welled from a deep spring of gratitude. Immeasurable, untappable gratitude. He'd not left on his ship for better places and better women. He'd come here. For her. She didn't know whether to fall to her knees or run and throw herself on top of him and cover his handsome face with kisses.

She did neither. With such an enormous storm of love gusting inside her, the best she could manage was his name. "Jarrod," she said shakily.

He looked up at once. When he saw her standing there, he pushed quickly to his feet, staring at her as if he didn't quite believe she was real. It was exactly how she felt about him.

She tried a smile, but it wobbled badly. "Jarrod, I—"

"No," he said softly. "I've got something to say to you first, and I need you to hear me out."

Unsure whether she could string any syllables together right now anyway, she nodded.

"I apologize for giving you that ultimatum yesterday."

She opened her mouth to speak, but he lifted his hand to stop her words before they could come. "I stood alone on that dock today waiting for you and feeling like a damn idiot. I don't blame you for not coming. Why would you? I finally told the ship to sail." He took two steps toward her, stopped. "The truth is . . ." A troubled expression crossed his face. "Well, the truth is that I'll take you any way I can get you, job or not. I don't even care if you only love me a little, because I swear to you, Sophia, that I love you enough for us both."

Her bottom lip dropped open in astonishment.

He reached into the inside pocket of his suit as he approached her, smiling a self-deprecating smile that fisted around her heart. He stopped at her side, ran a knuckle lovingly down her cheek to wipe away her tears, then flipped open a tiny satin box. "Marry me."

A ring box, she realized, as she gaped at the diamonds sparkling up at her. Lots of diamonds. A huge oval one in the center, surrounded by a circlet of round diamonds— all of them set in a sumptuous bed of platinum.

"Are you going to throw this one back in my face the way you did all the others?" he murmured, humor warming his voice.

"This one," she said, looking up at him, "I'll keep."

He grinned at her, and her belly did a slow flip. He lifted her left hand, kissed the heart of her palm, then slid the ring onto her third finger.

"May I speak now?" she asked.

"May I kiss you now?" he countered, his gaze turning hot as it dropped to her lips.

"No." She planted her hand against his chest. If he so much as nibbled on her ear, all sense would be lost and she wouldn't get a chance to set him right and say what needed to be said. "First of all . . ." She placed her hands on his cheeks, wanting to be sure he could see the truth in her eyes. "First of all, I did go to the dock today. And I don't just love you a little. I love you so much that I went to the dock ready and willing to give up everything, *everything*, for you, including Blackhaw."

He took her head in his hands and kissed her. The contact was sensual and adoring. Endlessly soft. She felt as if they were exchanging souls in that kiss, promising and accepting promises for a thousand golden things to come.

He pulled away just inches, so close their foreheads were still touching. "Tell me you didn't give up Blackhaw for me."

"I did," she said, pulling away just enough so that she could look into his eyes. "And as for my career . . . I thought we did pretty well that night we broke into the stationery shop together. Maybe we can work as a team from now on. Or not. It doesn't matter anymore."

"Tell me, Sophia, that you didn't give up Blackhaw for me."

She laced her fingers into the hair at his nape. "I couldn't pay the taxes on it, so the state auctioned it today at noon, and I couldn't be in two places at once."

He groaned and kissed her forehead, the corner of her eye, her cheek, her earlobe. "I cannot *believe* you gave up Blackhaw for me. Especially because"—he kissed her chin—"I've already taken the liberty of redecorating the great room."

"Redecorating?" she asked. His kisses must have muddled her mind because that made no sense.

Holding her hand snugly in his, he pulled her across the foyer and threw open the door to the great room. Beyond, a cheer arose. Sophia gaped at the assembled crowd. The Dewberrys and Collier sat before a makeshift pulpit someone had doubtless stolen from a local sanctuary. Jarrod's brothers stood to the right of the pulpit, clapping. And Maggie stood to the left, clapping and laughing. A minister stood behind the pulpit, robes in place, Bible in hand. Her favorite flowers, wisteria and daffodils, spilled from vases on pedestals. Garlands of white ribbon swagged the windows.

It looked for all the world like a wedding.

"Are you trying to blackmail me again?" she whispered.

"If it'll work." His expression glinted unrepentantly.

"You're incorrigible."

"You're irresistible."

Delight spun in heady circles inside her. "Will you . . . will you just excuse us for one moment?" Sophia asked the occupants of the great room. She pulled Jarrod into the hall, out of earshot and view. "I'd love to marry you here, now," she said sincerely. "Only I worry about the new owner. I've no idea when he'll arrive to claim this place, and I'd hate for him to interrupt us, for anything to spoil our wedding."

"Sophie," he chided. He smiled and seemed to wait for her to comprehend the joke.

"What?"

"Do you honestly think I'd let this place go?" he asked. "Knowing how much it means to you?"

He was so beautiful and he loved her and he smelled good and he was actually *hers* and maybe that was why she was having trouble understanding. "Jarrod, I spoke with the gentleman who purchased Blackhaw—"

"Tidy fellow. Wears good suits. Bowler hat?"

". . . yes."

"He's Collier's assistant. I couldn't very well send Collier could I, and risk him missing our wedding?"

Shock cleared her thoughts with a powerful sweep. "You knew about the auction?"

"Of course. I've excellent sources. I ought to, I pay them well."

"You bought this house?"

"No, you did. I purchased it for you in your name."

She gazed up at him, stunned.

"I've always had a hankering for this old place," he said, taking in their surroundings before focusing on her once more. "Ever since I begged at its gates as a kid and a little girl in a white dress gave me fruit from her trees."

Goose bumps flowed over her body as she looked into the green eyes of a man and saw in them the green eyes of a scrappy boy. A boy who had been desperately hungry and equally proud and equally determined. The memory slotted into place with what she knew of Jarrod and suddenly she could see it, how that boy had become this magnificent man.

"Speechless?" he asked.

She nodded, thoroughly overcome. Who knew a body could hold this much happiness without shooting like a firework into a million points of light?

"It looks as if I finally found the gift to melt the heart of an ice princess."

"No. It was you who melted my heart." She lifted onto her tiptoes to press a kiss to his lips. "Thank you for my house."

"It's nothing compared to what you've given me." He walked her backward, pressing her against the wall and deepening the kiss.

"How long you going to make us wait?" J. T. yelled from inside the great room.

Jarrod pulled back. Grinned at her. "Shall we?"

She laughed and let herself be drawn to the open doorway. Jarrod's brothers straightened to attention when they saw them. Maggie jerked her besotted gaze from Clint to them, then beamed.

"You sure about this?" Jarrod asked, as he tucked her hand in the crook of his arm. "This will make you the first Mrs. Stone."

"I've had seven years experience handling criminals, Mr. Stone. I believe I can manage you and your brothers."

Jarrod laughed and led her down the aisle.

Dear Reader,

If you've enjoyed the Avon romance you've just read, then you won't want to miss next month's selections. As always, there's a wonderful mix of contemporary and historical romance for you to choose from. And I encourage you to try a book you might not regularly read. (For example, Regency historical readers might want to be brave and give a different setting a try!) I promise that *every* Avon romance is terrific.

Let's begin with Rita Award-winning and *USA Today* bestselling writer Lorraine Heath's THE OUTLAW AND THE LADY. Angela Bainbridge has spent her life dreaming of the perfect marriage . . . but she knows that this will never be. So when she's kidnapped by the notorious Lee Raven she's angry and captivated. His powerful kisses leave her breathless, but can she ever reveal the truth about herself?

If you love medieval romances, then don't miss Margaret Moore's THE MAIDEN AND HER KNIGHT. Beautiful Lady Allis nearly swoons when she first sees the tall, tempting knight Sir Connor. She is duty-bound to wed another, someone of wealth and privilege . . . but how can she resist this tantalizing knight?

Blackboard bestselling author Beverly Jenkins is one of the most exciting writers of African-American historical romance, and her newest book, BEFORE THE DAWN, is a love story you will never forget. Leah Barnett can't believe how fate has taken her from genteel Boston to the towering Colorado Rockies . . . and into the arms of angry, ruggedly sexy Ryder Damien.

Readers of contemporary romance should not miss Michelle Jerott's HER BODYGUARD. Michelle's books are hot, hot, hot . . . and here, pert pretty Lili Kavanaugh hires sexy Matt Hawkins as her bodyguard—and soon finds herself wanting more from this tough guy than his protection.

Until next month, happy reading!

Lucia Macro

Lucia Macro
Executive Editor